THE PHRASE "RUNNING AMOK" WIDELY ENTERED THE ENGLISH LANGUAGE AT THE TURN OF THE CENTURY, WHEN IT WAS USED TO DESCRIBE THE FRENZIED, HOMICIDAL FURY IN BATTLE OF SOME FILIPINO REBELS AGAINST THE AMERICAN MILITARY OCCUPATION OF THEIR HOMELAND.

HOWEVER, IN THE ORIGINAL MALAY, *AMOK* IS A NOUN.

AMOK

A NOVEL BY

George Fox

FAWCETT CREST • NEW YORK

AMOK

THIS BOOK CONTAINS THE COMPLETE TEXT OF THE ORIGINAL HARDCOVER EDITION.

Published by Fawcett Crest Books, a unit of CBS Publications, the Consumer Publishing Division of CBS Inc., by arrangement with Simon and Schuster, a division of Gulf & Western Corporation.

ISBN: 0-449-23995-0

All the characters in this book are fictitious, and any resemblance to actual persons living or dead is purely coincidental.

Alternate Selection of the Literary Guild
Dual Main Selection of the Playboy Book Club

Printed in the United States of America

10 9 8 7 6 5 4 3

A last time—

for Steve

1

AGAIN HE HAD BEEN drawn back to the valley of the Cagayan, where it had started. He found a shadowed vantage point below a high ridge, squatted on his haunches, peered down at the valley with eyes as flat and black as crushed cockroach shells, his sword lying across his massive thighs. Once, long ago, he had smoked the gleaming blade over a fire, afraid that a chance reflection of the sun might betray him to pursuing soldiers. But after a few days, ashamed of his cowardice, he had polished away the offending darkness. Now the sword rested in a sheath stitched together from strips of carabao hide.

Despite the ache of hunger in his belly, he waited motionless, as he always did before entering open country. For more than an hour he waited, shoulders forward, huge hands dangling straight down over his knees, like palm fronds touched by a malignant rust. He studied the valley of the Cagayan the way a child stares at the box-front illustration of a jigsaw puzzle, memorizing every detail of the picture before trying to join the pieces together. The vista seemed unchanged: mile after mile of brown tobacco fields, broken by expanses of tall cogon grass or the groves of shade trees surrounding a barrio. One of the tiny farming settlements was so close that he could make out the roofs of nipa huts through the sheltering branches. Unless he found easier quarry, he would raid the barrio that night. When infiltrating an area where he had not hunted for years, he preferred at first to avoid even the smallest communities. By confining his strikes to isolated, outlying houses, he often could complete his mission before the enemy discovered his presence, fade back into the jungle as unobtrusively as he had come. However, in four days he had eaten nothing except a monkey and a few handfuls of wild berries. His hunger was too great to permit endless patience.

He finally detected an unfamiliar feature in the panorama below: a two-lane blacktopped highway. The last time he had come to this part of the valley, there had been no paved roads. The only vehicle in sight was a red sports car, racing north toward the sea. Without quite knowing why, he was angered by the artificial brightness of the distant automobile, as if it were a deliberate, provocative violation of the gray and dark green and umber landscape in which he had survived for so long.

His gaze followed the open-topped car as it turned right onto a dirt road. The driver briefly slowed down, waved to a man approaching on horseback. The rider, without breaking his mount's easy canter, returned the wave. The car picked up speed, was soon out of sight. When the horseman reached the highway, he rode a few hundred yards south along the shoulder, cut off on a narrow trail through a tobacco field.

If the rider stayed on the trail, he would pass nearby.

Perhaps there would be no need to raid a barrio after all. He rose to a crouching position and began descending a steep slope into the valley, moving with silent, scuttling speed, keeping whenever possible to gullies and other depressions in the ground, like a gigantic land crab capable of clawing its way into the earth at a hint of danger.

When he was below the direct light cast by the sun, already setting behind the mountains, he unsheathed the sword. . . .

LESTER Braden tried to confine his personal inspections of the plantation fields to the early morning and late afternoon. Like his father and grandfather, he had been born with a fair complexion and pale blond hair. From childhood he had avoided the pounding glare of northern Luzon's midday sun, knowing that even an hour of direct exposure would irritate every inch of unclothed skin. "The Bradens were meant for fog and snow and long, overcast winters," he had remarked to Cara before their marriage. "So, naturally, we settled in the Philippines. My brother, Mike, is the only one of us who could stand the climate. So, naturally, he was the first Braden in sixty years to move back to the States. I just wanted you to know what kind of a crazy family you're throwing in with. . . ."

His final task of the day was checking two acres of experimental seedlings west of the new highway. Hundreds of delicate green plants had perished the previous week when a field boss had kept the irrigation system's sluice gates open a few minutes too long. The seedlings were a hybrid variety imported from the Canary Islands.

With careful nurturing, Lester Braden believed, they would produce a strain of Philippine cigar tobacco light and moist enough to compete in the North American market, a decades-old Braden dream.

Planning to set out shortly after lunch, he had lingered to watch Cara give their four-year-old daughter, Eve, a swimming lesson. He had originally opposed putting in a pool. After all, the Cagayan River, less than a quarter of a mile from the plantation's sprawling main house, had been good enough for him and Mike. As usual, he had surrendered to his wife's wishes. He had soon come to understand her insistence. That white-tilted, rectangular pit and its contents of chlorinated water—fenced in by green plastic mesh, equipped at ridiculous expense with nondescript California redwood patio furniture—was another of Cara's symbolic links to the States.

It was nearly four o'clock when, a broad-brimmed reed hat pulled almost to eye level, he headed toward the experimental field on his roan mare. In his father's day, the stables had held at least a dozen saddle horses. But now, even with the jump in gasoline prices, four-wheel-drive vehicles were cheaper to maintain. Most of the other large planters in the valley had long since sold their animals. Lester Braden had kept only the roan and a docile piebald gelding, the latter as an eventual starting mount for Evie. He had never felt like a truly free man behind the wheel of a jeep.

Approaching the highway, he saw Harry Dietrich's new red Ferrari roaring toward him, exchanged waves with the balding, heavyset tobacco buyer. He idly wondered how long the man hoped to race that low-slung sports car along rutted back roads without breaking an axle. Two more weeks at the outside, he guessed. Whatever else you could say of Harry, he didn't fit the cliché about the Swiss being excessively cautious.

Past the highway, he spurred the roan to a trot. It was a warm day for early April. The air had a morose, spongy quality, the way it did before the start of the monsoon, not due to break for at least a month. A heavy preseason rain would destroy the weakly rooted imported seedlings. I worry too damned much, he told himself wryly, glancing at the cloudless sky. I always worry too damned much. His apprehensions were forgotten as he allowed the motions of his upper body to merge totally with the roan's rhythmic gait. He always felt at his best when riding alone over this expanse of dark, serene earth, as if he had been magically detached from time and change.

The Canary Island seedlings were located in a sheltered, semiwooded area, away from the producing fields. He was glad that he had decided to make the inspection on horseback, since he would save half an hour by cutting over a rocky ridge, impassable by jeep. As he urged the roan up a steep, lightly graveled slope, the animal unaccountably began straining at the bit, its head thrashing nervously. An odd, stifling odor—like a mixture of rancid human sweat and rotting vegetation—reached Lester Braden's nostrils. . . .

A giant shape detached itself from the earth ahead, like a puff of gray smoke rising from a mound of gray ashes. A guttural, bestial howl erupted as the man ran down the hillside, a samurai sword brandished overhead in both hands. Lester Braden knew instantly that he was facing the monster in whose existence he had never believed. But the charging figure was exactly as it had been described for more than thirty years by terrified jungle tribesmen: overpoweringly huge; black, blood-hungry eyes staring berserkly from a dark-bearded face, primeval in its gnarled ugliness.

The taste of fear souring his mouth, Lester Braden struggled to avoid panic. His only chance was to ride straight for his attacker, use the roan's hooves and bulk to keep the man at bay. If he turned and tried to flee on this loose-soiled slope, he would expose his back to the four-foot-long sword. He dug his spurs into the horse's lathered flanks. The animal responded, lunging upward at a near gallop. They were almost on top of the figure when—with amazing speed for his size—he darted aside, still sounding his maniacal battle cry.

The roan veered toward the noise, broke stride, reared, hooves losing their hold on the gravel. It toppled on its side, flinging Lester Braden out of the saddle. His reed hat flew from his head.

He rolled to the bottom of the hill, came to rest with his face in the dirt. Fear-triggered vomit spewed out of his gaping mouth. Stunned, fighting to breathe, he pushed himself over on his back, blinked loose earth out of his sweat-stung eyes. When his vision cleared, the attacker stood directly above him. The sword descended in a motion so swift that the shining steel blade could be perceived only as a silver-gray blur. He tried to scream, but the still-gushing vomit soaked up the sound, like straw absorbing water.

It was as if an invisible rope had been tied beneath his armpits, then savagely jerked by a tug-of-war team. He saw his lower body seem to slide away from his torso at incredible speed, the booted right foot making a single, spastic kick. Then consciousness drained downward, past his deflating lungs, merged with the torrent of blood gushing into the soil. . . .

THE attacker ran to the mare, caught the dangling reins just as it regained its footing. After making sure that the horse hadn't been lamed by the fall, he pulled it down the hill, secured the reins to a scrubby tree.

He went back to the dead man, grasped the lower half of the severed body by both ankles, dragged it into a thick patch of cogon grass, leaving a dark crimson trail over the ground, like the smear of a bloated mosquito crushed on a windowpane by a loosely rolled newspaper. Returning to hide the torso, he saw for the first time that he had slain a white man, possibly an American. There had always been many Americans in the valley of the Cagayan. He grabbed a limp wrist, suddenly released it. Kneeling, he studied the lifeless face's glazed blue eyes and pale, freckled skin and high-bridged, sunburned nose. All of the features were puzzlingly familiar.

I have killed this man before, he decided, wondering how such a thing could be possible. . . .

CARA Braden hated leaving the patio for the perennially shadowed interior of the plantation house, with its smooth teak staircases and somber yacal-wood paneling. After Eve's nursemaid took the protesting child, who had inherited her father's sensitive skin, inside, Cara continued to lie next to the pool, allowing the last rays of the tropic sun to play over her lithe, tanned body.

She wasn't precisely sure when she had begun to dislike the house; not during the first year of her marriage, certainly. The daughter of a U.S. Air Force officer, she had grown up in what seemed to be a series of identical bungalows. West Germany or Alabama or Thailand might lie beyond the base's fenced perimeter, but that tiny-roomed structure with its plasterboard walls, always perforated with ragged holes where the last tenant's pictures had hung, never changed. The Braden house's solidity and size, and the vast fields surrounding it, had promised a physical freedom she had never known—until she discovered that limitless space could be even more constricting than a military bungalow's walls.

She didn't rise until the light deserted the pool yard. Then she entered through the kitchen door, climbed the service stairs to the second floor, carrying her rubber sandals in her hand. From an open door halfway down the long corridor came splashing noises, her daughter's surprisingly low-pitched laughter, incomprehensible orders in the Ilocano dialect. The nursemaid had already fed Evie and started her bath. Cara slipped quickly past the door, hoping she wouldn't be noticed. She had less than half an hour to get ready for dinner.

Cara reached her bedroom without being diverted by childish cries, removed her bikini, quickly showered. After toweling herself and donning a slip, she sat by a window and brushed her shoulder-length chestnut hair, watching the dying traces of the sun disappear behind the Cordillera Central mountain range. A few workers were still straggling home through the rows of tobacco. Cara glanced at her watch, saw that it was twelve minutes to seven, wondered why Les had not yet returned.

Oh, God, I'm going to be left alone with him again, she thought as she pulled a cotton dress over her head.

Her husband's grandfather had a remarkable number of personal quirks, even for a ninety-three-year-old man. The most annoying to Cara was his refusal to sit down to a meal if any woman present was wearing slacks or jeans.

Sam Braden was already at the table when Cara entered the dining room. As usual, he stood when she appeared, forcing his wasted body erect by savagely pushing with both hands on the table edge, knocking over the pepper shaker.

"Please don't, Grandfather," she said, as she always did, righting the shaker. "It isn't necessary."

His inevitable reply was a curt nod as he sank back into his chair. He directed a disapproving glance at Les's place setting, opposite Cara's. "Not home yet?" he asked. His whisper of a voice still carried a hint of steely strength, like the bone handle of a straight razor so ancient its blade has rusted away.

"No, Grandfather."

The old man didn't speak again during the meal, to Cara's relief. Until a few months ago, he had been given to rambling monologues on his early days in the Philippines. He had come to the island as a young Marine, right after the Spanish-American war, fought in the bloody campaign to put down the native *insurrectos*. Cara often wondered why the repetitious stories had stopped so abruptly.

The maid brought in the main course: again roast mutton, one of the few meats with a flavor strong enough for Sam Braden to taste. Cara, listening for her husband, ate very little, spent most of the meal toying with her water glass, occasionally taking a sip. Why had Les picked today of all days to linger in the fields? It was as though he had guessed what she planned to say after the old man had gone up to his room and Evie was asleep.

She had mentally framed the ultimatum while lying beside the pool: *I haven't been home in seven years, Les. In a few weeks the rains will start and you won't have all that much to do. Just a month would be enough to sight-see a little bit and visit my folks in Arizona. Why, they've never even met Evie! If you turn me down this time, I've made up my mind to take her by myself. I really have. . . .*

Cara had never understood her husband's reluctance to make the trip. This was the third year she had asked —and the third year he had found an unconvincing reason to postpone a Stateside vacation. In some curious way, she sensed, he was afraid to visit the homeland he had never seen.

At eight o'clock exactly, Sam Braden began his long, painful ascent of the curving main stairway, withered, blue-veined hands clutching the balustrade. He had never permitted anyone but Elpidio, the last chief houseman, to assist him. After the servant, almost as decrepit as his master, had died two years before, the old man had insisted on making the arduous climb alone.

Cara waited until she heard Sam Braden's door close, then went upstairs to kiss Eve good night. "Daddy will look in later," she said, stroking the child's lustrous, pale blond hair. Later she mixed herself a bourbon and water, went out on to the west veranda, stared into the almost subterranean blackness of the Cagayan valley's night. She considered summoning Romolo, the plantation's foreman, have him send someone to look for her husband, decided she was silly to worry. Les often missed dinner—especially when he knew mutton was being served. The chances were he had stopped off at Dietrich's or the Tullys' place for a few drinks, would return with a lame excuse when he was sure the despised meat had been safely cleared from the table.

The only break in the familiar pattern was that Les had departed on horseback. He always took the pickup truck or a jeep if he planned to drop in on a neighbor. Neither the Tullys nor Harry Dietrich had a stable, and Les would never leave a sweated mount outside after sunset. Suppose he had been thrown, was lying alone and injured in the fields?

To hell with it, she decided. I'm getting Romolo.

She was turning to go back into the house when she saw distant automobile headlights. In the clear night air, the twin beams remained unchanged in brightness for an eerily long time, as if they were stationary beacons. At last she could hear a motor, being pushed to its limits. A moment later a jeep swerved off the road, came to a stop near the veranda steps. She recognized the man at the wheel—the young field boss in the remote area where Les had planted the Canary Island seedlings. His eyes were wide with alarm as he scrambled out of the jeep.

"What's the matter?" Cara asked, descending halfway down the steps. "What's happened?"

The man halted, started to speak, gestured helplessly. Then Cara realized that, like most of the field workers, he didn't understand English. Finally, a single, almost strangulated word emerged from his twisted lips: *"Amok!"* He repeated it again and again, his voice gaining in volume and stridency: *"Amok . . . Amok . . . Amok . . ."*

2

IT TOOK THREE DAYS to find Lester Braden. Members of the Philippine Constabulary had joined local police and plantation workers in a sweep of the countryside that bordered the trail to the experimental-seedling area. They went over the same ground more than a dozen times, ranging farther out with each search. Even so, they might have missed the body if a constabulary trooper hadn't stumbled across a reed hat halfway up a hillside, far from the trail. The hat—identified as Braden's by Romolo, the foreman—had been crushed flat, only a section of mangled crown showing above the gravelly earth. They used the spot as the center of a more concentrated sweep. Less than an hour later, a Tuguegarao town policeman saw a booted foot jutting out of a clump of cogon grass. . . .

MAJOR Virgilio Ramos, the constabulary's chief of criminal investigation for the province, was informed of the discovery by field telephone. The officer in charge of the search, obeying Ramos' contingency plan, had cleared civilians out of the area before transferring the corpse to a rubber body bag. When Ramos heard how Lester Braden had died, he was doubly glad he had taken precautions—though he knew the mass panic was probably inevitable. Fear, fed by rumor, would spread through the valley of the Cagayan like a fungous infection in a steam bath.

Ramos hung up the phone, lit a Benson and Hedges; he had never been able to stand Philippine tobacco, even before he could afford American brands. A troubled frown crossed his handsome, olive-skinned *mestizo* features, touched with a trace of fleshly sensuality often created by the merging of Spanish and Malay blood. He mentally ticked off the probable events of the next few hours. It shouldn't take the command truck more than forty-five minutes to reach the government clinic in Tuguegarao, where Dr. Mapitang would perform an immediate autopsy on Braden. The results would determine the content of Ramos' next bulletin to his superiors and the press.

Awaiting Mapitang's call, he again studied the file that had been delivered to his office after the Philippine Constabulary took over the investigation. The only document of real significance was the statement of Pio Cikalik, field boss of the area Lester Braden had been scheduled to inspect on the afternoon of his disappearance.

The typed words—crudely translated from the Ilocano dialect by a police interrogator—had an awkward, almost childlike quality. *The* patrón *did not come,* Cikalik had declared. *It was growing late, so I let the other workers go home. I stayed, sitting in the front seat of my jeep. I was afraid that he might come and be angry with me for not staying. Last week I put too much water into the fields and many plants died. I wanted him to see that I would make no more mistakes. Waiting, I fell asleep. When I awoke, the sun had set. I knew then that he would not come.*

I started home. I had not driven far when I heard a horse. Fast hoofbeats and snorting. The noises were from the field to the south of the trail. It must be the patrón, *I thought. I wondered why he was riding so far from the trail, especially after dark.*

I have a spotlight on my jeep. I turned it toward the sounds and I saw him. The amok. *On the* patrón's *mare. He was so big that the mare looked like a* calesa *pony beneath him. His eyes were red as fire and his face and arms were covered with thick black hair. He carried a sword—one of those long Japanese swords. He did not attack me. I do not know why. Instead he rode on toward the mountains. I have never seen a horse run so swiftly. He must have turned it into a demon, like himself. . . .*

Ramos' secretary entered his office, told him that Dr. Mapitang had completed the autopsy. Dropping the transcript onto his desk, he quickly rose. . . .

"WHAT do you want from me?" Dr. Isidro Mapitang asked drily as Ramos came into the clinic's narrow, drably painted examination room. "When a man has been cut in half through the abdominal area, the causes of death should be obvious."

Ramos detected the mockery in the elderly physician's tone. Like all members of the national police force, he knew that he was resented, even hated by many people in the valley of the Cagayan. Dislike of outside authority was to be expected in a province where deep-jungle

Ilocan tribesmen still occasionally took heads. However, sarcasm from another government employee was another matter.

"I am interested in *how* it was done," he replied stiffly. "Could a machete or bolo knife make such a wound?"

A tiny smile on his thin-lipped, parchment-tight Malayan face, Dr. Mapitang indicated the X-ray he had just fastened to an illuminated plate. "Machetes and bolos are clumsy weapons," he said. "Lester Braden's spinal column was severed with an incredibly sharp instrument, wielded by a man of enormous strength. The break in the cartilage was so clean that I failed to find even minute splinters of bone. A master surgeon, using the finest orthopedic saw, could not have done so perfect a job."

Ignoring the No Smoking sign on the wall—which proclaimed its message in Tagalog, Ilocano and English—Major Ramos lit another Benson and Hedges. "Then he *is* back," he said in a low, harsh voice. "I prayed to God that tobacco worker had seen an ordinary bandit, imagined the rest!"

Mapitang stared at Ramos in astonishment. Since 1946, he had filed twenty-seven medical reports to the Philippine Constabulary on victims of the *amok*. He knew that at least ninety other men and women had been butchered in neighboring provinces over the same three decades. The majority were backcountry peasants; a few—like Lester Braden—prosperous farmers or tradesmen. All they had had in common was their deaths—by vicious, precise sword strokes.

Now, for the first time, a high-ranking police officer had conceded that one madman might be responsible for this seemingly meaningless history of slaughter. Wondering if Ramos would have the courage to make his belief public knowledge, Dr. Mapitang absentmindedly asked him for a cigarette. . . .

THE moment she saw Pio's stricken face in the dim light of the veranda, Cara Braden had known her husband was dead. Her reaction had little to do with the stories she had long heard about an improbably gigantic Japanese soldier who had refused to surrender at the end of World War II, hidden himself deep in the jungles of the Cordillera, emerging on periodic rampages of murderous fury. Les himself had always scoffed at the *amok* legend. Nonetheless, an inexplicable, numbing certainty that she would never again see him alive had overcome her. When, three days later, a Philippine Constabulary captain arrived to report that the body had been found, the first crippling waves of grief were already past.

"I can provide no details," the captain said in an apologetic tone, as if he held himself morally responsible for the murder. "I wasn't there when they discovered him. In fact, Major Ramos was still waiting for a full report when I left Tuguegarao."

"It doesn't matter," Cara Braden murmured. She sat slumped on a leather sofa in the den. She had converted the former billiard room, long unused, by hanging groups of floral prints on the dark paneled walls, putting in a bar and a television set which, with the help of a seventy-foot antenna, picked up two of the Manila stations. She knew that the TV set put an expensive drain on the gasoline generator, the plantation's only source of electricity, but Les had gone along with it. He had gone along with so damned much. . . .

"You will not be required to make a formal identification," the captain said. "Major Ramos told me he will obtain a waiver of the law in this case."

For the first morning since Les had vanished, Lenore Tully, their nearest neighbor, had failed to stop by. Cara had been grateful for her friend's attempts to provide comfort, but she was glad Lenore wasn't in the house when the policeman arrived. It would have meant one more person to tell, and there were already so many. . . .

She sat in the corner of the sofa for a long time after the captain departed. Never in her life had she felt so isolated. But strangely, she could hear household sounds with unaccustomed clarity: the clanging of a pot in the kitchen; Evie singing an improvised, droning little tune on the east veranda; even the rough whisper of a broom over patio tiles. The only pocket of silence was Sam Braden's bedroom. The old man hadn't come downstairs since he had learned that Les was missing.

So many people to tell . . .

Evie wouldn't understand. *Daddy's gone away,* I'll say. At what age in a child's life did dead people stop "going away"? Six? Seven? Maybe she was already too old for that particular lie. In any event, she wouldn't understand.

And the old man? How could she tell *him*? All of his children had died, and now another generation was slipping into oblivion. *We've still got Evie,* she could say. Not that Sam Braden had seemed more than distantly aware of his great-granddaughter's presence, not even enough to complain of the noises she made when playing in the house. Anyway, *We've still got Evie* would also be a lie. Cara knew that she and the child would soon be leaving. A few days ago, going to the States had been all she could think about. Now she shrank from the prospect—or any prospect except immobility.

She would have to tell the servants—or at least Antonio, the houseman. He could inform the others. No, she decided quickly, that would be wrong. Inez, the cook, had known Les since his boyhood. She would be hurt if she learned of his death from Antonio, who had worked for the Bradens less than two years. It would have to be Inez. . . .

On and on she went, compiling her list, fingernails digging deeper into the moist palms of both hands. Until no more names occurred to her, she wouldn't have to act, wouldn't have to move. The next to the last name was that of her husband's older brother. . . .

THE Pan American 747 remained in a holding pattern over Manila International Airport for nearly an hour, giving Michael Braden a repeated view of the city he had last seen twenty-one years earlier. In his letters, Les had often predicted he wouldn't recognize the place when he came back. It wasn't true. All of the landmarks were there—the scabrous, fifteen-foot-thick walls of Intramuros, the ancient Spanish fortress; the too-narrow bridges, perpetually congested with traffic, across the brown, winding Pasig River. The only unsettling change was the lack of World War II debris, still piled in vast mounds when he had left in 1955. Even the rusted superstructures of the dozens of ships sunk in shallow water were gone from the bay. The former enemy had returned in the '60s, duly paid the Philippine government for salvage rights to the bombed-out hulks, cut them up and hauled the scrap back to Japan.

Michael Braden was perfectly aware that he smelled bad, would smell even worse when he left the air-conditioned plane and the cloying heat of Manila got to work on his dirty, sweat-soaked woolen clothing. "If it makes you feel any better, I itch like hell," he had remarked to the Dacron-clad traveler who had been assigned the seat next to him. Appalled, the man had spent most of the flight in the lounge section, which was fine with Michael; it had allowed him more sleeping room. Less than forty-eight hours earlier, he had been supervising a construction crew at a remote Alaskan oil-drilling site, setting up a prefab mess hall in slightly above-zero temperatures. Then the project engineer had come over, taken him aside, said that an overseas phone call had just been radio-relayed from Anchorage . . .

Northeast of the 747's right wing, the ornate eighteenth-century Spanish towers of Santo Tomás University came into sight for at least the twelfth time since the airliner had started circling. During the war, the campus had been the main internment center for American civilians trapped on Luzon by the invading Japanese. Michael had been five when the Bradens passed through the barbed-wire gates; Les, a two-year-old carried sleeping in his father's arms. Their sister had not even made it to Santo Tomás. . . .

The rage started building again. He tried to shut it off. Airliners weren't the place to show rage. Stewardesses came over and nervously asked if you had any complaints about the service. He was sure that his unshaven face and cold-weather gear already made them nervous enough. There hadn't been time to change clothes—much less buy a tropical-weight suit—if he was to make all the connections in his long journey.

It was past noon when the 747 finally landed. In San Francisco, Michael had sent a cablegram to Ken Tisak, operator of the two-plane charter line that was the only dependable air link between Manila and the valley of the Cagayan, more than 250 miles to the north. Ken, an old friend of Michael's father's, was waiting for him beyond the customs area.

"Mike, I'm sorry," the tiny, narrow-shouldered bush pilot said with a fatalistic grimace. "We can't take off for at least another hour."

"Why not?"

"The airport security office ordered me to wait for the next JAL flight from Tokyo. Some VIP going to Tuguegarao."

"Jesus!"

Ken shrugged helplessly. "I tried to explain about the funeral, but they wouldn't listen. And I can't turn them down—not with a mail contract to look after."

"I never figured I'd make it on time anyway," Michael said in disgust.

Again struggling to control his anger, he bought a cotton sport shirt at a terminal shop, went to the men's room, where he stripped to the waist, washed as much of his compact, hard-muscled upper body as he could reach. He tried to shave, discovered that his hands were shaking too badly to hold the razor. Cursing under his breath, he shoved the toilet kit back into his flight bag, put on the new shirt. On the way out of the men's room, he dropped his black woolen sweater into a trash receptacle.

The other passenger was already in the rear seat of Ken Tisak's Cessna when Michael came aboard. As he climbed into the copilot's seat, he nodded to the man, a stocky, middle-aged Japanese wearing a worsted business suit no more fit for the Philippine climate than Michael's Arctic garments. Trickles of perspiration ran down both sides of his thin, arched nose, and the lenses of his heavy-framed sunglasses were fogged. He did not return the nod. Michael wondered when Japanese had again begun moving freely about Luzon. As late as ten years after the occupation, the U.S. military had refused to station *nisei* troops there, fearing attacks upon them by Filipino civilians.

The Japanese didn't utter a word during the flight north. Assuming that he couldn't speak English, Michael and Ken Tisak almost forgot his presence. "You want to know anything about Les?" Ken asked after breaking radio contact with the Manila air-traffic-control tower.

Michael shook his head. "Jack Tully told me enough over the phone. . . ."

He felt a painful tightness in the pit of his stomach when, an hour and a half later, the Cessna came out of a cloud bank and he saw the valley of the Cagayan far below. To his brother, the valley had been the home he had never wanted to leave, the only place on earth where he really belonged. At ten thousand feet, Les's illusions almost made sense; the mountainous jungles on either side of the Cagayan plain resembled green, rolling suburban lawns. But from the distant era when the Ilocans had been Luzon's most-feared warrior tribe through the turn-of-the-century insurrections and the battles of World War II and the Hukbalahap Communist rebellion of the 1950s, the Cordillera jungles had been staging areas for endless human slaughter. *Les would never carry a gun,* Jack Tully's distant voice had crackled faintly over the telephone. *Crazy . . . Riding all over unarmed . . . Everybody told him . . .*

A rasping sound jolted Michael Braden out of his brooding revery. He glanced over his shoulder, saw that the other passenger's breathing had suddenly become harsh and rapid. His fingers were clutching the edges of an attaché case on his lap, so tightly that the knuckles and tendons were dead white. For a moment, Michael thought the man was going to be airsick. Then, noticing Michael's stare, he made a visible effort to relax, managed an embarrassed half-smile.

A dusty pickup truck was the only vehicle parked next to the semiannually bulldozed dirt landing strip that served as the town of Tuguegarao's airport. The driver—a Braden plantation worker—ran on to the field, took Michael's flight bag as he emerged from the Cessna. No one had come to meet the Japanese. He stood erect and impassive beside the strip, watching Ken Tisak taxi about for the return flight to Manila, his attaché case and a leather valise at his feet.

Tuguegarao was at least an hour's walk from the field. Not expecting to be understood, Michael gestured toward the pickup truck and asked: "Could I give you a lift into town?"

"No, thank you," the Japanese replied in unaccented English. "A car will be along."

Michael nodded, followed the driver to the pickup. Puzzled, he watched the isolated figure in the rearview mirror as they drove away from the landing strip. Whoever he was, the Japanese had had enough clout with the Philippine government to ground Ken's plane until he could board it at Manila. What, then, could have caused a foul-up at this end of the line?

Lester Braden's burial had been scheduled for three o'clock. It was well past four when the pickup halted in front of the plantation house. The driveway was lined with automobiles, mostly four-wheel-drive American makes and a few Volvos and other European models built to take the back roads of the Cagayan. The literally glaring exception was a scarlet Ferrari sports car which had already accumulated half a dozen paint scrapes on its lower body.

They didn't wait, Michael thought with relief when he entered the foyer of the silent house. He glanced through the open double doors to the dining room. A cold buffet had been set out on the long teakwood table. A maid—too young to have known Michael when he lived here—was lining up bone-china cups and saucers in front of an antique silver coffee urn.

He went upstairs to Sam Braden's bedroom, whose windows provided a view of the family cemetery, near the river. It was all over and the mourners were walking back toward the house, between the rows of ragged eucalyptus trees that Michael's father had planted just before the war. The altitude was too great for eucalyptus, but somehow the trees had survived in a kind of semi-dwarfed state. Everyone was still so far away that he couldn't distinguish faces, but he thought he recognized his grandfather, leaning on the arm of a young woman. In the distance, three men were filling in Lester Braden's grave. Unless they were old-time employees, they probably weren't aware that no one lay buried beneath two of the tiny cemetery's headstones.

Michael left the window, sat down on the edge of his grandfather's bed. Maybe they don't know I'm here yet, he thought when he heard murmuring voices on the floor below. The driver of the pickup truck, after dropping him off, had headed toward the equipment sheds. And the maid in the dining room hadn't even glanced in his direction.

Then he heard slow, dragging footsteps outside the door. It opened and Sam Braden entered. The old man halted, gazed at Michael uncertainly. "Mike?" he said at last.

"I tried, Grandfather, but none of the planes were on time," Michael said. He went over, gently touched a gaunt shoulder. "I didn't come back for Les's funeral anyway. I came back to kill the *amok*."

IN a brush-filled mountain ravine west of the Braden plantation, three Philippine Constabulary trackers had finally accomplished the mission assigned to them by Major Ramos. They had found Lester Braden's roan mare. The animal's head, lower legs and entrails had been discarded in the undergrowth after the butchering. The still-greasy bones projecting jaggedly from the dead coals of a roasting pit showed what had happened to the rest of the animal.

Crouched in a shallow cave high in the ravine wall, he watched the soldiers move about below. They always wore the same cumbersome-looking helmets and green uniforms. In the beginning, the faces beneath the helmets had been white. Now most of them were brown. But the uniforms never changed.

As he had anticipated, the soldiers soon started out of the ravine, back the way they had come, toward the valley of the Cagayan. If he followed and destroyed them, more soldiers would search for their missing comrades. Possibly they would drive him into the deepest jungles, where the hunting was poor at this time of the year. The most desperate of measures again might have to be taken in such an event. Only eight times since Captain Shimura had given his final order had he found it necessary to eat human flesh.

3

SEVERAL MINUTES after the Braden plantation pickup departed, a Philippine Constabulary jeep pulled on to the road paralleling the Tuguegarao airstrip. Despite the late-afternoon warmth, the jeep's canvas top had been raised, the rough-weather side flaps lowered and fastened. So I am to be put in quarantine, Takei Shimura thought as the jeep halted in front of him. It is probably for the best.

The driver—a constabulary corporal—apologized in English for being late. "Major Ramos told me not to show myself until any other passengers had gone," he explained as they drove toward town.

Shimura was relieved that the young policeman hadn't addressed him by name. Ramos had promised on the telephone that the truth about his identity would be shared only with the district commanding officer. *The war has been over more than thirty years,* he had said, *but men still kill each other because of blood feuds that started during the occupation. We are not an especially forgiving people, Mr. Shimura.*

Why am I here? Shimura again asked himself, with a twitching, involuntary shake of his head. He already knew the answer, of course: he had accumulated too many debts to both the living and the dead, obligations that could be met only in the valley of the Cagayan. But he hadn't anticipated the surge of fear that had gone through him during his first glimpse of the plain from the descending Cessna. It had all come back in a sickening rush: the long, doomed retreat to Aparri; Kurusu, reeking of blood and cheap rum, huddled in a corner, panting like some great predatory beast brought to bay but still capable of a last surge of lethal energy; his decision to use that energy . . .

"You have visited the Philippines before, sir?" the driver asked idly.

"A long time ago," Shimura replied.

They had reached the outskirts of Tuguegarao, which resembled an oversized jungle barrio more than a town. The majority of its buildings were nipa huts mounted on stilts, indistinguishable from backcountry dwellings. Only the homes within a few blocks of the town square were constructed of mortar, all surrounded by the high walls that well-off Filipinos erected to shut out their poorer neighbors. Shimura winced at the odor from the street's open sewers; during the occupation it had taken him months to get used to the perpetual stench.

As they crossed the main square, he picked out familiar buildings, unchanged since the war. There was the inexplicably named New Reno Hotel, whose bar had been a gathering place for the white tobacco planters—and later, his regiment's officers' club. Dozens of malnourished

Ilocano peasants—their bodies covered with open sores, bulbous tumors, other signs of wasting diseases—still huddled on the tin-roofed porch in front of the government clinic, just as they had in 1942. How many of those corrugated roofs had rusted away and been replaced in the decades since, he wondered. And could Dr. Mapitang still be in charge? Probably not. He must have died or retired years ago. Shimura smiled tightly when he recalled the physician's icily polite defiance of dozens of minor occupation edicts. He could never have known that he had escaped arrest solely because all the other civilian doctors had fled south to Manila after the invasion. Colonel Haruna, the garrison commander, had a history of gall bladder attacks and didn't trust the universally despised regimental surgeon to perform an emergency operation on him. Why he expected to fare better at the hands of an obvious Filipino patriot had amused and baffled Shimura.

By the time they reached Major Ramos' residence, both men were perspiring heavily beneath the jeep's raised canvas. Another constabulary trooper opened the gates to admit the jeep. "The major has gone to a funeral," the driver said as he and his companion—a middle-aged sergeant with a .45 automatic on his hip—removed Shimura's luggage from the jeep. "Sergeant García will show you to your room."

The corporal uncovered the jeep before driving back out of the courtyard. "I'll take one of those," Shimura said to the sergeant, who had picked up both his valise and his attaché case. When the man started toward the house without answering, Shimura realized he didn't understand English. It suddenly occurred to him that in nearly three years of duty on Luzon, he couldn't have learned more than half a dozen phrases of the occupied nation's language. Conquerors never have to, he mused as he followed the noncom.

He was led to a shadowed bedroom on the second floor of the small house. He nodded his thanks to the silent trooper. The man abruptly returned the nod—and for the first time since stepping off the JAL airliner in Manila, Shimura felt the reaction he had anticipated with dread. For a fraction of a second, limitless hatred had flickered in the sergeant's eyes. The door closed after him.

Shimura removed his sunglasses, placed them on the top of a dresser. He blotted the sweat off his upper lip with a pocket handkerchief, longing more than ever for the cool green pines of Mt. Nangoyama. If he were home now, he would be working in his garden, possibly pruning the tangerine trees in anticipation of the brief growing season that he might miss this year.

He wished that Major Ramos had been here when he arrived, able to provide a clearer picture of what was expected of him in the days ahead. The driver had said that Ramos was attending a funeral. From the conversation he overheard on the Cessna, he gathered that the angry-looking young American had flown to Tuguegarao for the same purpose. Undoubtedly they were interring Kurusu's latest victim.

Kurusu's victim, Takei Shimura thought bitterly, and mine. . . .

CARA Braden had awakened that morning with a half-guilty sense of relief. Today Les would be buried, freeing her to concentrate on the future. She had almost longed to plunge into the mass of details that would accompany her and Evie's return to the United States: buying airline tickets, packing, distributing unwanted clothing and other possessions among the women of the household staff. She didn't believe that the long flight home would lessen her grief, but at least it might still the voice that had nightly haunted her dreams: Pio Cikalik's voice, repeating its one-word message—*"amok"*—until, inevitably, she was jolted back to trembling consciousness. . . .

Maria, Evie's young nursemaid, had already given the child breakfast when Cara came downstairs. "Let her play on the patio this morning," Cara whispered to the girl after taking her aside. "But when they start arriving, I want her upstairs."

The nursemaid nodded in understanding. "Evita might be happier in the barrio," she suggested timidly.

The village housing most of the plantation workers and their families was less than half a mile downriver. Maria occasionally took Evie there to play with the barrio children, following a worn carabao path along the riverbank. It might be a good idea, Cara thought. She was bound to hear unfamiliar noises downstairs, wonder what was happening, resent being confined to the nursery. Then Pio's voice again reverberated chillingly in her mind.

"No," she said, instantly regretting the sharpness of her tone. "I don't want Evie away from the house."

Since the servants had begun laying out the china service for the dining-room buffet, Cara ate breakfast in the kitchen. Sam Braden had insisted that a meal be served after the funeral. "Some of them will travel hundreds of miles," he had explained. "We have our obligations."

She had finished her third cup of coffee when Lenore Tully arrived unannounced through the outside kitchen door. "You okay?" Lenore asked, putting down a large overnight bag.

"Yes."

"Figured you'd need help today," Lenore said. A tall, full-bodied woman with gray-streaked auburn hair, she had always reminded Cara of the chin-held-high farm wife in old Hollywood Westerns, prepared to shoot herself rather than accept degradation at the hands of the Comanches. Not even the Halston dresses and prefaded Paris jeans she brought back from regular shopping trips to Manila shattered her aura of indomitability.

Cara was about to ask Lenore what was in the overnight bag, abruptly realized that since she was wearing a khaki pants suit, it must be her clothing for the funeral. She thought of her own mourning dress—black linen trimmed with fine lace—hanging stiff and freshly ironed in the bedroom closet. Inez, the elderly cook, had spent most of the past two nights making it. None of the stores in Tuguegarao carried Western-style garments of sufficient quality for a prominent planter's widow, and there hadn't been time to travel to Manila. Forget it, she had wanted to say. I don't give a damn what I wear. He won't be able to see me. But as usual, she had gone along with the rituals imposed upon her.

Inez brought Lenore a cup of coffee. "You still planning to head right to the States?" she asked, sitting down at the old-fashioned zinc-topped kitchen table.

"As soon as I can manage it."

Lenore took a tiny saccharin pill from her shoulder bag, grimaced as she dropped it into her coffee. "What's back there, anyway?"

It was a question Cara had been trying to avoid considering. After her father's retirement from the Air Force, her parents had bought a mobile home outside Phoenix, Arizona. "Now, don't you worry about a thing," her mother had said over the telephone the previous day. "Dad picked a trailer with three bedrooms and a bath and a half, specially for when you and Evie came to visit. We'll all settle in fine." The shower would have sheet-steel walls. They always did. . . .

"*Home* is back there," she said with more certainty than she felt.

"I guess," Lenore replied, shrugging. "Anyway, I'm being selfish, wanting you to stay. It was nice, having another American girl within ten miles of the house. I'll kind of miss it."

Cara knew that the older woman's casual attitude was feigned, that her departure would deepen Lenore Tully's loneliness far more than her words had implied. What use were Halston dresses when the only place you could show them off was the bamboo-partitioned dining room of the New Reno Hotel? However, Cara had never heard Lenore utter a genuinely bitter remark about her existence in the valley of the Cagayan. Like Les, she seemed to accept everything that happened to her with almost annoying calmness. Two summers before, a fire had wiped out hundreds of acres of export-quality cigar tobacco on the Tully plantation. "It'll be years before they see a profit again," Les had told Cara. But only hours after the conflagration was extinguished, Lenore and Jack had turned up at the Braden house for their weekly bridge game. Lenore's only voiced complaint was about a new maid who had washed a load of drip-dry garments in boiling water. "Should have seen the stuff," she had sighed. "Every damned thread dissolved!" Jack had drunk himself into a semistupor before the game was over —but of course, he nearly always did. . . .

"Have you told Sam your plans?" Lenore asked.

Cara shook her head. "You can't talk to him," she sighed. "About anything except the funeral. God, why do we have to be put through this anyway? Most of the people he asked are almost strangers to me. You and Jack and our other local friends would have been enough!"

Lenore sipped her coffee; studied Cara with kind but puzzled eyes, realizing that the girl still had no concept of the bonds that held together the white families of the Cagayan. You don't understand, she wanted to say. Funerals are a luxury for us. My father died in Santo Tomás prison camp. So did Les's mother and both of Jack's parents. In the morning the Japs took away the bodies. We never knew what they did with them. They were simply taken away, like all the others. And Les wasn't just a neighbor's kid. When he was three years old, he sat on my lap while I fed him a stew my mother made from half-rotten vegetables she scavenged from the guards' refuse pails. The rancid, stringy bits of meat running through it were the remains of a rat that little Mike Braden beat to death with a stick the night before. . . .

She shoved her coffee cup into the middle of the table, muttered disdainfully, "You'd figure they could invent an artificial sweetener that didn't make everything taste like kerosene."

"I wouldn't leave so soon if Les's brother weren't coming to take over."

"You sure he'll stay on?"

"Who else is left to run the plantation?"

Lenore smiled ruefully. "Don't count too much on

Mike, honey. He was never much like the other Bradens. Or any of us, for that matter."

Antonio, the houseman, appeared in the kitchen doorway, knocked tentatively on the frame. "They are here, ma'am," he said in a hushed voice. "Mr. Tully and the men from Tuguegarao."

A sinking sensation in her stomach, Cara rose. Lenore steadied her arm as they followed Antonio. When they reached the front veranda, plantation workers were already removing the sealed coffin from the rear of the Díaz Brothers mortuary's 1937 Packard hearse. Jack Tully, who had followed the hearse from town in his jeep, came up to the veranda steps. His puffy but still almost theatrically handsome face was flushed except for two white, strained crescents at the corners of his mouth. "Everything ready inside?" he asked in his gentle growl of a voice.

"Yes," Cara whispered.

Her gaze remained fixed on the coffin as the workers carried it through the open double doors of the house. She struggled desperately to avoid picturing the body inside. "He could have felt no pain," old Dr. Mapitang had told her. But didn't they always say that to the relatives of men who had died violently?

The coffin was borne to the seldom-used rear parlor, laid on a black-draped catafalque fashioned from planks and sawhorses. The workers silently departed. What should I do now? Cara wondered, staring at the coffin, unable to really believe that her husband was encased in that dark, polished wooden rectangle. Should I cry? Go over there and touch it? What should I *do*? She remembered her grandmother's funeral, more than a decade earlier. The waxy head cradled on satin hadn't particularly resembled the old woman she had loved, but at least it had been something for the family to focus on. She hadn't been chopped in half, left to rot in the sun for days! And there had been banks of flowers around the casket, impossible in the valley of the Cagayan. The orchids and other local blooms were so frail that they turned brown minutes after cutting, even if immediately put in water.

"Should one of us stay?" Jack Tully asked, jarring Cara out of her revery.

"It isn't necessary," she said.

As they were turning to leave, Sam Braden limped through the parlor doors, walked past as if unaware of their existence. He sat on one of the folding chairs the Díaz Brothers had brought out the day before, his thin shoulders hunched, heavy-veined hands resting in his lap. Cara had never liked the old man, resented the faltering but tyrannical grip he had maintained on her and Les's lives. But now, swept by pity, she went to him, lightly stroked his thin, yellowish-white hair.

"I'll be back and sit with you as soon as I change my clothes," she said.

"No," he said. "Not for a while."

Cara and the Tullys left the shadowed parlor. Jack looked questioningly at Cara. Understanding, she nodded. He closed the teak doors. "Go upstairs and rest," Lenore suggested. "Jack and I will take care of everything."

For the remainder of the morning, Cara lay on her bed gazing at the mosquito netting overhead, furled like flimsy ship's sails. Just before noon a door slammed down the hall and she faintly heard Evie complain to the nursemaid that she wasn't hungry yet. Maria had been ordered to serve the child an early lunch, so that she wouldn't encounter the arriving mourners. Perhaps I'm wrong not to let her attend the funeral, Cara thought. Lenore had criticized the decision. "They can take a lot more than you'd believe at that age," she had said. If Les had died naturally—even in an accident—Cara would have agreed; she knew that children needed to understand the finality of such a parting. But the horror of what had happened—the need to protect her daughter from a truth she herself was unable to fully accept—had overwhelmed her.

A few minutes before one, Lenore, again carrying her overnight bag, quietly entered the bedroom, saw that Cara was awake. "Antonio is about to open the doors."

"I know," Cara said. "Grandfather explained my duties."

Cara put on her black linen dress and went downstairs, where she joined Sam Braden in the parlor. They sat side by side while plantation workers and their families filed past Les's coffin. None of the tiny, brown-skinned men and women displayed any external emotion or even spoke to Cara and the aged planter. They might have been figures in a strange, semianimated tapestry. It suddenly occurred to her how little she understood the inhabitants of the land that had been her home for more than seven years. She had seen barrio dwellers sob frenziedly over their own dead; many of them had known Les since childhood. But they might as well be observing the passing of a distant, formal ruler whose life had never personally touched their own. The household staff, the last group to enter the parlor, behaved with the same rigid formality.

"Has someone gone to pick up Les's brother in Tuguegarao?" Cara asked when she at last joined the Tullys in the den.

"Half an hour ago," Jack said, pouring himself a double Scotch.

"Could I please have one of those?"

Jack handed her his own drink, which she downed in three shuddering gulps. For an instant her legs had felt drained of energy, as if the reed-mat carpeting had started sucking her life downward. Then the whisky took hold. "They might have been lining up for a movie," she gasped. "Inez, too—and I *know* she loved Les!"

"He was the *patrón*," Jack Tully said, making another drink. "The Ilocans figure it's rude to show their feelings when one of us dies. Damned if I know why. It's always been that way."

Cara returned to the parlor, waited with Sam Braden as the guests arrived, murmuring their condolences. Most of them were members of American families that, like Sam's, had settled in the valley of the Cagayan early in the century—Cushings and Millers and Thomases and Lydeckers, the men towering over the few native Filipinos present. Cara felt a brief surge of resentment when she saw Dr. Mapitang and Major Ramos—the latter wearing a heavily starched dress uniform—enter together. Of all the people in the room, only those two could have seen the maimed reality of the body in Lester Braden's coffin; their presence was a violation of the artificial sense of order generated by the somber clothing and muted voices of the gathering mourners.

Stop it, she told herself, ashamed of her reaction. Dr. Mapitang is one of Sam's oldest friends. The major is performing a routine official courtesy.

Across the room, Ramos had caught the look of reproach Lester Braden's wife had darted toward him. It was a side effect of feminine grief to which he had never quite adjusted. He had seen it in the eyes of hundreds of women. My son or my daughter or my husband is dead, the look always said. You will share the murderer's guilt as long as he remains free. The reaction was senseless but inevitable.

Equally expected was the resentment—verging on anger—that touched the faces of many of the planters. The day before, he had issued a statement to the press, declaring that he would base his investigation on the probability that Lester Braden had been murdered by a World War II Japanese straggler. Within minutes of the first radio broadcast of the story, several of the men now gathered in this room had made indignant phone calls to the constabulary's district commander. The messages had all been roughly the same: *I'm trying to get in a harvest before the rains. . . . Half of my workers are already too frightened to go into the fields. . . . Giving official support to that ridiculous legend is irresponsible. . . .*

Mapitang had also sensed the hostility. "They will remain polite until after the burial," he said with his taut, knowing smile. "Then, Virgilio, you must prepare yourself."

A decade ago, protests from the American planters of the Cagayan would have guaranteed Ramos a reprimand and possible transfer. Their influence, although no longer so powerful, could still cause him trouble if he failed to prove the *amok*'s existence. And they were not alone in wanting to avoid focusing public attention on the theory that one man had been responsible for more than a hundred murders. During the years of the Hukbalahap rebellion, dozens of unsolved killings in the Cagayan had been routinely blamed on Red terrorists. Many of the men responsible for this politically expedient policy, now high-ranking members of the army and government, would undoubtedly prefer to see the *amok* remain a phantom. His own commanding officer had been furious when he learned that Ramos had issued the news release without consulting his superiors.

I am too old to be a rebel, he thought ruefully.

At ten minutes to three, Cara and Sam Braden and the Tullys took their seats in the front row of folding chairs. "Is Mike here yet?" the old man asked. His watery blue eyes were already glazed with fatigue.

"No, Grandfather," Cara said.

The brief service was conducted by the Reverend Mr. Eilers, a young, pudgy Seventh-Day Adventist missionary summoned from the northern coastal city of Aparri. There were no Protestant clergymen in Tuguegarao. As his hesitant sermon droned on—vague praise for a man the missionary had never met, of whose religion he was probably uncertain—Cara mentally shut out the words. Toward the end of the service, she heard low, apologetic voices, the muted scraping of chair legs over parquet flooring as someone took a seat in the back of the room. Sam Braden started, almost imperceptibly. Cara glanced over her shoulder, saw that the late arrivals were Harry Dietrich, the tobacco buyer, and his wife, Luz, a delicately beautiful *mestiza* still in her teens. Despite the circumstances, Luz Dietrich's ivory-skinned face wore its usual shy, eager-to-please smile.

"It isn't him," Cara whispered, taking Sam Braden's hand. To her surprise, his dry, sinewy fingers tightened slightly around her own. It was the first time that the old planter had in any way communicated a need to merge their sorrows.

By four-thirty, it had all been done. The coffin was carried to the family cemetery in the Díaz Brothers' hearse, the funeral party following it on foot. The Reverend Mr. Eilers pronounced his final benediction over the grave, and they walked back to the house along a eucalyptus-bordered path. Sam Braden, breathing heavily, clutched Cara's arm during the last few hundred feet of the journey, went up to his room as soon as they reentered the house.

And now the worst part of Cara's ordeal began. Please go away, she wanted to shout. Drink your coffee and eat those ridiculous little sandwiches and just go away! The figures gathered around the dining-room buffet reinforced rather than diminished the sense of isolation that had overcome her after Les's murder. They seemed flat and unreal, like life-sized photographic cutouts Scotch Taped to the paneled walls. The incomprehensible, respectfully low hum of their conversation might have emanated from a poor-quality electronic speaker mounted in the opposite end of the house.

She edged her way into the empty foyer, leaned back against a cool stuccoed wall, hoping to snatch a few seconds of peace before the ever-watchful Lenore Tully reached her side. Then she saw the man standing at the top of the curved central stairway. He wore a cheap, floral-printed orange sport shirt, disconcertingly bright in contrast with the sober garments that had surrounded her all afternoon. For some reason, his coarse, dark brown hair glistened wetly, and drops of water clung to cheek and eye furrows so deep that they seemed to have been chiseled into his swarthy, blunt-featured, angular face. She could almost physically feel the gaze of his narrow hazel eyes upon her.

Les's brother had made it home after all.

By the time the three green-uniformed soldiers were out of sight in the ravine, he had come to a decision. Retreat into the Cordillera was impossible; he must replenish his food caches before the monsoon broke or face starvation. Drought and spring fires—the most widespread he could recall—had blighted or destroyed the sparse fields of yams and brown rice planted by the primitive tribesmen of the deep jungle. Raids upon their villages would prove increasingly unproductive in the days ahead. Only the valley of the Cagayan offered the nonperishable supplies he needed to survive the monsoon season.

It had been prudent to spare the lives of the soldiers, he thought as he started back toward the valley, taking a roundabout route to avoid an accidental encounter with them. When they reported that they had tracked him to the mountains, the main force of troops was certain to begin pursuit at the spot where he had butchered the mare, assume that he had fled farther into the jungles. With luck and care he could finish his task and be gone before they discovered their error.

Slaying the horseman had been a mistake, he now realized. He had filled his belly for a few days at the cost of betraying his presence. As he moved silently through the brush, carrying the great sword across his shoulders, he again recalled the dead man's white, freckled face, the feeling of certainty that he had killed him before. It could not be, he brooded; days of nagging hunger must have temporarily weakened his senses.

He came to a graveled stream bed, dry except for a trickle of brownish water running jaggedly through the middle of the channel, like an enlarged vein descending an old woman's leg. Squatting, he dipped up liquid in the cupped palm of his left hand, drank. And then, with startling clarity, he remembered the first time he had killed the pale man.

It had happened on the bank of this stream, many years before. A rifle slung over his shoulder, the man had been on foot, leading a mule. He had not risked a direct attack, patiently paralleled his quarry's course, waiting for an opportunity to strike. His chance had come when the man halted beside the swift-running stream, stripped the canvas cover off the mule's pack yoke. Watching from a cluster of thick-leaved scrub palms, he had been surprised to see that the animal's burden consisted of large glass jars, filled with water; each held hundreds of tiny fish, swimming in circles like streaks of silvery light. Assuming the man was a hunter, he had expected the pack to contain food and camping supplies. But the mule would be prize enough. The pale man had propped his rifle against a tree, removed one of the jars from the yoke, unscrewed the lid, poured the fish into the stream. More than fifteen feet of open ground separated him from his weapon.

He had unsheathed the sword, raised it overhead, lunged out of the palms. The pale man, kneeling beside the stream, looked around just as he charged. "Stop!" he had shouted in Japanese. It had been so long since he had heard his own language that at first the word had had no meaning for him. The sword had already begun its remorseless descent, which he checked only inches from his helpless victim's head. The man hadn't flinched or raised his arms protectively; his fair, sunburned features remained astonishingly calm. "I know who you are," he had continued. "You have no reason to kill me, no reason to live like this. The war is over. It has been over for more than eight years."

The self-serving lie had dispelled his brief longing to again hear Japanese spoken, even by a barbarian. He had taken a half-step backward, flicked the sword in a tight, contemptuously casual arc. The outer tip of the blade had skimmed over the man's throat, cutting so finely that, for an instant, only a scarlet, hair-thin line marked its passage. Then the wound had opened like an invisible zipper and red waves pulsed down the man's sweat-stained shirt. His face still oddly calm, he had toppled backward into the water; the liberated fish had darted through his blood as it flowed downstream. . . .

It *was* the same man, he thought, feeling a prickly coldness in the hand that cupped the water. He had to find a natural explanation or endure the possibility that he was going mad—the only fate he truly feared.

He squatted in the dry stream bed for minutes, considering a plan of action. When first seen, the man on the roan mare had been riding along a dirt road through the tobacco fields. In the direction from which he had come, the road led straight to a large house with broad verandas and a red-tiled roof, probably the rider's home. The answers to the tormenting mystery might be found there.

He stood up, resumed his trek toward the valley of the Cagayan.

4

For minutes Michael Braden stood unnoticed at the top of the central staircase, studying the mourners through the open double doors to the dining room, trying to decide which of the men he would ask to aid him in tracking down the *amok*. After leaving his grandfather, he had shaved, held his head under the bathroom sink's cold-water faucet in an effort to dispel the fatigue that was closing in on him like a gray-gloved hand slowly forming a fist.

They were all there, as he had known they would be—the same dozen or so American families. Except for the servants and a scattering of Filipino guests, the reception could have been taking place at the home of a prosperous Ohio or Kansas farmer. Pity and bitter amusement fought for control of his emotions as he continued to watch them, aware that their effort to impose an alien way of life on this remote Asian valley—hopeless to begin with—was nearing its quietly doomed climax. Since 1974, even Caucasians who had assumed Philippine citizenship were barred from owning land. All of those proud, stern-faced heads of families had signed documents recognizing that the earth their forefathers had tamed three quarters of a century before was now the property of the republic, which, however, had been charitable enough to lease it back to its current occupants. Poor Les, who had given his life to the Braden plantation, now lay buried in rented ground.

Some of them seemed unchanged. Like his boyhood friend Walt Lydecker, who looked almost exactly as he had the morning he and Les had driven Michael to the Tuguegarao airstrip for the first leg of his flight to Los Angeles. A slight, narrow-shouldered man with the kind of amiably boyish face that turns into a cracked leather mask in late middle age, he stood just beyond the doors, talking to his father, who managed the largest plantation in the valley.

Jack Tully came out of the billiard room, crossed the foyer to the dining room, where Lenore was waiting for him. With an irritated, reproachful glance, she grabbed his arm, pulled him inside. It had taken Michael a few seconds to recognize the couple. When he left, Jack had been lean and muscular, had moved with casual grace. Everyone had known he drank too much, but somehow it had fitted his dashing image as the American settlers' only hero of World War II. At the age of sixteen, rather than accept internment by the Japanese, he had taken a rifle and headed into the Cordillera jungles, fought until liberation with the guerrilla forces of Aurelio Villamor. Now soft, alcohol-puffed flesh hung loosely on his raw-boned frame, and his walk was slow and fatalistic.

The changes in Lenore were not as startling. A potential for heaviness had always been present in her tall, long-limbed body. In a mature, voluptuous way she was still beautiful. Nevertheless, he couldn't make any nerve-end connection between the fortyish farm wife below and the vibrant, milk-skinned girl, face framed by cascades of deep red hair, who had shared a hotel room with him on his last night in Manila. But then, I'm twenty-one years older too, he thought ruefully.

Other familiar faces appeared in his line of vision. Dr. Mapitang, as arrogantly erect as ever, walked past the doors like a testy nineteenth-century schoolmaster, his hands clasped behind his back. Harry Dietrich joined Walt Lydecker and his father, Anson—and, to Michael's surprise, was greeted with friendliness. The Swiss seemed as untouched by time as Walt: wispy strands of hair still brushed straight back, his ruddy face set in a familiar expression of wary amusement, as if he had just learned a scandalous bit of gossip that he didn't quite have the courage to pass on. Michael was about to start down the stairs when a slim girl emerged almost stealthily from the dining room, leaned back against the wall, out of the other mourners' view. Even though he knew Cara's features only through an overexposed wedding-day snapshot sent by Les, he realized instantly that she must be his sister-in-law. Her stunned eyes, set in a soft, regular-featured, but not-quite-pretty face, looked more uncomprehending than anguished, like those of a small animal whose legs had been snarled by underwater weeds while it was crossing a stream, aware that the pain of drowning would come, not yet feeling it. She noticed him, quickly stepped away from the wall.

"You're Michael?" Cara asked unnecessarily as he descended to meet her.

"Yes." He took the hands extended toward him. Despite the warmth of the afternoon, her fingers were cold. "I'm sorry about the way I'm dressed. There wasn't time to buy anything proper."

"Grandfather went up to his room."

"I've already seen him."

Should I welcome him home? Cara thought. After all, it's *his* home, really, not mine. She felt strangely ill at ease with this man her husband and Sam Braden had mentioned nearly every day—and about whom she knew virtually nothing.

Lenore Tully came out of the dining room, started a little when she saw Michael. Cara wondered why, since she had been aware for days that he was coming.

"Hello, Mike," Lenore said with a hesitant little smile.

"You look great, Lennie."

"They don't call me that anymore. They haven't for years, not even Jack." She went to him, brushed her lips across his cheek.

An instant later, Walt Lydecker also spotted him, began to grin broadly, then, remembering the circumstances, straightened his face. "Man, I'm really glad to see you," he exclaimed, clapping his hand affectionately on Michael's upper arm. "I wish to hell it wasn't like this, though."

He allowed Walt to lead him into the dining room. One by one they came up to him—these people whom in many cases he barely recalled—reciting their clichés: *Everyone loved Les. . . . A terrible tragedy . . . It must have been a maniac. . . . He never hurt anybody in his life but isn't that usually the way in these things. . . .* And all the while he was thinking: You helped kill him. He even helped kill himself. . . .

Relieved that the focus of attention had been shifted from her, Cara watched Michael greet his former neighbors, his orange sport shirt standing out like an exotic flower that had perversely taken root in a field of gray shale. Everyone had told her that he didn't resemble the other men in the Braden family, but she hadn't anticipated so extreme a difference. Contrasted with her husband's and Sam's Nordic paleness, he might almost belong to another, darker race. Even more striking was his manner, displaying no trace of the lanky, charming near-awkwardness that had first attracted her to Les. His movements were as intensely controlled as those of a stalking cat.

At last the mourners began to leave, murmuring their final condolences to Cara at the front door. Michael went outside with Walt Lydecker. "You still have a regular Friday-night poker game at the New Reno?" he asked as he and his friend walked toward the Lydeckers' Land-Rover. He noticed for the first time that Walt still favored his right leg. Almost crippled by malnutrition and rickets in Santo Tomás, he had been hospitalized for more than a year after liberation, forced to use crutches until he was nearing adolescence.

Walt glanced at him in surprise. "Sure."

"Who sits in these days?"

"Jack Tully. Harry Dietrich, once in a while. Anybody else who feels like it. Les hardly ever missed."

"Mind if I fill his chair, then?" He smiled reassuringly. "Not callousness, Walt. I want to talk something over with you and the rest of Les's friends."

"Fine," Walt replied, sounding puzzled. "We usually start around eight o'clock."

Michael was about to head back toward the house when he heard an agitated but oddly muted voice. Anson Lydecker stood beside an olive-drab jeep, talking to a Philippine Constabulary major. Michael hadn't caught the man's name when he had been introduced earlier.

Others nearby had noticed, were moving toward them. By the time he and Walt reached the jeep, Dietrich, Jack Tully and Dr. Mapitang had joined the cluster of onlookers.

There was a nearly comic quality to Lydecker's attempts to vent his anger and still maintain the correct manner for a funeral. A heavy blue vein pulsed in his left temple, and his hands shook, but the tone of his words emerged in subdued contrast to their meaning, as if being censored by his teeth: "You aren't going to convince me—or anybody else in his right mind—that a Jap holdout killed Les. You've thrown the whole district into panic for no damned reason!"

Ramos listened with outward patience to the semi-strangulated tirade. All of Lydecker's arguments had been turned over and over in his own mind during the long hours of indecision before he had issued yesterday's news release. He had been present at the capture of dozens of Japanese stragglers—timid, confused men, frightened by their own government's propaganda into believing surrender inevitably meant torture and death. Most of them had survived by planting subsistence gardens in remote hills, had invaded settled lands only long enough to steal vegetables from a farmer's field, perhaps kill a duck or chicken or a dog for meat. All had been taken within a few miles of the places where they had first gone into hiding. Not one had been seven feet tall, had carried a samurai sword and had roamed over vast areas, slicing human beings to shreds on whim. . . .

"Pio Cikalik saw him, Mr. Lydecker," Ramos said. "So have many others in the past."

"No white man ever has!"

"Only superstitious, unreliable, childlike Filipinos?" Dr. Mapitang asked.

Lydecker flinched at Mapitang's sarcasm. "That isn't what I meant."

"Dad, not here," Walt pleaded, gesturing toward Michael.

"He knows what I'm saying is true."

"You're wrong," Michael declared. "The *amok* did kill Les—and our father."

The calm certainty of his words and manner produced seconds of nervous silence, finally broken by Anson: "Frank Braden was ambushed by the Huks."

"There aren't any Huks in the Cagayan now," Michael said.

"But we've always had bandits. And jungle Ilocans on ritual murder binges. Getting killed around here was never hard!"

"Anson has a point," Harry Dietrich said, his voice tinged by the faint remnants of a Swiss accent. "We need the *amok* the way Dachau needed Jack the Ripper."

Walt Lydecker released a half-embarrassed laugh, cut off when Michael said, "Not funny, Harry. Especially coming from a man who's never been inside barbed wire. Santo Tomás wasn't Dachau, but it came close enough."

As a citizen of a neutral country, Dietrich had escaped internment during the war, managed to keep his then-small plantation intact while the fields of his neighbors rotted into grayish-brown dust. Later, he had added hundreds of acres to the property, bought cheaply from men and women impoverished by three years of confinement. After liberation, many local families—including the Lydeckers—had refused to speak to him or deal with the tobacco export firm he had set up in Aparri.

Dietrich's face drained of color. Walt Lydecker quickly stepped between him and Michael. "No call for that, Mike," he said reprovingly.

Michael had already realized that near-exhaustion had blunted his judgment. If his plan was to succeed, he couldn't risk alienating any of these men. "I'm sorry, Harry," he said.

The apology went unheard by Dietrich, striding toward his red Ferrari, his thick shoulders rigid with anger. His young *mestiza* wife was waiting in the sports car. He slid behind the wheel, gunned the Ferrari hard, roared off on squealing tires.

Jack Tully spoke for the first time: "Let's get on home. We came here to bury a friend, not fight the war all over again."

Michael watched from the veranda until the last remaining sign of the mourners' cars was a thin smear of rising dust far down the dirt road that led to the new highway. Anson Lydecker might not believe in the *amok,* but Michael had noticed a rifle mounted in his Land-Rover's gun rack. He was certain that there were weapons in all of the other vehicles.

He lifted his gaze to the mountains. The highest peaks were partially obscured by the pale violet mists that often settled over them before dusk. As a small child he had believed that nightfall literally flowed down from the Cordillera, like an engulfing wave of black, cool water.

Maybe I wasn't too far wrong, he thought, turning to enter the structure that had once been his home and, he knew, could never be again.

"YOU were right, Doctor'" Major Ramos said as he

swung his jeep on to the highway, headed toward Tuguegarao. "Lydecker didn't even wait until the grave was filled."

Mapitang, sitting beside him, chuckled raspingly. The sound reminded Ramos of wind rustling dry, brittle leaves. "Did you expect otherwise?"

"No," he admitted.

"For thirty years they have denied the truth about the *amok,* even among themselves. I don't entirely blame them. Monsters *should* be imaginary."

The Lydecker Land-Rover was directly ahead. Ramos hit the jeep's horn with the heel of his hand before passing it. "All they care about is harvesting their filthy crops," he grunted.

"That's what a farmer is supposed to care about, Virgilio."

Realizing that Mapitang was teasing him, Ramos forced a smile. "You and the Americans have always gotten along, haven't you?"

"I rarely concern myself with them. Few have been my patients, except in emergencies. And, among the young ones, an occasional case of gonorrhea they are afraid to take to a white doctor."

"You see the rest of us only as patients?" asked the amused Ramos.

"A broad view of mankind is a luxury available only to physicians with lucrative private practices," Mapitang remarked dourly. "Now that you have put yourself on the side of the superstitious, unreliable and childlike, what will you do next?"

Ramos hesitated. He knew that Dr. Mapitang had miraculously managed to keep his clinic open throughout the war, had observed at close hand the sickening aftermath of atrocities committed by the occupation force headquartered in Tuguegarao. Instinct told him that Mapitang could be trusted. Nevertheless, remembering his promise to keep Takei Shimura's mission a secret as long as possible, he attempted to change the subject:

"I didn't realize Lester Braden's father had also been murdered."

Mapitang nodded. "In nineteen fifty-three or -four. The circumstances were strangely similar. He went alone into the mountains—I forget why—and someone cut his throat. Naturally, since the Huk war was at its peak, they were held responsible."

"I myself might have given the *amok* the benefit of the doubt. A samurai sword is a rather oversized weapon for throat slashing."

Mapitang put a cigarette between his lips, leaned close to the jeep's windscreen when he lit it. "Lester was killed at about the same age as his father. It is almost enough to make one believe in family curses."

As soon as the last guest had departed, Cara Braden hurried upstairs. A moment before, she had heard a child's impatient cries. She entered the nursery and found Eve sitting on the edge of her bed. Maria was vainly attemping to interest her in a coloring book and crayons.

"I'm sorry, ma'am," the nursemaid said. "She went out into the hall when I wasn't looking."

"It's all right. They've gone." She picked up her daughter, gently rocked her in her arms. "We didn't mean to keep you up here so long, honey."

Evie had still not asked about her father's absence, but Cara knew the dreaded questions had to come soon. I'll tell her tonight, she thought. When everything has settled down. She wondered if she could actually gather the courage to do it.

Cara lowered Eve to the floor and she skipped from the room, started descending the stairs. Halfway down, she saw a strange man come in from the veranda, stopped in her tracks, clutching the smooth, dark-grained banister. The man looked up at her silently. Frightened, the child ran back to the nursery.

Michael's gaze followed her until she was out of sight. He had known that Les had named his daughter after their sister but the resemblance to the long-dead other child had shaken him, stirring memories that he had always attempted, unsuccessfully, to banish from his mind. Now they returned with dizzying immediacy: the young Japanese officer with the clipboard, reading off his family's names in a flat voice; soldiers using long, bayoneted rifles to herd them into the back of an open truck, where Jack Tully's parents and at least a dozen other neighbors were already under guard; his mother, holding Les on her lap, trying to calm the older children by playing word games during the long, jolting, dusty ride to the port of Aparri; and, finally, the ship. A wood-hulled coastal steamer, probably built before the turn of the century, it lay moored at the end of a rickety pier. Before they boarded, the Japanese officer smilingly passed out small bags of candy to the children, while a military photographer took pictures. And then they joined more than a hundred other civilians in a foul-smelling cargo hold, crammed so tightly that it was impossible for even the smallest child to fully recline. "It won't be too bad," his father promised. "Shouldn't take more than a day to get to Manila." With a clanking groan, the steamer's engines started up and it moved slowly out of the harbor. Rigid with fear, Michael lay with his head in his eight-year-old sister's lap. Eve hummed soothingly as she stroked his hair, the sound broken every few seconds by a cough. She had been recovering from a racking cold when the Japanese came for them. At last he fell asleep, lulled by the wheezing, rhythmic chug of the ancient engines; awoke with a cry of terror when the noise abruptly ceased. "Damned hulk has broken down," his grandfather growled. It was the beginning of the real hell. For days the steamer wallowed helplessly in the South China Sea, the heat of the tropic sun searing its decks like a gigantic, invisible compress. Time disintegrated, became measurable only when crewmen opened the overhead hatch to lower buckets containing steadily smaller rations of water and cold rice. Before being raised, the buckets were filled with excrement dipped from the open fifty-gallon drums that were the hold's only toilet facilities. In the beginning, moans and whimpers and sobs, even bursts of lunatic laughter, emerged from the surrounding darkness but finally the heat and the stench turned all the prisoners into units of voiceless flesh. Eve, her lungs ravaged by pneumonia, was among the first to die. His throat and mouth too dry to release the screams of anguish he wanted to utter, he watched crewmen pull her in a cargo net toward the temporary square of sunlight above, her long, golden hair and one pale arm dangling through the strands of the net. Only minutes after they heard the faint splash when her body was thrown over the side, the ship's repaired engines started up again. . . .

CARA, leading her reluctant daughter, came down the stairs. "Don't be afraid," she told the child. "This is your Uncle Michael."

"Hello," he said, reaching out to take her free hand. She squirmed from her mother's grasp, ran toward the kitchen.

"Evie, come back here," Cara snapped, but the little girl paid no attention.

"We'll make friends later. Anyway, it was my fault. I should have introduced myself instead of staring at her like an idiot. But she looked so much like . . ."

"Your sister?"

"Yes."

"Lenore and Jack said the same thing out back, when I noticed the headstone. It may sound odd to you, but I'd never been in the family cemetery before."

"Who wants to be reminded of death?"

"She wasn't actually buried there?"

Michael shook his head. "After the war, my father insisted on putting up markers for both her and my mother. No one could talk him out of it. Les never told you what happened?"

"He seldom mentioned the war, even when everyone else in the room was going on and on about it. I suppose he was too young to remember very much."

Even as a boy, Michael recalled, his brother had lived totally in the present, as if afraid of venturing beyond the moment of current existence. It wasn't an uncommon quality among men and women who had begun childhood in places like Santo Tomás. That Les should have been murdered by a lone, twisted survivor of the hated past had already struck Michael as cruelly ironic.

"I'd better get unpacked."

"Dinner will be late this evening," she said.

"A sandwich is fine. To tell the truth, I've about had it. Why doesn't sleep on airplanes seem to count?"

"I've never known."

Michael lit a cigarette, went to one of the tall windows overlooking the veranda. "When do the guards go on duty?" he asked.

"I don't understand."

He quickly turned to face her, wincing in disbelief. "You haven't put on night guards?"

"No."

"What the hell is the matter with Grandfather, anyway?"

"Nothing," she replied, "except, perhaps, being ninety-three."

He strode away from her down the ground-floor hall, entered Les's study. Startled by his sudden brusqueness, Cara again reflected that everything she knew about her brother-in-law could be summed up in a few seconds.

He had left Luzon to study engineering at the University of Southern California, quit in his junior year without explanation, joined the army. His sole contacts with his family since then had been Christmas cards and occasional brief letters, yet only once could she recall hearing either Les or Sam express resentment over his neglect.

They had all been watching a television news film on the fall of Saigon to the Communists. "Mike fought in Viet Nam," the old man had grumbled. "You'd have thought he might have flown over to see us. It's only a few hundred miles." Les had replied: "I've heard it's damned near impossible to get leave from a combat zone, Grandfather." "I suppose," Sam Braden had sighed.

Sometime in the mid-1960s—again giving no reason to his family—he had resigned his commission, gone into construction work in the Pacific Northwest.

Michael returned, buckling on the holstered revolver that, as far as she knew, Les had never removed from the glass-enclosed gun rack in the study. "I'm going to the barrio," he said as he hurried out the front door into the gathering darkness.

Cara found it disturbing—and unaccountably, a little frightening—that this stranger, faceless until today, was already assuming rule over the Braden household. But what does it matter, she thought. Evie and I will soon be gone from here forever.

5

LENORE AND JACK TULLY didn't speak during the drive to their plantation, which bordered the Braden land on the northeast. "I'm sorry I sneaked into the den for a drink," he muttered after they entered the house. "Hell, Cara wouldn't have minded."

"I wasn't even thinking about that," she replied, truthfully.

"Could really use one now. It's been a rough day." He went to the living-room liquor cabinet, poured a Scotch on the rocks. "Mike Braden sure grew up into a mean-looking bastard."

"I didn't notice."

He sat on the couch, took an almost delicate sip of the Scotch. She watched him coldly, knowing that the second sip would be just as slight—and that after dinner he would be emptying his glass in under five minutes. As always, on nights like this, she would go to bed alone, and in the morning she would find him sprawled on the couch in the small office where he kept the plantation accounts. Ordinarily the prospect was depressing; but tonight, she didn't want him lying beside her.

"What happened over by Major Ramos' jeep?" she asked. "I thought that old fool Anson was going to hit him."

Jack described the argument. "Surprised me, Mike taking after Harry Dietrich," he concluded. "Christ, when was the last time anybody worried about *that*? Was poor Harry supposed to volunteer for a prison camp?"

"You're right, I guess." She noticed that his latest sip was perceptibly deeper than the one before. It would happen earlier than usual this evening.

"Mike's been away too long. If he sticks around awhile, he'll realize how much things have changed."

But things *haven't* changed, Lenore suddenly wanted to scream at him. Not in any important way! We all just sit here, pretending that we still count in a country that no longer wants us! We're as stuck in the past as that madman who killed Les—and you won't even admit that *he's* real!

Aloud, she said in a calm voice, "I'm going to take a bath before dinner."

Jack nodded, quickly finished his drink, rose to fix another.

Lenore went up to their bedroom, began removing the black dress she had bought last year for her mother's funeral and hadn't worn again until today. It's like peeling off a scab that formed twice, she thought with revulsion as she stepped out of the clinging garment.

She filled the bathtub, eased down into the warm, comforting water. Why had seeing Mike Braden been so unsettling? she wondered, resting her head against the back of the tub. It couldn't really have been their brief affair, an impulsive encounter between two half-forgotten children. Nonetheless, her renewed memories were surprisingly precise. . . .

ON that late-August afternoon in 1955, Lenore had been among hundreds of travelers stranded at the Manila airport. She had come to the city the day before to attend a ball at the United States Embassy, had stayed overnight with an aunt. The morning radio news had reported a typhoon alert for Mindanao and the southernmost islands, but no severe effects upon Luzon were anticipated. Drizzling rain had been falling when she left her aunt's building in a taxi; by the time she reached the airport, it had become a near-deluge, accompanied by infrequent but savage gusts of wind.

Learning that all flights were postponed, she reluctantly decided to return to her aunt's apartment. After what had happened at the ball, she felt a desperate need to get home, to drive the city and everyone in it from her thoughts. She had started toward the terminal entrance when she noticed Michael Braden sitting alone in the coffee shop. Although they had known each other most of their lives, they had not been especially friendly since the start of adolescence. Lenore was three or four years older—a wide gap among the young even in so small and isolated a group as the Cagayan's foreign community. The fact that she didn't belong to a plantation family—her stepfather ran a farm-equipment agency in Tuguegarao—had limited their contacts outside school to the Fourth of July picnic and occasional dances at the New Reno Hotel. Not that most of the kids his own age had been much closer to him. He had always been considered a loner by the clannish children who attended Tuguegarao's ill-named American Academy. Still, he was totally familiar—which was the sort of company she craved at the moment.

"You stuck too?" she asked as she entered the coffee shop.

He stood up, smiled crookedly, an expression of unfathomable loneliness melting from his swarthy, angular face. . . .

What happened afterward never quite made sense to Lenore. It was as though she were a swimmer entering a calm lagoon, only to find herself caught in a freak riptide from the distant sea. They were nursing Cokes when the loudspeaker announced that flights would be delayed another two hours. "A storm like this will keep up at least until morning," he said with mildly irritating certainty. "You want to catch a movie? There's a picture with Gary Cooper and Barbara Stanwyck downtown. One of those new wide-screen things."

"*Blowing Wild*? I saw it. She gets her head stuck in an oil-well pump . . ."

They ended up in one of those womb-dark hotel cocktail lounges on Rizal Boulevard, the kind where middle-aged American men in short-sleeved white shirts listlessly played poker dice for drinks. Many years later, she would often meet Jack at the same place, after finishing a day's shopping. She and Michael found a rear table. He ordered a bottle of San Miguel beer; Lenore, a martini. She didn't really like martinis—especially when she was certain they would be made with the peculiar, aromatic liquid that the Filipinos called gin—but she ordered one anyway, refining her self-cast role as a twenty-three-year-old woman tolerantly shepherding a lonesome boy of . . .

How old had *he been? She tried to remember. No more than nineteen, certainly. . . .*

"Maybe we ought to phone Ken Tisak's office and leave the phone number," she said, grimacing toward the cocktail lounge's narrow front window, still pounded by sheets of gray rain. "Not that those puddle jumpers of his take off on time even when the weather is good."

He gave her a look of almost injured surprise. "I'm not going home, Lennie. I'm on my way to America."

"Really?" She suddenly recalled her mother mentioning, a week or two before, that the older Braden son had enrolled in a Stateside college.

"I'm never coming back," he announced, without bravado. It was a flat declaration. "Not to live, anyway."

"Why?"

"Because I don't belong here."

"Where *do* you belong?" she asked, trying to hide her amusement. Like Lenore and most of their friends, he had been born in the valley of the Cagayan, knew little of the world beyond.

"That's what I'd like to find out."

He went on explaining himself for nearly an hour, in clipped, intense bursts of words. Since she automatically wrote off the monologue as juvenile self-dramatization, little of it lodged in her memory. She just sipped her drinks and nodded sympathetically from time to time, thinking about the young American vice-consul who had escorted her to the embassy ball. He had been her lover—her first and, so far, only—for more than six months. The evening had ended when he told her he had been transferred to a European post, would be leaving in less than a week. Actually, she had been planning to break off the affair herself, tired of making the long, expensive weekend trips to Manila to see a man whom she was beginning to realize she didn't particularly like. But the cool smugness with which he announced his departure had stung her. "I only got the news this morning," he had said. "That's a lie!" she had lashed back. "Even I know the silly government doesn't do anything that fast!" She had left the ball alone, angry tears streaming down her cheeks. . . .

"I was right," Michael Braden said. "It isn't going to stop."

The change in his tone jarred her back to the present. For an instant, she even found it difficult to recall who was sitting opposite her in the shadowed bar. "What isn't?" she asked.

He nodded toward the window, so streaming with water that it might have been the porthole of a submarine. "The bad weather. It'll last the night."

"Probably."

"I'm going to check into the hotel here, Lennie. Would you like to stay with me?"

It took her a few seconds to fully accept what she had heard. He can't mean it, she thought. The shift from nervous kid to casual seducer was too outrageously abrupt. If there had been some kind of preliminary—a kiss, even a touching of their hands—the invitation wouldn't have been so startling. Of course not, you silly little creep, she intended to reply with an appropriately scornful laugh. Instead, to her own astonishment, she heard herself say: "All right."

Later, when she tried to figure out why she had done it, none of the possible answers made sense. Had she been seeking oblique emotional revenge on the vice-consul? Hypnotized by the limbo—divorced from time and personal responsibility—into which stranded travelers are inevitably cast? Knocked off the normal, accepted course of her life by two martinis and a wave of self-pity? Years went by before she realized her decision had actually been rooted deep in the past, during the endless nights she and Mike and the other children of Santo Tomás had huddled together in tents, listening to the monsoon rains attack the flimsy, rotting canvas overhead. . . .

An interior door connected the cocktail lounge with the hotel lobby. Michael excused himself, went through it, returned a few minutes later and told her that he had registered. Lenore felt a pulsing tightness in her stomach when he picked up their flight bags. She followed him back into the lobby, glad that it was a small, third-class hotel and they weren't likely to run into anyone they knew. The desk clerk stared at her with open curiosity as they crossed to the tiny self-service elevator; white female guests were probably rare. She was relieved that there was no bellboy.

Their room was on the top floor, overlooking the boulevard. As she had expected, the hotel must specialize in assignations. A long mirror had been set in the wall next to the bed. I must be out of my mind, she thought as Michael put down the flight bags and took her into his arms, kissed her in an oddly tentative fashion. It wasn't the kind of kiss she had anticipated, suddenly suspecting that he was as jumpy as she was. His right hand traced slow circles over her back, producing a staticlike crackling from the surface of her white nylon blouse. She tried to relax, but every muscle he caressed involuntarily tightened.

"You don't have to go through with it," he murmured, his hand ceasing its motions.

"Why did you ask me to?" she replied. "So you'd have a souvenir of your last few hours in the Philippines?"

"I just didn't want to be alone tonight. I sort of figured you didn't either."

"How could you tell that?" she said, surprised again by his air of certainty, disconcerting in someone so young. "I hardly said a word downstairs."

He shrugged. "A look in your eyes . . . Something . . ."

All the time you were talking, I was thinking about another man, she almost confessed, wanting to laugh. Then, listening to the rain pelt the window glass, she knew that his instinct had been right. Sleeping by herself on the rickety daybed in her aunt's living room would have been unbearable. She took a step backward, studied his almost-too-familiar features, realized that she had never once considered whether she found him attractive. Before she could make up her mind, he started to look away. She gently stroked his left cheek with her fingertips. Until this second she had felt no desire for him—but now, unexpectedly, a tiny core of excitement began to build within her, like a dormant electric cell activated by a distant radio signal.

Lenore unfastened the top button of her blouse, but his fingers reached the second before her own. With the vice-consul, she had always disrobed in the bathroom of his apartment, emerged to find him waiting for her in bed. This was better. Michael's hands removed the blouse, clumsily released the buckle on her black patent leather cinch belt, pulled the zipper on her skirt, which fell to encircle her ankles. He reached behind her, eased out the hooks on her white lace brassiere, tossed it to the floor, knelt to unclip her stockings, fastened to the low-cut style of pantie girdle that Lenore and all her girl friends habitually wore in the mid-1950s, no matter how flat their stomachs. His coarse hair brushed tantalizingly against the bottom arcs of the full, round breasts she had then considered embarrassingly large in contrast to the slimness of the rest of her body.

"You'd better let me do the rest," she said, voice trembling, when he had stripped the stockings from her long, firm legs.

"No," he insisted. "All of it."

She revolved her hips to help him as his strong, blunt fingers eased down the pantie girdle. He paused several times to kiss the indentations pressed into her gradually exposed white skin by the elastic material, like a parent "curing" a child's minor bruise. With the vice-consul, it had taken at least ten minutes of foreplay to make her ready, but now an area of moist warmth was already spreading outward. When the pantie girdle slipped free, she clutched the back of his head with both hands, pressed his face against her belly.

Michael rose, his right arm sliding up between her legs until the inner bend of his elbow cradled her loins. His other arm slipped over to support her shoulders, and she felt herself lifted free of the floor. As he carried her toward the bed, his lips and tongue found one of her brown, straining nipples.

"Oh, God, hurry!" she moaned after he had lowered her to the bed.

But he took an almost maddeningly long time to remove his own clothes. Finally, he stood naked above her. She stared up at his dark, youthful body, saw that he was fully erect, reached out to clutch him, didn't relinquish her grip until she had guided him into her.

She had been afraid that he might be too inexperienced to sustain their lovemaking, at least the first time. But of course, she realized later, he must have long since been initiated by those ritual weekends with the whores of Manila that the white teen-agers of the Cagayan whispered about. There was something almost threatening in his implacable thrusts. The vice-consul had groaned and whined and murmured unconvincing obscenities against her ear, but Michael remained silent; he didn't even seem to breathe, as if all his physical functions had been diverted to the rigid force stabbing relentlessly into her body. The only sound in the room, besides the ever-present patter of the rain, was the *slap-slap-slap* of their meeting forms.

Then she heard a guttural whimper, realized that it had come from her own throat. As if two invisible demons had encircled her neck with a silken cord and started jerking it back and forth, her head began thrashing on the pillow. Whenever it was pulled to the right, she saw an unfamiliar face reflected in the mirror beside the bed. The woman's dark red hair was beaded with sweat, damp wisps adhering to her flushed cheeks and brow. Her lips were bared in a snarl, her tongue flicking against her teeth, as if it were a separate living creature trying to wriggle free of her mouth.

That can't be *me,* she thought as shuddering spasms of total release coursed upward through her. . . .

The storm passed a few hours before dawn. Lenore saw Michael off to America at nine twenty-six in the morning, less than thirty minutes before she boarded Ken Tisak's shuttle flight to northern Luzon. Seventeen months later, she married Jack Tully. . . .

THE water in the bathtub had started to cool. Lenore looked down, ruefully thought that it had been a long time since she had worried about her breasts' being out of proportion with the rest of her body. She touched the soft swell of her belly, the smooth fullness of an inner thigh, made a mental promise to again take up the exercise program she had abandoned in February.

The vividness of her recollection of that long-ago night with Michael Braden disturbed her. It wasn't that important, she told herself. Just a casual, friendly screw, the kids today would say. But *had* it been important, in ways she hadn't realized? At one point, lying in the sleeping Michael's arms, she had fantasized a moment in which he would ask her to go with him to the States, declaring that he had secretly loved her since childhood. She giggled at the memory. God, but I was silly, she mused. But she couldn't help trying to imagine how different her life would have been if the scenario had worked out. . . .

She forced herself back to reality, glanced at the wristwatch she had placed on the rim of the tub. It was past seven, so the maid must already have set the table for dinner. A hissing in the wall told her that Jack was in the downstairs bathroom, washing up before the meal. She experienced an abrupt surge of guilt over her thoughts about Michael. The only real defect in her marriage had been Jack's alcoholism—and that could have been worse. He was one of those quiet, self-disciplined drunks, a seeker of periodic oblivion, never missing a full day in the fields, never stumbling or incoherent, never driven to anger or violence. That he had killed at least fifty Japanese soldiers during the war had always struck her as grotesquely improbable. Sex with him had always been good, except when he was drinking really hard. They both would have been happier with more than one child, of course—their sixteen-year-old son, Kevin, was a student at a Manila boarding school—but that hadn't been Jack's fault. . . .

Sixteen, she reflected. *Kevin is sixteen—only three years younger than Mike, the time we shacked up.* A sob erupted from her throat.

6

As soon as he turned the jeep into the dirt main street of the field workers' barrio, Michael Braden could sense the terror gripping the inhabitants. Even though the sun had been down less than half an hour, only a few human figures were visible. Li Tung, the Chinese storekeeper, sat alone behind the dimly illuminated bar in the open-faced nipa shack that served the barrio as a café. Normally at this hour, a dozen or more men would be inside, sipping warm beer, letting the ache of the day's labors ooze out of their muscles. Farther down the street, two ancient women squatted beside a sewage ditch, smoking cigars in the inexplicable backcountry fashion, lit ends inside their toothless mouths. He and Les had tried it once as kids, burned their tongues so badly that they couldn't eat solid food for two days.

Romolo, the plantation foreman, lived in the barrio's largest hut, on the edge of the river. As a precaution against floods, the building was mounted on eight-foot-high stilts. He braked the jeep in front of it, saw that the ladder to the porch had been raised—normally a breach of hospitality so early in the evening. The house, like all of its neighbors, was dark.

Forgoing courtesy, Michael repeatedly hit the jeep's horn. The door opened and the foreman emerged, an oil lamp held high at the end of his short, plump arm. The last time Michael had seen Romolo, he had been an ordinary worker. Time and supervisory duties had added at least a hundred pounds to his slight frame. The guttering orange light from the lamp seemed to bounce off the curve of his vast stomach and disintegrate, leaving his lower body in darkness.

"It's Michael Braden," he snapped.

"I recognized you, *Patrón*," Romolo said. Handing the lamp to an early-teen-aged girl who had timidly walked out behind him, he lowered the ladder to the ground.

Michael climbed to the porch, preceded Romolo and the girl into the house. The main room was furnished only with sisal mats and a low table. A central oil lamp hung from the ceiling. Romolo lit it, blew out the smaller lamp, which the girl quickly carried into the kitchen.

"Welcome back to the Cagayan, *Patrón*," Romolo murmured, his round face expressionless. Vague rustlings sifted through the beaded curtains over the doors to the bedrooms, where his wife and the rest of his children were undoubtedly hiding.

Michael repressed the anger that had been building inside him since he had left the plantation house. He knew that upbraiding the foreman within his family's hearing was an act that might never be forgiven. Before he could speak, the girl came back out of the kitchen. Her trembling hands bore a lacquered reed tray, on which sat a glass half-filled with a dark amber liquid.

"Thank you," he said, taking the glass. He sipped the liquid, realized it was the potent cane rum that was home-distilled all over the valley. The taste had always reminded him of sugar-impregnated furniture polish. "Could we talk outside, Romolo?"

The foreman gave him a tired nod, the brief glint of guilt in his eyes revealing that he already knew what the conversation would concern.

"Why haven't guards been posted at the main house?" Michael asked when they had returned to the porch.

"I was given no orders to do so," Romolo replied in a near-whisper.

"You shouldn't have needed any."

"We are without guns now, *Patrón*. And what use would machetes be against *him*?"

Two years earlier, the national government—under the martial-law edicts that had given President Marcos dictatorial powers—had confiscated firearms throughout the district, part of a program to cripple potential revolutionary movements. Only major landowners had been exempted. "I have guns at the house," Michael said. "I'll need three men."

Romolo hesitated. "*Patrón,* each time he comes, the fear is greater than before. None of them want to leave the women and children alone throughout the night."

Fire anyone who refuses, Michael almost said. The words were on his lips when he recalled the pointless quarrel he had provoked earlier with Harry Dietrich. Most of the men in the barrio probably weren't even aware of his existence—and nothing was more deeply resented than the tyranny of strangers. He didn't want Cara and his grandfather to have to face that resentment after he returned to America.

"Ask for volunteers only at houses where there are three or more grown men."

Romolo lumberingly descended to the ground. With a mild shudder, Michael finished the rum and put the empty glass on a porch rail. Then he followed the fat foreman down the ladder, which Romolo's daughter hauled up immediately. To an outsider, her frantic haste might have seemed amusing; the terror of the villagers, excessive, even childish. Michael knew better. Like them, he had grown up with accounts of how the *amok* had descended on small, deep-jungle settlements, wiping them from the face of the earth in storms of homicidal rage. It had never happened in the valley of the Cagayan—perhaps it had never actually happened anywhere—but thirty years of fear could paint a hard glaze of probability over even the wildest stories.

Michael drove his jeep into the middle of the street, stopped and waited with the lights on and the motor running. He knew that he was visible from nearly all the barrio huts—and that if he were forced to leave alone, every man in the village would be shamed. He disliked such theatrical tactics, but the need to quickly establish personal authority over the plantation workers was vital.

More than five minutes passed before the first volunteer—a boy in his late teens—approached the jeep, his thin shoulders hunched, his face taut and anxious. "I am from the house of José Mariano, *Patrón*," he said in Ilocano.

Michael hadn't spoken the dialect since leaving the Philippines. "I know your father," he said haltingly. "He used to be the stablemaster."

The youth's abrupt smile showed that Michael had picked the right family. He climbed into the rear of the jeep, sat with his hands clasped between his legs. Soon a second volunteer, no older than the first, came to join him. A third, even younger man was accompanied by Romolo, flushed and wheezing. As Michael had hoped, workers who remembered him had sent out their eldest sons. It was a trick he had seen his grandfather use again and again: turning a man's pride inward upon himself, twisting it like a knife until he did what you wanted him to do. However, he had been away from the islands for years before he realized it worked just as well in Los Angeles or Seattle or Anchorage as it had in the valley of the Cagayan. . . .

"See me in the morning," he told Romolo. "I want the area around the house fully lighted, like in the old days." During the Hukbalahap rebellion, most of the plantation owners had ringed their homes with a network of floodlights as a precaution against nighttime guerrilla raids.

"The bulbs and wires have been stored away for many years. I am not sure they still work."

"Buy all the new equipment you have to. Just make sure the system is operating by tomorrow night."

No one was downstairs when Michael and the three field

workers entered the house. He led the way into the study, unfastened the chain running through the trigger guards of the weapons lined up in the gun cabinet. From the too-oily odor that rose from them, he could tell they hadn't been fired in years but at least his brother had had enough sense to keep them clean. He took out a 12-gauge shotgun, loaded it with a shell from the cabinet's ammo drawer, passed it to the stablemaster's son. He armed the others with light rifles—again placing a single round in the firing chambers, checked to be certain that the safety catches were on. The awkward way they held the weapons showed him that they were unfamiliar with firearms.

"One of you will sleep while the rest patrol the verandas," he said when they had returned outside. "Spell each other every few hours. If you see something suspicious out there, yell a warning, *don't* shoot. Chances are it's only a carabao wandering loose."

"If it is not a carabao?" asked the stablemaster's son.

"All I need from you—right now, anyway—is a lot of noise. I'll handle the rest. And thank you for your help. It will be remembered."

He went to the servants' quarters, told Inez to serve breakfast to the guards the following morning. The cook acknowledged his order with a familiar, sour nod, as if only days—not two decades—had preceded their last meeting. He managed to hide his amusement until he left her room. Obviously, she disliked him as much as she had when he was a child. He had never known why.

Still wearing his holstered .38, Michael climbed the stairs. Since no one had told him where he was to sleep, he assumed it would be in his old room, at the west end of the hall. A headache was trying to settle in behind his eyes, like a tiny, razor-clawed animal digging a burrow in unyielding soil. His hand was on the doorknob when he heard a woman call his name. He turned, saw Cara standing outside the open door of the bedroom his mother and father had shared. She had changed into a white terry-cloth robe; with her long chestnut hair unbound, she looked softer, more relaxed.

"I saw you drive up," she said, her tone vaguely troubled. "Was it necessary, bringing those boys here?"

"Very necessary."

"But don't they have their own homes to protect?"

"That's taken care of. And the danger to the main house is greater. We have more of what he wants."

"The *amok*?"

"Of course."

"Then you believe in him?"

"Once we were just a few yards apart. Maybe less."

"I don't understand."

"It takes a while to tell," he said, "and I'm right on the edge, Cara. If I don't get some sleep soon, I'll fall on my face."

"I'm sorry. Good night, Michael." She forced a smile, went down the hall, entered the nursery.

Michael found his flight bag on the narrow bed, which smelled of freshly washed linen. Looking around the room, he realized how young he had been the last time he had seen it. Everything seemed unchanged—from the faded spines of the Mickey Spillane and Carter Brown paperbacks in the bookcase to the Ilocan crossbows and spears and brightly stained carabao-hide war shields mounted on the walls. The primitive weapons had been gifts from his grandfather. So had the heaviest rifle in the gun cabinet downstairs, a .375 Browning given to him on his fourteenth birthday. It was capable of bringing down a lion.

Since the biggest game in the Cordillera jungles was wild boar, he had fired the rifle only at tin cans and paper targets. Now, twenty-six years later, he at last had a proper use for it.

Michael unbuckled the gun belt, draped it over the back of a chair, removed only his shirt and heavy boots before lying down with a gut-deep sigh of relief. He figured that he would fall asleep in seconds, but for more than an hour, his muscles stubbornly fought all attempts at relaxation. The mosquito netting around the bed seemed as solid and confining as the whitewashed concrete walls of a prison, and distant sounds took on uncanny resonance: the soft footsteps of one of the reluctant guards passing below, the baffled fluttering of a moth's wings against a screen.

He finally rose, went to a window, gazed out at the blackness of the Cagayan. His headache had turned into a steady throb, grinding against the inside of his brow. He could be anywhere out there, Michael thought. Twenty miles away or twenty feet, using the night as armor, wrapping it around himself like protective layers of steel.

On another moonless night, when he was seventeen, Michael Braden had tried to pierce that armor—and failed. . . .

THAT morning—a Saturday—Michael's father had ridden alone into the heavily wooded foothills at the eastern edge of the Braden land, leading a mule behind his saddle horse. Tied to the mule's pack yoke were half a dozen jars containing trout fingerlings, air-shipped from New Zealand. Frank Braden regularly stocked a netted-off section of a cool stream flowing down from the Cordillera.

"It'll be just like last year," his grandfather grumbled to

Michael and Les as they watched him leave from the veranda. "First time the temperature gets over a hundred, every damn one of those fish will float belly up."

The week before, a platoon of Philippine Constabulary troopers had been ambushed by Huk guerrillas ten miles north of the plantation. As a precaution, Frank Braden had taken along his old Savage hunting rifle, but no one expected him to run into trouble. Like most big farmers in the valley, the Bradens secretly paid a monthly "tax" to the rebel command, in return for a promise to avoid their lands. This extortion-based truce had rarely been broken. However, when his father hadn't returned by lunchtime, Michael began to grow concerned. Frank Braden had promised to join Sam in the southwestern fields—where the old man was supervising a harvest of cigarette tobacco—as soon as he stocked the stream. The round trip into the hills shouldn't have taken more than three hours.

"Maybe Dad went straight on to meet Grandpa," his twelve-year-old brother suggested. Both boys had been excused from their weekend duties to study for exams at the American Academy.

"Take too long on horseback. He'd come here first, get a car. I'm going to look for him."

Accompanied by Romolo—then a slim young farmhand—Michael set out by jeep; he had never shared his family's enthusiasm for horses. He drove the vehicle hard, bouncing so wildly over rutted back trails that Romolo was forced to clutch the top of the windscreen with both hands. At last they saw Frank Braden's saddle horse ahead, tethered to a spindly tree at the end of the dirt road. Michael braked the jeep, hurried over to the animal. From the yellow caking around the horse's mouth, he could tell that it hadn't been watered for hours. Obviously Frank

Braden had considered the terrain beyond too rough for his mount, had proceeded on foot, leading the mule. Seriously worried now, Michael slammed a cartridge into the firing chamber of his .30/30 Winchester before he and Romolo began the climb into the hills.

They discovered Frank Braden lying on his back at the bottom of the trout stream, blue eyes staring lifelessly upward through the clear water, his ripped throat gaping open like a torn white linen pocket, his face already bloated beyond recognition. Michael released a strangled cry, threw his Winchester to Romolo, leaped into the water, hauled the body on to the bank.

He was never able to completely sort out the crosscurrents of emotion that went through him as he held his father's limp form in his arms: grief, hatred of the unseen murderer and, strongest of all, rage. Another one had been violently taken from him. His sister, his mother, now his father, all thrown away like chunks of refuse in this mad battleground of a country. Always the gentlest, he thought. Even in the hell of Santo Tomás, his father had tried reason, learning Japanese in his endlessly rebuffed attempts to build some kind of human bridge between the starving, diseased prisoners and their jailers. Always the gentlest . . .

"For what?" he muttered. "A mule? A few pesos? How is it going to help their filthy revolution?"

"The Huks did not kill him," Romolo said in a frightened whisper.

For the first time Michael noticed the almost panicked apprehension in his companion's eyes. "What do you mean?"

Romolo jerked his head toward a nearby tree. Propped

muzzle up against the trunk was Frank Braden's Savage hunting rifle.

"*He* does not need guns."

Later, of course, he realized Romolo had been right, that the poorly armed guerrillas would never overlook such a valuable prize. But he was still too disturbed to think clearly. "I don't have time for that *amok* bullshit," he growled. "Drive straight to Tuguegarao, tell the constabulary what's happened. I'm going to pick up their trail."

Romolo exchanged the Winchester for the jeep's ignition key, headed back toward the valley at a near-run. Michael paused for a second, staring down at his father, wishing that he had something to cover him. But at least Frank Braden's headstone would mark a real grave, not a pitiful, self-deluding fiction.

In the beginning the trail was easy to pick up. It had rained the night before, and tracks left by the mule's shod hooves were plentiful. Still, he knew that the odds were against his finding the murderers. He had often hunted in these hills with his grandfather, knew that ahead lay stretches of hard, rocky ground, where the animal's droppings would be the only clues to follow. If he didn't spot his quarry before dark, it would be useless to continue. He hadn't brought food or a water canteen, and without them he couldn't sustain a long pursuit.

The sun was low in the sky when Michael got his first—and only—break. For hours he had climbed higher and higher into the mountains, twice lost the trail, only to pick it up again. Now it had vanished for the third time. He had reached the top of a ridge overlooking a shallow, bowl-shaped valley, wooded with banyan and tall, skinny highland bamboo. He was familiar with the area, had bagged a deer nearby only a few months before. He squatted on the ground, removed the kerchief knotted around his neck, wiped the sweat from his grimy face. By now he regretted this impetuous chase. He should have gone back to the plantation with Romolo, recruited help from among the many jungle-wise Ilocan field workers.

And then he saw the dark, indistinct forms ascending a rocky hillside on the far side of the valley, at least three miles away. He threw himself face down, shaded his eyes with his hands, squinted against the red glow of the dying sun as he sought a clearer view. At this distance, it was impossible to fully make out the figures. They could be a man leading a mule—or, just as likely, a party of hunters moving close together, even a group of timarau buffalo. If only I had binoculars, he thought in frustration.

Michael quickly conceived a plan. He knew an old game path across the valley. By following it, he could reach the spot where he had seen the figures before dark, resume tracking from there, gain hours. The hitch was that if he hadn't spotted his father's murderers, he might lose the trail for good. He decided to take the gamble. In his zeal for vengeance, it didn't occur to him that, facing the sun, he had been far more visible atop the ridge than the men or animals he had observed. . . .

Soon after reaching the jungled valley floor, he realized that he was in trouble. The path, remembered as clear, had become overgrown with brush and trailing vines, generated by the unseasonal rains of the past few weeks. Without a machete to clear the obstructing tangle, he moved far more slowly than he had anticipated. By nightfall, he was close to exhaustion—and not even halfway to his goal.

Hungry and thirsty—he had not encountered a stream in hours—Michael left the path, entered a stand of banyan trees, whose broad leaves would provide shelter if it rained during the night. He sank down wearily, rested against a thick tree trunk, the Winchester across his lap. He knew there was no point in going on until morning; he would never be able to keep to the path in darkness. Overhead, a band of chattering monkeys rustled the leaves, the sound gradually diminishing as the night deepened.

He didn't realize he had dozed off until he was jolted awake by the sudden resumption of the monkeys' annoying chatter. Branches shook as the tiny animals fled the tree, squeaking in alarm. Within seconds, the jungle again fell silent except for the inevitable muted chorus of insects and tree frogs. He glanced at the illuminated dial of his wristwatch, saw that it was past one in the morning. The temperature had plunged at least twenty degrees, as it always did in the Cordillera after midnight. Shivering, he lowered the rolled sleeves of his thin khaki shirt, buttoned the cuffs. The monkeys must have been startled by a binturong, he decided sleepily. The night-prowling civet cat was their greatest enemy.

Then he detected the smell. It was like the distilled essence of all the jungles in the world, compounded of mold and blood and green-scummed swamp water and great decayed trees, the way the whole world must have smelled in the age of the dinosaurs. At first it was faint, soon grew so strong that he almost retched. Has to be an animal, he thought, already knowing better. His father's murderer had backtracked, was now hunting *him*! And for the first time he knew that the *amok* actually existed. Fear unlike anything he ever experienced—before or after—coursed through his body, turned his hands into rigid claws, tightening around the Winchester. He exerted all his will just to make his right hand relax enough to free the safety catch on his weapon. He performed the familiar motion with semiparalytic slowness, afraid that whatever was out there might hear the slight click. He reached over, eased his left shirt cuff down over the glowing watch dial.

According to the legends, the *amok* was armed only with a sword—and *he* had a rifle. His conscious mind screamed an order over and over again: *Go after him, goddamn you!* But the fear was too great. All he could do was crouch down, struggle to keep his breathing inaudible despite the searing, expansive pressure in his chest and throat, hope frantically that the unseen predator would miss him in the dark. More than a dozen times he imagined a giant form materializing out of the blackness, swung the rifle toward the apparition, barely restrained himself from squeezing the trigger and betraying his position.

It was nearly dawn when the sickening odor at last faded from his nostrils, the monkeys swarmed back into the banyans and he knew that he was safe. His hands had gripped the Winchester so long and hard that the skin over the knuckles had split, was crisscrossed with thin rivulets of blood.

Defeated, ashamed of his cowardice, he began the trek back home. A few hours later he encountered a column of Philippine Constabulary troopers, accompanied by Romolo and his grandfather. He wanted to tell Sam everything that had happened but was unable to force the humiliating confession from his throat. All he said was that he had followed the stolen mule's trail until nightfall, had been forced to turn back by lack of water.

Sam Braden and Romolo returned with him to the plantation, while the troopers took up their futile pursuit of the murderer. As Michael expected, a constabulary report later blamed the crime on the Huks. Even before it was issued, he knew that the Philippines was no longer his home.

IF I hadn't lost my nerve, Les might be alive, Michael Braden thought as he peered out the bedroom window at the vast, night-shrouded fields. Years before, he had shed his guilt over failing the first real test of his adult life. After all, he had been only seventeen, had taken on a job for which he was wretchedly unprepared. That was no longer true—and this time he would make no rash moves. Every step of the hunt would be planned, every possible contingency covered in advance. Even more important, the science of killing and stalking other human beings—in darkness or the full light of day—had long since ceased to be alien to him. The *amok*, no matter how bestial his actions, *was* a human being, he again reminded himself. The cunning, unpredictable brain of another man guided that monstrous body.

But what kind of man?

7

"HIS NAME WAS KURUSU," Takei Shimura declared. "He served as a warrant officer in the *kempeitai*."

"I recall the organization," Major Ramos said drily. The Japanese military police—charged with suppressing civilian resistance—had been the most hated troops in the occupation force. He was suddenly glad that his wife was visiting her family on Mindoro. Two of her brothers, accused of distributing anti-Japanese pamphlets, had been tortured and executed by the *kempeitai*. Listening to this conversation would have put a severe strain on her sense of hospitality. "Were you a member?"

A self-mocking smile flitted across Shimura's lined features. "Even the Imperial Army had its share of commissioned clerks, Major. Outside of training, I didn't fire a shot during the entire war. I wish that I had. Just one."

Ramos' left eyebrow formed a puzzled arch.

"You will understand when you have heard more about Kurusu," Shimura said.

After a late dinner, the two men were having coffee. Shimura had been politely distant during the meal, limiting his end of the conversation to bland remarks about his flight from Tokyo or the changes in Tuguegarao since he had last seen it. Nothing in his manner had suggested that he was an agent of the Japanese government sent to aid in apprehending a mass killer. Ramos had resisted his natural urge to ask the dozens of questions nagging at him, sensing that, behind his formal facade, Shimura was struggling to resolve an unvoiced problem, would speak when he was ready.

"How can you be certain this Kurusu is the *amok*?" Ramos asked.

"He was a giant, twice the size of any other man in our regiment."

Ramos shrugged. "I've met several Japanese well over six feet tall. Surely there must have been at least a few hundred among all your troops on Luzon. And we have no way of being sure that the murderer was even stationed in this district during the occupation."

The look of wary thoughtfulness returned to Takei Shimura's thin-nosed face. He drained his coffee cup, then announced firmly: "It is Kurusu. And he did not, as you probably believe, go mad after hiding out in the jungles. He was an insane butcher years before the war ended. He may well have been an insane butcher before it began. It is best that I tell you everything. As a policeman, you should be used to hearing confessions."

"A confession of *what,* Mr. Shimura?"

The Japanese shoved away the empty cup, as if abruptly realizing it had contained poison, and said in a quiet voice: "All of Kurusu's crimes were committed under my orders."

THE conquest of the Philippines had almost been completed when—on April 11, 1942—Lieutenant Takei Shimura joined his new regiment on Luzon. Only a handful of American and Filipino soldiers still held out on Corregidor island, the last Allied bastion. The valley of the Cagayan was virtually untouched by the war, since all of the major battles had been fought hundreds of miles to the south.

Most of the young officers who accompanied Shimura on the four-day voyage from Yokohama to the port of Aparri had expressed disgruntlement about being posted to garrison duty in a backwater area. Although he echoed their complaints, Shimura was secretly relieved that he had so far avoided front-line action. The son of a former Japanese diplomat who had opposed conflict with the

United States right up to the attack on Pearl Harbor, he considered the war an act of national suicide, wanted only to survive and resume his architectural studies. He had enlisted in the army to help ease the pressure on his parents, ostracized because of his father's political views.

The regiment was quartered in tents on a nine-hole golf course, built by the local white planters, just outside Tuguegarao. Although soldiers' boots and the wheels of military vehicles had turned the course into a brown, stubbled wasteland, several of the greens' flags incongruously remained upright in their cups, like the ragged banners of defeated medieval knights. Shimura, assigned to share a tent with three other newly arrived junior officers, had not yet finished unpacking when a sergeant entered the tent, asked him to report immediately to Captain Hisao Tanape, commander of the regiment's *kempeitai* unit. Trying to ignore the surprised stares of his tentmates, he followed the messenger outside. *Even here,* he thought bitterly as he walked toward the headquarters building, formerly the course clubhouse. Without the influence of his uncle—a director of the Mitsubishi aircraft corporation—Shimura knew he would have been denied a commission after enlisting. Even so, during training, his superiors had made a point of reminding him that his father had been forced to resign in disgrace from the foreign ministry. He had foolishly believed that the harassment would end once he had left Japan.

The office of Captain Tanape was cast in shadow by a broad awning over the single window; the only interior illumination came from a small gooseneck desk lamp. Tanape proved to be a slender, mild-looking man in his mid-thirties. However, Shimura knew better than to be deceived by his appearance and comparatively low rank.

Commissions in the elite *kempeitai* force were limited to professional soldiers who had proved unswerving allegiance to the militaristic *bushido* code; in matters of internal security, his authority probably exceeded that of the regimental commandant.

Without looking up from a file he was reading, Tanape acknowledged Shimura's bow by waving him to a chair opposite the desk. For more than three minutes, Shimura sat at stiff-backed attention in the prescribed manner, hands resting on his knees, while the captain ignored him. At one point Tanape lifted the file high enough for Shimura to see his own name on the cover. Sweat broke out in his armpits.

"I see here that you are fluent in English, Lieutenant," Tanape said at last, putting down the file.

"Yes, sir."

"Good. It is a badly needed skill. The regiment was ordered to the Philippines so suddenly that we weren't provided with a single interpreter."

Shimura repressed a sigh of relief, believing that he had been spared the usual hints that he was not considered fully trustworthy. The captain's next question made him realize he had been optimistic.

"Where did you learn English? In school?"

"No, sir," Shimura replied as the sweat started gushing again. Obviously, his family background must be included in a *kempeitai* dossier. Tanape was coldly baiting him. "When I was a child, my father served in our Washington and Ottawa embassies. I picked up the language there."

Tanape gestured toward the window, which overlooked the mangled ninth green. "Did you play this game in America?"

"Once or twice," Shimura said, startled by the unexpected change of subject. Tanape's tone had implied that hitting a golf ball was virtually a treasonous act.

"It is comforting to know that so foolish a pastime could never catch on in Japan, isn't it?"

"Yes, sir." Tanape's remark often came to mind in the postwar years, especially after he had waited for hours to tee off at one of Tokyo's surreally overcrowded golf courses. Nothing else the man said was to give him the slightest amusement, even in retrospect.

"Report here in the morning," Tanape muttered. "And change your blouse. It is stained with perspiration. This vile climate is no excuse for failing to look like a soldier."

Shimura had risen, bowed again and turned toward the door before realizing that he and Tanape had not been alone. Seated behind a desk in a corner of the room was an immense, shaven-skulled figure wearing the insignia of a *kempeitai* warrant officer. The man's strong, thick almost colorless face reminded him of the stone carvings of warriors found in out-of-the-way areas of ancient Shinto temples—their swords invariably sheathed, armored bodies monolithically erect but with an aura of suppressed energy, as if awaiting the incantantions of a magician to bring them to ferocious life. His flat black eyes failed to acknowledge the young lieutenant's presence.

Takei Shimura knew instantly that he was facing the *kempeitai*'s executioner. And even three years later, when he possessed life-or-death power over Kurusu, he would fear him. . . .

"I never learned his surname," Shimura said, "never heard him speak. Few people did, except Tanape. For a while, I actually believed he might be mute."

"You recall nothing of the man's background?" Major Ramos asked. They had finished their coffee, moved into the living room for brandy and cigars.

"He was a native of Shikotan, one of our northernmost islands. A strange, barren place. Even today, the inhabitants are primitive fishermen and hunters of seals and whales. I have no idea how he came to be in the *kempeitai,* although it was not uncommon for them to recruit and train such large, powerful men for the lower ranks. If your purpose is to inspire the maximum amount of terror, large, powerful men are by definition more useful than small, weak men. All I ever knew about him beyond these few facts was that he was fearless—and capable of any brutality Hisao Tanape ordered him to perform. Kurusu worshiped the man."

Shimura held out his glass, which Ramos refilled. "During the time I served as his interpreter, Tanape frequently lectured me on *kodo,* the doctrine that the Japanese Empire had been divinely chosen to bring a millennium of peace, justice and order to all of Asia," Shimura continued with a rueful grimace. "Like most fanatics, he was afflicted with the need to proselytize—especially when he believed his listener had been partially corrupted by foreign cultures. Since I knew my life might depend on it, I put on a proper show of interest. Kurusu was usually present during these sessions, but there was nothing fake about *his* response. He might have been listening to the voice of God! In his own fashion, Tanape equally respected Kurusu. 'He is the perfect soldier,' he once told me. 'So perfect he has passed beyond humanity and become a pure weapon.' I didn't know what he meant then. It was before the slaughter began."

"How long did you work for the *kempeitai*?"

Shimura hesitated briefly; chronic suspicion must be to policemen what perfect manual reflexes were to surgeons. "Only a short time," he said casually. "Until enlisted men skilled in Philippine dialects were assigned to the regiment. My duties didn't amount to much—chiefly translating for Tanape at meetings with the civilians who took over the local government. Most of them understood English."

"I helped hang a few such men after the war," Ramos said, taking a deep, satisfied draw on his cigar.

"Eventually I became a company supply officer. Life in the early months of the occupation wasn't unpleasant for a man without military ambitions. Your guerrillas had not yet begun operations, and our high command still deluded itself with the belief that most Filipinos had welcomed liberation from the American colonial yoke. Then, of course, the raids started—and Kurusu went to work. . . ."

BY the end of the 1942 monsoon, Takei Shimura's regiment had settled in. Barracks for the enlisted men replaced the tents on the golf course; the New Reno Hotel had been requisitioned as quarters for the officers. The inhabitants of Tuguegarao had begun to nervously accept their conquerors, aided by the fact that the anticipated orgy of rape and massacre had not occurred and most of the displaced officials had been spared imprisonment or execution.

This false peace was irrevocably shattered when guerrillas ambushed a truck convoy hauling supplies from Aparri, killing all the drivers and guards before removing their booty into the jungle on muleback. An immediate pursuit of the raiders was ordered. Shimura and other administrative officers suddenly found themselves back in the infantry, commanding platoons. After the war, he was astonished to read that the Americans and British considered the Japanese to be masters of jungle warfare. They would have changed their minds if they had seen the frightened faces of the conscripts he led into the Cordillera that afternoon. To them—and to Shimura himself—the black-green wall of mountainous rain forest looming on either side of the valley of the Cagayan was an alien, forbidding environment, as mysterious as the landscape of another planet.

For more than a week the Japanese force—following outdated maps, guided by Filipino collaborators who, it was soon clear, knew little more about the jungle than they did—plodded along trails that led nowhere, slapped futilely at the hordes of poisonous flying insects that always sought out eyelids or nostrils or other sensitive areas, stunned by the heat pounding relentlessly through the blanket of overhead foliage. Twice, encamped for the night, they were awakened by distant rifle fire, learned the next morning that the enemy had attacked neighboring units. At last—demoralized, many of them suffering from dysentery or skin infections—they staggered back to Tuguegarao. Twenty-three men did not return. Nineteen had been cut down by guerrilla snipers; the other four had simply vanished in the forest, like beads of water hitting a hot skillet. Not a single enemy had been slain—or even glimpsed.

The next day Hisao Tanape, now a major, was put in charge of suppressing the guerrillas. His first measures were predictable: erecting barbed-wire barricades on all roads into Tuguegarao; issuing identification cards to the town's permanent residents; lowering the civilian curfew from ten P.M. to eight; ordering crash training programs in antiguerrilla tactics. Shimura was one of the few men in the regiment who knew that the real basis of the upcoming campaign had been established months earlier. Tanape had anticipated the rise of an insurgent movement after the monsoon, recruited civilians for a clandestine intelligence network. Just as significantly, Kurusu and a battalion of crack *kempeitai* troops had disappeared from Tuguegarao only hours after Tanape was given his new responsibilities.

During the next two weeks, the guerrillas struck again and again. The largest bridge over the Cagayan was dynamited; a river patrol boat, raked by machine-gun fire from a tree-shrouded bank. The battle soon reached into Tuguegarao itself. Three soldiers left a brothel in the early morning, minutes later were hacked to death with bolo knives in an unlit alley. Some of the officers began expressing muted scorn for Tanape. "Why doesn't he retaliate?" a disgruntled veteran of the North China war asked Shimura. "If this were Nanking, we'd already have shot hostages."

"I'm sure he will get around to it," Shimura observed.

Later that same afternoon, suffering from the recurrent indigestion that had plagued him since he had joined the army, Shimura turned the company supply office over to a sergeant, quit work half an hour early. He had intended to lie down—until he encountered Tanape on the front steps of the New Reno Hotel. The man's delicate, almost feminine eyes glistened with excitement. "Come along to my room, Shimura," he said. "There is something you must see."

The invitation—and Tanape's unprecedented friendliness—startled Shimura. The *kempeitai* commander's quarters were on the hotel's third floor, overlooking the main square. As soon as they entered, Tanape looked at his wristwatch. "We have a few moments," he said, smiling. "Would you care for some *sake*?"

"Thank you, sir," the increasingly dumbfounded Shimura replied. While Tanape poured two bowls of wine, he glanced around the room, furnished in the traditional Japanese manner. A rolled sleeping mat had even replaced the original hotel bed. Mounted on the wall above it was a magnificent nineteenth-century samurai sword, its handle wrapped with gold wire and tightly braided strands of scarlet silk.

"The Emperor Matsushito presented it to my grandfather in nineteen five," Tanape said, noting Shimura's interest in the gleaming blade. "He conceived the plan that led to our conquest of Port Arthur."

"I believe I read about him in school," Shimura lied—before it struck him that Tanape had not mentioned the grandfather's name. Suppose the man had been his mother's father? He waited tensely for the acid question that would expose him.

However, Tanape's thoughts were rooted in the present. He handed Shimura a bowl of *sake*, again checked the time. "Let us drink outside," he said. "By the way, Kurusu is back."

Shimura, his indigestion suddenly growing worse, followed Tanape to the narrow wrought-iron balcony. It was nearly six o'clock, and the square below remained crowded, although some merchants were already lowering corrugated-steel shutters over their shop windows. Women carrying market baskets haggled with food vendors, squatting beside wares displayed on brightly covered cloths spread over the ground. Directly opposite the hotel, Dr. Mapitang, his work finished for the day, sat on a folding canvas lawn chair in front of the government clinic.

Then a Japanese labor battalion dump truck turned into the open square, growled slowly toward the center. The driver of an empty *calesa* lashed his pony out of the truck's way. A *calamansi* lime vendor, less quick, watched helplessly as the vehicle's huge wheels crushed the fruit into green pulp. Shimura had raised the *sake* bowl to his lips, lowered it when he saw the truck's cargo. From a distance, the load might have been mistaken for bundles of stained rags, but the stench already rising in the hot, still air betrayed its true nature.

"Kurusu was not able to find the guerrillas' central force," Tanape said. "There are fewer than fifty of them hiding in those filthy mountains—but they have hundreds of supporters in the barrios. We have, of necessity, begun with them."

The truck had halted in the middle of the square. With a whining metallic rumble, the rear elevated, began spilling bodies through its loose tailgate. Some of the slaughtered men, dead for days, were as rigid as logs; others had been slain so recently that their arms and legs hung limp and the blood on their garments had not yet turned brown.

Terrified Filipinos—the women and children screaming and sobbing—fled the square as the grisly cascade continued. When the last corpse flopped in the dust, only Dr. Mapitang remained, staring up at the balcony where Shimura and Tanape stood side by side. Shimura's *sake* bowl fell from his hand, broke on the deserted sidewalk below. Mapitang rose, unhurriedly folded his lawn chair.

He tucked the chair under his arm, like a bather departing the beach after a full day in the sun, carried it into the clinic.

"Kurusu?" Shimura asked, struggling to keep his voice calm.

"Yes."

The driver of the dump truck descended from the covered cab, came to attention beside the heaped bodies. To Shimura's surprise, he was a small, round-shouldered corporal.

"He has already started back into the jungles," Tanape said, anticipating Shimura's question. He dismissed the driver by slashing the air once with his fine-boned right hand. . . .

"I am already familiar with what you did here," Major Ramos said, interrupting Shimura's reminiscences. The Imperial Army's effort to destroy the resistance force led by Aurelio Villamor, a young lawyer from Tuguegarao, had been unparalleled in its ruthlessness. Eventually more than two thousand innocent civilian hostages had been shot, hanged or beheaded—ten for each Japanese soldier killed by guerrilla action.

The faint street noises filtering through the walls around Ramos' house had long since ceased. The enveloping silence reminded Takei Shimura of the final, ominously quiet nights before Tuguegarao's fall. "We saw little of Kurusu after the first executions," Shimura continued. "He and his men stayed in the mountains for months at a time, stalking and killing guerrillas, sending their bodies back for public display.

"By the end of 1944, we actually thought the battle had

been won. Kurusu discovered that Villamor's central headquarters was an Ilocan village, more than thirty miles into the jungle. He led a surprise attack on the place, killed most of the hard-core insurgents. Villamor and a few of his followers escaped, but the backbone of the revolt had been broken.

"Of course, ten thousand such 'victories' would have meant nothing at all. The Americans had already crippled our navy at Lingayen Gulf, landed in the southern islands. Their B-29s had begun mass bombing raids on our homeland. What did the security of an isolated Luzon valley matter? The *kempei* were like coffinmakers obsessed with building a casket so strong that maggots or rats could never penetrate it, not even considering that all they had accomplished was the safeguarding of the dead . . ."

ON March 26, 1945, only a skeleton Japanese force held Tuguegarao. The bulk of the regiment—led by Colonel Haruna, the commandant—had moved south to reinforce a defensive line against the advancing Americans. Most of the troops left behind to secure the town were members of the *kempeitai,* with Lieutenant Colonel Hisao Tanape as the garrison's senior officer. Shimura—who had reached the rank of captain through routine promotions—had also remained, in charge of a squad of overage soldiers and three decrepit trucks. His assignment was to move supplies to the front—if, by some miracle, any Japanese ships were to get through to Aparri.

Tanape had scheduled a staff meeting for seven that evening. Certain that it would be an excuse for another harangue about the Empire's ultimate triumph, the restless Shimura took a walk after dinner. Even six months earlier, no Japanese in his right mind would have moved alone through the narrow streets of Tuguegarao. However, little resistance survived in the weary minds and gaunt bodies of the town's civilians, who had suffered more than their conquerors from the U.S. Navy's successful blockade of the Philippines. Virtually all the crops grown in the Cagayan now went to feed the occupation forces. Starvation and disease had done a far better job than the *kempeitai* in defeating insurrection.

At least we've never lacked for tobacco, Shimura thought as he lit a cigarette hand-rolled from the local dark leaf. In the clear twilight air, the rumble of distant artillery was audible. He knew it had to be enemy fire. The last of the defenders' shells had been used up weeks before.

Shimura was about to start for headquarters when he heard female screams, a man's piercing howl of agony, the sounds of splintering wood and smashing glass. The uproar came from a building about half a block away. Shimura knew the place—a brothel frequented by noncommissioned officers. He didn't quicken his pace, assuming it was simply a soldiers' brawl. Then, with incredible speed, a tan-uniformed human figure flew through the bamboo-shuttered window of the brothel's ground-floor bar, crashed head on into a wooden telephone pole. It reminded Shimura of an exaggerated bit of action from those foolish American Western films he had enjoyed before the war. The difference was that in the films, the man rose a few seconds later, comically clutching his brow. His skull didn't burst like an overripe pomegranate, scattering puddles of blood and brains and bone shards all over the sidewalk.

By the time Shimura reached the brothel, half a dozen

armed *kempeitai* troops were running down the street from the main square. Now the only sound emanating from the bar was deep, harsh, rumbling groans, like waves of molten lava trying to burst through the resisting earth. Shimura briefly paused by the dead man, saw that his sleeve bore a master sergeant's insigne.

When the military police burst into the bar, they found Warrant Officer Kurusu standing in the middle of the tiny dance floor, his giant torso swaying to an uncertain rhythm, like the blade of a defective metronome. Shimura, entering on the soldiers' heels, realized that the groans were part of a keening, wordless song issuing from Kurusu's lips. The front of his torn jacket was wet with blood, and his black eyes had rolled high in his head.

Across the room, amid the wreckage of shattered tables and chairs, lay the twisted forms of three Japanese soldiers. Five young Filipina prostitutes, too frightened to move, huddled against the walls. A sixth girl—thin, pretty, gold front teeth gleaming in her slack mouth—had slumped to the floor. Her face was gray with shock, and her left arm —torn from its shoulder socket—dangled lifelessly, secured to her body by a few strips of ripped muscle and skin.

In those first, confused seconds, the soldiers naturally assumed that Kurusu had been wounded by assassins who had fled out the rear door. They had lowered their rifles and were going to his aid when Shimura shouted: "No! Stay where you are!" He knew of only one person in Tuguegarao strong enough to hurl a fully grown man like a javelin. The soldiers paused, peered at Shimura in bafflement. Then one of the Japanese on the floor twitched slightly. Kurusu lurched over to him, sent a booted foot crashing against the side of his head. His neck broken, the Japanese lay motionless.

The military policemen were raising their rifles, prepared to fire, when Kurusu fell to a kneeling position, still chanting his meaningless song. Again the *kempei* hesitated, unwilling to shoot the man they respected above all others. Their problem solved itself when Kurusu toppled on his side, unconscious, his enormous legs drawing upward until his knees touched his chest. He snored drunkenly, saliva coursing from the corners of his mouth, turning pink when it encountered his crimson-stained jacket.

"Take no chances with him," Shimura warned.

The corporal leading the *kempeitai* patrol nodded dazedly. He removed manacles from his belt, ordered another soldier to train his rifle on Kurusu's shaven head while he secured the giant's hands behind his back. Kurusu's wrists were so thick that he was barely able to close the manacles around them.

Shimura heard excited voices behind him, turned to see one of the *kempei* barring Dr. Mapitang's way into the bar. "Let him in," Shimura snapped.

Mapitang, his worn black medical bag already open, went to the girl. Shimura knew that it was duty to demand that he treat the Japanese first, but he said nothing. A quick glance at the bodies showed there would be no point. Two had been beaten to death; the stem of a broken bottle protruded from the chest of the third.

After four straining, gasping soldiers had hauled Kurusu from the room, one of the prostitutes calmed down enough to tell what had happened. Kurusu had been in the brothel since late morning, drinking straight rum between bouts of lovemaking with the women. "Every few months he would come here like a crazy animal," she sobbed, "force us to do terrible things! We always obeyed! We had no choice!" By the end of the day, his sexual needs satisfied, he had settled down at a corner table and started on his third quart of rum.

Four sergeants, also drinking heavily, had entered, sat down at another table, where they were joined by the gold-toothed girl. One of them—the man with the jagged bottle-half twisted into his heart—had loudly told his friends that the war was lost, that they were all idiots to just sit around and wait to be killed by the Americans. Without a word, Kurusu had risen and started toward them, smashing off the end of his rum bottle on a table edge. The slaughter began. . . .

"So you have finally taken to murdering each other," Mapitang remarked in English to Shimura, snapping shut his medical bag. A pair of clinic helpers carried the girl out on a stretcher. Mapitang followed them, trailed by Shimura's irritated stare. During the past two years, Shimura had often supplied the clinic with small amounts of medicine and drugs from army stores, risking court-martial if the diversion were discovered. Without the quinine he had provided Mapitang during a virulent malaria outbreak the previous spring, dozens of civilians, weakened by malnutrition, would have died. But the arrogant physician had never given him a single word of thanks.

Shimura was already half an hour late for the staff meeting called by Hisao Tanape. Wondering what the *kempeitai* commander would say when informed that his "pure weapon" had gone berserk, he hurried across the ravaged golf course toward the headquarters building. He was still fifty yards from his goal when the American planes—a flight of the dreaded P-61 fighter-bombers—zoomed out of the sullen red ball of the setting sun, their cannon and machine guns roaring. Shimura ran to a nearby sand trap, threw himself face down in the loose soil, huddled frantically against the three-foot-high trap wall. As explosion after explosion reverberated through the earth, he pressed his hands over his ears, didn't lift his face from the gritty, stinging sand until the sounds of the air raid had passed.

When Takei Shimura crawled out of the sand trap minutes later, he was to find himself in command of the Tuguegarao garrison. The headquarters building had taken at least three direct hits, been reduced to a blazing mound of wreckage—and all the officers who outranked him had been attending Tanape's staff meeting inside. The devastation of the area was almost total. Every truck and car in the motor compound was burning; the enlisted men's barracks, leveled. And even worse destruction had to be on the way. The far-off artillery reports—sporadic an hour earlier—had become an endless rumble. It could only mean that the Americans were launching a major attack.

After improvising a temporary headquarters in the New Reno Hotel, Shimura and the handful of surviving junior officers waited for orders that never arrived. Garbled radio reports had already told them that the Imperial force to the south had been routed. By dawn hundreds of exhausted, leaderless troops—from every unit in the Cagayan—had poured into Tuguegarao, their first stop on what was to become one of the most hellish retreats of the war. The rumor had spread that a fleet of transports had slipped through the blockade, was waiting at Aparri to take off survivors of the battle.

"Do you think it could be true?" a nervous young lieutenant asked Shimura.

"Yes," he lied. "Thousands of our men were evacuated from Guadalcanal and Attu, right under the enemy's noses." He did not add that these epic rescues had been accomplished earlier in the war, when Japan still possessed the remnants of a navy. Still, since the Americans would be in Tuguegarao within hours, the garrison had no choice except to join the exodus north—and false hopes were better than none at all.

"What shall we do with Kurusu?" the lieutenant said.

The question startled Shimura. In the last few hectic hours, he had almost forgotten the madman in the Tuguegarao jail. As commander of the garrison, he had the right to put a revolver bullet into Kurusu's head. Then it occurred to him that the hulking killer might still serve a function; anything that could slow down the advancing Americans, even for a few minutes, had to be used.

"Go to Colonel Tanape's room," Shimura ordered. "On the wall is a ceremonial sword. Bring it to me. . . ."

Only a Japanese rear guard remained in Tuguegarao when Shimura, carrying Hisao Tanape's sword, unlocked the cell in which Kurusu had been confined. The giant—now sober—sat on the bare stone floor, his back to a corner, immense hands clutching his knees. Shimura had half-expected him to defend last night's massacre, argue that the men he killed had expressed defeatist beliefs, a serious military offense. But he remained silent, emotionless black eyes staring at Shimura without apparent recognition.

"You know me, Kurusu?" he asked, almost gagging on the stink of dried blood and vomit and rum that rose from the man's befouled uniform.

Kurusu nodded slightly.

"Colonel Tanape was wounded in an air raid last night," Shimura said, extending the samurai sword. "He realized that Tuguegarao had to be evacuated—and that men too badly injured to walk must be left behind. Rather than accept the disgrace of capture by the Americans, he ripped open his own belly with a short sword. I used this—his most treasured ancestral weapon—to behead him and end his suffering. But first he made me promise that I would give it to you afterward, tell you what you must do to expiate your crimes."

The single, grief-racked moan that emerged from Kurusu's twisted mouth convinced Shimura that his *bushido*-drenched fantasy had been accepted without question. He dropped the sword at Kurusu's feet. "In half an hour the rest of us will be gone," Shimura continued. "You will stay behind and continue to fight, do everything in your power to delay the enemy. It is a better way to end your life than hanging. As Colonel Tanape once told us: *The greatest privilege a soldier can attain is to choose the time and place of his own death.*"

Shimura strode out of the cell. He didn't look back, but the faint whisper of steel being drawn across the stone floor told him that Kurusu had picked up the sword.

"MORE than three thousand of us started out for Aparri," Takei Shimura told Ramos in a weary voice. The hands of the antique clock on the living-room wall were nearing eleven. "We figured that we could reach the port in a few days. Then the American planes began their strafing runs. Your guerrillas, armed by parachute drops, attacked our flanks at night. We finally broke up into small, undisciplined groups, hid in the jungle for weeks at a time, afraid to travel in the open. When our food ran out, some men resorted to cannibalism. Others committed *hara-kiri*. Officers, by the sword, in the traditional manner. The enlisted men—six or seven at a time—would usually squat in a circle around an activated grenade. They would join hands, like schoolchildren at their games, wait for the blast. In the beginning I tried to stop them, but, after a while, it didn't seem to matter much. Only thirty-two out of our regiment reached Aparri—where, of course, the Americans were waiting to put us in prison camps. I had accomplished the goal I had set for myself at the start of the war. I had survived. It never occurred to me that Kurusu might have also."

HE thought again of the morning, three days before, when he had read a newspaper article about Lester Braden's murder—and the theory that a gigantic Japanese straggler armed with a samurai sword had been responsible for it, along with dozens of other killings since the end of the war. Hours of indecision had preceded his telephone call to the government's repatriation commission in Tokyo.

He had not anticipated, during an interview with a commission official the following day, that the government would ask him to make a personal attempt to talk Kurusu into surrendering. "In these cases, a former comrade is often the only man able to establish contact with the poor wretches," the official had said. This is preposterous, Shimura had almost replied. I am a retired architect . . . a widower with grandchildren . . . too old to crawl around in jungles searching for homicidal lunatics. . . .

But in the end he realized that he must return to the

valley of the Cagayan—not so much because of what he had done but because of his motives for doing it. His real reason for unleashing Kurusu had not been military, he had slowly come to understand; that had been a self-deluding ruse, permitting him to avoid the responsibilities of his involuntary command. Unlike most of his fellow officers, he had never believed in the cause for which he had fought, despised any kind of fanaticism—yet he, out of all of them, had succeeded in the mindless prolonging of horrors that should have ended in 1945.

Sergeant García entered the living room, spoke to Ramos in a rapid stream of Tagalog. The major quickly rose from his chair, excitement gleaming in his dark eyes. For an instant, his expression disturbingly reminded Shimura of the look on Hisao Tanape's face when he was waiting for Kurusu's first victims to be dumped in the main square.

"A patrol just returned from the hills, Mr. Shimura," Ramos said, looking about the room for his visored cap. García found it on a bookcase shelf, handed it to him. "They have discovered the place where the *amok* killed Lester Braden's horse. I would advise getting to bed. Our hunt will begin early."

Troubled, Takei Shimura watched the two policemen hurry out of the house. Obviously Ramos had not comprehended a word of what Shimura had told him, failed to understand that he had not come here to help destroy Kurusu. He had come to save him. . . .

By now the soldiers had reported finding the remains of the pale man's horse, he thought with satisfaction. The search for him had probably begun—in the wrong place.

He had reached the base he had chosen for the coming operation—an area of thick cogon grass about two miles north of the plantation house from which the pale man had ridden—but much work remained to be done. However, he had already found the necessary tools, guided by the torn, brown-edged map he had carried in an oilcloth pouch since the first day of his mission.

He removed a chunk of horsemeat from his canvas food sack, sniffed it, took a cautious bite, spat it out before swallowing, realizing the meat had grown rotten. Another day of hunger lay ahead. He threw the meat to the ground; gazed across the fields to the pale man's plantation house, dark except for a single light gleaming in a second-floor window. He wondered who lived in the room.

In time I will find out, he promised himself as he moved farther into the grass, his sheathed sword over his shoulder. But first he had to set his traps.

8

IT WAS PAST TEN O'CLOCK when Cara Braden awoke the next morning, realized she had fallen asleep on top of the coverlet, still wearing her white terry-cloth robe. She had even forgotten to turn off the lamp on her night table. Against the vivid tropical sunlight pouring through the bedroom's north window, the illumination from the bulb had a negative quality, as if contaminated by the darkness of the preceding night.

She propped herself on an elbow long enough to flip the lamp switch, then fell back against her pillow. On most mornings, she rose without effort, her mind instantly clear. Les, who needed two cups of coffee just to manage his socks, had constantly teased her about it. "You ought to be the planter, honey," he had mock-grumbled only last week. "You've got the right metabolism. God meant *me* to be a blackjack dealer." But today, though she had slept hours longer than usual, she felt drained of energy. Why shouldn't I be, she thought, nevertheless struggling to wrench free of the lethargy that had settled over her body like a coating of warm, sticky, semiliquid plastic. How are you *supposed* to feel the morning after your husband's funeral?

She would have to begin seriously thinking about the move to America. Although she had lived all over the world, she had never once made personal travel arrangements, really wasn't sure how to go about it. Whenever, during her girlhood, she and her mother had joined her father at an overseas post, an Air Force enlisted man had simply delivered an envelope containing tickets and a typed itinerary. After her marriage, Les had handled all the details. Was it possible to make airline reservations over the telephone, or would she have to go to Manila? Would she be required to turn in her permanent-residence papers to the Philippine government? She felt foolish for not knowing the answers.

I've always had someone to take care of me, she reflected a little bitterly as she got out of bed, pushed a dangling strand of hair out of her eyes. Years ago, in one of those silly women's-magazine articles, she had read that many widows actually felt resentment against their husbands for having died, unconsciously regarding it as a form of abandonment. At the time, the notion had struck her as ludicrous; now she understood.

Cara put on jeans and a cotton blouse, went downstairs to the kitchen, where she found Maria seated alone at the table, embroidering a handkerchief. "Where is Evie?" she asked the young nursemaid.

"With the *patrón,* ma'am. They went for a walk together."

Cara felt a peculiar, shocked tingle in her stomach at Maria's casual use of the title *patrón.* Only Les had been addressed that way by the plantation workers. For a confused instant, she imaged that the events of the past week had been a nightmare, that any second Les would come through the door, holding their daughter by the hand. Then she realized the girl must have been talking about Michael.

After a meager breakfast of coffee and toast, Cara walked out on to the patio, looked around for Michael and Evie, glad that the child had gotten over her shyness with him. A few minutes later, she glimpsed their distant figures approaching the house, along the eucalyptus-bordered path that led to the river—and the family cemetery. He couldn't have, she thought. He had no right!

"Mama, Michael showed me where Daddy is," Eve announced calmly after she had run up to kiss her mother on the cheek. "It's so pretty there."

"Run along inside," Cara said, trying to hide her distress. "I want to talk to your uncle."

Eve took a few half-skips toward the kitchen door, then turned and gazed upward into Michael Braden's dark-skinned face. "Are you really my daddy's brother?" she asked in a doubting voice.

"Yes."

"You don't look like him."

Michael reached down and stroked the little girl's delicate blond hair. "Later I'll prove it, okay?"

"How?"

"You'll see."

"Did you have to take her to his grave?" Cara snapped when Eve was out of earshot.

"She asked me to, Cara."

"But Evie had no idea that—"

"Then why did she ask?" he said firmly, cutting her off. "You never told the kid her father was dead?"

Without knowing why, Cara took a step backward. "Last night," she said, "but not in those words."

"The words don't matter. They understand anyway—and they're afraid. Better to go all the way, so the healing can start."

"That should have been my decision!" she cried.

"I'm sorry."

The anger suddenly left her, replaced by a kind of numb relief. Michael's action had probably been right. Eventually, back in America, Evie would have wanted to be told where her father was buried. Now the question would not have to be answered. Cara was free of it—but uncertain that she had wanted to be freed by a stranger who happened to be Les's brother.

"I'm going to inspect the fields," Michael said. "I wish you'd come with me."

"All right," she replied reluctantly, "but I don't see the point."

"There's a point. I'll pick you up out front in a few minutes."

Michael left her, went to the equipment shed to get a jeep. Romolo and two workers were inside, untangling coils of electric cable, part of the long-stored grounds floodlight system. "How we doing?" he asked the foreman.

"The wires look all right," Romolo said, "but the lights are corroded. I have sent someone to Tuguegarao to buy new ones."

"Will you be finished before dark?"

"I believe so, *Patrón*."

Cara was waiting on the veranda when Michael pulled up in the jeep. She gave him a nervous half-smile as she climbed into the front passenger seat.

Within minutes after starting the tour of the plantation, Michael realized that his sister-in-law knew virtually nothing about its operation. The original purpose of the drive had been to let the field workers see them together, help establish the legitimacy of his temporary overseership. However, he soon found himself providing her with a running lecture on tobacco growing, explaining the function of the long, rectangular, open-walled drying sheds, telling her why certain varieties of the plant had to be sheltered beneath broad muslin sunshades until almost fully grown. He hadn't expected Cara to be steeped in the technicalities of her husband's work, but total ignorance had been unanticipated.

Remembering his brother, Michael thought as he drove along a dirt trail north of the main house, it made sense. Even as a boy, Les had compartmentalized his life, constantly striving for a manageable simplicity—so many hours and no more given to schoolwork, so many to sports, so many to private reading. Everything in its niche. He must have chosen a wife in the same manner, seeking someone content to manage the house, supervise the servants, care for the children. A beautifully efficient system—unless you happened to get sliced in half by a maniac and no one was left to assume your responsibilities except a ninety-three-year-old grandfather and a young woman who behaved as if she were living in an upper-middle-class suburb of Los Angeles. . . .

"Why was nothing ever grown in those fields?" Cara asked, indicating one of the dozens of high-grass areas dotting the plantation, like tufts of artificial hair jutting out of a clown's rubber skullcap. The road went right past it.

"They were cultivated before the war," Michael explained, "but when the Japs retreated in '45, they planted land mines and booby traps all through here. In the worst places, we just let the cogon grass take over."

"It's still dangerous?"

Michael shrugged. "Wouldn't make any difference after all these years. Once cogon is deeply rooted, the only way you can clear it is to bulldoze out all the decent soil. Not much point."

"Have we gone far enough, Michael?" Cara asked.

"Want to start home?"

"If you don't mind. I have a lot to do today."

IN the brief time it took the driver of the jeep to brake his vehicle, back to the edge of the narrow road and swing around to head toward the plantation house, he could easily have rushed over and slain the man. The jeep had halted less than twenty feet from his hiding place. However, such an action would have been senseless. He had no need for an automobile—wasn't even sure he remembered how to drive one—and he had already seen that the rear of the jeep held no food or useful supplies. Besides, with the soldiers searching for him, he must not chance a daylight raid.

What could be the relationship between the occupants of the jeep and the pale man? The girl was almost certainly American, with that look of mingled openness and hauteur he had noticed on the faces of female tourists before the war. He decided that she couldn't be his victim's wife, since she would have been too young for marriage the first time he had killed the pale man. His daughter, perhaps? Or a younger sister?

He had possessed an American woman once, a high-priced whore in Shanghai. To be with her an hour had cost him all of his savings—he was a young recruit then—but he had never regretted it. Her legs had been long and sleek and firm, had locked around his waist with sinuous strength, urging him further into her; unlike most of the Oriental women he had known, she had not feared or found grotesque the hugeness of his body. He wondered if the girl in the jeep possessed such legs. Since she was seated, it had been impossible to tell.

Again hearing the distant hum of an aircraft engine, he pulled shut the camouflaged lid of his underground shelter. . . .

"IT'S an L-19," Michael said as the small airplane with Philippine Constabulary markings flew over the jeep. A second plane of the same type was distantly visible, above the green peaks of the Cordillera, moving in lazy, ever-widening circles. "We used them in Viet Nam to spot guerrillas. Didn't do a hell of a lot of good there either."

"Are they—"

"—looking for the *amok*? Sure. Ramos must have a big operation under way. I saw truckloads of PCs go by on the new highway this morning."

Cara glanced at him, curious about the cynical undertone of his words. "You don't believe they'll find him?"

"No," Michael declared flatly.

"Why not?"

"Because they're pulling the same old dumb stuff. During the Huk war, the PCs and the army had at least a thousand troops stationed here. They used to mount artillery batteries in the tobacco fields, lob tons of shells into the jungle. The war lasted more than six years. You know how many guerrillas they killed in all of the valley of the Cagayan?"

Cara shook her head.

"Eight." He released a burst of dark laughter. "Plenty of civilians, but only eight confirmed Communists."

Last night Michael had told her that he had once been separated from the *amok* by only a few yards. She had intended, sometime during the drive around the plantation, to ask him to explain. But suddenly she didn't want to know. She had already realized that her brother-in-law was a deeply troubled man—and that attempting to understand the source of his emotional pain could only add to her own.

They were nearing the plantation compound when Cara casually revealed that she intended to take Evie to her parents' home in Arizona as soon as the arrangements could be made. "The two of us will only be in your way here," she concluded.

It had never occurred to Michael that she might assume he had returned to manage the plantation. He planned to stay only long enough to kill the *amok* and hire a permanent overseer. Although stunned by her revelation, he managed to keep his manner calm; telling her the truth immediately might be a serious error. "I wouldn't make any firm plans until we see Luis Delgado," he said.

Delgado had been the Braden family's lawyer since the late 1940s. "Luis called me from Manila two days ago," Cara replied. "He said the terms of Les's will were clear-cut. His share of the plantation was divided equally between me and Evie."

Michael slowed down as they passed the equipment shed. Romolo and his assistants were stringing floodlight cables over the ground, like a huge set of Christmas-tree bulbs. "Philippine law is tricky," he said, "especially where foreign citizens' property rights are concerned. For your own good—and the kid's—I think you should stick around at least until Delgado gets his documents filed. You know lawyers—everything is easy to start with. Then they keep bringing up new details until you figure your head is going to split."

"You may be right," she said thoughtfully.

"I'll phone him this afternoon, make an appointment. By the way, have you told Grandfather your plans?"

"No."

"I'd wait a few days. He looked pretty rocky when I talked to him yesterday."

"You actually believe he'd care that Evie and I are leaving?"

"Of course."

"I don't. He hardly knows we exist."

AFTER lunch, recalling his promise to Evie, Michael

Braden went up to his room, opened an old footlocker. His scrapbooks were still there, resting beneath layers of clothing. He had intended to pick out photos of Les and himself together as children, show them to his niece as proof of their relationship. However, he found himself caught up by the snapshots and clippings neatly taped to page after page of black construction paper. Soon the faint sounds of human voices and hammering—Romolo and his men beginning to mount floodlights in the trees around the house—disappeared from his consciousness. . . .

The collection had begun with fourteen ragged-edged photos found on the floor of a closet in his parents' gutted bedroom, his only links to the way of life that had existed before the Braden family was sent to Santo Tomás. He had been nine years old the day he, Les, his father and his grandfather—after months of physical rehabilitation in a U.S. Army hospital—had returned to the plantation house, discovered that the Japanese or local vandals had stolen the furniture and everything else of value. Only debris—and the photographs—were left.

He had carried the pictures with him everywhere, like religious relics, until he was able to buy the first of the scrapbooks, obsessed with somehow re-creating his own past. Throughout most of the following year he had eagerly sought additions: photos of family members in the possession of neighbors or plantation servants; stories clipped from yellowed copies of the mimeographed newsletter put out before the war by the Tuguegarao country club, bland items about his father taking third place in the American Legion golf tournament or his mother's participation in a flower show.

To his baffled annoyance, Les had been indifferent to

the project, even reluctant to pose for new photos if he knew they would enter Michael's collection. Years later, of course, he understood why. His younger brother's first conscious memories had been of the prison camp. In his stumbling, child's fashion, he must have set out to begin a new life from scratch, trying to remain untouched by events that had gone before. Each of them had chosen his own way of dealing with the emotional destruction inflicted by the war years, Michael thought. Maybe Les's had been better.

There they all were: his mother pregnant with Les, a smile brightening the dark, usually somber features that Michael alone had inherited; his father and a bored-looking Sam playing croquet; Eve, uncannily like her namesake, grinning in the back row of her fourth-grade group portrait. His sister appeared again—her arm protectively around Michael's shoulder—on the front of a faded Japanese propaganda leaflet celebrating the Imperial Army's humane treatment of civilian internees. The setting was the dock at Aparri, minutes before the Braden family joined the other American prisoners in the foul hold of the steamer that was to transport them to Manila. Michael, gazing upward, was accepting a bag of candy held out to him by the young Japanese officer in command of the guard force.

Where in the hell did I find *that*? he asked himself grimly, flipping the page. A moment later, as he was examining a newspaper shot of liberating GIs entering Santo Tomás, a grotesque possibility struck him. He turned back to the propaganda photo, stared in disbelief at the nameless officer, imagining the same features creased by deep eye and jowl lines, the black hair gone gray. Beyond doubt, it was the face of the middle-aged Japanese who had flown up from Manila with him yesterday. . . .

SINCE a few minutes before seven that morning, Shimura, Major Ramos and a squad of Philippine Constabulary troopers had been encamped in a wide clearing at the edge of the Cordillera jungles. Overhead, two L-19 spotter planes had dropped leaflets in Japanese on dozens of square miles of forest before beginning constant patrols of the area. The message to the *amok* stated that no harm would come to him if he surrendered, that his former comrade-in-arms Takei Shimura would meet with him alone and offer proof that Japan was at peace with the rest of the world; every half hour a smoke flare would be set off to mark the spot where Shimura waited.

Now late-afternoon shadows were inching out of the mountains; the planes had already flown back to Tuguegarao. Shimura shifted in his canvas camp chair, watched yet another flare spew its orange trail high into the air. He wondered if Kurusu was watching from the nearby trees, trying to decide if this actually was the same man who had released him from prison, given him orders to fight on until death.

Ramos walked over from the command car, uttered a disgruntled sigh. "It is not going to work today," he said. "Tomorrow morning we will try a few miles farther north. However, he must have read our message by now. He couldn't have reached deep jungle in so short a time."

"Tomorrow it might be best if the planes left after dropping the leaflets," Shimura suggested. "He may not leave hiding as long as they are in a position to fire upon him."

Ramos slumped into the camp chair next to Shimura's, irritably chewed on a thumbnail. "I have already assured you that I will live up to the agreement between our governments. No matter what the *amok* has done, he will be regarded as a legitimate prisoner of war as long as he gives up without resistance. Actually, it is of no concern to me whether he spends the rest of his life in a Philippine prisoner or a Japanese insane asylum."

"I am not suspicious of your motives," Shimura said with quiet amusement. "*He* is."

"Mr. Shimura, I have taken part in at least a dozen of these manhunts since the war," Ramos remarked with a baffled shake of his head. "I have talked to most of the stragglers after their capture—and I still lack the faintest comprehension of such stubbornness. I know your people believed that surrender to the enemy was the ultimate disgrace, that the Allied forces would torture and kill all prisoners. But after more than thirty years, how can even a madman like the *amok* believe that the war is still on?"

Shimura gestured toward the constabulary troopers, clad in olive-drab fatigues, lounging around a nearby truck. "Why not?" he asked. "Look at those soldiers. Or yourself. You all wear the same uniform and helmets the Americans did when they landed here in nineteen forty-four. For that matter, so do the men in the Japanese Defense Force! And the Cuban Communists! To a fugitive hiding in the jungle—unable to speak or read the language of the country, devoting every waking moment to staying alive—it would seem as if nothing had changed. We—and Kurusu—are victims of Yankee standardization. And there is another possibility."

"What?"

"That he *does* know Japan lost the war—and doesn't care. He may be performing an act of *gekokujo*."

Ramos stared at him without understanding.

"There is no exact equivalent of the concept in English. 'Respectful insubordination' is the closest I can manage. Kurusu may feel that our forces, in allowing themselves to be defeated, betrayed the Emperor. By not surrendering, he is symbolically expiating the shame of his own government, demonstrating to the world that the essential spirit of the nation remains intact, if only in his person."

"Then nothing you or I do can make him surrender?"

Shimura laughed sardonically. "Even worse, from my viewpoint. If he is performing *gekokujo*—and has read your leaflet—he must regard me as a traitor. Any meeting between us would begin with Kurusu cutting off my head!"

Ramos stood up, glanced at the rapidly darkening sky. "I can think of still another reason why he failed to make contact today," he said, walking back toward the command car. "He may not be in the jungle at all."

FOR more than an hour he had crouched amid heavy reeds on the riverbank, waiting for the last lights in the barrio to be extinguished. He knew it would be a brief wait. Whenever his presence in an area was discovered, he had long since learned, the people in these tiny villages invariably—and foolishly—sought darkness, providing him with the element most vital to the performance of his missions.

Finally a lamp in a distant building flickered out and the barrio merged fully into the night. He waited a few minutes more and then left the shelter of the reeds. He had already picked out the object of his raid: the village store.

If its shelves were sufficiently stocked with canned goods—and he could move the food without being detected—it might yield enough supplies to last him through the monsoon.

The store was the only two-floor building in the barrio; the owner probably lived on the second. Fortunately, there was a large, tree-shrouded yard behind the structure. He hid for another quarter hour in the shadow of a rusted pickup truck, listening to make sure no one was moving around inside the store. Finally satisfied, he unsheathed his sword, scuttled silently across ten feet of open ground to the back door, secured with a heavy padlock. He enclosed the lock with his right hand, squeezed until the mechanism came apart in his palm. He carefully opened the door.

As he had expected, a stockroom lay beyond. Its shelves were heavily laden, he saw with relief; often country merchants kept only a few days' goods on hand. Large burlap bags filled with rice were stacked against the far wall. He flicked one open with the tip of his blade, poured its contents on to the floor.

He was filling the sack with canned meats when shuffling footsteps approached the interior stockroom door. He lowered the sack to the floor, grasped his sword in both hands, held it in the horizontal attack position. He moved over to face the door, waited. Dim yellow light gleamed through the crack below the panel. It creaked open and an old, bent-shouldered Chinese entered. He clutched an oil lamp in his right hand, a baited rat trap in his left.

The surprise in the old man's eyes had not yet yielded to fear when the blade descended on the right side of his neck, cut through bone and flesh and muscle with surgical precision, emerged from the left armpit. His head, left shoulder and arm—fingers still clutching the lantern—

spun away like a bird crippled in midair by a shotgun blast, landed in a far corner with a soft thud. The rest of the body crumpled, spewing blood; the rat trap hit the floor face down, loudly snapped shut.

He darted across the room, stamped out the flames licking over the floorboards from the shattered lamp. Now he had no choice except to kill everyone in the house before an alarm could be given. Even if the people upstairs had heard nothing, they would soon come to look for the Chinese. He went into the shop's front room, ascended a flight of steep wooden steps to the living quarters.

There were only four rooms on the second floor. The bathroom, kitchen and living room were dark and unoccupied. Perhaps the storekeeper had lived alone. Then he eased open the door to the bedroom, saw an elderly Chinese woman lying in a double bed. Faint moonlight from an open-shuttered window bathed her ash-white face, reflected from her open, glazed eyes. Whimpering, she turned over, pressed her face into her pillow, her withered fingers clutching the edge of the mattress, shoulders quivering beneath her faded cotton nightgown.

Why, he wondered, did so many of them accept their fate without struggle? The back of the old woman's neck was exposed. By severing a vital cluster of nerves between the first and second vertebrae, he knew he could induce instant, painless death. He brought the sword down with a movement so gentle that it was almost a caress.

9

"WE HAVE TO GO into the mountains and kill him," Michael Braden said. "If it takes a week or a year. There's no other way."

Seconds after he spoke, he realized that the other men at the poker table would probably refuse their aid. It showed in Jack Tully's tired, bemused half-smile; the embarrassed, uncertain flush that rose in Walt Lydecker's cheekbones; Harry Dietrich's grimace of disbelief. The other players—Lyle Miller and Tim Cushing—had still been children when Michael had left the valley of the Cagayan. They merely looked confused.

The game—held in the same shabby New Reno Hotel room used in Michael's youth—had been under way more than an hour when he sat down at the table. No mention had been made of his brief quarrel yesterday with Dietrich, though Jack Tully had pointedly recalled that the Swiss had risked his life by providing food to the guerrillas during the Japanese occupation.

Jack had also brought up the subject on all their minds: "Walt said you wanted to talk something over with us."

Michael's terse reply temporarily ended the game. Dietrich pushed back his chair, went over to a table holding plates of cold cuts and an ice bucket filled with bottles of San Miguel beer. "I figured that was it," he grunted, slapping a thick chunk of ham on a slice of bread. "And I will take no part in such madness. You have been away a very long time, Michael. The government has ceased regarding white landholders as a privileged class, believe me. Any foreigner caught joining a vigilante force would be jailed or deported."

"Besides, Major Ramos must have put a hundred PCs up into those hills today," Walt said. "They're really zeroing in on him this time."

"The PCs will fail," Michael stated with total certainty. "They're political cops. They don't have the training—or the commitment—to go all the way into the jungle, wait him out on his own terms. They'll just pick around the hills a couple of weeks and then head home—until he butchers somebody else."

"Why would we do any better?" Tim Cushing asked.

"Most of us have hunted in the Cordillera. So did our fathers and grandfathers. We understand the jungle Ilocans, hired them as trackers. Our workers have family links with them. The tribesmen must have some notion of the *amok*'s movements, the areas where he appears most often. They hate the PCs too much to cooperate with them, but they might talk to us. Half a dozen men, if they made up their minds to keep at it until they nailed him, could do the job."

"No, they couldn't," Jack Tully said tonelessly. Every eye turned toward him. For three years, fighting with Aurelio Villamor's guerrillas, he had lived in the Cordillera, had explored more of its dense, tangled terrain than any other white man.

"Why not?" Michael said, irritably riffling the stack of

red chips in front of him. He forced himself to stop, determined to keep his temper even if they opposed his plan.

"The *amok*—if there is an *amok*—has stayed alive in the Cordillera since World War Two. He must have worked out defenses and ways of hiding so tricky we can't begin to imagine them. Mike, you said you'd be willing to keep up the hunt for a year. *Ten* years might not be enough—and I'm already out of shape for that sort of thing."

Dietrich returned to the table, took a grinding bite out of his sandwich. Drops of mustard spattered his collar. "When you've calmed down about Les, you'll see that we're right," he told Michael.

He surrendered to the red haze of anger forming behind his eyes. "It's more than a personal vendetta with me—and it ought to be with you," he said. "The son-of-a-bitch has been up there too fucking long."

Michael cashed his chips, curtly nodded goodbye, left the hotel room. "He'll try it alone," Walt Lydecker said with a dismayed shake of his head. "Jesus!"

"Deal me out of the next hand," Jack Tully said, standing up. He went to the sandwich table, opened a San Miguel, realized that beer wouldn't be enough to take the edge off the self-contempt seeping into his consciousness, like ground water slowly rising in a cement basement wall. Every word Michael Braden spoke had been the truth—and he had lacked the strength of will to back him up.

Jack had been out of the room a full minute before the other men, again engrossed in the game, noticed his absence. . . .

I should have expected it, Michael thought as he descended the front steps of the hotel. Maybe he had no right to get mad over their reluctance to take part in a dangerous and time-consuming manhunt. They had farms to run, families to look after. Besides, in a way that years of absence made it impossible for him to share, the existence of the *amok* must long since have become an accepted danger, like typhoons or the dry-season field fires that could wipe out decades of work in minutes. Perhaps such matters had to be left to exiles, if only because they had so little to lose.

He had parked his jeep on a street off the opposite side of Tuguegarao's main square, bustling with strollers, *calesas* and sidewalk vendors even at this late hour. He headed across the square, passed among a chattering crowd of people leaving the first show at the town's only movie house. The garish poster above the theater door showed a burly man in a striped T-shirt tearing off a luscious *mestiza*'s lace-topped peasant blouse. Tearing-off-the-girl's-blouse was a traditional key scene in Tagalog-language films, he recalled. How many hours had he and Les spent in the place, not understanding a word of the dialogue, hoping that just this once, the girl's breasts would be revealed? They never were.

Already past the theater, he heard someone call his name, turned to see Lenore Tully. The gray streaks had vanished from her auburn hair, which had been freshly cut in a shorter, more youthful style. "Like to buy me a cup of coffee, Mike?" she asked. "I have a lot of time to kill."

They went to an outdoor café, sat at a bamboo table near the sidewalk. "Since Kevin went away to school, I come in with Jack on poker nights," Lenore said, sipping the black, gritty brew that passed locally for demitasse.

"We take a room at the New Reno—not that he uses it, except to shave in the morning after the game. I see if the drugstore has gotten in any new American paperbacks, have dinner in a restaurant, catch a movie if I'm not meeting a friend."

"How was the picture?"

She laughed lightly. "Boobs falling out all over the place."

"I was born twenty years too soon."

"Actually, I've never understood why they hardly ever run American movies. To most Ilocans, Tagalog is as foreign a language as English." The amused expression left her face. "How was Cara feeling today?"

"All right, as far as I could tell."

"Do you mind?" Lenore plucked a cigarette out of the pack jutting from the pocket of his khaki work shirt. "I always felt so sorry for the girl, even before this happened. Les had really trapped her in that nineteenth-century dream world of his—mistress of the plantation, everything except crinoline skirts. You almost expected the field hands to sing spirituals on the front lawn after dinner. Can't you hear it—*Swing Low, Sweet Chariot* in Ilocano?"

He raised a plastic throwaway lighter to the cigarette between her lips. "It's as easy to die in a dream world as the real one."

"I'm sorry," she said quickly, reaching over to clutch the back of his hand. "I wasn't really making fun of Les."

"I know."

Her hand remained on top of his own. "What about *your* world, Michael?" she asked softly. "Did you ever learn where you belonged?"

For a few seconds, he didn't understand what she was talking about. Then he faintly remembered his self-dramatizing monologue in a Manila cocktail lounge. He was startled that after all this time, she would make even an indirect reference to their long-ago one-night stand.

"Not really, Lennie," he replied.

"I didn't think so," she said, lifting her hand. . . .

NEITHER of them noticed Jack Tully standing beneath a dusty-leaved curbside tree just beyond the pool of light cast by the café terrace's pastel paper lanterns. He had followed Michael from the hotel, intending to tell him the real reasons why he could not join a private expedition against the *amok*. He had still been halfway down the square when he saw the meeting between Michael and his wife. By the time he had reached the café, they were seated at a table.

He had retreated into the shadow of the tree, watched them. It all came together: her tense, inexplicable coolness to him last night; her decision this morning to have her hair tinted and restyled for the first time in months. He had always known that Lenore had had lovers before their marriage. That young Mike Braden might have been one of them had never occurred to him. He tried to convince himself that his suspicions were foolish—but even at this distance the look in his wife's pale green eyes when she touched Michael's hand was unmistakable. It was a look he had not seen in years.

Jack slowly walked back to the New Reno Hotel, bought a bottle of rum at the bar, took it up to their room. He poured a glass full of the dark brown liquid, downed it quickly. If Lenore and Michael wanted to resume the liaison, they could easily manage it tonight. As far as they knew, he was still at the poker game, would play halfway into the morning. Where could they go, he wondered. Not the New Reno; too much chance of encountering acquaintances. Of course, since Lenore was already registered, Michael might take another room and she could secretly join him there. Perhaps he should have entered the café, ended it, at least for this evening. But he wouldn't have been able to hide his jealousy, no matter how hard he tried.

He poured another glass of rum, sat on the bed, stared with dead eyes at the image reflected from a dresser mirror across the room: the tiny rolls of fat at the corners of his jaw; the flabby-fleshed hand holding the glass; the bulge of his gut, concealing his belt like fresh bread oozing over the edge of a baking pan. How much older than Michael was he? Not more than ten years, probably. Enough.

The door opened behind him and Lenore entered. "Did the game break up early?" she asked in surprise.

"I didn't feel like playing anymore."

"God, I'm tired," she said, bending to pull a nightgown from the open suitcase on the floor beside the dresser.

"Go anywhere after the movie?"

"I met Mike Braden on the street," she replied casually. "We had coffee."

After she went into the bathroom, closing the door, his shoulders sagged with relief. Obviously, back at the café, his imagination had tricked him. What evidence did he have to back up his suspicions? A childhood friend touching another on the hand; a fleeting facial expression that, in retrospect, could have been a look of sympathy, not desire.

"I guess Mike told you he sat in tonight," Jack said, raising his voice in order to be heard through the bathroom door. "He asked us to help him track down Les's killer."

"You won't do it, will you?" she asked sharply when she returned to the bedroom. The brown circles of her half-dollar-sized nipples were hazily visible through the nightgown's semitransparent fabric. Despite the easing of his jealous doubts a few moments before, he mentally pictured Mike Braden's lips and hands moving over her breasts.

"No," he said.

She went around the bed, slid between the sheets, as usual gave a kick with both feet. The movement inevitably dislodged the bedclothes on her side. By morning she would be uncovered, huddled against him for warmth, her arms around his waist. He had told her again and again not to kick away the bedclothes, but she always did.

Jack turned off the light, undressed, joined Lenore in bed, tried to make love to her, failed. It had happened before but always when he had been drinking heavily. Except for the two glasses of rum, he'd had nothing all day. . . .

He believed it. Just a touching of hands. A look. And still he believed it. . . .

"Go to sleep, honey," Lenore murmured in the darkness. The bedsprings creaked as she pulled down the nightgown he had raised to her throat.

"Mike Braden talked about how we could do a better job than the PCs because we knew the Cordillera so well," he said. "And he looked at me. Hell, I haven't been up there since nineteen forty-five! What for? To shoot a wild pig or a scrawny deer?"

Lenore placed her hand on his naked left shoulder, patted him twice. She kept the hand there, the inert fingers slowly separating, like a ridge of tidal sand worn away by a mild but relentlessly intrusive surf.

"It wasn't like they think," he said. "Being with Villamor. In the beginning, we did what we were supposed to do. We shot up trucks, blew bridges, distributed leaflets."

"I remember the war, Jack," Lenore said drowsily.

"You were in Santo Tomás."

"Same thing."

Nevertheless, he told it all again: how the Japanese had surprised the Cordillera guerrillas in a remote jungle barrio; how he, Villamor and a handful of others had fought their way out of the trap that took the lives of thirty-three of their comrades; how for more than a year they had hidden in the depths of the forest, always on the verge of starvation, constantly pursued.

"They must have sent a special unit after us," he said. "We never saw them, but we knew they were there. Time and again we'd reach an Ilocan village where we'd been helped before, find it burned down, the people dead, the crops destroyed. Another month or two and we'd have had it. Then the Americans reached the valley and everything turned around."

Lenore's breathing had become heavier, more rhythmic. Her fingers had ceased to move.

He had never told anyone the full truth about his part in the attacks on the shattered Japanese army retreating north through the valley of the Cagayan. Now the words came out in a whispered torrent:

"They airdropped food and guns to us. It only took a few days to recruit a new force from the barrios, men who had been too afraid to join the guerrillas before. We had contempt for them, but that didn't matter. What mattered was killing Japs. And we did kill them. A couple thousand, I guess. No point to it militarily. Aparri and the other coastal towns were held by the Americans, so they couldn't have escaped anyplace. It was easy. They had no ammo left, nothing to eat. And the planes had scattered them into small bunches.

"In the beginning we paralleled the retreat, set up ambushes. Then we got tired of shooting them. A waste of bullets, Villamor said. So we used clubs and machetes. One afternoon I bashed out the brains of eighteen soldiers, so weak from dysentery they couldn't walk. Another day we bottled up three platoons in a ravine, stoned them to death from the cliffs. Took hours, but that's how we did it, instead of firing a few rounds with our submachine guns. We burned them alive with gasoline, staked them on the ground, let the sun cook their eyes before we cut their throats. They hardly ever fought back, not after the first couple of weeks.

"They still had grenades but they used them on themselves, not us. We got mad whenever we stumbled on a bunch who had blown out their own guts, as if they had deliberately cheated us of our pleasure. And it *was* pleasure, Lenore. In the beginning I told myself I was simply getting revenge for what they had done to us and our people, but it wasn't true. I killed with joy.

"All of a sudden, it was over. I got hit with malaria, and Villamor and the others carried me to a GI field hospital. I was delirious a couple of weeks—not much quinine was available yet—and when my senses finally came back I vomited all over my bedsheets. Not from the malaria—from realizing what had happened to me during the retreat. A man should never learn how much he's capable of. That's why I don't hunt, why I refused to help

Mike Braden tonight. Up there, I'd turn into an animal again. I know that I would."

Her arms encircled his thick waist, tightened. Already the bedclothes on her side had worked free. He tugged the blanket back over her hips, realizing that she must have been asleep for minutes, hadn't heard his warning. . . .

Did you ever learn where you belonged?

Lenore's question still nagged at Michael's mind as he turned off the new highway on to the plantation's main road. How long *had* he counted himself among the dispossessed? Probably the full realization had come in Viet Nam, but, days after entering USC, he had sensed part of the truth. The distant homeland that no Braden had seen for half a century had proved to be more illusory in fact than it had been in his imagination. He spoke colloquial English, had dressed like an American all his life—but he was just as much a foreigner to his open-faced, annoyingly childlike classmates as he had been to the Ilocans. That was probably why his brother had never visited the States. America was part of the past—and Les had been wise enough to know the past would always betray you.

Michael still wasn't sure how he had gotten through even two and a half years at the university. He hadn't known until he started classes that he was barely literate. His family's position in the valley of the Cagayan—and the deeper ignorance of the region's natives—had shielded him from the truth. But how could it have been any different? Because of wartime imprisonment, he had been eleven when he entered Tuguegarao's American Academy, run by an elderly Australian and his usually drunk wife. In the early postwar years, struggling to rebuild the plantation, his father couldn't have afforded to send him and Les to a decent school in Manila. Anyway, he must have figured, all of the other white kids around here are in the same fix. And, of course, they were—but only Michael had decided he didn't want to be a tobacco farmer.

After quitting USC—aware that years of further study wouldn't gain him entrance to advanced engineering courses—he had joined the army, obtained an OCS commission. Like millions of men before him, he had realized that the military was as good a place as any for the dispossessed. He might still be in, counting the remaining years to retirement, if he hadn't fractured Colonel Blassingame's skull. After that had come a decade as a construction worker, always in the wilderness or its edges—power projects in the Pacific Northwest or the Rocky Mountain states, finally the Alaskan oil fields. Occasionally, he had thought about returning to the valley of the Cagayan—his brother had often urged him to in his letters—but he had known it would be a mistake, especially after Les wrote that his wife had given birth to a daughter and Michael realized that, quite accidentally, he had mislaid a generation. . . .

The house was dark except for the window of Cara's bedroom. Remembering the foreman's promise to have the grounds floodlights operating by evening, he drove the jeep through the open doors of the equipment shed, found Romolo, his round face flaccid with fatigue, wrapping rubber tape around a spliced cable. "A few more minutes, *Patrón*," he said. "The lead wire from the generator was broken."

"Did you put on guards?"

Romolo nodded. "The same three volunteered again. It is easier work than a day in the fields."

Michael took his gun belt and .38 revolver out of the glove compartment, carried them in his hand as he walked toward the house. He would have been arrested if a policeman had seen him wearing a weapon in Tuguegarao. "Who is coming?" a voice nervously challenged from the shadowy veranda. The pale sliver of moon had long since set.

"Michael Braden," he said, mounting the front steps.

Suddenly the floodlights in the trees flared to brilliant life, bathing the area for hundreds of feet around the house in a flat, pitiless glow. He recognized the stablemaster's son, who was again armed with a shotgun. His face was contorted, his eyes wide. For a second Michael assumed that he had been temporarily blinded by the lights. Then he realized the youth was staring in appalled surprise at a distant object.

Michael turned quickly, glimpsed a gigantic, semihuman form on the periphery of the field of light. An instant later, the shape melted into the darkness beyond.

"It's him!" Michael shouted, yanking the .38 from its holster. More to arouse the household than in hopes of hitting anything, he fired a single shot, leaped down the steps, ran toward the spot where the figure had vanished. He plunged into the darkness—and the flesh-numbing fear that had incapacitated him during his first encounter with the *amok*, years before, returned with unexpected force. Every instinct urged him to hurry back to the light but he continued to move ahead through hip-high tobacco, keeping to the furrows between the rows of plants, so that the rustle of the leaves against his body wouldn't give away his position. Every few seconds he paused briefly, listened for his enemy, aware that the *amok* might backtrack and try to waylay him, as he had done in the Cordillera.

Michael's eyes gradually adjusted to the dim starlight.

About ten feet ahead, an unfamiliar mound blocked the furrow. He threw himself on his elbows, rested the barrel of the .38 across his left forearm, sighted in on the hulking outline. When it failed to move, he inched forward, keeping his weapon trained, saw that the object was a heavily laden burlap sack. Its neck had opened, spilled half a dozen food cans over the ground. Clinging to the burlap was a phantom's trace of the *amok*'s rancid, primeval odor.

He heard breathing and uncertain footfalls to his left, swung the revolver toward the sounds, his sweating forefinger tightening on the trigger. It can't be the *amok*, Michael told himself. He wouldn't be that clumsy. Michael glanced back toward the plantation house. It was less than a hundred yards away—but from the black isolation of the field, the building and its surrounding pool of glaring light seemed unreachably distant. Cara stood near the open front door, beside two of the teen-aged guards. The jeep Michael had taken to Tuguegarao—Romolo now at the wheel—was just squealing to a stop near the veranda. But there was no sign of the stablemaster's son. With incredulous horror, he realized that the kid must have followed him, was making the noises to the left.

"Go to the house!" he yelled.

A shotgun blast rumbled over the flat earth. Before its reverberations faded, they were overwhelmed by a piercing cry of agony.

Michael pounded toward the source of the merging sounds. Two bobbing shafts of light stabbed across the furrows as Romolo steered the jeep into the fields. The foreman reached the body of the stablemaster's son only seconds after Michael. The boy sprawled on his back, his belly ripped open, wisps of vapor rising from his exposed intestines as the heat of his abdominal cavity met the cool night air. The shotgun lay a few feet away.

"I'm going ahead," Michael told Romolo, rising from beside the body. "Follow in the jeep."

"What will we do about the boy?"

"What the hell *is* there to do? Just follow me, goddamn it!"

He found the first sticky smear of blood on a tobacco leaf; a larger pool, sinking into loose dirt about three yards beyond. Judging by the almost instantaneous convergence of the shot and the boy's dying scream, he and his murderer must have been only a few feet apart when they fought. Even a monster couldn't take a load of 12-gauge shot at that range and escape major injury.

For nearly an hour, Michael Braden walked in front of the slow-moving jeep, pursuing the trail of blood revealed by its headlights. Time and again the stains ran out but he spotted others in parallel furrows. The *amok*—unable to stanch the telltale flow—must be taking a zigzag course across the fields, the only means left to obscure his tracks. Michael cursed the fact that the jeep wasn't equipped with a movable spotlight which would have enabled them to penetrate the darkness on either side.

The trail ended at the same broad patch of cogon grass Cara had questioned him about that afternoon. "We are not going in after him, are we, *Patrón*?" Romolo wheezed uneasily.

Before Michael could reply, they heard the blare of a klaxon. Four Philippine Constabulary vehicles—a command car and three heavy trucks—were roaring up the dirt road that ran past the eastern border of the cogon. Cara must have telephoned Tuguegarao for help. Michael quickly boarded the jeep, told Romolo to head for the road.

They intercepted the convoy at the edge of the grass. "He is in there?" Major Ramos asked Michael as he stepped out of the command car. Constabulary troops, obeying Sergeant García's guttural orders, were scrambling from the rear of the trucks, slamming the breeches of their M-16 rifles into automatic-fire position.

Michael nodded, his gaze traveling past Ramos' shoulder to the command car's interior. The lights of the truck behind it shone through the rear window, dimly illuminating the face of the Japanese officer who had headed the roundup of American civilians during the war.

"How large is the field?" Ramos asked.

"Four or five acres," he muttered, still staring at the Japanese.

Ten minutes later, dozens of troopers ringed the cogon. A hurried reconnaissance had failed to turn up fresh traces of blood leading out of the grass, so their quarry—if alive—must be hopelessly trapped. And already, Michael Braden had begun to feel that something was wrong. Why would anyone as jungle-wise as the *amok*, even wounded, have staggered two miles to a hiding place that lacked a single avenue of escape?

10

CARA BRADEN SIGHED with relief when Michael and Romolo came into the living room. Her brother-in-law's face and hands and clothing were smeared with dirt and dried sweat, but he seemed unhurt.

"What is happening?" asked the young constabulary lieutenant who, along with three troopers, had been left at the house by Ramos.

"They've penned him up in a patch of cogon a couple of miles north," Michael said. "Major Ramos won't try a sweep until morning. Hard enough moving through that grass in broad daylight. You found the Mariano boy?"

"We took him to the barrio in one of your trucks. I have already sent for Dr. Mapitang and the priest from Tuguegarao."

Michael told them about the burlap sack of canned goods dropped by the fleeing killer. "There was too much of it to have come from a farmhouse kitchen. You'd better check Li Tung's store."

With a startled nod, the lieutenant hurried on to the front veranda, barked orders in Tagalog to the troops posted outside. A moment later, they heard a jeep drive off at top speed. "Go on home, Romolo," Michael told the weary-eyed foreman. "Nothing else you can do. And thanks for coming after me. It took guts, especially unarmed."

"The barrio will be without sleep tonight, *Patrón*."

"I know," Michael said. "Tell the men they won't have to work tomorrow, except for monitoring the irrigation."

When Romolo had shambled from the room, Michael sank on to the couch, poured himself a cup of coffee from a pot Inez had prepared for the troopers. Cara noticed that his hand shook as he raised the cup to his lips and took a deep swallow. "It must be cold," she said. "I'll start some more."

"It's fine."

"Michael, did you actually see him?"

"Just a glimpse."

"And there's no way he can escape?"

"Doesn't look like it."

"It's over, then," she said, shuddering beneath the bathrobe she had flung on over bra and panties when she heard the first gunshot. Even now the events of the past few hours seemed fragmented and unreal: rushing downstairs and on to the veranda, just in time to see Michael vanish into the blackness beyond the floodlights; the blending of a shotgun blast and a human scream; Romolo following Michael in the jeep; desperately telephoning the Tuguegarao constabulary post for help, knowing it would take the troopers at least forty-five minutes to reach the isolated house; going upstairs to comfort the shrieking Eve and her equally terrified nurse; the arrival of Ramos and her confused attempt to give him a sensible account of what had happened; flinching away from a living-room window when she saw troopers carrying the limp body of the stablemaster's son back into the light. At least Sam Braden hadn't been roused by the turmoil; the drugs he took to control his high blood pressure usually plunged him into deep sleep.

"Romolo was right," Cara said. "None of us will sleep tonight."

"Try, at least. You'll have to call on the Mariano family in the morning. They'll expect you."

Again Michael had sounded uncannily like his grandfather. "Is it necessary? I can't speak Ilocano. And Les was buried only two days ago. . . ."

"Makes it even more important that you go. The boy died trying to protect Les's family."

"You're right," she reluctantly agreed. "Will you come with me?"

"If I'm back in time. I have to be there at the finish, Cara. You understand."

"Of course," she said, starting toward the center hall. "Perhaps I *should* try to sleep. Good night, Michael."

"What were you doing when the floodlights came on?"

She halted, puzzled by the unexpected question. "Getting ready for bed. Why?"

"With the shutters open?"

"I may have forgotten to close them. No one can see through a second-floor window from the fields."

"It's not important," he assured her. During the drive home, he had pondered why—if the canned goods were from the barrio store—the *amok* had traveled across open ground after stealing them, approached needlessly close to a large house. The brush-and-reed-filled banks of the river would have offered far better cover. Obviously, something had drawn him to the plantation. Remembering the light in Cara's bedroom window, he had suddenly realized that she might have been the unknowing lure.

When Cara left the room, Michael rested his head against the back of the sofa, aware that she had misunderstood his eagerness to return to the cogon at sunrise. I'm not some bloody comic-book avenger, he had wanted to tell her. I just have to be certain it's really done.

After Ramos had ordered him and Romolo away from the siege area for their own safety, he had briefly resented losing a personal chance to finish off the unseen killer. But the feeling had soon left him, to be replaced by a dull sense of relief, as if he had just had an agonizingly painful bad tooth extracted and were waiting for the Novocain to wear off. All that counted was losing the source of infection, not who wielded the instrument of release. . . .

Cara was nearly to the head of the stairs when she noticed Sam Braden's bent figure in the doorway of his darkened bedroom. "Is Mike all right?" he whispered.

So the old man had been aware of the emergency after all, she thought, wondering why he had remained upstairs. "Yes, Grandfather," she said.

"I figured he'd be. Boy always knew how to take care of himself." Sam backed into the bedroom, softly closed the door.

Cara looked in on Evie, made sure she slept soundly, then went to her own room. Instead of lying down, she stripped a blanket from the bed, wrapped it around her shoulders, sat at a chair beside a front window. The floodlights still poured their scalding white glow from the trees. She clutched the blanket tighter over her breasts; the predawn chill was creeping out of the Cordillera.

When she went downstairs for breakfast, at a few minutes before eight, Michael had left the house. A mound of twisted cigarette butts in the coffee-table ashtray showed how restlessly he had spent the final hours of darkness. . . .

"IT is no use," Major Ramos declared. "We will have to go in."

All night, Takei Shimura had urged Kurusu to surrender, blaring his message through a bullhorn. No answer had come from the cogon grass. Now it was past eight A.M., and the heat of the sun had already grown uncomfortably strong. Perspiration bathed the constabulary troopers' taut faces—as always, looking incongruously small beneath steel helmets designed for Americans. Seventy-three men, summoned from neighboring units, had joined Ramos' original force.

Shimura rested the bullhorn on a front fender of the command car, wiped his forehead with a pocket handkerchief. "Do you think he is still alive?"

Ramos shrugged. "From the amount of blood he lost, I would say it was impossible. But what about him *hasn't* been impossible, at least to rational minds?"

A strong wind from the south bent the tops of the cogon, dry stalks rustling like the legs of giant insects rubbing against each other in a mating signal. If the wind had not risen, shortly after dawn, Ramos might have considered Sergeant García's suggestion that they set fire to the grass and burn him out. But the combination of wind and weeks without rain presented too much danger that a blaze would spread to the surrounding tobacco.

"Excuse me, Mr. Shimura," Ramos said. "I must begin the preparations."

Shimura watched Ramos walk toward García, who was seated in front of a field radio. He debated whether to deliver his message again, realized that it couldn't do any good. If he was conscious, Kurusu must have heard him dozens of times, decided to reject his plea. He again remembered what Hisao Tanape had told both of them: *The greatest privilege a soldier can attain is to choose the time and place of his own death.* Perhaps this windblown plain was the site Kurusu had picked for his final, demented stand against an imaginary enemy. If so, other men might die this morning.

He banished this pessimistic vision, tried to concentrate on the fact that within twenty-four hours he would be back at his home below Mount Nangoyama. Whether Kurusu was dead or alive, Shimura's self-imposed responsibility had ended.

He looked away from the field of swaying grass—and again found himself the object of Michael Braden's relentless stare. Last night, just before the American and the fat plantation worker had driven off, Braden had directed a glance of implacable hatred at him. The animosity baffled Shimura, especially since Braden had been courteous during the flight from Manila, had even offered him a lift into Tuguegarao from the airstrip. At sunrise, Braden had returned alone, halted his jeep beyond one of the sawhorse barricades Ramos' men had set up to keep civilian traffic off this section of road. His eyes had rarely been diverted from Shimura in the hours since. It was inconceivable that the man's attitude stemmed from a wartime grudge; he must have been a child during the occupation.

A constabulary jeep, coming from the direction of the river, halted by the barricade. To Shimura's amazement, Dr. Mapitang was sitting beside the driver. His bony mask of a face was darker and even more parchment-tight, but otherwise he seemed little changed by the years. While the guards were removing the sawhorses to let the jeep through, Mapitang spoke briefly to Michael Braden, who reacted to the message with a fatalistic nod. A trooper waved the jeep ahead. It passed within a few feet of Shimura, but the old physician gave no sign of having recognized him.

Why should he? It had been too long ago. . . .

MAJOR Ramos had already sent García to summon the unit's officers and senior noncoms when Mapitang's jeep halted by the field radio. "Where did you find Shimura?" Mapitang asked as he stepped to the ground.

Ramos immediately regretted having allowed the Japanese to leave the command car. But, expecting the hunt for the *amok* to be over in a few hours, he had seen no danger in it. After all, Shimura would probably be on a JAL airliner by midnight. "You remembered him out of all the soldiers stationed here?" Ramos said with a distressed smile. "I should have expected it."

"Many will remember him. He was with the *kempeitai.*"

"Only as an interpreter," Ramos said quickly. "In any case, it does not matter, Isidro. He is an official agent of his government, under my protection."

"I will tell no one," Mapitang promised.

"We got a radio report from Lieutenant Díaz about Li Tung and his wife. I suppose that's where you've come from."

Mapitang grimaced in disbelief. "I will go to my grave without the faintest understanding of how that brute's mind worked. Li Tung had been split in two like a pear. But it took me minutes to find the wound that killed the old woman. A hairline cut!"

The assault force's platoon and squad leaders were leaving the ring of men around the cogon. "I would appreciate it if you would stay here until the search is over," Ramos said.

Mapitang nodded in understanding, took his medical bag from the back of the jeep, started toward the red-cross-marked constabulary ambulance parked on the other side of the road. The paramedics standing by it grinned in nervous relief when they saw that the physician was not leaving. He passed Ramos' command car, then impulsively turned back and approached the Japanese. "You have been well, Captain Shimura?" he asked.

Shimura started to extend his hand, lowered it quickly, not sure the physician would take it. "Well enough, Dr. Mapitang."

For seconds the two men looked at each other without speaking. Up close, the toll of the years showed in Mapitang's features. His flesh had taken on the arid fragility of a long-abandoned spiderweb in a corner of a seldom-entered room; a single slam of a door might be enough to turn it into wisps of dust. If any of them had truly cheated time, Shimura thought, it was the fugitive in the cogon. The world had not changed for him since 1945, and the eyes of no living man or woman had reflected his own decay.

"The giant from the brothel?" Dr. Mapitang asked at last, gesturing toward the high grass.

"Probably."

"I often thought it might be. Such ferocity is rare."

"His name is Kurusu."

"I wonder if even he remembers that. And you, Captain Shimura? Have you prospered?"

"Reasonably. I am an architect."

"Not a totally unworthy profession." Mapitang nodded his approval. "Perhaps it is good that I spared your life after all."

"When was it in your hands?" Shimura asked with a puzzled frown.

"After your surrender," Mapitang said, as if he were discussing an almost-forgotten baseball game both had attended. "The names of all Japanese prisoners were sent to me so that I could pick out anyone who I knew had taken part in the murder of civilians. It was before the procedures for atrocity trials were set up. You would simply have been handed over to the guerrillas for execution."

"I committed no crimes."

"Of that I was never certain. In most circumstances, serving the *kempeitai* would have been enough to doom you. All I had to balance against it was the fact that you gave the clinic a small amount of drugs and once allowed me to treat an injured Filipina prostitute ahead of Japanese soldiers."

"Not very much," Shimura agreed, shaken.

"I had already put your name on the condemned list. Then I thought again about the afternoon you and that pig Tanape watched from a hotel balcony while the bodies of butchered peasants were dumped in the town square. You were both drinking from bowls. Tanape continued to drink, but your bowl fell from your hand and broke. It seemed to indicate that you had not known what was about to happen. So, on impulse, I erased your name."

"Just the dropping of a bowl," Shimura mused in a barely audible voice, recalling the dozens of fellow officers who had been taken out of the barbed-wire compound at Aparri, never to return.

"Sufficient," Mapitang replied, "in a time without justice."

DOZENS of field workers had joined Michael Braden behind the barricades. He could see others approaching across the fields, many of them from the neighboring Tully and Dietrich plantations. Soon, as the word spread throughout the countryside, hundreds of Ilocans would gather, wait in expectant silence for the destruction of the creature that had held them in terror for decades.

He looked over again at Mapitang and the middle-aged Japanese, annoyed that the physician could calmly chat with a man who had helped bring destruction on his own people, even if he had been sent here to help capture the *amok*. In the past, other diehard stragglers had been talked into surrendering by fellow countrymen. But Michael had never heard of an Imperial Army veteran returning to the scene of his occupation duties, especially in a district as cruelly governed as the valley of the Cagayan. There had to be countless local men who, if they learned his identity, would kill him on sight. Mapitang's friendly manner seemed especially inexplicable in view of the fact that he had been the chief of the Tuguegarao resistance, had lost his only son in the Japanese raid on Aurelio Villamor's jungle headquarters.

The knot of officers around Major Ramos started to break up, platoon leaders hurrying back to their troops with the stiff-legged gait of men preparing to deliver bad news. The first sweep of the cogon would begin soon, Michael guessed. His attention was diverted from the assault preparations by the hum of a high-powered auto engine. Harry Dietrich, his teeth clamped on a half-smoked cigar, halted his Ferrari convertible at the eastern barricade, about 200 feet down the road. He stared at the assemblage of men and trucks for a few seconds, then swung the car in a tight U-turn and drove toward the new highway.

Dietrich must have been coming home from the poker game at the New Reno Hotel. Michael idly wondered why he hadn't asked the barricade guards to let him pass; he wasn't the kind of man who accepted delays without question.

The tobacco buyer's uncharacteristic behavior soon faded from his thoughts. Ramos' platoon leaders had conveyed their orders, and the ring of men around the cogon was breaking up, the troopers quick-marching toward the road. At the shouted commands of Major Ramos, who had taken over the bullhorn, they formed a skirmish line along the entire face of the cogon field. Dr. Mapitang left the Japanese, went over to the ambulance. Three squads remained outside the rapidly coalescing formation, standing by to give pursuit if the main force flushed their quarry.

The maneuver was familiar to Michael. He had taken part in dozens of such sweeps, experienced the fear that must already be drying out the throats of the troopers. In Viet Nam they had called the stuff elephant grass instead of cogon but, no matter what the name, it afforded concealment so total that a soldier could brush an enemy's elbow without seeing him—until the instant before a bayonet was rammed into his body.

Major Ramos and Sergeant García, both carrying M-16s, took their places in the center of the skirmish line.

Ramos wore a whistle around his neck. He raised it to his lips, blew two sharp signals. The troopers moved forward. . . .

HALF an hour later, the line of uniformed men had advanced less than two hundred feet. As he prodded stalks of grass with the muzzle of his weapon, Ramos recalled the instructions he had given to the force's platoon leaders: "You have probably been telling yourselves that he is either dead or too badly injured to offer resistance. Foolish assumptions. We will proceed on the theory that he is not only alive but in full possession of his physical powers. No man is to take a step forward unless he is able to see the troopers on either side. It is easy, in high grass, to drift away from each other, provide a corridor for the enemy's escape."

Ramos had not led this kind of mission since the Huk war, twenty years earlier, had forgotten the sense of isolation that gripped a man once he had entered tall cogon. He now realized how difficult his orders would be to follow, especially with the wind worrying the tops of the twelve-foot-high stalks of grass. The troopers were less than a yard apart, but he was rarely able to get more than broken glimpses of García, on his right, or the young private to his left. The harder gusts bunched the grass into solid masses, cut visibility to a few inches, painfully whipped the sharp edges of the larger stalks against his exposed face and hands. No sounds reached his ears except the wind rustling the grass and, faintly, the footfalls of the flanking troopers. The cogon's thick, clustered roots provided near-perfect insulation.

The search continued, step after cautious step. Like the

others, Ramos looked for traces of the *amok*'s blood but by this time, he knew, the sun had dried the stains the same dingy brown as the cogon. Despite his own words earlier, he found himself peering downward constantly, hoping to spot a huge, lifeless body.

Off to his right, he heard an abrupt, swishing noise—perhaps a frightened bird fluttering up out of a ground nest—followed by the sound of a heavy object falling to earth. Sergeant García vanished from his line of vision. Puzzled, Ramos edged over toward his aide, found him lying face down.

"I tripped," García muttered dully, pushing himself up on his right elbow. His worn, flat-nosed face was putty gray; his eyes, coated by the onslaught of massive physical shock. Ramos' stare traveled the length of the sergeant's body, saw that García's legs had been severed above the knees. The lower sections of limb were grotesquely pointed toe-to-toe, blood coursing from them to merge in a deepening puddle with the torrent gushing from the stumps of his thighs, as if trying to form a bridge between the mutilated segments of flesh.

Ramos thrust his whistle between his teeth, blew three times—the signal for the formation to halt. He swerved the muzzle of his M-16 in brief, spastic arcs as he tried to spot the fleeing swordsman, found nothing. Everywhere he looked, the grass seemed undisturbed. *He couldn't have gotten away that fast!* Ramos thought with frantic anger, almost ready to believe that the *amok* was the invincible, supernatural demon of the Ilocans' imaginings.

He blew the whistle twice, to summon the medics. The second shrill signal was drowned out by an explosion, so deadened by the cogon that it resounded no louder, inside the field, than the ignition of a stubborn gas oven. Another followed; then a third, so near that the impact flattened the grass. He saw fragments of uniformed bodies shoot into the air, heard the cries and groans of wounded men, the stutter of automatic weapons as panicked troopers fired wildly. A cloud of black, greasy, lung-searing smoke swirled around him, cutting his vision even further as more explosions rocked the field. He lifted García, started carrying him back toward the trucks.

A trooper, blood coursing into his eyes from a jagged scalp wound, stumbled past them. "This way!" Ramos yelled after him—then realized that he himself had lost all sense of direction, might well be headed into the heart of the cogon. The trooper vanished in the grass—and seconds later the spot where he had disappeared became the nucleus of another blast, so close that Ramos was knocked off his feet, taking García down with him. Shrapnel slashed off stalks all around them, like the jaws of invisible steel locusts. Ramos struggled erect, seized García beneath the arms, dragged him through the cogon.

Then the final explosion came, generating a wave of heat that washed over him with blistering force. Orange-tinted balls of flame arced through the air, started fires wherever they landed. Sergeant García finally began to scream. . . .

At the first blast, Michael Braden had instinctively thrown himself to the ground, realizing from the flat, crumping brevity of the report that a land mine had gone off inside the cogon. All around him, the Ilocan spectators had either followed his example or fled in fear.

Michael crawled behind his jeep, watched one charge after another detonate, the sounds overlapping into a single terrifying roar. A pall of impenetrable gray smoke settled over the grass—until, like a bright-winged moth emerging from a drab cocoon, a column of reddish-orange fire rose more than thirty feet into the sky, spewing gobs of liquefied flame back into the smoke. The explosions faded, were replaced by the crackle of burning grass and the distant cries of trapped, dying men.

The troopers held in reserve broke formation, milled about at the edge of the cogon. Some of them ran into the grass to help their comrades, were driven back by the flames. Others stood and gaped. The Japanese, like Michael, had hit the dirt. Survivors began stumbling out of the cogon, coughing and retching. A trooper, the back of his fatigue jacket ablaze, ran a course of ragged figure-8s until a paramedic wrestled him to earth, began beating at the burning cloth with his bare hands. Dr. Mapitang rushed over, grabbed the medic by the back of the neck, pulled him away from the man he was attempting to help.

"Don't burn your hands!" Mapitang shouted. "I will need them!" He seized the thrashing trooper by the ankles, twisted until he had flopped him on his back, placed his foot on the man's throat, ruthlessly held him down until his own squirming movements against the dry, loose earth had extinguished the fire.

Michael rose, started toward the cogon, intending to join Mapitang and the other rescuers. Then he realized that he had a greater responsibility. Already the wind-driven fire had spread to rows of tobacco north of the grass; within minutes, the entire area would become an inferno. He scrambled into the jeep, started the engine.

The last thing he saw before driving off was Major Ramos hauling a legless figure out of the cogon.

11

CARA WAS BEING driven home from the workers' barrio by Antonio, the houseman, when they noticed the black, curling smoke on the northern horizon.

She had dreaded going to the barrio—but, to her surprise, the ritual moments spent with the murdered boy's family had breached the benumbed isolation that had closed in on her after Les's death. The rawness of their pain had altered Cara's perception of her own, made her sense for the first time that it would eventually end. She had felt more at peace than she had in days—until Antonio raised his right hand from the wheel of the car, pointed at the smoke.

"Go faster," she said, realizing that the distant fire was in the area where the constabulary had trapped the *amok*. Anger, held at bay until now by grief, swept through her. Les, the Mariano boy, Li Tung and his wife—and now a new, undisclosed horror. Even at the end he must have found a means of wreaking havoc on his pursuers. She suddenly understood why Michael had wanted to be on hand when the constabulary searched for him, why nearly everyone in the barrio had rushed to the cogon. The destruction of so monstrous an evil had to be witnessed, details memorized so that they could be told later to those who had not been present; the legend, as well as the man, had to be eradicated. If it was not, fear would remain, perhaps even grow.

They were pulling into the drive to the main house when the plantation fire alarm began howling. Michael and a dozen field hands were hauling armloads of picks and shovels from the tool-storage shed, throwing them on to a flatbed truck. Other vehicles, even tractors, were already leaving the work area.

Cara ordered Antonio to halt, jumped out of the car, hurried over to her brother-in-law. "How did it start?" she asked.

He quickly told her what had happened in the cogon, while continuing to help load the truck. "Soon as I saw it was spreading, I pulled out," he said. "Christ knows how, but I managed to turn about half of the crowd back to fight the fire. . . . I guess the rest are still running. . . . A break, having that many men on the spot. . . . But they'll be helpless without tools. . . ."

"I know what to do here. I helped Lenore when they had that bad fire two years ago."

He forced a smile, gave her arm a reassuring squeeze, climbed into the back of the truck. The other men were already aboard. Even before the truck drove off, Cara was heading toward the house. "Get the whole staff into the kitchen," she told Antonio, who was trotting along beside her.

Sam Braden was sitting in a chair on the front veranda, his yellow-filmed eyes staring out at the cloud of smoke, ten times larger than when Cara had first seen it from the barrio road. "How bad?" he whispered.

"We don't know yet," she said. "Would you mind keeping an eye on Evie? I'll need Maria."

Sam Braden nodded. "The wind will give them trouble. Coming from the south. Always the worst."

Cara was inside the house before it occurred to her that she had never before asked the old man for any kind of help, even to perform so simple a task as watching the child. She found Evie and Maria on the rear patio, told the nursemaid to help Inez in the kitchen, took her daughter by the hand and led her to the veranda. "Now, you be good with Grandfather," she said.

Sam and Eve regarded each other with what to Cara seemed an equal degree of suspicion. He couldn't have spoken more than a hundred words to the child since her birth. Evie, in turn, had obviously regarded him as a sort of unthreatening family ghost, sharing her home but on another plane of existence. "You want me to tell you a story?" he finally asked. "Like I used to?"

"You *never* did!"

Sam blinked in surprise—and Cara abruptly understood that he must have confused Evie with her long-dead namesake. She went back into the house.

Inez, Antonio and the maids were already at work making mounds of sandwiches, cooking rice and quickly preparable Ilocan foods. On the patio, Maria was using a hose to fill jerry cans—kept on hand for such emergencies—with drinking water. It often took a full day or more to extinguish a raging field fire. The men would have to be fed at the scene in shifts, requiring an endless supply of meals.

"We will need more bread and meat," Inez said, stirring a vat of *pancit* on the gigantic, old-fashioned cast iron range. "More of everything!"

Cara turned to Antonio. "Go back to the barrio, get into Li Tung's store."

"What if the police will not let me? They were still there when we left."

Cara gave him a small, irritated shove toward the door. "Lieutenant Díaz knows what's happening in the fields. If he has any questions, send him to me."

"A lazy coward," Inez grumbled after Antonio had reluctantly departed. "Not like old Elpidio. *He* would have shot anybody who tried to stop him from doing his duty!"

A flushed Lenore Tully burst into the room, hugged Cara in sympathy. "Jack and I were driving back from Tuguegarao when we saw the smoke," she said. "I dropped him off at the fire, then went home and ransacked the pantry. Come help me unload the pickup."

Cara and the two maids went outside with Lenore, started carrying canned goods and vegetables into the kitchen, unceremoniously dumped them on the floor before hurrying back to the pickup truck. On the second trip, a trio of Philippine Army helicopters flew low over the house, heading north. "They must have sent for them to bring out the wounded," Lenore said with a dismayed wince. "I haven't seen anything so awful since the war. My God, it was a regular battlefield! Dead PCs everyplace!"

Hour after hour the grueling routine continued—cooking the food, carrying it to waiting trucks in any available container, washing the pots and pans and refilling them as soon as they were returned. Antonio had come back from the barrio with only a few sacks of rice and vegetables. "The police let me into the store," he had said with a baffled shake of his head, "but the shelves were almost empty. The *amok* must have stolen everything." Cara waved him away impatiently. During his absence, trucks from every farm for miles had brought in more supplies than they could use.

The only news they had of the fire fighters' progress came from the drivers of the trucks that carried food and water to the workers. The confused snatches of information passed through the kitchen from woman to woman: tractors had plowed under a fifteen-foot-wide swath of tobacco north of the flames . . . wind-driven sparks had bridged the firebreak, started new blazes . . . Michael had opened irrigation sluice gates along a half-mile stretch of river, flooding acres of prime leaf but blocking the fire's westward course . . . a group of field hands frantically shoveling earth on flames at the eastern edge of the fire had been inundated with waves of smoke by a sudden cross-wind, had nearly been asphyxiated before rescuers reached them. . . .

At a few minutes past noon, Sam Braden entered the turmoil of the kitchen, declared: "Kid's hungry." Cara yanked two sandwiches—without any notion of what might be lying between the slices of bread—from a stack, threw them on a plate, shoved it into the old man's hands. He nodded his thanks, left, was soon back to ask for a glass of milk. At two, Cara went on to the veranda, planning to take Evie upstairs for her nap. There was no sign of either her daughter or Sam Braden. She found them in Evie's room. The little girl was asleep in her bed. Sam sat in a chair by the window, peering out at the fields.

"You shouldn't have done it to me, Cara," he said without looking around.

"A few hours of baby-sitting is asking too much?" she gasped in astonishment. "At a time like this?"

"Not that." His tear-filled eyes moved toward the sleeping child. "Can't you understand? Now I'll miss her."

THE SUN was low when Major Ramos—olive skin slack and pale at the corners of his mouth—entered his home in Tuguegarao. For the past two hours, he had been interrogated by the constabulary's district commander. Even now the enormity of what had occurred had not fully registered in his dazed consciousness. All he could think of was the numbers—twenty-seven troopers missing in the cogon and presumed dead, eight men so mangled or burned that they were not expected to live more than a few hours, twelve who had lost arms or legs—running them over and over in his mind as an alternative to picturing actual bodies and faces.

Takei Shimura and Dr. Mapitang were waiting in the deep-shadowed living room. As soon as he came through the door, Mapitang poured a glass of brandy, handed it to him. Shimura was seated on the edge of a chair, his lined face carefully watchful, hands between his knees, fingertips touching, almost in a position of prayer.

"Why aren't you at the clinic?" Ramos asked Mapitang after gratefully gulping half the brandy.

"The army flew up a team of surgeons and burn specialists from Manila," the physician explained with an ironic half-smile. "They didn't say so, of course, but I knew they thought I would be in their way."

Ramos slumped on a couch. "Sergeant García? Is he all right?"

"He will live."

Mentioning his longtime aide's name destroyed the wall of mental defenses Ramos had built up; abruptly, they were men again, not report statistics or names on a row of medical charts. "So many dead," he said huskily, more to himself than to his companions. "Dead—or worse. I wish I had left poor García in there. Six months from now he will be a street beggar, pushing himself along gutters in a cart. He won't even be able to stir pity by wearing his old uniform jacket. Too many people would spit on it . . ."

"Enough, Virgilio!" Mapitang commanded sharply, sensing that Ramos was close to breaking down.

"It is true," Ramos insisted. "We both know it. Perhaps that is why I ignored my superiors' advice and pushed so hard in this matter. I have no illusions about the constabulary's function. Whether it was fighting the Huks years ago or the Moro rebels in the south or people who simply want to recover the liberties they had before martial law, I was a political policeman. Once, before I retired, I wanted to perform an act I could be proud of, end a threat to all of our people, not the handful with money and power."

"I would not broadcast those sentiments publicly," Mapitang sighed.

Ramos finished his brandy, his face contorting with self-disgust. "It no longer matters. I have been suspended from my duties. The commandant has scheduled an official hearing Tuesday to determine whether court-martial papers are to be filed. I am afraid, Mr. Shimura, that you will have to remain in Tuguegarao until then. You will be called as a witness."

"Insane!" Mapitang snorted, pouring himself a glass of brandy even larger than the one he had given Ramos. "You did nothing improper."

"I failed to examine the charts of the area. The cogon

had been mined by the Japanese at the end of the war. It was plainly designated."

"Those things couldn't have lain there more than thirty years," Mapitang insisted. "One, perhaps even two old mines going off I might accept—but more than a dozen? It's ridiculous! The last was a firebomb. How could its chemical elements withstand decades of monsoons and drought without breaking down?"

Shimura spoke for the first time since Ramos' return. "Thermite," he said in his polite, measured tones. "We used it often for booby traps, especially in the jungle. Primitive, compared with the Americans' napalm, but effective in a limited way. Dr. Mapitang is quite correct: thirty years of exposure would render the compound harmless. Kurusu set the incendiary charge—and the others as well—using mines and matériel he preserved and hid away in nineteen forty-five. We left many crates of explosives in the regimental arsenal when we retreated to Aparri."

"But *why* did he do it?" Ramos exclaimed with a gesture of weary helplessness.

"*Gekokujo,*" Shimura again suggested. "He chose to destroy as many of the enemy as possible, even if it ensured his own death. The final gesture of defiance."

Mapitang had begun moving aimlessly about the room with his vexed-schoolmaster's stride. "How is it possible, Captain Shimura? We know he was wounded when he entered the grass last night. Even an uninjured man couldn't rig such an intricate series of traps in so short a time. The mines and charges must have been planted *before* the murder of the Lis, when he didn't have the faintest inkling that he would be under siege within hours."

"Why, then, did he mine the cogon?" Ramos asked.

"I don't know," Mapitang conceded.

"At least he is dead—even if at too great a price."

"Kurusu has been found?" Shimura asked.

Ramos shook his head. "The army sealed off the area. Before trying to recover bodies, they plan to cover every inch of ground with mine detectors, in case some of the charges weren't detonated. But few of the men caught in the grass will be identified. What can be left of them—after the explosions and a thermite fire—except bones and a few pieces of charred meat?"

A frightening possibility took root in Shimura's mind. "Major Ramos, did you see Kurusu after he cut off García's legs? Even for an instant?"

"If I had, I would have killed him."

"Did the sergeant see him?"

"García was still under sedation when I left the clinic," Mapitang said. "I will question him tomorrow, if you think it is important."

"Who else but the *amok* could have attacked him?" Ramos snapped.

"No one," Takei Shimura replied, already certain that Kurusu was alive—and that to prevent further slaughter, the task of apprehending his countryman now belonged to Shimura alone. . . .

By sunset, the black, clenched mass of smoke on the horizon had given way to twisting gray wisps, like the tentacles of a beached octopus thrashing upward into an environment suddenly unable to sustain life. Even before Jack Tully came to report that the fire in the northern fields had been put out, Cara and the others could see that the battle was over. Within two hours, all but one of the plantation trucks had returned, after dropping off the exhausted workers at their barrios.

Only Michael had remained in the fields. Cara and Sam waited for him in the living room. The old man didn't speak a word, as if ashamed of his emotional confession earlier. The exposure of his vulnerability had touched Cara—but how had he guessed that she planned to take the child to America? Keeping her promise to Michael, she hadn't even hinted to Sam of her intentions.

It had been a day full of surprises. She felt almost guilty about the paradoxical release from tension that the emergency had induced in her body and mind, temporarily wiping out her brooding preoccupation with Les and her and Eve's uncertain future. The torment would return, she knew, but perhaps less intensely. She had even been spared, for the first time since her husband's murder, Lenore Tully's bullying benevolence. *If, just once, she tells me to go and rest, I'll bang her on the head with a skillet,* Cara had promised herself at the height of the frenzied activity in the kitchen. However, Lenore had suppressed her usual urge to take charge and calmly worked beside the other women.

"Where the hell is Mike?" Sam grumbled. "Past nine-thirty."

"He's all right, Grandfather. Jack said no one was hurt except the men overcome by the smoke."

At last, the old man went to bed. Cara decided to stay downstairs a few minutes longer, afraid to shed the fatigue that had helped provide a buffer against despair. She glanced out a window, saw that the floodlights ringing the house had gone on again, remembered Michael explaining that they were controlled by an automatic timer in the vehicle barn.

Cara was barely able to recognize her brother-in-law when he came through the door. His face and clothing had been blackened by smoke; his coarse, wiry hair, gray with ash, was plastered lankly against his skull. "We lost more than a hundred acres," he told her, collapsing into a reed-framed chair. He rubbed his temples with his fingertips, leaving pale tracks in the soot adhering to his skin. "Would have been a lot worse if the wind hadn't died late in the afternoon."

"Michael, why didn't you come home with the others?"

"Checking to make sure the damned thing was really out," he lied. Actually, he had sat for hours in the cab of his truck, staring at the greasy black plain, dotted with wind-shifted piles of ash, that had been the cogon field, dimly illuminated by the moon and the portable lanterns of the soldiers guarding the area. The cloying, repugnant odor of burned human flesh still hovered. This is crazy, he had thought. Go home. You have nothing to do here. But he had continued to watch, clutching the top of the steering wheel with both hands. . . .

Cara hesitated before asking the question he must know was inevitable: "Did they find . . . *him*?"

"Anyone who didn't get out of the cogon within two minutes after the mines went off is dead," he declared in a flat, hollow voice. "He didn't get out."

His adamance disturbed Cara; it was the tone of a man trying to cover up deep uncertainty. Then she realized that the yard floodlights had not been turned off, even though he must have been only a few feet from the switch when he drove the truck into the vehicle barn. He just forgot, she thought, already guessing the truth. The floodlights would burn all night—and every night to come. . . .

HIS strategy had gained him only a few more hours of life. When the sun rose he would be exposed on the open plain, too weak to fight his enemies. In the beginning, after leaving his hiding place, he had crawled westward through stubbled, acrid-smelling rows of burned tobacco, hoping to find shelter among the trees and brush of the riverbank. But after covering less than a mile, he realized that he could not survive on his own. Although he had deflected the shotgun barrel with his sword, part of the charge had torn into his left thigh, now swollen to twice its normal size. The pain rose from the infected wound in pulsing waves, stabbing through his groin like jagged steel rods dipped in acid. He needed a place to rest until the injury had healed, a place where he could sleep without fear of being stumbled upon by a field hand or a fisherman.

For the first time since Captain Shimura had given him the sword, he decided to seek the help of another human being. He had recognized the house days earlier but had no way of being sure the same man still occupied it. With death as the alternative, he would have to take the chance.

Crawling, he could never reach his new destination before dawn. However, the lanterns of the soldiers guarding the leveled cogon were no longer visible behind him. He pushed himself up on his hands, then to his right knee—but his other leg was so stiff that he could not bend it. He drew his sword from the sheath carried over his shoulder in a sling, plunged the blade into the soft, plowed earth, supported himself on it as he lurched erect, grinding his great yellow teeth to keep from crying out against the fresh pain that surged through him when he shifted the injured leg. . . .

He moved toward his goal, using the sword to balance himself, like a skier who has lost one of his poles, afraid the blade would break under the repeated pressure. He had carried the treasured weapon so long that it had become virtually part of his body. Losing it would be like losing a limb. . . .

More than two hours later, he reached the top of a hill and saw the familiar building below, different from the other large plantation houses in being constructed from mortar, like the homes in Tuguegarao. He was surprised to see light glowing from three of the ground-floor windows. Afraid of showing himself against the horizon, he went the rest of the way on his belly. Grunting with effort, close to the end of his strength, he crawled to the nearest window, stood, peered through it. The man was there, sitting alone in a room crowded with dark, massive furniture, unchanged since his last visit.

He moved toward the narrow front porch, hauled himself up a short flight of steps, fell against the locked door. Again and again he weakly pounded the heel of his hand against the wooden panel. He would have called out the man's name, but he could no longer remember it. After what seemed hours, the door slowly opened inward. The man, holding a .45 automatic pistol, backed away from him, mouth agape.

"Kurusu!" Harry Dietrich whispered hoarsely, staring at the monolithic form filling the entire frame of the door. It took all of his will to avoid squeezing the trigger of his .45, blasting this foul apparition back into the darkness where it belonged—even knowing that if he did, his own life would be destroyed.

Dietrich lowered the pistol, went to help the man he hated above all others.

12

TOMORROW MORNING I will kill him, Harry Dietrich silently vowed, peering through the window of his office at the low, cement-walled shed where he had hidden Kurusu four days earlier. The building, used by his first wife as a storeroom for her preserves, had not been opened in years; the only key to its thick plank door now lay in Dietrich's pocket. It would be easy: just go in and shoot, tell the police that he had discovered Kurusu hiding, been attacked, fired.

It would not be easy much longer. Each night, when he took Kurusu food and water, he was astonished to see how much stronger the man had grown. On that first, shocked morning, Dietrich had been convinced that he would die of his obviously pre-gangrenous wound. The giant—using sign language and scraps of English—had asked for bandages, disinfectant and a container of boiling water. While Dietrich looked on with awe and revulsion, unable to believe that anyone could function so nervelessly in the face of excruciating pain, Kurusu had used his sword to lance the abscessed wound on his thigh. The stench of pus and corrupt flesh had almost driven Dietrich from the shed. But by the following night the swelling had gone down and the fever flush had departed from the portions of Kurusu's face visible through tangled masses of black hair.

At this moment, the Philippine Constabulary hearing on Major Ramos' fiasco was probably still under way in Tuguegarao. When he had definite word that Takei Shimura had given his evidence and departed, Dietrich could finally rid himself of this curse. Even so, he was taking a serious risk that his wartime collaboration with the *kempeitai* would be revealed. Back in Japan, Shimura might read how his former comrade had died—and at whose hand—expose him to Ramos or Dr. Mapitang. But it was far more likely that, so distant from the scene, he would allow the past to remain buried. Besides, Dietrich told himself, he might not even remember me. I met Shimura once; Kurusu, at least a dozen times.

He lit a cigar, forced his attention back to the plantation account books he had been going over. The numbers seemed to scuttle off the ruled page like burrowing insects fleeing from a descending boot. None of it was his fault, he thought bitterly; he had been caught in a trap. . . .

SINCE the beginning of the occupation, Dietrich and his first wife, Inge, pregnant with their daughter, Frieda, had struggled desperately to maintain their farm, the smallest in the valley owned by a white man. Although the war had closed off all but a few local markets for tobacco, they were determined to keep the fields in arable condition, looking forward to the day when they could at last sell the ever-growing stocks of cured leaf in the plantation warehouse.

It had been a strange, isolated existence for the young couple, the only Caucasians left in the district after their American neighbors were transported to Santo Tomás. Dietrich had tried to avoid contact with the Japanese, going into Tuguegarao only once a month for supplies, always uncomfortable under the curious stares of off-duty Imperial Army soldiers. Even before the American blockade, meat and canned foods were scarce, but he figured they would be able to make it. Wisely—and against his wishes, since he had wanted to use the land for their cash crop—Inge had insisted when they bought the farm that an acre be devoted to a vegetable garden. Along with two milk cows, pigs, chickens and a few head of carabao, it had given them the means to survive.

Then Captain Tanape and Lieutenant Shimura had come; like the *amok,* at night. He had sent his wife upstairs, already feeling the growth of dread deep inside him, offered his visitors a drink. Through Shimura, his interpreter, Tanape had declined for both of them. In a matter-of-fact voice, Shimura went on to deliver the message Dietrich had anticipated. Inevitably, the lieutenant declared, a resistance movement would grow in the valley. Harry Dietrich was to report suspicious activities among his workers.

"I am a citizen of a neutral nation," Dietrich protested. "I cannot involve myself in hostilities."

"Any man living under the authority and protection of the Empire has the duty to oppose insurrection," Shimura explained after translating Dietrich's remark to the suddenly frowning Tanape.

"Why would the Filipinos confide in a foreigner?"

Dietrich asked nervously. "My wife and I came to this country only two years ago. Except for a few of the Americans—and they're all gone—we know barely anyone."

From the curtness of the stream of words Tanape released in Japanese, Dietrich realized that his arguments would go unheeded. "Captain Tanape says that you must make the necessary contacts," Shimura stated. "Also, that the benefits of cooperation will be great. The army is authorized to confiscate civilian food crops and domestic animals in case of emergency. The edict does not exempt neutrals. Especially unfriendly neutrals."

Dietrich's position was impossible. He and his wife were alone in a foreign land, without friends or relatives to depend on. The war might last for years, eliminating income for tobacco farmers in so remote an area. When, as Tanape threatened, military confiscation of foodstuffs began, he and Inge and their soon-to-be-born child would face starvation.

After the Japanese officers departed, Dietrich went upstairs to the bedroom, told his wife everything that had happened. "What will you do?" she asked.

"I'm not sure," he said, gazing at the rounded swell of her belly. "I promised them I would help, merely to stall for time."

"But what help *could* you give them?" she wailed. "You know nothing about politics! Even if a resistance movement started, no one would ask *you* to join!"

"I explained all that, but they would not listen. Anyway, who would be foolish enough to fight the Japanese now?"

He had spoken these words merely to reassure his wife. It was common knowledge that a few days before the enemy arrived in Tuguegarao, dozens of men had taken guns and all the supplies they could carry, headed up into the Cordillera jungles. He had been on friendly terms with two of them—Aurelio Villamor, a local lawyer, and Jack Tully, the teen-aged son of his American neighbors to the east. I should have given their names to Tanape, he thought. The Japanese must have them anyway. It would have done no harm.

Throughout the months of the monsoon, Dietrich heard no more from the *kempeitai,* decided that the visit of the two officers had been part of an area-wide program of intimidation, that he had not been singled out as a potential informer. The child was born, helping to fill Inge's hours during the long days she was imprisoned inside the house by the rain. Then, late in September of 1942, the weather cleared and guerrilla attacks began against the Japanese.

He was never to see Shimura again. But on a dark night three days after the first guerrilla strike, a warrant officer named Kurusu appeared at the back door of the plantation house, accompanied by an enlisted interpreter. Dietrich, himself over six feet tall, was startled by the man's physical immensity, even more by the unfathomable blackness of the eyes that met his own, like the terminal ends of round, narrow tubes that had their beginnings in the depths of outer space. Had he any information for the *kempeitai,* asked the interpreter. No, Dietrich replied fearfully, half expecting to be executed on the spot. The giant warrant officer and his companion simply turned away and vanished into the darkness—but when Dietrich went to the barn the next morning, one of their milk cows lay dead in its stall, its neck broken, head wrenched half off its body.

He returned to the house, looked at his wife sleepily warming a bottle for their infant daughter, knew what he must do. Two nights later, Kurusu and the interpreter again appeared. Dietrich gave them the name of a field hand he had chanced upon reading a mimeographed leaflet urging defiance of the occupation authorities. He expected the man to be reprimanded or, at worst, jailed for a week or two. Instead, he turned up in the first truckload of bodies dumped in Tuguegarao's main square. . . .

In the months that followed, Dietrich repeatedly told himself that he had no choice except to go along with the *kempeitai;* the lives of his wife and child must take precedence over those of the brown-skinned semiprimitives who inhabited this remote valley. At least, if they didn't want to submit to the Japanese, they could go back to the jungles from which they had emerged. His and Inge's and Frieda's only possible refuge was Switzerland, halfway across a war-ravaged, impassable world. We're completely alone, he thought in despair.

As he had anticipated, he was able to provide little information to the *kempeitai.* Because his knowledge of Ilocano was rudimentary, his conversations with native workers were limited to giving simple orders on their duties. Any attempt to question them about the guerrillas in the hills would have met with immediate suspicion. A few times he found the tracks of large groups of men crossing his land, assumed they were raiders, reported the movements to Kurusu, always too late for the Japanese to follow the trail. A quarter of a century would pass before telephone lines were strung to the plantations of the Cagayan. However limited his usefulness, there were no more incidents like the slaughter of the cow. But Dietrich knew the harassment would eventually resume if he failed to perform a major service for his tormentors.

In 1944, when the tide of the war had turned against

the Japanese, his opportunity came. He had finished his work in the fields, was returning to the house on horseback. Suddenly, half a dozen raggedly dressed men carrying rifles leaped out of a drainage ditch beside the trail, blocked his way. He was about to try to flee across the fields when one of the group shouted in English: "Hold on, Harry!"

Dietrich pulled back on the reins. When he had last seen his neighbor, Jack Tully had been little more than a child. In two years he had seemingly aged a decade, his handsome features hard and gaunt, skin marked with the sallowness of chronic malaria.

"You oughtn't to be here," Dietrich gasped, hoping that the guerrillas would ask nothing of him, go on their way.

His hopes were soon dashed. Jack told Dietrich that he and his Filipino companions had come down from the hills on a scavenging expedition. Japanese counter-insurgency forces, in a series of brutal sweeps, had destroyed most of the jungle Ilocans' rice and yam crops in order to deprive the guerrillas of food. "We're starving up there," Jack said in a nearly apologetic tone. "I know things aren't a hell of a lot better in the valley, but anything you can spare will help."

"I will put it out behind the barn after dark," Dietrich said, before riding on to his house.

Not telling his wife of the encounter, he filled sacks with potatoes, turnips and other vegetables Inge had laboriously grown in unfriendly soil with seeds she had brought from Europe years before. Along with two burlap-wrapped hams, they were deposited outside the windowless rear wall of the barn before he went in to his dinner, his mind seething with fear and doubt. To betray Jack Tully seemed unthinkable. He was another white man, the son of a neighbor. But if he came once, he was certain to come again—and if Kurusu discovered that Dietrich had fed the guerrillas, the *kempeitai* might murder his entire family.

The following night, Kurusu and his nameless interpreter again visited the kitchen of the plantation house. Dietrich had decided not to report the contact with Jack Tully. However, in the warrant officer's towering presence, he found himself blurting out the story, as if a secretly administered drug had taken possession of his lungs and vocal cords, compelling words that his brain fought against releasing. "We have long known about the young American," the interpreter said as Kurusu's voice droned on behind him. "He is one of Villamor's chief lieutenants. Did he tell you where their headquarters is located?"

"We barely spoke."

"Did they say when they would come again?"

"I'm sure that they won't. It would be too dangerous."

Kurusu's broad nostrils tightened slightly after Dietrich's last answer was translated. For an instant, Dietrich thought the warrant officer was angry. When the interpreter spoke he realized that, on the contrary, Kurusu had been amused. "No action is too dangerous for a hungry man" was the message the interpreter passed on.

"What do you want me to do if they come?" Dietrich asked.

"Nothing," the enlisted man translated as Kurusu rose from a kitchen chair. "You have done all that is necessary."

Less than two weeks later, Jack Tully and a small band of guerrillas again intercepted him on a back trail, asked for more food. Half expecting to be caught in a hail of Japanese gunfire at any second, Dietrich managed to conceal his apprehension, promised to leave supplies behind the barn that night. Surely Kurusu must have the farm under surveillance, he thought in bafflement as he put out bags of vegetables and salted meat. Why hadn't he already moved in with troops?

For hours Dietrich lay awake beside his wife, waiting for distant shots that would mean the Japanese had caught up with Jack Tully's band. But the night remained silent. The next morning he saw that the supplies were gone, again wondered why the *kempeitai* had permitted the guerrillas to escape. Days later, he heard that an Imperial Army brigade had discovered the deep-jungle refuge of Aurelio Villamor's hard-core force, wiped out all but Villamor and a handful of his men. Kurusu must have followed Jack from the Dietrich plantation into the mountains, figuring rightly that he would lead the way to the insurgents' base.

After the slaughter of the guerrillas, the *kempeitai* never approached Harry Dietrich again. His usefulness to them had ended. However, Tanape continued to protect him. Except for a few minor confiscations—obviously intended to shield the fact that Dietrich had suffered far less than the area's other farmers—his fields and livestock were untouched by military foragers. In the years immediately after the war, the fact that he had succeeded in preserving his land—and the enormous cash value of the leaf in his warehouse—enabled him to enlarge the plantation at small cost, establish a profitable tobacco-export firm in Aparri.

At first, he had constantly feared that his collaboration with the *kempeitai* would be exposed. When he first learned that Jack Tully had survived and planned to rebuild his dead parents' farm, he had considered fleeing home to Switzerland with Inge and Frieda. Then, thinking it over, he saw no reason why Jack would suspect him of betraying the resistance; he had not sought out the guerrillas or asked them questions, the way a real informer would have done. His estimate of the situation proved correct. Jack greeted him as a friend, was one of the few white settlers who didn't resent his postwar prosperity. In turn, Dietrich gratefully lent the impoverished American thousands of dollars to get his plantation running again, gave him unlimited use of his tractors and other equipment.

However, Dietrich never fully lost his fear of retribution. Aurelio Villamor, the guerrilla leader, was named district magistrate after independence, relentlessly prosecuted collaborationists. Since there was no statute of limitations on such crimes, men were still being tried and shot years after the war. Hundreds more—untouchable because of political influence or lack of evidence—were murdered by former members of the resistance. Several of Dietrich's own field workers were the brothers, fathers or sons of men slain in Kurusu's invasion of Villamor's jungle stronghold.

As the years passed, his apprehensions faded. Occasionally, after the growth of the *amok* legend, he mentally toyed with the possibility that the murderer was Kurusu—simply because of the warrant officer's monstrous size—but he always rejected the notion. The odds were overwhelming that Kurusu had perished on the retreat to Aparri. Probably, if the *amok* was ever caught, he would prove to be a normal-sized man, blown up to gargantuan proportions in the Ilocans' frightened imaginations. The links to Dietrich's wartime actions fell away one by one. His wife, Inge—the only person who knew of the nighttime visits of the *kempeitai* to their home—succumbed to cancer in 1969. Less than two years later, Aurelio Villamor was stricken with a heart attack, died on Dr. Mapitang's operating table.

I will end my days like the rest of the foreigners here, Dietrich decided somberly on the afternoon in 1976 that Frieda and her new husband—an Australian mining engineer—departed for Sydney. Spending my evenings playing cards or sitting around the New Reno bar. Pretending that I still do useful work, even though I've turned everything over to foremen and clerks and lawyers. A good life—and I will hate it.

Then he met Luz Ramírez, the shy, flawless-complexioned daughter of his office manager in Aparri. He guessed from the start that Ramírez—like most middle-class *mestizos,* rooted in a peculiar distillation of the islands' long-vanished Spanish culture—was attempting to arrange an advantageous marriage. Initially he had been amused at the notion, accepted his employee's dinner invitation in order to see how far Ramírez would go in his ludicrous scheme. And of course, by the end of the evening, he was entranced by Luz.

During the ten months of their marriage, he had been happier than ever before. He realized that the other white settlers were bound to be amused by a man in his late fifties wedding an eighteen-year-old mixed-blood girl. The usual clichéd guesses about their sex life—or lack of it—were undoubtedly being made behind his back. But to his own amazement, none of this bothered him. Luz's sleek, fresh body engendered a fervor he hadn't felt since the early years of his first marriage. In return, he had brought her out of the narrow world of a provincial *mestizo* family. They went to Manila twice a month, took long holidays in Hong Kong and Singapore, were planning a European trip after the monsoon broke. Nothing mattered except her pleasure and, through it, his own.

He had been looking forward to years of revitalized

existence, had even considered fathering another child—until, five days ago, he had been halted at a Philippine Constabulary roadblock, seen Captain Tanape's interpreter standing beside Dr. Mapitang on the other side of the barricade, known that despite the years and the deaths and the diminishing of memory, the danger to him had not ended.

In a daze, he had driven home along the twisting, little-used river road, found his plantation in turmoil. Through Luz, he finally learned what had been occurring back in the cogon. Absorbed in his own plight, he had not even noticed the muted explosions or the distant smoke to the south.

He performed all the proper acts—ordered his overseer to take every available man and help fight the fire in the adjoining Braden fields, told Luz to have the household staff assemble food for the workers—but only one thought echoed in his mind: *What if the little Jap bastard saw me at the roadblock, told Mapitang and Major Ramos what happened during the war?*

All day, reports filtered back: the blasts had killed or mangled dozens of constabulary troopers; the fire had been extinguished; it was certain that the *amok* had perished in his own demonic trap. No one even mentioned Shimura. However, the only logical explanation for his presence was that he had come to help Ramos capture the *amok*.

That night Dietrich remained downstairs after Luz went to bed, telling her, truthfully, that the day's events had made him too nervous to sleep. He sat in the living room for hours, slowly decided that he had exaggerated the peril to himself. With the *amok* dead, Takei Shimura would soon be gone. If Dietrich stayed on the plantation until

Shimura's departure, there was no reason why he should ever encounter the Japanese again.

Harry Dietrich was about to go to bed when he heard the muffled thumps on the front door. He hurried to his office, got the .45 automatic he kept in his desk, returned to the living room, cautiously opened the door—and saw Kurusu. . . .

THE sound of an auto engine cut into Dietrich's thoughts. He looked out the window, saw Luz bring the red Ferrari to a jolting halt, winced in dismay. Fully aware that the sports car was unsuitable for most of the Cagayan's roads, he had bought it to please his wife, had made her promise not to drive over fifty kilometers per hour except on paved highways. However, turning into the drive, she must have been going at least sixty-five.

A moment later—as usual, without knocking—Luz came into the office, a smile revealing her small, even teeth. Her delicate fingers were already at the pins holding her waist-length black hair in a prim bun. She always unbound it as soon as she entered the house. He was about to warn her again about pushing the Ferrari too hard over dirt roads. Watching her hair fall loose around the perfect oval of her face, he found himself incapable of uttering angry words, remembering how, when they made love with Luz on top, the dark strands fell over his face and chest like fine, warm, perfumed rain.

"How was Remi?" he asked. Luz had gone into Tuguegarao to have lunch with the daughter of the town mayor. To Dietrich's occasional annoyance, she had never attempted to make friends with any of the women in the foreign community, was even reluctant to attend such obligatory functions as Lester Braden's funeral.

Luz shook her head to release the hair still clinging to her shoulders and the back of her long, pale neck. "All she talked about was the hearing at constabulary headquarters," she complained petulantly. "She said her father told her poor Major Ramos might be court-martialed. Is that possible?"

"I suppose."

"It is not fair. After all, he killed the *amok*."

"Yes." Dietrich hesitated. "Was the hearing still on when you left?"

Luz shrugged. "How would I know? Now I must tell the cook about dinner."

She bent, brushed her lips over his brow, always sunburned in the area where his sandy hair was thinnest. When she had departed, he turned his gaze to the telephone, wondering whom he could call to learn if Takei Shimura had caught the afternoon flight to Manila, decided anyone he spoke to was sure to wonder why he was so interested. No matter how minor the risk, he feared arousing even the faintest traces of suspicion.

If Shimura did not leave today, he would undoubtedly go tomorrow. What possible reason could the man have to linger in Tuguegarao?

13

Entering a room in the New Reno Hotel was an unsettling experience for Takei Shimura. Nothing had changed since he had been quartered there as a young officer in the Imperial Army. The walls were painted the same shade of mustard yellow; the bed, without headboard or footboard, had the same casually contemptuous aspect, as if it were defying guests to sleep in comfort.

Not until he boarded the Philippine Constabulary jeep that had come to take him from Major Ramos' home to the Tuguegarao airstrip, where he was supposed to catch Ken Tisak's afternoon shuttle to Manila, had he been sure he possessed the courage to go through with his plan. "I have changed my mind," he had told the driver when the gates closed behind them. "Please drop me off at the New Reno Hotel."

Shimura went out on to the balcony, which overlooked a narrow, shaded side street. He was glad he hadn't been given a room facing the main square, a view that would have reminded him constantly of the old horrors. Time enough to think about them when he began his search for Kurusu.

He sat down on a wrought-iron outdoor chair, whose

intricate, curlicued design contrasted oddly with the plain furniture inside the room, let the coolness of the late-afternoon shadows envelop him, sought to temporarily cleanse his mind of the events of the past week. But recollections of the hearing at Philippine Constabulary headquarters soon destroyed his efforts at self-induced serenity. He had told the three-man panel of officers of his certainty that the mines and thermite bomb had been planted in the cogon recently. "If anyone was at fault, it was I," he had declared. "I regrettably did not inform Major Ramos that Warrant Officer Kurusu was an expert with explosives, had conducted our regiment's training program in the use of what the Americans called booby traps. The major could not possibly have realized what lay ahead."

A Philippine Army bomb-disposal specialist had also stated that so many World War II charges could not have remained intact after years of exposure to the elements. Michael Braden, the final witness, had testified that as children, he and his brother had often played in the tall grass, without their family's knowledge. "If those bombs had been there then, I wouldn't be here now," he had concluded. But Shimura could tell, from the stolid, grim set of the panel members' expressions, that Ramos was in serious trouble. When dozens of men had died or been crippled, a scapegoat inevitably must be found. Ramos, sitting pale and rigid at a bare wooden table, didn't seem to hear the witnesses, never sought to meet their sympathetic gazes. After Braden spoke, the panel had retired to deliberate. No word of their verdict had yet reached Ramos' house when Shimura left, ostensibly for the airstrip.

Shimura heard a sharp, irritable rapping, went back into the room. He opened the door and saw Dr. Mapitang's taut-parchment face, frozen in a grimace of annoyed disbelief. "Have you gone mad, Captain Shimura?"

"How did you learn I was here?" he asked as the old physician brushed past him.

"The driver came back to Virgilio's house and told us. Why didn't you get on that airplane?"

"There is something I must do."

Mapitang snorted his disdain. "The news is out of your testimony at the hearing. Hundreds of people now know that a former officer of the *kempeitai* is among them. They'll soon be sharpening bolo knives all over the valley!"

"I was not a member of the *kempeitai*."

"You served them." Mapitang picked up Shimura's valise. "I doubt that you will be safe even here in the hotel. You must stay at my house, take the morning plane to Manila."

"Has Major Ramos received any word yet?"

"He got a telephone call a few minutes ago. The commandant wants to see him at nine tomorrow morning. Is *that* why you stayed? To find out what will happen to Virgilio?"

Shimura realized that he had no choice except to tell Mapitang his suspicions. "I do not believe that Kurusu is dead. No body was found."

Mapitang slowly lowered the valise, stared at Shimura in perplexed astonishment. "You heard my report today. Nearly half the men trapped in the cogon were so burned and mutilated that identification was impossible. Nothing left of them but burned and splintered bones. We brought out the pieces in small bags!"

"And Tanape's sword?"

"Do you have any idea of the temperatures generated by

burning thermite? They found odds and ends of fused, misshapen steel all through the grass."

Shimura shook his head stubbornly. "Only in the immediate area of the firebomb explosion. Sergeant García was supposedly attacked hundreds of feet from it—and the thermite charge went off seconds later."

"*Supposedly* attacked? The poor devil has no legs! What you are saying is impossible, Captain. The *amok* could not have escaped without being seen. It all happened in broad daylight."

"He was never *in* the grass—at least, not that part of it where the fire burned most heavily."

"Ridiculous!"

"Do you have a car?" Shimura asked in a tired voice, realizing that he could never verbally convince Mapitang.

"Of course."

"It will not be dark for a few hours yet. If you take me out to the cogon, I will try to show you how he did it."

Mapitang nodded his reluctant assent.

"FOR a while, it was like before the war," Sam Braden whispered. "No gunfire in the hills at night. No fear. I knew Cara didn't much like me, but that wasn't important. All that mattered was seeing life go on. With some kind of happiness, some kind of peace. 'Sam,' I told myself once, after the little girl came, 'you were wrong. It's going to work out. Everything you dreamed of and fought for so long is going to work out.' "

A few minutes earlier, Michael had returned home from the constabulary hearing, been surprised to find his grandfather alone in the front parlor. At this hour Sam Braden was usually napping upstairs. Slumped in a black carabao-leather armchair that had already been cracked and flaking when Michael was a teen-ager, the old man had begun to ramblingly describe the years that Les had run the plantation.

"But it didn't work, did it?" Sam Braden said. "Always the madness . . . I guess you don't remember your sister. . . . You were too little."

"I remember her."

"Wasn't until she died that I knew the madness had beat me. Should have known. Hell, I was old even then! Sixty, anyway. But I didn't know. Always had things my own way. The big things. I'd complain when the rains were late and I lost most of a crop. But that wasn't a big thing. The land was still there, my family was still there. It'd all go on. . . . You remember the boat?"

"I remember the boat."

"That's when I knew. In the boat. Watching Eve die and not being able to do a damn thing about it. Watching your mother and father start to die because she had and not being able to do a damn thing about it. Wanting to die myself—the way it's supposed to be, before the rest of you—and not being able to do a damn thing about it."

"A long time ago, Grandfather," Michael said gently.

"Funny—but in Santo Tomás I always knew I'd make it. People who shouldn't be alive nearly always make it. You ever notice that?"

"Yes."

"Your mother didn't make it."

"I know."

"Your dad either. He came out alive, like we did, but he didn't make it."

"I know."

"Kind of just piddled around after that. Did peculiar things. You remember the trout?"

"I remember the trout."

"Shouldn't have tried it. Nothing lives up in those mountains unless it was born there. Usually not even then."

"I know."

"But we got another chance, didn't we? Les and Cara and Evie. I thought it was going to work out."

"It'll work out."

"You ever notice how much she looks like your sister?"

"Yes."

"Just like your sister, even when she was a baby. Kind of scared me, Mike. Sounds crazy, doesn't it? That it scared me?"

"No, it doesn't sound crazy."

"Tried to keep away from her. That was a mistake. Selfish. But she was so much like the first one, I didn't want to get too close. Just selfish. What if something bad happened, I used to figure, and I lost her twice? Don't think I could have taken that." The old man's head had settled back on the webbed leather of the armchair. His eyes were closed; the jagged whisper of his voice faded even further. "They'll be gone soon . . . Cara and Evie. . . . Maybe for the best. . . . They'll be away from the madness."

"They won't leave, Grandfather," Michael said. "I'll see to it."

He realized that Sam had already been asleep when he made his rash promise. Nevertheless, Michael was determined to keep it. More than three quarters of a century ago, his grandfather had come alone to the Cagayan, turned a few acres of cogon-covered wilderness into the beginnings of a rich farm, held on through war and imprisonment, seen virtually everyone he loved perish in degradation and violence. To permit him to spend the final months or years of his life again alone would be an act of merciless cruelty. Michael had no illusions that staying himself would help ease the old man's pain. Sharing the house with a grandson who had given his own life to sterile drifting would only emphasize to Sam the long, relentless disintegration of the Braden family.

Luis Delgado, their attorney, was flying up from Manila tomorrow to meet with him and Cara. It would be a cut-and-dried affair, devoted to signing documents clearly defining Cara and Eve's share in the plantation's future profits, necessary because of the tortuously complex Philippine laws on foreigners' property rights. Realizing what he had to do, Michael checked to make certain Cara was not in the house, then placed a call to Delgado. In clipped, emotionless sentences, he described the additional document he wanted drawn up.

"Are you sure about this, Mike?" the attorney asked incredulously.

"Yes."

"It will mean the end of the Braden plantation."

"Already happened," Michael replied. "It died with Les."

He replaced the phone on its cradle with a trembling hand, went upstairs and donned khakis. That morning, Romolo had asked him to inspect the cleanup work on a section of land damaged by the fire. He had promised to drive over when he got back from Tuguegarao. The illusion of the plantation's existence would have to be maintained, for a while longer anyway.

Michael was heading toward the vehicle barn when he

heard the soft clopping of hooves, saw Cara ride into the utility-building compound on a piebald gelding, the last horse in the plantation stable. Eve sat in front of her on the Western saddle, clutching the horn with both tiny hands, her sneaker-clad feet rhythmically kicking the piebald's upper shoulders. The animal obviously didn't notice. Maria hurried past him, arms upraised to take the child as Cara lowered her.

"Uncle Mike, can we look at the picture books again after dinner?" Eve asked as the nurse led her away.

"Sure," Michael said, watching Cara effortlessly dismount, her faded, skintight jeans emphasizing the lithe, just-full-enough curves of her hips and legs.

"Where did you ride to?" he asked, falling in beside Cara as she walked the piebald toward the stable.

"The river and back. Evie loves horses, just like her father."

"I wish you wouldn't go out alone like that. Not quite yet."

Cara halted, looked at him quizzically. "You aren't sure the *amok* is dead, are you?"

"I can't figure out any way he could possibly be alive—but excess caution never hurt anybody."

He didn't tell her that for days a team of field hands had been exploring the area between the plantation house and the workers' barrio, trying to locate the rest of the canned food stolen from Li Tung's store. The single sack-load abandoned by the *amok* had amounted to less than a tenth of the missing goods. It was obvious that he had hidden the rest, intending to transport it into the jungle later in small lots. If the cache was found intact, it would prove that the murderer had not returned for his loot, dispelling Michael's doubts.

They entered the stable, where Michael helped her unsaddle the piebald. Cara began brushing its hide. "I told Romolo to put the stableboy to work in the fields," she explained. "I never understood why Les insisted on having a man to care for only two horses. All he ever did was hang around the kitchen and annoy the maids."

"Well, I have an inspection to run," Michael said, starting toward the door.

"What happened at the hearing?"

He turned back toward her. "I gave my evidence, not that it helped. Ramos has had it."

"You mean they'll actually put him on trial?"

Michael shook his head. "Too many embarrassing questions would come up. For example, why the government and the constabulary brass refused for years to concede that the *amok* existed. But no matter how they do it, Ramos' career is finished."

Cara was surprised at the inexplicable bitterness in her brother-in-law's voice. He wasn't a friend of Major Ramos', had met the man only twice. Suddenly, she began to understand. "Michael, why did you quit the army after putting in so many years?"

Michael again headed for the door. "I didn't quit," he said without looking around. "I was thrown out. The same way Ramos is going to be thrown out—the sneaky, gentlemanly way. Be back in an hour or so."

Driving north in his jeep, Michael wondered why he had answered Cara so readily. He had never told anyone the full truth about his discharge from the U.S. Army. A captain in the Special Forces, he had spent nearly eighteen months as adviser to a South Vietnamese force operating in the jungles east of An Tuc, an area so heavily pro-

Communist that government units had to operate out of fortified hamlets.

Late in the afternoon of October 13, 1965, Michael had accompanied Colonel Hugh Blassingame, the district's senior American adviser, on a low-level helicopter inspection of the area. They had come under fire from hidden riflemen, and a slug had smashed through one of the rotors. The chopper had crashed in deep brush, and only Michael and Blassingame had escaped alive from the burning wreckage. For the next two days—armed with a single carbine—they had struggled toward An Tuc, several times narrowly missed being spotted by Viet Cong patrols. Waiting at the crash site for air rescue would have been impossible in a guerrilla-infested region.

On the morning of their third day in the jungle, the nearly exhausted Americans had come on a winding trail that, Michael knew, led to a fortified hamlet fifteen miles to the east. They had risked following the path instead of keeping to the bush, as they had done earlier.

It had been a bad decision. Rounding a curve minutes later, they had encountered one of those tattered, wandering families that turned up everywhere in this ravaged land—an old woman; a couple in their thirties; four children, the youngest a boy of about six, all clutching cloth bundles. His carbine at hip level, Michael had questioned them in his limited Vietnamese. The man had stated that they were refugees from a village bombed out the day before, were on their way to the home of an uncle.

Michael had relayed the information to the wary-eyed Blassingame, who declared in English, "Not one chance in a hundred they aren't Red sympathizers. They'll have the bastards on our asses in half an hour. Kill them."

When Michael heard the order, he was looking at the

six-year-old boy, who stared up at him with the same terrified incomprehension that must have been in his own eyes when he saw the Imperial Army lieutenant who had come to take him and his family to the Aparri death ship. In an instant, reflexive outburst of rage, he had swung around, smashed the barrel of the carbine against the side of Colonel Blassingame's head. The man had crumpled into the dirt like a wash-and-wear suit falling off a bent wire hanger. The Vietnamese had dropped their bundles, run away along the path.

He had carried Blassingame on his back the rest of the way to the fortified hamlet, where the colonel, still unconscious, was airlifted to a military hospital in Saigon. When Blassingame finally regained consciousness—with a minor skull fracture—he had declined to bring charges against Michael, not wanting to put on a court-martial record that he had ordered the murder of civilians. It would be two or three years before such actions became routine among the American forces.

Nonetheless, Michael had realized he was through in the army. The message had been delivered personally by a one-star general, a West Point classmate of Blassingame's. The man had curtly told him that the paperwork had already been set in motion for Michael to resign his commission. The alternative would have been an assurance of negative efficiency reports and eventual discharge for incompetence. Forty-eight hours later, Michael had been on his way back to the United States and separation from the service. He had even been denied a brief leave to visit his family on Luzon. . . .

As he drove through the tobacco fields, he thought again about how deeply his childhood memory of the Japanese officer had affected his life. And now this phantom from his past even had a name: Takei Shimura. Michael had studied him while he testified at the constabulary hearing. He seemed like a decent man—reserved, soft-spoken, gentle-mannered; a man who, moreover, had come here to help end a lingering evil. And Michael still hated him with an intensity that made every muscle in his body as tight as stretched steel cable. . . .

"IMAGINE his predicament," Takei Shimura said as he and Dr. Mapitang slowly walked along the border of the blackened cogon field. The constabulary guard force had been ordered out after the last of the bodies were recovered. "In a few weeks the monsoon would begin, making hunting impossible. He came down from the mountains intending to raid in his customary manner—striking at outlying farmhouses or small barrios, killing all witnesses to prevent word of his crimes from reaching the police before he accumulated enough supplies to last him through the rains. But, by murdering a prominent planter instead of obscure peasants, he inadvertently prompted a full-scale manhunt."

"I am aware of all that," Mapitang remarked drily. "What are you looking for?"

Since they had left Mapitang's wheezing 1953 Saab, Shimura's gaze had been fixed on the ground; he had occasionally paused to prod the earth with the tip of his heavy walking boot. "Kurusu's *takotsubo.*"

"I understand little Japanese."

Shimura struggled to find the English equivalent for the word. "His 'octopus trap.' We called it that because of its shape, like a net used by fishermen to snare shallow-water creatures. One of the reasons he has remained at large so long is that even capable policemen like Major Ramos knew too little about the military system that produced him. Kurusu's life is the essence of *bushido,* of its rules and traditions.

"For example, the Americans prized mobility. When they took a position, their troops would dig shallow foxholes, be ready to move out quickly in the event of a counterattack. A Japanese soldier's training taught him that that conquered ground must be held to the death. So he would construct a *takotsubo,* a curved excavation running deep into the ground, even shored up with wood when materials were available. If his officers forbade retreat, he would have to be literally rooted out of the earth by the enemy.

"But I am getting ahead of myself," he murmured distractedly, nudging a thick hummock of grass. "After Lester Braden's body was discovered, Kurusu faced two possible courses of action—flee into the jungles or stay in the valley of the Cagayan, plan a single raid that would yield him everything he needed. That meant attacking a rich planter's home or entering a barrio large enough to support a store like Li Tung's. He chose to remain in the valley, after first drawing off the constabulary with a false trail into the mountains.

"It was a dangerous plan, since he might be caught in open country. He decided that if the enemy were to again pick up his scent, he would make a final stand in a place where he could kill as many of his pursuers as possible, perhaps even trick them into destroying themselves, enabling him to escape. So, using weapons he had preserved and hidden at the end of the war, he mined the cogon, dug his *takotsubo* in a place where he would avoid being caught in his own trap."

"All this is supposition," Mapitang protested.

"Of course."

They had reached the western edge of the cogon. Shimura crossed the road and started back the way they had come, through rows of tobacco plants that had been untouched by the fire. They were halfway to the Saab when his probing boot struck a concealed, solid object. Shimura knelt, dug at the ground with his fingers. Mapitang dropped to one knee beside him, looked on in fascination as the Japanese's swift-moving hands gradually revealed a broad disk fashioned from reeds and bamboo, like the lid of a large basket. Stalks and leaves of tobacco had been ingeniously woven into the bamboo, providing camouflage so perfect it would be undetectable two or three feet away.

"So it is true," Mapitang sighed in dismay.

Shimura yanked hard, pulled the disk free. A narrow tunnel slanted into the earth, the faint odors of dried blood and sweat still rising from its black depths. "When he was chased by Michael Braden, Kurusu went a few yards into the cogon, far enough to leave traces of his blood on blades of grass, then doubled back and hid in the *takotsubo*," Shimura said. "Major Ramos later arrived with his men, assumed that Kurusu had fled into the heart of the cogon, like an animal seeking cover."

"But who cut off Sergeant García's legs?"

Shimura, after carefully replacing the camouflaged lid of the *takotsubo,* stood up, wiped the dirt off his palms with a handkerchief. "He was caught in a type of booby trap that Kurusu and his counterinsurgency battalion often placed on jungle trails they thought heavily traveled by your guerrillas. A simple device, actually—just a thin strip of flexible, razor-sharp steel staked a few feet above the ground, bent double and attached to a trip wire. There may have been others in the grass, but only poor García was unlucky enough to spring one of them."

The words of the Japanese stirred memories in Mapitang of at least half a dozen mysteriously maimed back-country Ilocans who had been brought to the clinic during the occupation. He now recalled Aurelio Villamor's telling him that the guerrillas had actually avoided well-beaten paths out of fear of such traps. "It was so unbelievably long ago," the physician said.

"Not to Kurusu," Shimura said as they started back to the car. "He remained in his *takotsubo* until nightfall then, under cover of darkness, crawled off through the fields."

"To where?"

"I have no idea," Shimura replied with a shrug. "However, he could not have been as seriously wounded as Major Ramos believed. By now he is probably deep in the jungle."

"Why did you not report your suspicions immediately?" Mapitang asked, although he had already guessed the answer.

"Until I actually saw the *takotsubo,* I prayed that I might be mistaken. The insanities of the present are painful enough to face."

Mapitang's thin lips arched downward in a grim smile. "You intend to go after him yourself?"

"Yes."

"I thought as much."

"He could not have read the leaflets Major Ramos dropped in the jungle—or, buried deep in the ground, heard the messages I shouted into the cogon. He still does not realize I am here. If I meet him face to face, I may be able to persuade him to surrender. If I am wrong, no one but me will be harmed."

He is as crazy as the *amok,* Dr. Mapitang mused to himself. Then he considered what would happen if he told Major Ramos' successor—whoever he might be—about Shimura's discovery. Virtually nothing, he decided. New teams of trackers might be sent into the foothills. Every night, for a week or two, helicopters with searchlights would send futile beams of light stabbing over empty tobacco fields. Then they all would settle down to wait for the next massacre.

Until today, Mapitang had thought of the *amok* as a mindless beast but the diabolical cleverness that had created the trap in the cogon proved that intelligence—no matter how twisted—still existed in that grotesque body. And if intelligence remained, so did memory. Shimura had told him earlier that Warrant Officer Kurusu had run the *kempeitai's* rural informants' network. If he was the *amok* —and could be taken alive—he might provide the answers to questions that had long haunted Mapitang and other survivors of the World War II resistance movement. . . .

"You cannot enter the Cordillera alone," Mapitang said. "You would not live forty-eight hours."

"That is why I have confided in you, Doctor. I thought that perhaps you could recommend a reliable guide."

They had reached the Saab. For a few indecisive seconds, Mapitang drummed his thin fingers on a front fender. "I will take you myself," he said at last. "The government maintains medical stations—pitiful affairs, usually run by midwives—in several of the larger Ilocan villages. Before the monsoon, I go into the mountains to deliver enough medical supplies for the rainy months, try to squeeze in typhus inoculations and any other treatment I have time for. I see no reason why we cannot combine our missions."

"When would we leave?" Shimura asked.

"In a few days." Mapitang slid behind the wheel of the Saab. "Until then, as I said back in Tuguegarao, you would be wise to live at my house. I don't believe you fully comprehend the danger you are in as long as you remain in Tuguegarao."

Shimura got into the car, and Mapitang drove toward the new highway. Absorbed in their conversation, neither of them noticed the jeep halted on a slight rise to the north.

MICHAEL Braden had finished his inspection of the fire cleanup, was heading home over a narrow back trail when he glimpsed the two distant figures standing next to Mapitang's ancient green Saab on an intersecting road ahead, realized that the physician's companion was Takei Shimura. Still haunted by his grandfather's recollections of the Aparri death ship, he had barely restrained himself from reaching for the .375 Browning he had carried in the jeep since the night of his encounter with the *amok*. It would be so easy: just raise the rifle, frame Shimura in its telescopic sight, put a bullet through his head. He was prevented only by the knowledge that seeing his last surviving grandson jailed for murder would crush the fading vestiges of Sam Braden's once unconquerable spirit.

When the Saab had turned and driven off, he began to speculate about what the men had been doing here. A single explanation made sense. Like himself, they were uncertain that the *amok* had perished in the fire, had been searching the burned-out cogon for evidence to back up their suspicions. They could have found nothing, since he and Romolo had gone over every foot of the leveled field as soon as the constabulary guards departed.

Why had Shimura stayed in the valley of the Cagayan? It was as if he were deliberately inviting execution. If Michael had encountered the Japanese under other circumstances—alone, at closer quarters, in a less exposed area—he might well have given way to his murderous impulse.

Go home, he wanted to shout after the Saab. *Let us at least try to forget what you did here!* But Michael knew that he would never forget.

14

CONFUSED AND UNCERTAIN, Cara Braden looked up from the typed legal document she had just read, gazed across the study at Michael and Luis Delgado. "I'm sorry," she said, "but I don't understand this."

"The wording is quite clear," said the slender, white-haired attorney in his studied English. "Michael hereby agrees to sign over his interest in the plantation to you and Eve—with the provision that you both continue to live here until his grandfather's death. It will make you the sole owners, since Sam transferred full title to Michael and Lester many years ago."

Cara had come into the room expecting to go over a few routine papers. However, the first document Delgado had handed her was the agreement. "Why?" she asked Michael in a shaken voice. "Why would you give away your own home?"

"Sam is ninety-three," Michael said. "He's already survived two strokes. For whatever time he has left, I want him to feel that the family will remain intact, that our control of the land will go on."

Why didn't he just ask me to stay, she wondered with sudden anger. Why did he have to offer a bribe? Then she recalled her conversation with Michael the afternoon they had driven around the plantation together, her confession that neither she nor Evie had ever been able to get along with the old man. Nevertheless, a trace of anger lingered behind her words when she said: "But it's so . . . so *fake*!"

"Sam will never realize that," Michael replied with a matter-of-fact shrug.

"I couldn't run this place all alone," she protested.

"You won't have to. I'll stay as overseer. Pay me whatever salary you feel you can afford."

Cara, shaking her head, started to rise from her chair. "No . . . I couldn't . . ."

"You have any idea, if you and Evie go back to the States, how little money you'd see from the plantation?" he asked, almost brusquely. "Tell her, Luis. You've been sending me checks all these years."

Delgado looked mildly embarrassed. "Less than five thousand dollars annually."

"That's impossible," Cara gasped, sinking back into the chair. "Why, this is one of the biggest farms in the Cagayan!"

Antonio had wheeled a serving cart into the study after Delgado's arrival. Michael went to it, poured himself a cup of black coffee. "You used the word *fake* a minute ago, Cara. You were a lot more right than you knew—and for a lot longer. In economic terms, this and most of the other white-owned plantations have always been part fake. Sure, we maintain fancy houses and plenty of servants, but both are cheap on Luzon. The simple truth is that large, family-operated tobacco farms have never made much sense here, not in terms of cash income. Americans are conspicuous in the Cagayan because we work our own land, but actually, most of the valley is owned by fat-cat *mestizos* who live in Manila off rents collected from hundreds of small tenant farmers."

"And there is now the complication of the Laurel-Langley agreements," Delgado added. "Are you familiar with the law, Mrs. Braden?"

Cara nodded. "Of course. I remember how disturbed Les became when the Philippine Supreme Court finally upheld it."

"Then you are aware that since nineteen seventy-four, actual title to foreign nationals' land belongs to the government, although it has been leased back to you at minimal cost. All you own here is the house and outbuildings, valueless without the property on which they sit."

"Are you trying to tell me we're broke?" she asked in disbelief.

Delgado gave her what was supposed to be a reassuring smile; it emerged on his lips as an edgy grimace. "Quite to the contrary. However, proper utilization involves delicate legal problems."

Michael put down his coffee, untasted. "What Luis means is that after Grandfather is gone, you and Evie could be well off for the rest of your lives without ever setting foot in the Philippines again."

"How?"

"By establishing a land company with enough Filipino stockholders to conform to the Laurel-Langley rules. The company would take over our government leases, sublet acreage to independent farmers. Including my share, it ought to assure you . . ." Michael paused, cocked an inquiring eyebrow at the lawyer.

"A conservative estimate would be forty thousand dollars a year," Delgado said.

Still stunned by Michael's offer and the disconcerting facts thrown at her by the attorney, Cara stood up. "I'll have to think it over."

"Mrs. Braden, I assure you everything we said is true. To refuse would be foolish," Delgado declared.

"How long can you stay with us, Mr. Delgado?"

"To catch the afternoon shuttle to Manila, I will have to leave for Tuguegarao by three."

"I'll give you my decision by two-thirty," Cara said, walking toward the door. Delgado stared after her in astonishment. Michael, on the other hand, didn't look at all surprised. . . .

Cara spent the rest of the morning in the nursery with Eve, who was forced to stay in by a slight cold. As she watched the sniffling little girl lay out toy china dinner plates on her play table, she thought about the strange contradictions in her brother-in-law's nature. When she had first met him, less than three weeks ago, he had struck her as cold, even potentially ruthless. Not until the evening when, like a primitive tribal historian, he had patiently spent hours showing Eve the photographs and clippings in his boyhood scrapbooks, telling the child about her grandparents and other relatives she had never seen, had Cara realized that his detachment masked a need for emotional contacts he seemed incapable of making with anyone in the present. Surely Les must have known of the albums' existence, but he had never taken them out, the way most fathers would have. More than anyone else she had ever known, he had possessed a knack for starting his life over again each morning, forgetting any petty squabble they might have had the night before, meeting the events of the day with an easy calmness.

When Michael showed them the scrapbooks, she had realized that Les's personal serenity had been one of the underlying causes for her dissatisfaction with life on the Braden plantation; he had placed her in a bland, loving limbo, divorced from time. Now Michael had jolted her again. Even if he was acting out of affection for his grandfather, his willingness to break up the property was as disturbing as if, while Evie and Cara looked on, he had doused his treasured books with kerosene and set them afire. . . .

Michael and Delgado had eaten lunch, were sitting in the front parlor when Cara came back downstairs. "May I see that agreement again?" she asked the lawyer.

Delgado hurried to the study, returned with the thin sheaf of papers, handed it to her. Almost physically feeling the pressure of Michael's expectant stare, she calmly tore the documents in half, passed the pieces to the lawyer.

"A mistake," Delgado sighed with sincere regret. He had already been mentally computing his fees for setting up a company to manage the Braden lands.

"Does going home mean that much to you?" Michael asked in disappointment.

"I'm not going home," Cara said. "I'll do what you

asked me to, Michael—but not at the price of looking at Sam's face every day and telling myself that I'm *really* not waiting for him to die. We'll talk about the future of the farm when the proper time comes. Now I must get back to Evie. Goodbye, Mr. Delgado."

"I did not expect her to do that," Delgado said when Cara had returned upstairs.

"Neither did I," Michael Braden said.

THAT night Harry Dietrich finally set out to destroy the *amok*.

He had abandoned his earlier scheme to shoot Kurusu and claim that he had discovered him hiding in the preserves shed. Takei Shimura's continued presence in the valley made it impossible. To his bafflement—and that of everyone else who had learned of the arrangement—Dr. Mapitang had taken the Japanese into his home, a surer protection than surrounding him with platoons of armed guards. Not even men seeking to avenge wartime atrocities would defy the physician's judgment. Besides having been the head of the anti-Japanese insurgency, he was the most respected—by some, even revered—man in the Cagayan.

Dietrich now had no choice except to kill Kurusu and secretly bury the body. He could not risk using a gun. Their servants lived in a cluster of nipa huts less than twenty yards from the plantation outbuildings; the reports of a weapon powerful enough to fell Kurusu with one or two shots were certain to be overhead, even through the shed's cement walls. It would have to be done silently. The means were available in the barn—containers of arsenic, used by local farmers to poison bait for field rats.

At Dietrich's suggestion, Luz had driven to Aparri that

morning for an overnight visit with her parents. "I would like to come," he had told her, "but I am too busy getting in the crops." "Oh, Harry," she had chided, stroking his cheek with her fingertips, "you never really *do* anything yourself. Besides, isn't it more important to be at the warehouse during the harvest? My father told me on the phone that this is the first year you've allowed him to supervise the buying. He is worried about the responsibility." "I am not likely to fire my own father-in-law," he had replied wryly. "Now go on and have a good time."

For dinner, Dietrich had ordered *pancit,* knowing that the heavily spiced stew had to be prepared in large quantities. As he had anticipated, he found nearly a full pot in the refrigerator when the cook left for the night. He waited until eleven o'clock before heating the pot on the stove, stirring in enough poison to slay a full-grown carabao, taking gingerly, tongue-flicking tastes to assure himself that the arsenic was undetectable, spitting the tiny morsels of food into the sink. He had no doubt that Kurusu would eat it. Dietrich was able to smuggle a meal to him just once a day, and as his strength returned, his appetite had grown nearly insatiable.

For a few seconds—after the *pancit* was fully heated—Dietrich considered replacing it with a bowl of rice, forgoing his dangerous plan. After all, Kurusu's wound was nearly healed. Dietrich could release him from the shed, give him supplies to take into the jungle. No, he decided grimly as he filled a plastic gallon container with water, it must be done now! Convinced that he had found an ally, Kurusu would return again and again, turn Dietrich's life into a nightmare of apprehension. Besides, as long as the man remained alive, there was always the risk that he might be captured, reveal Dietrich's wartime dealings with the *kempeitai.*

Struggling to control the trembling of his hands, Dietrich shifted the *pancit* and water bottle on to a tray. A bristling knot of fear formed in his stomach as he carried the tray across the darkened rear yard toward the shed. The building's low, hunched outline resembled that of a crypt in a Swiss country cemetery. He put the tray on the ground, unlocked and opened the wooden door, wincing at the odor that assaulted his nostrils. Kurusu's harsh, heavy breathing seemed to slap against his face in solid waves. He could not see the man himself, but pale moonlight streaming over his shoulder reflected faintly off the blade of his drawn sword. Dietrich wordlessly put down the tray, backed out of the shed, again locked the door.

I've done it, he thought with shuddering relief as he walked back to the house, a strange coldness in his hands and legs. He went to the bedroom, set the alarm clock for three A.M., although he was certain that he would not sleep. A few more hours and it will be over, he brooded, lying on the bed. He had already chosen the spot for the grave, an isolated, brush-filled ravine where, last year, a field worker had been fatally bitten by a cobra. The area was now avoided by everyone.

Harry Dietrich did not realize he had fallen into a half-sleep until he heard faint, distant crashing sounds. He sat up with a start, glanced through befogged eyes at the illuminated hands of the clock. It was only a few minutes past midnight. The noises had ceased, and for an instant he believed he might have imagined them. Then, with a surge of nauseous horror, he guessed what was happening: Kurusu had felt the first effects of the poison, was attempting to escape from the shed!

His .45 automatic lay on the night table. He grabbed the pistol, cocked it, ran downstairs to the kitchen, yanked a heavy flashlight from a drawer, rushed into the night. As he feared, the plank door of the preserves shed had already been kicked open from the inside, the lock twisted and broken. He trained the flashlight beam on the dirt floor. The pot of poisoned food lay overturned, what was left of the green, creamy stew sinking into the earth.

Until dawn, Harry Dietrich searched the plantation's outbuildings, cautiously prowled the adjoining fields. But he found no trace of the Japanese. He must have crawled off to die somewhere, Dietrich told himself. Only a few mouthfuls of the *pancit* should have been enough to kill him. His body, despite its great size, was the same internally as any other human body. Blood gushed from his veins when they were cut. Food was digested and waste excreted through the same natural processes as that of normal men. Besides, even if his huge, rotting carcass was found, no one would know who had poisoned him.

Dietrich returned home when he spotted the first workers entering the fields. In an hour he had to give his foreman the orders for the day. It would look peculiar if he appeared unshaven and wearing dirty, slept-in clothes. Before going upstairs to shower, he locked all the ground-floor doors and windows.

WITH surprising ease, Michael Braden had reaccustomed himself to the rhythm of operating the plantation—at this time of year, a grinding, sweaty rhythm. He put in twelve- to fourteen-hour days supervising the premonsoon harvest; leading convoys of tobacco-laden trucks to Aparri, where the semidried leaves were weighed and graded before storage in Dietrich's curing warehouses; choosing the areas to be reseeded and with which varieties of plant. The last task was actually handled by Romolo, while Michael stood by trying to look self-assured. In fact, as a boy, he had gained little knowledge of the technical side of his family's business, was relieved that Les had been wise enough to educate field supervisors in all aspects of their work.

The endless labor served another function: that of blunting his almost obsessive need to be certain beyond all doubt that the *amok* was dead. The team of men he had sent out to locate the canned goods stolen from Li Tung's store had turned up nothing, but the search continued. However, he had disconnected the yard floodlights to avoid alarming Cara any further. If, by some miracle, the murderer was still alive, he must have fled back to the mountains by now. Of one fact he was sure: the Philippine Constabulary would be of no help if another killing occurred. Since Major Ramos had been compelled to accept early retirement as the alternative to court-martial, the new chief of investigations was unlikely to repeat the "mistakes" that had wrecked his predecessor's career.

Michael usually remained in the fields until dusk. Six days after his meeting with Cara and Luis Delgado, however, he returned from a run into Aparri in midafternoon, impulsively decided to quit early. The house was silent except for Eve's distant laughter, coming from the patio. She and her mother must be using the pool.

His guess proved correct. When he went up to his room to put on a clean shirt, the laughter and shrill, childish cries were much louder. He lit a cigarette, strolled to an open west window, overlooking the patio. Eve—her delicate blond hair tied in rubber-band-held pigtails—lay face down on a tiny Styrofoam float. Cara, clutching the bottom edge of the float, was swinging it in wide circles, drawing squeals of mock fright from the child. . . .

CARA gave the float a final twirl and, ignoring Eve's protests, swam to the other end with easy, graceful strokes, climbed up a steel ladder, pushed her chestnut hair out of her eyes with both hands. The movement elevated her small but perfectly shaped breasts, outlined her nipples against the wet fabric of her halter. Hiking the bikini bottom higher on her softly rounded hips, she sank on to a redwood patio lounge. Lenore Tully, reading the Pacific edition of *Time*, lay on the adjoining chaise.

"You'll never know what you did for me when you talked Les into a pool," Lenore murmured, pretending not to have noticed Michael standing at the second-floor window. "Though I guess I've gotten to be a pest about using it."

"Don't be silly," the younger woman replied. "I'm grateful for the company."

Lenore put down the magazine. "I think it's knowing that any day those monsoon clouds will move in and we'll have to live like fish for months. I'm trying to store up enough vitamin D to get through it."

She had been a daily visitor to the Braden plantation—for reasons more complex than she had told Cara. Since the night of the poker game at the New Reno Hotel, her husband had been continuously drunk in his unobtrusive way—and for the first time in Lenore's memory, had allowed his condition to interfere with his work. Delegating supervision of the harvest to their foreman, Jack rarely left the house, spent most of the day in the plantation office, alone with a quart bottle of Scotch that he invariably emptied before dinner. Nothing she tried—direct questions, pleas, angry shouting—provoked even a hint of explanation for his behavior. Rather than face the wall of quiet contempt he had erected between them, she had chosen to stay away as much as possible.

"Don't leave the low end," Cara called to Eve, who had paddled the float to the middle of the pool.

Lenore again stole a surreptitious glance at the bedroom window; Michael was still there. During nearly twenty years of marriage, she had remained faithful to Jack Tully—but she knew she was now closer to infidelity than at any other time. Her long-ago night with Michael Braden had come to dominate her thoughts, especially after Jack began ignoring her existence. Alone in bed every night, she had caressed herself, imagined Michael's driving hardness within her, the tingling warmth of his lips moving over her breasts and shoulders, the opening and closing of his hands on her buttocks as he started his final thrusts. . . . She wondered if he was having the same visions as he studied her from the window. . . .

"Better head home," Lenore said, rising from the chaise. "I think I'm starting to burn. Don't bother coming in with me. Evie's enjoying herself too much."

"Give my love to Jack."

"I will."

Lenore had used Cara's bedroom to change. She noticed, when she came off the back stairs, that the door to Michael's room, at the end of the hall, was open. She quickly entered the master bedroom, stripped off her swimsuit. I'm being silly, she thought, gazing at the slacks and blouse and underwear laid out on the double bed. Like a kid. It couldn't have been *that* great with Mike. I've built it all up in my head.

She had decided to dress and leave when she glimpsed her naked body in a mirrored closet door. It was still a good body. Her large, round breasts were almost as firm as they had been the night Michael undressed her in the Manila hotel room. Weeks of dieting and exercise had flattened her belly, restored the slim lines of her waist and hips. A body she had pampered and trained and molded —only to find it unused and unwanted by her husband.

With a surge of resentment, she opened the closet, took out one of Cara's robes, threw it on. She could still hear Eve's chattering voice below, knew that Cara and the child would probably remain at the pool for at least another half-hour. The servants had all been in the kitchen when she passed through, helping Inez begin preparations for the evening meal. Sam Braden would be napping in his room. Eventually, she told herself, either Mike or I will have to make a move. Why not get it over with?

Her heart pounding, mouth dry, she entered the hall, slowly walked toward Michael's room. There was so little time—but enough to let him know she desired him again. She would just enter wordlessly and remove the robe. He might want to make love to her immediately, she thought with excitement, imagining their locked bodies on the bed or, perhaps, the floor, to avoid the telltale creaks of bed-springs. Their mating would, of necessity, be over quickly, but they would make plans to meet the next day. . . .

Then she reached the threshold of his bedroom, saw that Michael was still staring out the window, a look of hungry, almost painful longing on his dark, lean face. Instantly understanding, she barely checked the bitter, humiliated laughter that had started to rise in her throat.

You damned fool, she wanted to scream. It can't work! Cara would pack up and leave the minute you made a move toward her! Don't you see it can't work?

Instead, she turned and went back to the master bedroom, her bare feet padding silently over the smooth mahogany floor. Michael had not even been aware of her brief presence in the doorway. . . .

Jack Tully was sitting slouched in a corner of the living-room sofa when Lenore got home, less than an hour later. "Quit the office early?" she asked with dispirited sarcasm, dropping the reed bag containing her swimsuit to the floor.

"Happened today, didn't it?" he said, after studying her for a few wordless seconds.

"What?"

"Mike Braden finally screwed you."

The memory of Michael at the window was still nagging at her when his calm, only slightly slurred remark sliced brutally into her consciousness. She could feel the blood rise in her cheeks, feel her facial muscles shape an expression of mingled guilt and shame.

"You're crazy," she said in a quivering voice, already realizing that no amount of words could wipe out the message her involuntary reaction had delivered. Even telling the truth—*I wanted him but he didn't want me*—would be damning.

"I think I'll skip dinner," Jack said, standing up.

How in the name of God could he have known, Lenore wondered in helpless desperation as she watched her husband leave the room, his heavy shoulders slumped forward. Even if something had really occurred between her and Michael, he couldn't have known. . . .

But he did know—and suddenly Lenore Tully was afraid. . . .

THE depression in the ground was roughly three feet deep, four feet wide and six feet long. The loose dirt scattered at its edges indicated that at one time a tarp or some other large piece of cloth had been stretched over it and covered with camouflaging earth.

Minutes earlier, Romolo had rushed into the house, told Michael that the men searching for the provisions stolen from Li Tung's store had made a discovery. They had immediately driven to the area, a fallow field near the river. Although only a few grains of spilled rice indicated that the excavation had held food, Michael was sure that it was the temporary hiding place of the *amok*'s loot.

"Very puzzling," Romolo said in English, since they had not told the triumphantly grinning workers the purpose of their search. "They went over this ground only four days ago, found nothing."

"That means he has to be alive," Michael replied harshly.

"We cannot be certain, *Patrón*. Suppose someone else found the food? A poor man would take it and tell no one —and in the valley of the Cagayan most men are poor."

The Philippine Constabulary would voice the same opinion, probably argue that Michael had no real evidence to support his suspicion that the *amok* had survived the explosions in the cogon, cite dozens of valid alternative reasons for the mysterious hole's existence. Going to them would be pointless.

"Who is the best tracker you know?" he asked Romolo.

"Nemelio Tegasay," the foreman replied without hesitation. "He has a small farm on the edge of the jungle, guides hunters to make extra money."

"I remember Tegasay," Michael said. "My grandfather used him often when I was a boy. Send for him. I'm going into the Cordillera tomorrow."

15

THAT MORNING he had seen that the red sports car always driven by the betrayer was gone from its usual parking space. Since the road ended at the plantation, the man, in order to get home, must pass the place he had chosen for the ambush, a sharp bend of the road about ten kilometers east of the highway to Tuguegarao. All day he had waited, crouched in the tall brush that grew on the roadside, his sword across his knees.

He had rarely killed for personal vengeance. But the betrayer's crime was an unforgivable insult not only to himself but to Colonel Tanape, who had protected the man and his family during the early years of the war. His anger was magnified by the betrayer's use of poison, the weapon of a coward and—in this case—a fool. From the very beginning, he had never bolted food that he had not prepared himself, had always eaten a single mouthful and waited for signs of illness before consuming the remainder. As soon as the abdominal pains began, he had quickly dug a hole in the shed's earth floor, vomited the tiny amount of *pancit* he had swallowed, poured most of the pot's contents into the hole before covering it up. If he could trick the betrayer into believing that he had taken a fatal dose, his task would be easier to accomplish.

After breaking out of the shed, he had hidden near the river for four days, used the nights to shift the food he had stolen from the store of the old Chinese to a new cache in the mountains. It had been slow, painful work, since the wound in his thigh had not completely healed. Only when the last of the supplies had been moved had he set out to trap the betrayer. He had made a new *takotsubo* on a wooded hilltop that afforded a clear view of the house, observed his enemy's comings and goings. The betrayer obviously was not sure he had perished, since he always wore a holstered pistol. A direct attack would be too risky; the man might post armed guards around the house at night. He had quickly realized that the sports car was the key to success. Even on straight sections of dirt road, the betrayer drove it at cautious speeds, slowed to a few kilometers per hour on sharp curves. It had simply been a matter of finding the best spot for the ambush.

The sun was descending behind the Cordillera. *Impatience is the father of error* had been the wisest of the precepts Colonel Tanape had taught him—but for one of the few times since he had undertaken his mission, he was unable to suppress it. Suppose the betrayer had gone away on a long trip, did not return for weeks? In order to survive the monsoon, he would have to move his food to the stronghold before heavy rains turned the jungle trails into impassable mires. Even spending a few more days in the valley might doom him.

Calm yourself, he thought sternly. If you do not kill him this year, you can kill him the next.

Then he heard the faint growl of a high-powered auto engine, realized that the car was still two or three kilometers away. Sound traveled far across the Cagayan plain. He moved to the edge of the brush, his sword clutched in both massive hands, waited eagerly, his flat black eyes focused on the eastern bend of the curve. Since the air was warm, the betrayer would be driving with the sports car's top lowered. It would be easy: just lunge out as the car passed, sever the betrayer's contemptible head with one sword stroke . . .

The car swerved around the bend. He had already leaped from the grass before he realized that it was being driven at a faster speed than he had expected, was bearing down on him like a juggernaut. With the instinctive delicacy of a bullfighter, he waited until the front bumper was only inches away before slipping aside. As the car roared past, almost grazing him, he swung his sword in a tight half-circle, flicking the very tip of the blade against the right rear tire. It exploded and the car skidded hard left, spun three times, shot off the road. The instant before it overturned, he heard a terrified feminine scream. . . .

The girl, thrown free of the wreck, was already dead when he reached her side. Shaking off his angry disappointment at having slain the wrong victim, he gazed down at her twisted body, wondering if she had been pretty. He had occasionally seen her on the porch of the betrayer's house, but at so great a distance that it had been impossible to judge her features. However, the long black hair streaming away from the scarlet pulp of her obliterated face had the perfectly cared-for sheen that comes from long periods of daily brushing. Yes, he decided, she had been pretty—and loved by the betrayer. A daughter, to judge by the youthful, unmarked skin of her naked legs.

He could not, of course, permit the betrayer to believe she had died in an accident. That would dissipate the man's fear as he waited through the monsoon for the retribution he knew must come. He raised his sword straight overhead, brought it down again and again and again. . . .

WHEN Luz had not returned home by dinnertime, Harry Dietrich grew even more alarmed. Their quarrel couldn't have justified her staying away overnight. What had it amounted to, really, but a few hot-tempered words about the restrictions he had placed on her?

At first, when Kurusu's corpse remained undiscovered, he had told himself that it might never be found. The Japanese must have sought a dark, secluded place to die, like the animal he had become. But the lack of confirmation of the madman's fate had inevitably worn at Dietrich's nerves, especially after Luz's return from her visit to Aparri. For the remainder of the week he had sought a variety of excuses to keep his wife close to home, finally refused to let her drive because of her habitual speeding in the sports car. He had known his decision puzzled and infuriated her. But how could he have told her the truth: *I want you near me because a mass murderer everyone else believes dead may still be at large—and especially dangerous to us.* He remained caught in the snare of lies and guilt and subterfuge that had been woven around him nearly thirty-five years ago by the *kempeitai,* would probably die still in it.

Except for her strained, uncharacteristic silence, Luz had not disobeyed his orders until that morning. It was

Thursday, when she usually shopped in Tuguegarao with her friend Remi Marqués. He had told Luz to stay home, been barraged by a string of incomprehensible but clearly unflattering Tagalog phrases. Later he had gone out to the fields to discuss the day's cutting schedule with their foreman, had come back to find both Luz and the Ferrari missing. Too worried to be angry, he had telephoned Remi, had been informed by a maid that Luz had already picked up her mistress. He had briefly considered heading into town after her, rejected the idea; his excessive reaction would have provoked questions he couldn't dare answer. Besides, what possible danger could she be in as long as she remained in a moving car?

When night fell, he again called the Marqués house, learned that Luz had started for the plantation more than two hours before. The journey shouldn't have taken more than an hour, even in the unlikely event that she had followed his rule about slowing down after leaving the highway. Dread eating at his mind like acid, he buckled on his .45, drove off in a spotlight-equipped jeep. . . .

Since the out-of-control Ferrari had careened more than thirty feet off the road before overturning, Harry Dietrich nearly missed the wreck in the darkness. Then his haunted, searching eyes saw skid marks in the tightly packed dirt roadway ahead. After hitting the brakes, he directed the spotlight to the right. The yellow beam swept over high, tangled brush, finally bathed the underside of the sports car, its intact tires outlined like a trio of fat sentinels.

Dietrich scrambled from the jeep, thrashed his way through heavy brush to the wreck. A hoarse sob was torn from him when he noticed a white, motionless lower arm and hand on the ground, jutting out of the area of the driver's seat. Kneeling, he clutched Luz's fine-boned wrist, tried to locate a pulse, felt only cool flesh. It's just shock, he thought frantically. He tugged on the arm, hoping to free the rest of his wife's slender form from the wreckage, was surprised by the ease with which he was able to move her—and then realized the truth. . . .

He lurched erect, dropped the severed arm as if a ten-thousand-volt electrical current had passed through it, stumbled backward. . . .

Although he was more than a mile away, beginning his trek into the mountains, he dimly heard the betrayer's howl of grief, sweeping across the fields like the ghostly wind gusts that assaulted his desolate, rocky home island of Shikotan. Yes, he thought again without breaking his stride, time enough after the monsoon to complete his vengeance. . . .

"I have to try to find him," Michael Braden told Cara. "Maybe he is dead—but I have to *know*."

For hours he had attempted to think of a convincing reason why, at the peak of the harvest, he would choose to journey into the Cordillera, realized full well that his sister-in-law would guess the truth immediately. He had waited until Sam and Eve had gone to bed before telling her about the discovery of the empty food cache. They had been in the den, watching an old Jackie Gleason *Honeymooners* comedy on television. She had risen and switched off the set.

"You'll do it alone?" she asked.

"Romolo is hiring a tracker. I told him to bring the guy straight to the house, no matter how late it is. I want to start as early tomorrow as possible."

Cara went to the bar, made a bourbon and water. Only

a few moments before, she had been reflecting about how comfortingly mundane life seemed that evening—a drink or two after dinner, staring at a TV program that had been taped when she was still in elementary school, made even more remote in time by its pale, flickering transmission from distant Manila—everything that would have happened if Les were alive. And of course, it had all been illusion.

"Is there any way I can help?"

Michael shook his head. "I've already given Inez a list of supplies we'll need. She'll have them ready in the morning. I can borrow a pack mule from the Lydeckers. Old Anson breeds them."

"How long will you be gone?"

"As long as I have to be."

"And the rains? They're way overdue. You can't live out there during the monsoon."

"The *amok* does," he replied. "Don't worry about the harvest. Romolo runs this place better than I ever will."

Cara left her inexplicably tasteless drink on the bar, returned to the couch. "I almost convinced myself it was all over," she said, looking away from Michael to prevent him from seeing the tears in her eyes.

"It'll be over when I'm certain he's dead. You and Evie will have the kind of life you deserve. We all will."

She felt his fingertips stroking the back of her neck, sensed that he was going to try to make love to her. She had suspected for days that it would happen—from the edginess that entered his voice during the most ordinary conversations, the way his eyes followed her when they were alone together in the evening.

As his hand slipped down her back, she turned toward him, startled at the expression of overpowering need on his face, more like an urge to devour her than like sexual desire. The intensity of his stare virtually paralyzed Cara as he pulled her to him. His mouth descended on hers and his free hand found and gently cupped her right breast. To Cara's surprise, she began responding to his caresses, her lips parting moistly beneath the pressure of his tongue. Then his hand left her breast, unfastened the top of her blouse—and she thought: *Les hasn't been dead a month* . . .

Cara pushed Michael away, shook her head. "No," she murmured in a barely audible voice.

"Going to happen eventually," he said with flat certainty. "We both know it. And we'll be living here together an awfully long time. It'd make it easier on both of us—and Evie—if we got married."

Her confusion gave way to anger. "I'm not a piece of furniture! Something that comes with the house!"

"You don't come with the house. You *belong* in it. And so do I—now."

Suddenly she understood why Michael had been willing to sign away his rights to the plantation to prevent her and Eve's departure. He didn't want to replace her husband; he wanted to *be* Les! She and her daughter had become part of his past, like the faded faces in the scrapbook photographs. They had found a measure of contentment on this remote farm that Michael had loved—and ultimately fled. Now he had returned, seen in them a chance to cancel his own failures, take over the life his brother had created.

"Good night, Michael," she said, rising. She left the room without a backward glance. . . .

We'll be living here together an awfully long time. . . . Michael's statement echoed in Cara's mind as she undressed for bed. The same thought had often occurred to her during the past few days, as she and her brother-in-law settled into the routine of their new lives—superficially like those of a husband and wife, she had soon realized. Eve always kissed him good night, the same way she had kissed her father. Then, after Sam went to his room, they would talk about the day's events or look at television. Usually, they would ascend the stairs together, part at the landing, go to their rooms, less than twenty feet apart. . . .

In time there would be another man, she brooded, slipping between the sheets. With the worst of her grief dissipated, the prospect of endless nights of cool solitude in this bed had already begun to nag at her. Possibly, as Michael had so confidently declared, the man might even have been himself. The monsoon would have imprisoned them inside the house for days at a time. She remembered how it had been with Les during the heavy rains, how they went to their room as soon as Evie was down for her afternoon nap, made slow and lazy and tender love until they heard their daughter's waking cries, her nursemaid's hurried footsteps along the hall. . . . Yes, it would happen again. . . . But not now. . . . Not quite yet. . . .

She had drifted into the truth-filled, semihallucinatory state before full sleep when she realized that she was deceiving herself: it had been Michael's proposal of marriage that had shaken her, not the fact that he wanted to possess her. She had already guessed that—and done nothing firm to discourage him. . . . Suppose he had gone on simply trying to seduce me, she wondered. Left the whole matter on the level of physical need? If he had, Cara sensed with uncomfortable suddenness, she wasn't at all certain that they wouldn't be lying now in each other's arms. . . .

Somewhere a telephone was ringing, faintly, distantly. . . . She ignored the sound, doubled a pillow under her head, clutched it. . . . Later—she wasn't sure how much later—she heard a light but insistent knock on the bedroom door, dragged herself back to consciousness. . . . Knowing it had to be Michael, since everyone else in the house must be asleep, she hesitated to answer. Suppose he had decided to force himself upon her? The knocking sounded again—louder this time.

Cara got out of bed, turned on the night-table lamp, started toward the chair over which she had draped her robe. She was lifting the garment when the door opened and Michael entered, his face taut. Aware that her body was fully visible beneath her transparent silk nightgown, she clutched the robe against her breasts, stared defiantly into his hazel eyes.

"He's murdered Luz Dietrich," Michael said.

THE first to come were Romolo and Tegasay, a squat, brown-faced man whose flat cheekbones still bore the eroded tattoo scars of a deep-jungle Ilocan warrior. They pulled up behind the plantation house, illuminated by the reconnected floodlights, in the foreman's jeep. Sprawled on the rear seat was a huge gray dog with a gentle, long-muzzled face. Familiar with Ilocan tracking animals, Michael knew that on Tegasay's command, the beast would become a ravening killer.

"We will be hunting the *amok*," he told Tegasay. "If you do not wish to help me, Romolo will drive you home."

Tegasay wordlessly climbed out of the jeep. Over his shoulder was a bedroll wrapped in a World War II GI rubber raincoat. At a guttural signal, the dog joined him. "Good," Michael said. He filled in the tracker about the killing of Harry Dietrich's wife, pinpointed the area where it had happened. "Try to pick up his trail but do not follow him alone. Wait at the river ford north of the Dietrich plantation for the rest of us."

Nodding, the tracker set off at a loping trot, the dog on his heels. . . .

Less than half an hour later, Walt Lydecker arrived in a truck. In the back of the vehicle were four mules, which waiting field hands quickly prodded down a loading ramp. "You were right, Mike," the boyish-faced planter said in a voice tinged with self-disgust. "It's up to us to nail him. It always was."

Walt, who had been in the New Reno bar when word of the murder had swept through the patrons, had made the phone call to the plantation. "Have you learned any more?" Michael asked as he and his friend walked toward the house.

"They'd just brought the body in when I left Tuguegarao. Christ, he chopped her to pieces! Why?"

"Who the hell knows—or probably ever will?"

"Rounded up anybody else?"

"Jack Tully and Virgilio Ramos."

"Major Ramos? Why him?" Walt said in surprise.

"Because he's tough and resourceful and he knows more about the *amok* than any of us."

"But suppose he tips off the PCs?"

"He won't," Michael said with absolute certainty. "Not after what happened in the cogon. A couple of dozen men died because of his error. You don't wipe out the memory of something like that by calling the cops, even if you used to be one yourself."

Cara, dressed in blouse and jeans, was setting out coffee and plates of sandwiches in the main parlor. "Michael, are you going to tell Harry Dietrich what you're doing?" she asked. "When none of you turn up at Luz's funeral, there are bound to be questions."

"He'll have enough on his mind tonight," Michael replied grimly. "Walt, grab a cup of coffee. Haven't had a chance to pack my gear yet."

When he returned downstairs with a rolled sleeping bag and a laden knapsack, Ramos had joined Cara and Walt. Somehow, in civilian clothes, the former constabulary major looked smaller, more Oriental. The ordeal of the past weeks showed on his face, which had lost its olive-skinned sleekness, grown almost gaunt. However, his tone still carried a note of military formality when he said: "Thank you for permitting me to accompany you, Mr. Braden. However, may I ask an additional favor?"

"Of course, Major."

"I do not keep personal weapons, and even if the stores were open this late, guns are no longer legally obtainable. Would it be possible to borrow a rifle?"

Michael and Ramos went into the study, inspected the hunting rifles and shotguns in the wall cabinet. After handling several weapons to test their weight and balance, Ramos selected a Marlin .444.

"Good choice," Michael said.

"Have any of you talked as yet to the police?"

"This trip is supposed to be secret."

"I have—to a former deputy I trust fully," Ramos said. "The constabulary does not believe the *amok* killed Mrs. Dietrich."

"When did any cop except you believe he killed anybody?"

Ramos lit a Benson and Hedges, inhaled deeply. "If you had not told me of the discovery of the empty food cache, I doubt that I myself would hold the *amok* responsible.

Even you don't have any idea how he escaped from the cogon. Other aspects of this matter are equally puzzling. The killing of Mrs. Dietrich was an act of sadistic butchery, a *personal* crime."

"And the others weren't?" Michael asked sardonically.

"I have read the dossiers on all murders attributed to the *amok*. He is an extremely consistent—in a sense, reasonable—killer, once you accept the mad premise upon which his actions are based. Every victim was slain by a single sword stroke, delivered with ruthlessly efficient skill. His motives were quite clear-cut: to secure food or other necessary supplies, to defend himself against threatened danger. There has never been a shred of evidence that he feels a psychological need to inflict pain. He kills without remorse—and without pleasure."

Impatient to complete the preparations for the hunt, Michael had barely listened to Ramos' words. "Major, we don't have time to explore his motives—if any. I don't care about them. I just want him dead!"

They heard a vehicle turn into the front drive. Michael hurried out of the study. Ramos, deep in thought, remained behind. He knew that he had made a mistake in speaking to Michael Braden while the American was in such an agitated state. But more than a quarter of a century of police work had instinctively told him that vital pieces of information about the Luz Dietrich death were missing.

Almost as disturbing was the fact that eight days ago, Dr. Mapitang had taken Takei Shimura into the Cordillera. In virtual seclusion after his forced resignation, Ramos had not learned of the two men's trip until he had spoken with his ex-aide. Clearly, Shimura had believed that the *amok* was alive, and somehow enlisted Mapitang's help in a rash personal search for proof. He could already feel lines of disorder starting to converge, like narrow but fast-rushing streams of water pouring into a gorge to form a deadly whirlpool. To learn the full truth—and through learning it, destroy the *amok*—he had no choice except to cast himself adrift on one of the streams. . . .

Cara had already admitted Jack Tully when Michael got back to the parlor. "I stopped off at Harry's on the way over here," Jack said with a bitter shake of his head. "The poor son-of-a-bitch couldn't talk straight yet. . . . When are we shoving off?"

"At least an hour before sunrise," Michael replied. "If the PCs have set up extra patrols, I don't want to risk running into them."

Michael had been surprised that after his earlier, vehement opposition to organizing a vigilante force, Jack had so readily agreed to join them. The man's manner was still inexplicably tense, even under the circumstances, and he avoided directly meeting Michael's gaze. To hell with it, Michael thought wryly. I'm getting to be as big a nit-picker as Ramos. He's coming and that's what counts.

"Am I the last one?" Jack asked.

"Yes. The smaller the group, the faster we can cover ground. He'll already have at least a twelve-hour lead on us by morning. Right now I think we should get any sleep we can. Going to be a rough trip."

"I've had the guest rooms made up," Cara said.

MICHAEL slept atop his bedcovers, fully dressed except for his boots. He was awakened by a gentle shaking of his right shoulder, sat up with a startled grunt, saw Cara standing above him. She wore the same blouse and jeans as the previous night, and her eyes were shadowed. "It's four o'clock, Michael," she said in a near-whisper.

"You didn't go to bed?"

Without answering, she started toward the door. "I'd better wake the others."

"Cara, I'm sorry."

She turned back toward him. "About what?"

"Making a fool of myself in the den. Won't happen again."

"That's all right."

"You'll be here when we get back?" He tried to make the question sound casual, failed.

"Of course," she said, shutting the bedroom door after her. . . .

FROM the open kitchen doorway, Cara watched the men check the bindings on the pack yokes of Walt Lydecker's mules. To make their departure as inconspicuous as possible, the floodlights had been turned off. In the black, shifting shadows, the four figures were almost indistinguishable. At last, Michael came to the open kitchen door, murmured goodbye. She kissed him quickly on the cheek, waved to the others. Only when the column of men and animals had vanished into the night—a matter of seconds—did she consciously face the fact that they might be going to the same kind of macabre, pointless death that had claimed her husband. She backed into the kitchen, shut the door to fend off an abrupt chill that she knew had been generated by her own body.

Cara reheated a pot of coffee, drank a cup at the kitchen table. She was finally forcing herself to go upstairs when the phone rang. She hurried to the parlor, answered it, heard the husky, worried voice of Lenore Tully: "Have they left?"

"Yes."

"I was afraid of that. I tried to talk Jack out of going but he wouldn't listen. Nothing I said would make him listen!"

"They'll be all right, Lenore."

"He told me it was crazy, that they don't have a chance of finding the *amok*."

"Then why—"

Lenore cut her off: "Something I wanted to tell Mike. I've sat here all night, trying to work up the nerve."

"What?"

"Never mind. It's too late. And I'm probably wrong anyway."

Without saying goodbye, Lenore hung up. Cara slowly replaced the receiver, experiencing the same ill-defined disquiet that had come over her the last day of Les's life, while she was waiting on the darkened veranda for him to come home. . . .

BY the time they reached the fording place, pale light was oozing upward on the eastern horizon. Since it was the end of the dry season, the Cagayan was only a few feet deep at this point, bedded with hard gravel. Even if Michael had not wanted to avoid well-traveled roads, for fear of being stopped by constabulary troopers, they would save valuable time by crossing here, since the nearest bridge lay more than ten miles to the north. A gray mist crawled through the reeds on the opposite bank.

Walt Lydecker had already started leading a mule across when they saw jouncing headlights coming toward them along the rutted riverside trail. Walt tugged harder on the mule's lead reins until Michael barked, "Just act normally. If it's the PCs, we'll tell them we're on a hunting trip."

However, they had not been intercepted by the police. Harry Dietrich's foreman was behind the wheel of the jeep. His employer—face ashen, eyes swollen and red—sat beside him, a rifle and bedroll across his lap. When the jeep halted, he got out, slung the rifle over his heavy shoulder.

"No, Harry!" Jack Tully cried in a pity-wrenched voice, hurrying to his friend. "Let us handle it."

"She was my wife," Dietrich said hoarsely, signaling the foreman to drive away. "I have to come with you."

"Catch up later, when you've had time to pull things together," Walt Lydecker urged.

"Her family can take care of the funeral. . . . I don't give a damn about funerals."

"Walt is right," Michael said, silently cursing Jack Tully for having told Dietrich their plans. "You're in no shape for this."

"I'm coming!"

Only Virgilio Ramos remained silent, his deceptively bland brown eyes examining Dietrich's haggard features. Yes, they showed inconceivable grief, a determination to right a hideous wrong, all the emotions that should be present. And just under the surface, rigidly controlled fear. . . .

Michael guessed that if he refused the Swiss permission to join the expedition, he would probably follow them anyway. "Let's go," he ordered, grasping the lead on the second mule. "It's getting late."

The Cordillera loomed ahead like a jagged black-green wall as they splashed across the shallow river. Waiting for them amid the thickening mists on the far bank was Tegasay, squatting on the ground, his dog crouched beside him. The tracker rose, gave Michael a brief nod to indicate that he had picked up the trail of the *amok.*

16

IN A THATCHED HUT more than thirty-five miles to the southwest, Takei Shimura was awakened by the laughter of children. He sat up on his reed pallet, hoping that the aching musces in his back and legs would unknot a little more easily this morning.

Seeing that Mapitang's pallet was unoccupied, he rose, rubbing the small of his back with both hands, and went to the slatted wooden door, pushed it open. They had reached the village of Ticlac the night before, gone to bed immediately in the hut used as a medical station. In daylight, the place looked little different from the other settlements they had visited during the eight days of their journey: a cluster of stilted huts on the bank of an almost dry stream, along which sat a row of now-unusable dugout canoes, like dusty artifacts from an earlier civilization. The inevitable flock of debilitated chickens pecked listlessly at the earth of the communal clearing.

The only evidence that they had entered deep jungle

was the clothing of the villagers. In the foothills, most of the Ilocans had worn Western clothing—ragged khaki or denim pants, cheap plaid shirts, faded but lovingly maintained floral-print dresses. As he and Mapitang had moved farther away from the valley of the Cagayan, the garments of civilization were seen less frequently. In Ticlac they didn't exist at all. The men wore bundled blue loincloths, carried bolo knives in brightly decorated reed scabbards, fastened around their waists by hemp belts; the women's bodies were covered, haphazardly, with loose white shifts. The children, like the giggling group staring up at him from the foot of the bamboo porch ladder, were naked.

Squinting in the bright sunlight, he looked around for Mapitang without success, decided the physician was probably conferring with the barrio's headman or explaining the use of a new drug to the midwife. He wondered again why the physician had been in such a hurry to get to this nondescript settlement. Usually, if they had not reached a village by sunset, they would set up camp. But last night he had insisted that they press on hours after the fall of darkness.

Shimura reentered the hut, opened a can of peaches for breakfast before one of the village women could present him with the usual morning meal of sticky, rancid yam paste wrapped in a banyan leaf. After eating, he shaved with his battery-powered electric razor, noticed irritably that it was beginning to lose power; he had not thought to bring extra batteries. When he went outside again, there was still no sign of Mapitang. He descended to the ground, confronted the children, repeated the word *doctor* three or four times, drew only shy, uncomprehending grins. Finally, he pantomimed the action of inserting a hypodermic needle into his arm. A gangling boy nodded vigorously, pointed at a high, scrub-covered bluff north of the village. The entrance to a narrow canyon cleft its center, like the imprint of an ax blade in a soft log.

The children running ahead of him, Shimura started toward the bluff. . . .

AT home, Takei Shimura had always prided himself on having escaped the physical flabbiness of most of his contemporaries. However, after he and Dr. Mapitang began their journey into the Cordillera, he had faced the fact that rounds of tennis or handball did not prepare a midde-aged architect for a trek through highland jungles.

The knowledge had come on the first afternoon, while they were tugging and pushing pack mules up a steep hillside covered with loose volcanic shale. "Wouldn't it be easier—and faster—to visit the villages in a helicopter?" he panted when they reached the crest.

The physician—who, although two decades older than Shimura, never seemed to tire—smiled tightly and replied: "Easier, but self-defeating, if you want to keep the trust of the jungle tribesmen. To them a helicopter is a threat. They have never forgotten the constabulary's airborne raids on their barrios during the Huk war, accept my help only because few of them know I serve the same government that used to attack them.

Remembering his regiment's ill-fated thrust into the Cordillera in 1942, Shimura had been relieved to discover that, except for the ever-present green flies, insects were merely an annoyance, not a constant source of buzzing, stabbing, itching torture. "It gave me pleasure to see you all marching off so confidently that day," Mapitang said when asked about their absence. "At the very end of the monsoon, just when fresh swarms of malarial mosquitoes and burrowing parasites are drying their wings."

"I am afraid we knew very little," Shimura sighed.

"You knew nothing," Mapitang said flatly. "But don't worry, Captain Shimura, if we are still out here through the first rains, the environment will grow more familiar. There is one microscopic bug—I don't believe anyone has ever named it—that flourishes early in the monsoon. It lays its eggs on human eyelashes. Days later, before the victim even realizes he is infested, the larvae enter his retinas, causing excruciating pain and irreversible blindness."

"I will be sure to wear my glasses at all times."

At first, Shimura had been perturbed that the old physician had not hired a guide to lead them into the wilderness. However, he soon realized that his companion knew the Cordillera as well as any of the inhabitants, surrendered himself to Mapitang's judgment as they climbed higher into the mountains, so gradually that on the single occasion when they reached a peak affording a clear view of the country behind them, he was astonished to see that the valley of the Cagayan was visible only as a featureless, off-brown corridor twisting through endless expanses of green hills.

"Every spring since nineteen thirty-seven—except when your army occupied Tuguegarao—I have made this journey," Mapitang said in his dry, rustling voice as they gazed out at the jungle. "And there is no place on earth that I hate so much."

"Why?"

"The jungles of the south offer hardship and disease—but also coconut palms and bananas and *calamansi* and soil that can sustain high yields of rice. The jungles of the

Cordillera—despite the forests and the rains—are as sterile as a desert where human needs are concerned. That is why the *amok* is often driven back to the Cagayan. When the hunted starve so do the predators."

At each village they visited, Mapitang turned over a package of medical supplies to the local midwife, treated as many of the ill as he could in the limited available time. "A dangerous year," he remarked to Shimura while inoculating a row of frightened-eyed children against typhoid, the most common epidemic disease in the mountains. "The dry season began early and is ending late. What little water is left has grown stagnant." Shimura did not have to be told of the drought's extent; almost every stream bed they passed had been dry, and the murky water given to them from village wells was virtually undrinkable, even after boiling.

When Mapitang's medical tasks were completed in each settlement, the physician set up a conference with the barrio elders, translated for Shimura as he asked the Ilocans about encounters with the *amok*. Obviously Mapitang was as well respected in the jungle villages as he had been in Tuguegarao, able to casually cut through the rituals and taboos ruling these isolated people's lives. He ordered them to tell Shimura the truth, and they obeyed, even though the Japanese was a stranger, did not even speak their language.

At every barrio, the accounts of the *amok*'s past depredations were similar. For years at a time he would leave them in peace. Then, usually at the harvest, the attacks would begin, last less than a week—farmers murdered for a basket of rice; young girls kidnapped and sexually assaulted with such brutality that they were usually found in a state of shock. "He never kills the women he rapes,"

Mapitang once mused. "No one knows why." Each scene of a raid—and its approximate date—was marked on a government map Mapitang had given him. In the beginning, the younger warriors had mounted pursuits of the murderer—from which no man had ever returned alive. Now his forays were regarded as supernatural visitations of doom, accepted stoically, like avalanches or jungle fires. Shimura's final question was always the same: Had any of them heard of villages that had been totally spared the *amok*'s fury? He had received half a dozen replies, based on boasts or rumors from infrequent visitors to the barrio. The jungle Ilocan's world was limited to his hut, his fields and the patch of forest where he hunted. What happened beyond was of little interest.

However, by the night they reached Ticlac, Shimura had gathered enough information to hazard a guess about the area where Kurusu dug in during the monsoon. Since it was well after dark when they arrived at the village, he decided to wait until morning to test his theory on Mapitang. . . .

THE naked children took Shimura to the canyon mouth, then ran back toward the huts. He went on alone through a high-walled gorge, which at some points was less than three feet wide, wondering what Mapitang could be doing out here. After walking over the rock-strewn ground for nearly a quarter of an hour, he was ready to turn back, wait for the physician in the village. Then he entered a broad area overgrown with coarse grass and vines. Mapitang, a cigarette held between the bony index and second fingers of his right hand, was sitting on a boulder, staring somberly at the ground. The cigarette ash had burned almost to his knuckles.

"Good morning, Doctor," Shimura said.

Startled, Mapitang glanced up at him—and for the most fleeting of instants, his eyes showed resentment bordering on anger. "You have no idea where you are, do you?" Mapitang asked."

"Should I?"

"I suppose not." The ash reached Mapitang's knuckles, and with a wince of pain he dropped the cigarette, crushed it under his boot. "Aurelio Villamor's guerrillas had their main encampment here. Just before dawn on September seventeenth, nineteen forty-five, a brigade of your troops infiltrated the canyon, slaughtered all but a handful of the guerrillas. My son Raúl was among those who died."

"I had not realized."

"You weren't intended to," Mapitang said with a distant smile. "As you may recall, immediate relatives of identified guerrillas were executed without trial by the *kempeitai*. None of them used their real names, even while talking to lifelong friends. At least, his mother and I were spared the sight of his body decomposing in the Tuguegarao square. Since it would take an unpleasantly long time to pack out corpses over such a great distance, your troops just let them lie. Ticlac was burned to the ground, of course, but a few of the villagers managed to escape. When they returned, they buried the victims in a common grave. No one quite remembers where but I am sure the spot is nearby, perhaps under our very feet."

"Kurusu led our forces that day."

"Major Ramos had already informed me."

"I thought he must have."

"You misunderstand," Mapitang said. "I no longer feel

hatred for the Japanese, even that obscene madman we are hunting. They were soldiers, performing their duty. Besides, Villamor's guerrillas never took prisoners either."

Since the afternoon they had found Kurusu's *takotsubo,* Shimura had not understood why the old physician had so willingly aided his efforts to talk the *amok* into surrendering. "What else did Ramos tell you about Kurusu?" Shimura asked warily, already guessing the answer.

"That he was the *kempeitai*'s liaison with civilian informers."

Shimura exhaled sharply between his teeth. "I see."

"Look at this place," Mapitang said, gesturing at the sheer rock walls of the canyon. "Do you honestly believe that an encampment could have been spotted from the air or discovered by one of your patrols—in the unlikely event that any of them penetrated this far into the jungle?"

"No."

"A traitor led them here. Or told them the location."

Shimura shook his head in dismay. "All that happened nearly thirty-five years ago. You executed hundreds of collaborators after the war. He might well have been among them. Even if he was not, he could have died of natural causes."

Mapitang lit another cigarette. "Quite true—but I would like the name. So would the families of the other men who died. Their parents are old now—many even older than I. They should not end their lives knowing such vermin will walk the earth after their passing. . . . I have shocked you, haven't I?"

"A little," Shimura admitted. "After all, you have devoted your life to healing."

"To heal, it is necessary to cut away diseased flesh." Mapitang stood up. "In nineteen seventy-one, after heart surgery both he and I realized would fail, Aurelio Villamor died in my clinic. I was with him during the final moments. 'Isidro,' he said over and over again, 'we will never know who it was.' I *will* know, Captain Shimura! I *must*! And only one human being can tell me!"

"Kurusu?"

"Yes."

"Shall we return to the village?" Shimura said after a few seconds of brooding silence. "I think I have figured out where he hides during the rainy season. I will explain further when we can go over our map."

He is wrong, Shimura thought as he and the suddenly eager Mapitang started back through the gorge. Someone besides Kurusu knew the identity of the collaborator responsible for the massacre of Villamor's guerrillas. Shimura still remembered Hisao Tanape's exultant words in the bar of the New Reno Hotel the evening after Kurusu reported his victory: "I learned in Shanghai that neutrals make the best informers. They will perform any act, no matter how foul, to preserve their precious state of nonbelligerency." Tanape could have been referring only to the Swiss planter he had tried to recruit for the civilian intelligence network a few weeks after Shimura arrived in Tuguegarao. . . .

LATE that afternoon—in a stand of dark, gnarled yacal trees—Tegasay's dog led Michael Braden and his companions to a second food cache. Like the one discovered on the plantation, it had been dug in the shape of a narrow grave, covered with a tarpaulin—probably stolen from Li Tung's store—and camouflaging dirt. But this time the excavation was not empty.

"Looks like only two or three sackloads," Michael said,

gingerly lifting a corner of the tarp, taking care not to disturb the cans themselves. "He must have carried the rest with him."

He hadn't expected to make a key find so early in the expedition. Seeking deep jungle before the monsoon broke, the *amok* might have neglected to cover his tracks with his usual meticulousness, depending upon the rains to eliminate the trail. It wasn't a particularly dangerous gamble, since shifting gray clouds had sent shadows rippling over the mountains since midmorning. Even a heavy drizzle might be enough to prevent the dog from following the scent picked up at the wreck of the Ferrari.

"He's bound to come back for the rest," Walt Lydecker exclaimed. "All we have to do is wait him out."

"The *amok* has not survived by doing the things he is expected to do," Major Ramos commented sardonically. "Suppose he has other hoards of food, makes a rule of not visiting a new cache until earlier rations have been consumed?"

"Why would he have taken such wild risks for the past month if he already had supplies?" Walt asked.

"Once again you are describing predictable behavior. He must have buried this food days ago, therefore had no 'predictable' reason to return to the valley of the Cagayan. But he did return. Otherwise, poor Mrs. Dietrich would still be alive."

The burly Swiss grimaced at Ramos' words, a flush further darkening his sunburned cheeks. Jack Tully drew in his breath, gave the ex-policeman a reproachful glance. No one had mentioned Luz's murder since Dietrich had joined them at the ford.

"Well, do we stay or not?" Jack snapped at Michael. "You're running this posse, so you decide."

His sarcasm startled Michael. In a week or two, when the strain and discomfort of living in the open had lacerated their nerves, displays of temper would be inevitable, even from so normally easygoing a man as Jack Tully. That acrimony should break out less than fourteen hours after their departure disturbed him. However, Jack had been moody and withdrawn from the beginning, rarely speaking to anyone except the almost equally silent Dietrich.

"I'm not running anything," he said quietly. "And you've spent more time in these mountains than the rest of us put together. What do *you* think?"

"I think it was too easy to locate this stuff. He figured he'd be chased by the PCs, left it here as a diversion. If it was a small party after him, they'd pin themselves down the way Walt wants us to. A bigger group would split their forces, leave three or four men behind while the others went on, lowering the odds in his favor if he had to make a stand later."

"What if you're wrong, though?" Walt protested. "It'd mean losing contact with the only place we're sure he'll come back to eventually."

"There is a simple way to resolve the question," Ramos said with a frown of bitter reminiscence. "After what happened in the cogon, I find it hard to believe that diversion would be his only motive in setting up so convenient a lure. Would you care to make the test, Mr. Braden? Your rifle will do the most damage at short range."

"Everybody take cover," Michael said, unslinging the .375 Browning. "At least fifty feet away. Get the mules even farther back."

They all moved into the yacals, crouched behind thick tree trunks. Then Michael rested the barrel of his weapon on a forked branch, sighted in on the camouflaged food cache, fired. The first slug from the powerful big-game rifle shredded the tarp. The second triggered an explosion that sent dozens of steel cans hurtling skyward, snapping off heavy tree branches as if they were dry thistles. For seconds after the ear-numbing blast faded, the only sounds in the grove were the whimpering of Tegasay's terrified dog and the frantic brays of the pack mules.

"I'm beginning to think the son-of-a-bitch *did* want somebody to find it," Michael said.

Walt and Major Ramos uttered bursts of tension-releasing anger. A slight, strained smile even touched Dietrich's harrowed features. However, Jack Tully just stared at Michael with cold, expressionless eyes, wondering if he and Lenore laughed at each other's jokes when they were in bed together. She had laughed at Jack's, no matter how silly, when they were first married. But of course, that had been a long time ago. . . .

"He won't do anything," Lenore Tully said. "He never actually said he would. Just a kind of nutty feeling I had."

However, Cara could sense the desperation behind her friend's self-calming words. Lenore had turned up at the plantation house that afternoon, stayed for dinner. It hadn't been until the two women were sitting alone in the den that Lenore had told her of Jack's obsessive belief that she was having an affair with Michael. She had already betrayed her nervousness by going three drinks beyond her usual solitary after-dinner Scotch and soda.

"That's what you wanted to tell Michael on the phone this morning?" Cara asked, stunned by her friend's revelation. Mingled with her surprise was another feeling, barely recognizable even to herself: the tiniest splash of jealousy. She had so long thought of Lenore as a kindly, helpful, older neighbor that she had ceased to notice her voluptuous, still-sensual beauty.

"Yes."

"What could have given him such an idea?"

"I'm not sure," Lenore said with a twitching shrug of both shoulders. "Jack seems calm to most people, kind of slow. But he sees things."

"Was there anything to see?" Cara asked, almost afraid to hear the answer.

Lenore hesitated, then said in a low voice, "Once, about a year and a half before Jack and I got married. And I guess I wanted it to happen again."

"But if it *didn't*—"

"What's the difference as long as Jack believes it did?" Lenore replied, already regretting having blurted out the story to Cara. None of it had been the girl's fault—or Michael's, for that matter.

"He just . . . flung this at you? For no good reason?"

Lenore knew how improbable her account must sound to anyone who hadn't witnessed her husband's behavior since the night he had first accused her of the affair. He had begun sharing her bed again—but not to sleep or make love. He had lain motionless, questioned her for endless hours in his diffident voice about the details of her nonexistent meetings with Michael.

For three nights she had continued to insist that nothing had ever happened between them. On the fourth—worn down by fatigue and growing fear, wishing that he would show any kind of emotion, even anger—she had told him about the night they had spent in the Manila hotel room.

"But that was all," she had concluded pleadingly. "Just a few hours. We were kids!"

After a moment of silence, he had asked: "How many times did he screw you? Three? Four?" "I barely remember it," she had lied. "Any of it!" "He's older now, pushing forty. Can he still get it up again and again, or do you have to help him once in a while with your mouth?"

On the evening of Luz Dietrich's murder, convinced that Jack was going insane, she had made plans to flee to Manila as soon as he went off to the fields the next day. And then Michael had telephoned, told Jack about the killing, again asked him to join an illegal hunt for the *amok*. "I'll be over as soon as I get my gear together," Jack had said into the receiver in the same matter-of-fact voice with which he had tormented her with his obscene questions. . . .

"Better start home," Lenore said, quickly finishing her drink.

"You're afraid that he'll attack Michael, aren't you?" Cara asked. "It's hard to believe. Jack is so gentle."

"Not always. No one who fought with Villamor could be."

"But that was during the war."

"Oh, you Americans!" Lenore cried with a vexed sigh.

"You're an American."

Lenore shook her head. "I have an American passport, but I'm not an American. Neither is Jack or Mike or Walt Lydecker. Neither was Les. Americans are people who sail off to fight battles in other people's countries and then go home to neat, safe little families in neat, safe little houses and say dumb things like *But that was during the war*. This *is* the other people's country, Cara, but we were born in it and live here and can't go home because home doesn't really exist. Only the war exists, and it'll go on forever. Even the *amok* knows that."

Lenore rose from her chair, walked unsteadily toward the door. Cara, realizing that her friend was close to being drunk, hurried to her side, put an arm around her shoulders. "Sleep here tonight," she urged. "It'd be too depressing to go back to an empty house."

"*They'll never find him,* Jack said when he was packing," Lenore murmured, as if she hadn't heard Cara's invitation. "*I'd better go anyway and play the old games, at least try to keep the silly bastards from killing themselves.* Maybe that *was* his reason. Maybe. . . ."

Cara and Lenore had almost reached the stairs when they heard the patter of raindrops, a sound so unfamiliar that it took them a few seconds to recognize it. Lenore stumbled to the teakwood front doors, flung them open. Already sheets of dark water were cascading from the veranda roof. "It's started," she said, her voice weak with relief. "They'll never be able to follow his trail now! They'll have to turn back!"

"Yes," Cara said, forcing a note of hope that she didn't actually feel. *You can't live out there during the monsoon,* she had told Michael yesterday afternoon, remembered the implacable determination in his gaze when he replied: *The* amok *does. . . .*

17

Why does it always begin at night, Michael wondered as he listened to huge, pulpy drops of tropical rain splatter on the roof of the tent he shared with Ramos and Walt Lydecker. He threw off the unfastened cover of his sleeping bag, lit a cigarette, waited, hoping that the shower would not develop into a full downpour. But in minutes, rain drummed against the canvas with hard, steady force.

"Unfortunate," Ramos' voice muttered in the darkness. "Your tracker is excellent, far better than any I had in the constabulary. A few more clear days and he might have led us to the *amok*."

"He still might if this doesn't keep up too long. The early rains are usually localized. Maybe the next valley over is dry and the dog can pick up his scent again."

"Perhaps," Ramos said doubtfully. Like Michael, he was familiar with the monsoon's normal progression. The first rainfalls would be brief, followed by hours—even, occasionally, days—of clear weather. However, the wet periods would relentlessly grow longer and more frequent, finally merge into storms that continued for weeks, obliterating trails through the jungle, turning gullies and ravines into temporary rivers. "But if we *are* unable to track him further?"

"What would you advise?"

"We know that, so far, he has moved to the southwest. We could visit the barrios in that direction, question the villagers, on the chance that someone has seen him."

"A pretty slim chance," Michael said wryly.

"You have an alternative?"

"No."

The tent flaps parted and Walt Lydecker entered, his narrow shoulders trembling beneath his drenched shirt. "Your turn on guard, Mike," he said. Although they assumed the *amok* had not lingered in the area after mining the food cache, they had decided it would be prudent to mount watches.

Michael crawled out of his sleeping bag, groped through a knapsack for a hooded rubber poncho, pulled it over his head before picking up the .375 Browning. "Any place look even fairly dry?" he asked.

"Not a one," Walt sighed. "Why don't you just stay here? Can't see a damned thing out there."

Without replying, Michael flicked the Browning's safety and left the tent. Walt stripped off his sopping clothes, dried himself with a towel before getting into his sleeping bag.

In less than a quarter of an hour, the rain stopped. From the rhythmic sound of Walt Lydecker's breathing, Ramos knew that the American was already asleep. His own nights would be restless until he solved the personal dilemma created by the breaking of the monsoon. Lydecker had been closer to the truth than Michael Braden: without a solid trail to follow, the hunters would soon be reduced to an aimless march through the mountains, pursuing a phantom that nature had put hopelessly beyond their reach.

Obviously, none of his companions were aware that Dr. Mapitang and Takei Shimura had entered the Cordillera nine days earlier, might already have found leads to the *amok*'s whereabouts. The logical move would be to link up with them, combine forces and knowledge—but in this case, the logical move could have catastrophic results.

Although no longer a police official, Ramos felt responsible for Shimura's safety—and most of his companions possessed overwhelmingly valid reasons to hate ex-members of the Japanese occupation force. Jack Tully was one of the four survivors of the Ticlac massacre. Michael Braden and Walt Lydecker had been imprisoned as children in Santo Tomás, watched friends and relatives die of starvation and disease and beatings. Less than two days ago, Harry Dietrich had found the dismembered body of his young wife, slain by a *kempeitai* executioner, might be disturbed and angry enough to senselessly retaliate against a former Japanese officer with links to the despised security organization.

That Shimura's life should be endangered by events that had occurred in his youth seemed madness—but Ramos had long since learned that, in such matters, madness was the rule. . . .

THAT afternoon Takei Shimura had explained his plan to Mapitang, while both men knelt over a map spread on the floor of the Ticlac medical station. At the location of every barrio they had so far visited, Shimura had noted the approximate date of the *amok*'s past attacks.

"Each localized outbreak has been separated from the

last by from four to six years," he explained. "Never have two neighboring barrios been struck in the same year. By selecting widely spaced targets, he leaves himself clear avenues of escape in all directions, and the long waits between raids lull the villagers into a false sense of security, cut down the possibility of his encountering strong defenses. In short, rather than the uncontrolled monster you have all believed him to be, he is actually quite disciplined, even cautious."

"You may be right—but I fail to see how any of this reveals his hiding place."

Shimura indicated five spots circled in red. He took a pencil from his shirt pocket, linked them, forming a crude half-circle at the base of a ridge of mountains north of Ticlac. "According to the villagers we have spoken to, all of these barrios have escaped attack. As you no doubt notice, they are only a few miles apart. Again we see not mindless fury but caution. In any organized effort to track him down, pursuers would naturally assume the villages were spared because they are beyond the range of his hunting pattern. Actually, the opposite is true. Their very peacefulness—like the camouflaged entrance to a *takotsubo*—creates a buffer zone, sealing him off from his enemies. I am certain that his stronghold lies between these barrios and the immediate area north of them."

Mapitang irritably drummed his fingers against the naked wood of the hut floor. "The 'immediate area' consists of hundreds of square miles of wilderness! Even if you are right, it would take an army to find him."

"I intend to let Kurusu find *me*," Shimura said calmly. "I will start a signal fire in a high, easily visible area and wait. The presence of a stranger so close to his sanctuary is certain to disturb him. In time he will come to investigate."

Mapitang released a sarcastic snort, stood up. "And then you will ask him to surrender, he will do so and the two of you will go home to Tokyo hand in hand? Ridiculous! Even if he is where you say he is—and I doubt it—he would kill you."

"No, Doctor, he will not. I am his commanding officer."

Mapitang's eyes mirrored amusement and disbelief. "Captain Shimura," he said at last, "you have lived all over the world, speak English far better than I do—but for all that, you remain astonishingly Japanese!"

"So, despite his apparently insane actions, does Kurusu. This is a man imprisoned by bonds of ritual fanaticism, bonds from which only I can release him."

"I have visited the country you speak of. The few people who live there work soil so poor that, even in the best of years, they exist on the edge of starvation. Did it occur to you that the *amok* spares them because they own nothing worth stealing?"

"I do not ask you to accompany me. I doubt that he would make contact unless he were certain that no one else was near."

"And how do you propose to reach this region?"

"I am not foolish enough to believe that I can find my way alone," Shimura said. "You will ask one of the village men to guide me. After I have established a camp, he will return here. In a few weeks—however long it takes you to finish your work—he will lead you to the place where he left me and we will return to Tuguegarao together, with or without Kurusu. If I remain close to camp at all times, I will not be in great danger."

"Except from cobras, poisonous insects and the *amok*

himself." Mapitang shook his head. "I cannot permit it—and no one here will help you against my opposition. We will start for the next barrio in the morning."

However, as he went about his work, doubts formed in Dr. Mapitang's mind. During the months of the monsoon, the *amok* might remain inactive—but when the weather cleared, he would kill again. Mapitang returned to the map, studied the figures marked by the Japanese, noted that Ticlac had been free of attack for five years. If Shimura's theory about the murderer's basic strategy was correct—and it seemed to be—some of the people he had treated today would soon die under the *amok*'s blade. Besides, Shimura offered the only means of taking the fugitive alive, freeing the information stored in his diseased brain. . . .

He did not make his decision until that night, when the first rain in nearly seven months fell on the village. Although it had been dark for hours, he and Shimura could hear excited cries. They went on to the porch, watched children scurry down hut ladders, turn their faces to meet the downpour. Torches flared on other porches as the adults emerged to celebrate the end of the yearly drought.

"All right, Captain," he told Shimura, who had not mentioned his plan since Mapitang's refusal of help. "I will provide you with a guide. Perhaps you *are* destined to end this horror."

"Thank you," Shimura replied; he didn't sound even mildly surprised at the physician's about-face.

"However, I have a condition."

"What?"

"You already know it."

"That I ask Kurusu who told him Villamor's headquarters was located here?"

"Yes."

For an instant, Shimura considered lying to the physician, later telling him that he had been able to learn nothing from Kurusu. But the words would not come. "There is an agreement between our countries on these matters," he said. "If Kurusu gives himself up, he must be regarded as a legitimate prisoner of war, subject only to the Geneva Convention. He cannot be compelled to provide information not covered by the convention's rules."

Mapitang leaned forward, clutched the bamboo porch rail with both gaunt hands. "The Cordillera is not a place for the enforcement of civilized rules—no more than Kurusu was ever a soldier! My God, how can you insist he be regarded as an ordinary prisoner of war when you yourself ordered his arrest for murdering his own comrades? It makes no sense!"

"More than thirty years ago, a man who may no longer be alive committed a great wrong against your people," Shimura declared, nauseously aware that the statement he was about to make could just as well have emerged from the lips of Hisao Tanape. "No matter how despicable I personally consider his actions, they were done at the behest of the Imperial Army regiment of which I was an officer. If I aid you or any other former enemy in punishing him, I betray my own honor."

Mapitang gripped the rail so hard that the angry tremors of his body shook the bamboo. But his eyes remained fixed on the children playing in the rain. With agonized effort, he managed to uncoil his fingers, push himself erect. "Only a fool would sacrifice the living in order to avenge the dead," he said in a defeated whisper. "You will have your guide, Captain Shimura. Good night."

Takei Shimura remained on the spindly porch after

Mapitang went back into the hut, watched the villagers call in their children and extinguish the festive torches. The rain had tapered off to a misty drizzle when he reentered the hut, lay down on a pallet across from the old Filipino who had nearly become his friend. . . .

THREE days later, in a short-grass savanna northeast of Ticlac, Michael Braden finally admitted to himself that the *amok*'s trail had vanished irretrievably. Several times, despite the increasingly strong rains, Tegasay's dog had managed to pick up his scent in areas where the overhead foliage was so thick that only scattered drops of water penetrated to earth—but had lost it again within minutes. The few visual signs they discovered—crumbling indentations that might be the footprints of a large man, a wooden lean-to erected so recently that semihardened sap still clung to the broken ends of the branches used in its construction—were ambiguous, could as easily have been made by an Ilocan hunter.

While Tegasay scouted the country ahead, the others consumed a cold lunch from cans, since they had no dry firewood. Although it had not rained for hours, the ground was so wet that everyone but Walt Lydecker ate standing. Glancing down at his friend, Michael realized that his slight body, permanently weakened by childhood deprivation in Santo Tomás, would never adjust to the grueling regime of the trek, that he was keeping himself going on sheer will.

However, Ramos and Harry Dietrich had borne up well so far—and, to Michael's amazement, Jack Tully seemed to thrive on their hardships. From the beginning, he had been afraid that Jack's alcoholism might compel him to flee back to the Cagayan, provide the first defection. But he had never mentioned the need for a drink and each day his rangy but loose-fleshed body visibly grew harder, his movements firmer and more controlled, as if he were drawing some kind of mystic strength from the surrounding jungle. The face of Aurelio Villamor's ruthless young second-in-command had begun emerging through his slack, puffy skin like a newborn crocodile clawing and biting its way out of its semitransparent eggshell.

Tegasay returned, shook his head to indicate that he had found no signs of the *amok*. Walt Lydecker stood up, shivered slightly as he brushed at the damp, grass-stained seat of his khaki shorts. "Somebody has to say it," he muttered. "The rains have beaten us."

Michael glanced quickly at the unshaven faces of the other men. He appreciated the danger of becoming the only member of the party to continually urge going on; it would stir resentment, subtly compel the others to band against him. However, when no one else spoke, he said: "We have to change our approach, that's all. Check out the barrios, learn if anyone has spotted him."

"Why would he go near settlements?" Jack Tully asked. "He's already carrying as much food as he can manage."

"Do you want to turn back too?"

"No, but I think we ought to set a time limit. None of you guys except Tegasay has ever lived out here at the height of the monsoon. I did for three filthy years. You hunker down in the driest hole you can find, watch your shoes and clothes rot off and pray you haven't picked up some fungus that'll do the same thing to your balls!"

"How long do we have left?" Harry Dietrich asked.

"Three weeks at the outside. Then hiking overland will be damned near impossible."

Michael said nothing. He knew that Jack was right—and he also knew that if the others returned, he would stay in the jungle. Eventually the *amok* had to finish the supplies stolen from Li Tung's store, be forced to mount new, localized raids. When it happened, Michael didn't want to be sitting in a plantation house fifty miles away.

Ramos took a Benson and Hedges from his shirt pocket, tried to light it twice before noticing that his matches were water-soaked. He threw them to the ground in disgust. "Who is our enemy?" he barked, impulsively making the decision that had been nagging at his mind for days.

The others turned puzzled eyes toward the ex-policeman. "The *amok*, of course," Walt Lydecker said.

"And only the *amok*?"

"What are you driving at, Major?" Dietrich asked.

"I want a promise that you will raise your hands against no man except the *amok*."

For a stinging instant, Jack thought that Ramos had somehow read his mind, seen the vision that had tantalized him since the start of the hunt. They would have cornered the *amok*, be maneuvering to bracket him in a deadly crossfire. Michael Braden would cross his path just as he was about to fire; his finger would continue to close around the trigger, "accidentally" blowing off the top of his rival's skull. Even though he doubted that he was capable of turning vision into reality, Ramos' enigmatic words produced a surge of guilt so intense that he could feel the blood pounding hard in the veins of his forehead.

"Do you give me your word?" Ramos persisted.

Everyone except Jack Tully issued a baffled affirmation. "I won't promise anything," Jack muttered, meeting Ramos' expectant gaze, "until I know what I'm letting myself in for."

Realizing he had gone too far to back down, Ramos told them that Dr. Mapitang and Takei Shimura had journeyed into the mountains together more than a week before Luz Dietrich's murder.

"Then what you really want is my word that I won't harm Shimura?" Jack asked Ramos.

"Yes."

"All right," Jack said with a shrug. "You've got it."

"They must have discovered the *amok* was alive," Michael said, describing the afternoon he had observed the two men walking past the burned-out cogon. "Why didn't they tell the constabulary?"

"Shimura is convinced that he can talk that madman into surrendering," Ramos said. "Undoubtedly he thought he would have more luck on his own, rather than surrounded by police and soldiers."

"That doesn't explain why Dr. Mapitang went along. He *has* to know better!"

"I myself do not understand his motives," Ramos admitted.

"Major, you actually think we'd hurt this man just because he's a Jap?" Walt Lydecker exclaimed in disbelief.

"He served as an officer in the regiment that occupied Tuguegarao."

"We knew that," Walt said. "It was all over town after your hearing. But, Jesus, the war ended a long time ago!"

Michael Braden wondered, in silent bitterness, if Walt would be so charitable if he realized that Takei Shimura had led the roundup of American civilians in 1942, set in motion the events that had turned his childhood and adolescence into a marathon of crippling pain, caused the death of Michael's sister and mother and both of Jack Tully's parents. Almost certainly, Shimura had been a member of the *kempeitai*. An ordinary officer would never have been given such a detail. "So what do you suggest, Major?" he said aloud, with cool evenness. "That we link up with them?"

"Possibly they have learned nothing. However, since we have lost the *amok*'s trail in any case, we have no other leads."

"We do not know where they are," Dietrich said, the words rasping through his dry throat. He had come on this expedition to make certain that Kurusu was not taken alive, eliminating one of the two men who could reveal his collaboration with the Japanese. Even if Shimura had still been in Tuguegarao when they returned, none of the hunters would dare reveal their role in a civilian vigilante force without facing imprisonment. The news that Shimura was also in the Cordillera had hit him with brain-reeling impact.

"Before the monsoon, Mapitang takes medical supplies to many deep-jungle barrios," Ramos said.

"But which?" Michael asked. "Dozens of villages scattered through these mountains."

"I know one he always visits," Jack Tully said with grim nostalgia. "A place called Ticlac. His son Raúl is buried there, along with thirty-two other friends of mine."

"How far is it?" Walt Lydecker asked nervously.

"A day and a half if we move fast. Two, at the most. Even if Mapitang has already passed through, the villagers might know where he was heading."

Walt shook his head in weary, embarrassed defeat. "Mike, I'm not going to make it. I thought I could, but I was wrong. Don't suppose I have to spell it out."

"No, Walt, you don't," Michael said.

"The legs, mainly. Years go by and I think I'm over it.

Then I push myself a shade too hard and all of a sudden I'm as weak as a ninety-year-old woman with arthritis. I'd slow the rest of you down."

"Can you make it home?"

"Sure, setting my own pace."

"Okay, then," Michael said. "We'll leave you a mule."

For a few anguished seconds, Harry Dietrich considered going back with Walt to the valley of the Cagayan. But after he had forced himself on the expedition, vowing that he would endure anything to track down Luz's murderer, his quitting at the first opportunity would look suspicious. He knew that Ramos, although he had so far asked no questions, was curious about the circumstances of his young wife's death.

As a child on his father's farm in Switzerland, Dietrich had once watched a mountain owl hunt the wild pigeons that scavenged in the barnyard. It had alighted on a high farmhouse drainpipe where the plump birds liked to perch at dusk. The pigeons were beyond the reach of the predator's beak and talons as long as they remained on the drain. The owl had edged sidewise, pressing its folded wings against the nearest pigeon. It too had moved aside, started a chain of nudgings that pushed dozens of birds farther down the drain, like commuters waiting to file through a railroad-station turnstile. The movement had been repeated again and again—until one of the pigeons panicked and took flight, an instant later found itself impaled on the owl's claws, swept through the sky to be devoured at leisure.

Ramos' manner reminded Dietrich disturbingly of the owl in its position of false rest. The worst mistake he could make would be to abandon his present role. Besides, he thought, the chances were slight that they could find

Mapitang and Shimura in this endless wilderness. Even if they did, the Japanese probably would not remember him. . . .

We met once, Harry Dietrich told himself, as he had told himself hundreds of times a day since spotting Shimura at the Philippine Constabulary roadblock. *Just once. . . .*

It took the men another half-hour to reassemble the mules' yoke packs after gathering the supplies for Walt's homeward journey. He watched until his friends disappeared over a rise to the southwest, not certain whether the tears in his eyes were induced by humiliation or by the bright sun which had briefly appeared overhead. It would soon be gone, he realized. Dark blue clouds were stampeding in over the wooded hills to the north, linked to the earth by wispy gray columns. In the Cordillera, you heard and saw approaching rain minutes before it descended like a curtain of warm, wet gauze.

A forest of camagon lay a few hundred yards east. Months of drought had denuded the branches of leaves, but the trees might offer some protection from the rain. Walt turned, started toward the mule, realized that a dark, indeterminate form had materialized between him and the animal. His eyes had barely time to define the shape as human before the cutting edge of the sword cleft his brow, hissed downward through his nose and mouth and chin, divided his head into a pair of disintegrating scarlet profiles.

18

ALTHOUGH MICHAEL BRADEN had returned from the States more than a month ago, he had made no changes or additions to his bedroom furnishings, Cara realized with amusement. It was still a child's room, its walls decorated with pictures of long-forgotten American athletes—none of whom the young Michael could have seen play, even on television—and a display of Ilocan crossbows, bolos and spears. After Evie learned to walk, Cara had asked Les to take down the primitive weapons, afraid that the child would discover them and accidentally injure herself. Instead, he had ordered the maids to keep the room locked.

The evening news had reported a storm front in the Luzon Straits, the turbulent stretch of ocean between the northern Philippines and Formosa. Usually these systems —common during the monsoon—dissipated at sea after hanging on for days, but occasionally they moved south, building up winds of nearly typhoon force. Until the alert was lifted, the only sensible course was to close the house's heavy mahogany shutters before going to bed. Once Cara had forgotten to secure the windows in the rear parlor;

the casements had blown in during the night, and the room had been flooded.

As she locked the shutters in Michael's room, she could hear others being slammed shut by Inez and Maria, the only servants who slept in the main house. I must be getting claustrophobic, she thought with mild queasiness, staring at the slabs of dark wood that had closed off her view of the rain-washed tobacco fields and the mountains beyond. The already muggy air seemed to congeal into a semisolid state, like gelatin that had just begun to harden. She switched off the lights and hurried out to the hall.

Downstairs, she found Eve and Sam Braden sitting together on a couch in the front parlor. The old man, who now spent at least an hour or two a day with the child, was telling another rambling story about his service in the U.S. Marines' campaign against the *insurrectos*: "After a fight, the *negritos* would come," he said. "Don't have them up here. They live way south, mostly in Pampanga. They're little people. Full-grown *negrito*'s about your size, and their babies aren't much bigger than new puppies.

"Anyway, sometimes before all the shooting was over, hundreds of them would come out of the woods, dig at the ground and tree trunks with stone knives. What they were after was the lead from our bullets. No way to scare them, either. We'd fire a volley over their heads, and they'd run away for a couple of minutes, maybe. Then they'd be back again, grinning and chattering at us, working with their knives. They weren't afraid, those *negritos*.

"Funny part was they'd never beg for food or money or cigarettes. All they wanted was pieces of lead, do most anything to get them. Don't know what for—to make arrowheads, maybe, or necklaces for their ladies. And nothing ever seemed to happen to them. Bullets flying around everywhere, big cannons blowing holes in the jungle—but you never saw a dead *negrito*. Not even one with a scratch on him."

"They were safe because they were so little," Evie declared solemnly.

"I guess so, honey."

"Okay, bedtime," Cara said, sweeping Eve into her arms. Why, when they still faced so much unhealed horror and violence, did the old man have to resurrect seventy-five-year-old battles, she wondered resentfully as she carried her daughter to the nursery. However, she hesitated to speak to Sam about it, realizing how close he and Evie had grown in the past few weeks. She could not bring herself to help rebuild the barrier of shyness and fear that had so long separated them.

"Going to be a storm," Sam Braden said when Cara came back downstairs.

"We can't be sure, Grandfather."

"Not tonight. Maybe tomorrow. Or most likely, day or two after. They like to sit up there in the straits awhile, brooding kind of. Then they move on down fast, like they got to make up for lost time."

"I just hope Michael and the others will be all right."

"He will."

As always, Sam went upstairs at exactly eight o'clock. On most evenings, after he retired, Cara would sit in the den, which she considered the only comfortable room on the ground floor. But tonight she lingered in the formal, old-fashioned but far more open parlor, listening to scattered raindrops descend on the veranda roof with muffled force.

He will, the old man had said with the same disturbing certainty that often entered Michael's voice, as if they shared a supernatural power that permitted them to instinctively escape the fates that destroyed other men. As far as Cara was concerned, all the attitude really showed was stubborn, self-assured—and potentially dangerous—pride. Despite Lenore's desperate cry of relief when the first rain had fallen six days ago, the hunters had not returned. Cara was certain that her brother-in-law must be goading them on—but toward what goal? His death at the hands of a man he considered a friend?

I must stop thinking about it, Cara told herself. Lenore had been drinking, on the edge of hysteria, and Cara still found it impossible to believe that Jack Tully, even ravaged by jealousy, would attack Michael. Nevertheless, for a few minutes after hearing Lenore's story, she had considered sending the Philippine Constabulary after the party, though aware it would probably mean jail for all of them. But the onslaught of the monsoon had decreed that there was literally nothing to be done. The rains would eliminate the hunters' trail as fully as they had that of the *amok*.

Cara suddenly realized why the closing of the window shutters had upset her. It was as if the entire building had been magically sealed inside a gigantic mahogany coffin! She ran to the nearest window, unlocked the shutters, flung them open, expecting to feel a rush of clear coolness against her face. But the atmosphere outside the house was as impenetrably still as the air trapped within. . . .

THE following afternoon, the hunters reached Ticlac, where the villagers refused to give them any information on Dr. Mapitang's whereabouts—until Jack Tully and the elderly barrio headman recognized each other. "Gageng was a tracker for Villamor," he explained. "I'd better talk to him alone. They don't cooperate with strangers, even Ilocans from other areas."

While Jack and his old comrade conferred in the headman's hut, the others led their mules to the grassy, tree-covered riverbank, unburdened the animals of their packs to permit them to graze more easily. The stream—a narrow tributary of the Cagayan—had already risen several feet since the beginning of the rains. Michael sank to the ground, rested against a broad yacal, watched two naked children bathe the family carabao in midstream, pouring water from clay bowls over the huge buffalo's black, glistening hide. Ramos and Dietrich followed Michael's example. To judge by their tired faces and slumped shoulders, they would probably vote to turn back if Jack Tully failed to learn anything from the headman. Of Jack he was uncertain. Despite his early reluctance, the man now seemed to be as much caught up in the search as Michael himself.

Nearly half an hour passed before Jack joined them, a young Ilocan warrior striding by his side. "They were here, all right," he said. "Left five days ago—but not together. Mapitang headed west to deliver the rest of his medical supplies. Shimura went north."

"Alone?" gasped the startled Ramos.

Jack nodded toward the Ilocan. "This is Sacda. He guided Shimura into the jungle, left him two days' march from here. Just got back this morning. His orders are to wait until Mapitang shows up again, then lead him to the Jap's campsite."

"Makes no sense," Harry Dietrich grunted. He had experienced a rush of relief when they discovered that Shimura and the physician were not in Ticlac; now new fear had started to grow inside him.

"Sure it does," Michael said. "Shimura figured he could make easier contact with the *amok* if he were on his own."

"Will Sacda take us to him?" Ramos said.

"Already asked. He promised to wait for Mapitang and nothing will make him change his mind. They rate that sour old bastard a couple of notches above God! But he's agreed to explain the route to Tegasay." Jack frowned in puzzlement. "Also said it wouldn't be hard to find him. For some crazy reason, he's perched himself on top of a hill visible for miles."

"To attract the *amok*," Ramos guessed.

"Major, you spent a lot of time with Shimura," Michael said. "He must have told you what that maniac was like before he went into the mountains. You believe it's even faintly possible that he'd surrender?"

"Perhaps—but only to Shimura."

Ramos was glad that Michael Braden didn't pursue his questioning further. The less these men knew about Takei Shimura's wartime duties—especially his connection with the *kempeitai*—the greater his chances of safety in their company. Ramos himself had never been certain that Shimura had told the truth when he claimed his work for the Japanese military police had been occasional and involuntary.

Sacda squatted beside Tegasay, used the tip of his bolo to draw a crude map in the earth, muttering instructions in backcountry Ilocano. Jack Tully wandered off toward the village's central compound, his gaze fixed on a bluff, bisected by a narrow canyon, just beyond the farthest ring of huts. Michael got up and followed him, planning to make one more attempt to break through his neighbor's strange, intractable coolness.

"Is that where it happened?" he asked quietly.

"About half a mile up the canyon," Jack said, without looking at Michael. "The Japs shouldn't have been able to get at us without warning, even at night. We had a dozen sentries posted on ledges and in foxholes at both approaches to the camp. But they got through anyhow. Later, the villagers told us every lookout had been found at his post, his throat cut. They were all tough, trained, careful men, the best guerrilla fighters in the world—and whoever led the Japs figured out how to knock them off as easily as if they had been kids in a playpen!"

"The *amok*?"

"Maybe," Jack said with a fatalistic shrug. "What's the difference now?"

"We don't have to push on right away. If you'd like to—"

"Look at the place again?" He uttered a burst of mocking laughter. "It'd be like visiting my own grave!"

"All right," Michael said, starting to turn away. Apparently nothing could penetrate the barrier of moody contempt that had surrounded Jack since the start of the journey.

"I have a question."

Michael paused. "Go ahead."

"What if we find Shimura and the *amok* has already surrendered to him?"

The same possibility had occurred to Michael. "We kill him anyway," he stated in a flat, emotionless voice.

"I thought you'd say that," Jack Tully replied, arriving at a silent decision of his own. . . .

VIRGILIO Ramos, watching the two Americans from the riverbank, wondered what they could be discussing with such intensity. They were too far away for him to overhear their words. His attention warily shifted to Dietrich, still sitting under the trees, his troubled eyes staring at the stream. Ramos had noted the easing of the stress in the tobacco buyer's heavy features when they discovered that Mapitang and Shimura were not in the village, its return when Jack Tully reported that he knew where the Japanese could be found. He had grown more and more convinced that Luz Dietrich's murder had been an act of vengeance aimed at her husband. It was entirely possible that Harry Dietrich had known Kurusu during the occupation, injured him in some way. But, if so, why had the *amok* waited more than thirty years to obtain redress? And why would Dietrich suppress facts that would aid in apprehending his wife's killer? He suspected that Shimura had the answers.

Tegasay rose, went to Michael, nodded once to indicate that he was prepared to lead them to Takei Shimura.

ONLY an idiot would take an electric razor into a jungle, Shimura told himself in disgust, staring down at the useless instrument—its stainless steel casing already touched by rust—clutched in his right hand. Each morning he had flicked it on, run it over his cheeks, even though the batteries had grown so weak that the blades merely caressed his beard, as if trying to seduce the individual hairs. With an irritated sigh, he threw the razor into the ravine, watched it bounce down the steep, muddy slope, disappear in matted brush more than fifty feet below.

It had been seven days since he and the young Ilocan had left Ticlac. The last five, after his guide had started home, he had been alone. The rock outcropping he had chosen for his campsite lay below a ridge of gray volcanic mountains, their sides marked by twisting gullies, like deep wounds torn in a madman's face by his own fingernails. Southward, all the way to the horizon, lay the forest through which he and Sacda had passed.

On the third morning, he had awakened to find the jungle dotted with broad patches of delicately beautiful pink-and-white blossoms: orchids nurtured by the rain. Unfortunately, it had had the same effect on flies, mosquitoes and other insects, compelling Shimura to coat his face and hands with a foul-smelling—but effective—repellent salve given him by Mapitang. However, not until yesterday had he experienced a sense of genuine entrapment.

The nearest vegetation—a tangle of undergrowth and banyan—had originally been more than twenty feet from his tiny nylon tent. With astonishing speed, green vines had crept out from the shade of the banyan trees; the outermost tendrils were now within a few feet of the camp. When he went to refill his canteen at a narrow creek at the bottom of the hill, he discovered that the trail blazed by Sacda was already obliterated, forcing him to chop his way through with a machete. It was as if the jungle intended to encircle and swallow him, like a jellyfish consuming a minute limpet.

After his angry disposal of the battery-powered razor, he completed his morning routine. He pulled an Ilocan reed mat—so tightly woven that it was virtually water-tight—off his dwindling supply of dry wood, built a fire out of half a dozen spindly logs. When a trail of smoke began rising, he boiled a small pot of rice above the flickering flame, thankful that heavy rain usually held off until afternoon. After consuming the rice and a few tinned biscuits, washed down with swigs of water from his canteen, he had nothing to do but wait, prepared to kick over the fire and save the partially charred logs if it began to rain.

He sat cross-legged, peering off over the mountains, his machete across his knees. In the beginning, he had carried the weapon only when he had to cut wood or once again clear the path to the stream. But for the past two days, he had taken it with him everywhere. This is how it must have been for Kurusu at first, he thought: feeling real and imaginary fears accumulating in his nerve ends, watching the last vestiges of civilized humanity fade away, as if consumed by the mold that had already begun to attack his clothing.

For the first few days of his vigil, Takei Shimura had hoped that Dr. Mapitang would give him at least two weeks in the open. As the periods of rain became longer and the jungle thickened, he had begun to hope that the physician would complete his mission earlier than expected, might already be on his way to rescue Shimura from this hellish isolation.

I was wrong, he decided. *Kurusu is not here. No man would attempt to live in such a place.* Nevertheless, he continued his now-mechanical routine—building the fire, feeding it with damp leaves to create smoke perceptibly darker than the gray monsoon sky, waiting. . . .

"HE doesn't move at all," Michael said, lowering his binoculars. "Just sits there next to the fire."

The hunters had reached their goal late that afternoon, found a hiding place in a tree-shrouded hollow that afforded an unobstructed view of Shimura while concealing their own presence. Sacda's description of the campsite chosen by the Japanese had proved accurate; the stolid figure perched atop a spur of volcanic rock had to be visible from any point—high or low—for miles.

"All right, we've found him," Jack Tully said. "Now what?"

"Nothing," Michael declared. "If the *amok* is anywhere around here, he'll go for Shimura. Then *we'll* go for him."

Virgilio Ramos, tethering the party's string of mules to a rope line, stiffened when he heard Michael's words. "You intend to use this man as bait, Mr. Braden?"

"Yes."

"We should go up there, explain what has happened, give him an opportunity to cooperate willingly."

"And if he doesn't?" Michael asked. "You've already told us he's committed to taking the *amok* alive. Christ knows why. Suppose he tells us to go to hell and pulls out?"

"Impossible," Ramos exclaimed. "He could not find his way back to Ticlac on his own. If the *amok* should appear and we attack, Shimura is almost certain to be killed. If not by our bullets, by the *amok*'s sword."

It had never occurred to Michael that Ramos—after watching his own troops blown to chunks of bloody meat—might plan to honor his agreement with Shimura. God in heaven, he wanted to shout, my father and brother were butchered by that monster! So was Harry's wife! Do you honestly believe we'd let him surrender?

Before Michael could speak, Jack Tully stepped between him and the ex-policeman. "You're both getting ahead of yourselves," he said calmly. "Nine chances out of ten, the *amok* isn't within forty miles of this place—and wouldn't be if we stuck around straight through the monsoon. Dumbest thing a man can do is spend the winnings on a long shot before it comes in."

"You are right," Ramos conceded, pale furrows of anger disappearing from the corners of his eyes.

"So is Mike. Letting Shimura know we're here would be a mistake. Right now, he's the only link we have to the *amok*. We can't throw it away."

"We won't make a move unless we're certain the Jap is in the clear," Michael added.

He is lying, Ramos realized, studying Michael Braden's taut, swarthy face. If he sights the *amok*, he will pursue him even if it means expending Shimura's life. But at least it was an uncomplicated lie, unlike those of Harry Dietrich. Why had the Swiss, standing only a few feet away, voiced no opinion in the dispute? A week and a half ago, he had found the dismembered body of his young wife; he possessed the freshest, strongest motive of any of them to seek the killer. Yet after that first meeting on the bank of the Cagayan, he had fallen into the role of a cautious observer, leaving decisions to the others, as if afraid to call attention to himself. Before this expedition was over, Ramos intended to learn why.

"We will do it your way for the time being, Mr. Braden," Ramos said grudgingly. After all, he reasoned, it would be easy enough to alert Shimura. A single gunshot in the air would suffice.

The leaves overhead rustled as a sudden, sharp gust of wind shook the treetops. Tegasay's dog, lying at its master's feet, rose quickly, hackles rippling, yellow fangs bared in a nervous snarl. The tracker clucked softly, placed a comforting hand on the animal's shaggy neck.

"We may be in for rougher weather by morning," Jack Tully said, gazing at the dark clouds beyond the mountains. . . .

IT can happen, Harry Dietrich thought, unless I act now. Dr. Mapitang would finally come to retrieve the Japanese, and the hunters would no longer have a reason to stay in hiding. Takei Shimura would recognize Dietrich, tell Mapitang that he had been a *kempeitai* spy. Shimura might even be aware that he had aided Kurusu in setting up the massacre at Ticlac. Why wouldn't he know, since both he and the *amok* had served as aides to Colonel Tanape?

All Dietrich had to counterbalance this grim vision was the possibility that Shimura might not remember him or, if he did, would keep silent. It had been enough to sustain hope until he had actually seen the Japanese, sitting like a carved stone figure atop a hill less than a quarter of a mile from the hunters' camp. To predict the thoughts of a man capable of so bizarre an act seemed impossible. Clearly, he cared nothing for his own life—so why should he concern himself with Dietrich's? There was only one safe course: kill him. . . .

Dietrich had gone on guard duty at eleven P.M., relieving Tegasay. Since setting up camp, they had maintained constant scrutiny of the rock outcropping, spelling one another every three hours. Except for a brief shower, just after sunset, it had not rained all day—often the case when a heavy storm might be holding off to the north. He again looked through his binoculars, just in time to see Shimura rise and enter his tent, probably ending his vigil for the night. Even though the undergrowth ahead looked heavy, Dietrich estimated that he could reach the outcropping in less than an hour. Shimura would be asleep when he arrived. He could club the Japanese to death with his rifle butt, bury him and his gear in the jungle, be back in plenty of time to rouse Jack Tully for the next shift. With the fire extinguished, no one would realize until morning that Shimura had departed. His subsequent disappearance couldn't arouse suspicion; in the deep jungles of the Cordillera, the roads to annihilation were too many to count. . . .

The hunters had conducted their round-the-clock observation of Takei Shimura from the edge of the wooded hollow. Virgilio Ramos, standing in heavy shadow, watched Dietrich move off into the night. Certain that Dietrich, Shimura and the *amok* had been linked in the past, Ramos had silently slipped out of his tent a few minutes after the tobacco buyer's first nighttime guard shift began, watched him from hiding with intense, professionally speculative eyes.

He is going to Shimura, Ramos decided when Dietrich left his post. But why? To tell the Japanese that he was under surveillance? The action made no sense—assuming that, as he claimed, Dietrich's sole interest was in destroying the *amok*. To learn something from Shimura that would aid in the search but, for unknown reasons, Shimura could not share with his companions? Equally ridiculous. He had no evidence that Dietrich and Shimura had spoken to each other since the latter's arrival in the Philippines. In fact, a meeting was unlikely, considering that Shimura had been isolated for his own protection, first by the constabulary, later by Dr. Mapitang. So, since this was Shimura's first visit to the Philippines since the war, Dietrich's last encounter with him must have been during the occupation. Ramos could conceive of only one reason why the Swiss would so desperately try to conceal a wartime acquaintance with a Japanese officer: the fact that Shimura had served as interpreter for the commandant of the *kempeitai*. . . .

Ramos briefly considered telling the other men that Dietrich had left the encampment. But bringing him back would prove nothing. Dietrich could simply claim that he had broken under the pressure of grief and hatred, decided to force Shimura to reveal everything he knew about the *amok*—an explanation of his behavior far more believable than Ramos' cloudy, half-formed suspicions. Besides, Michael Braden and Jack Tully were white men, products of the colonial system that had dominated the valley of the Cagayan for so many years. It was inconceivable to the *mestizo* that they would side with him against a member of their own caste.

I will have to discover the truth on my own, he decided. He went back to the tent he shared with Michael, saw that the American was sleeping soundly. Picking up his rifle, he left the tent, headed toward Takei Shimura's dying fire. . . .

MICHAEL Braden was roused to instant, total consciousness by the slap of distant rifle fire—two shots in quick succession, followed by a third a few seconds later. He glanced at his watch, saw that it was past midnight. "Ramos, wake up!" he shouted before realizing that he was alone in the tent.

He grabbed his .375 Browning and hurried outside, at almost the same instant Jack Tully burst from the other tent. Tegasay, who preferred the shelter of a lean-to to canvas, joined them, the gray dog poised at his side. "Had to have come from Shimura's camp," Jack said. "Nothing else around. But Sacda told me the Jap didn't have a gun."

"Virgilio did," Michael said. "And he's gone."

"You figure he went to warn Shimura we were here?"

"Maybe," Michael said, abruptly wondering why Harry Dietrich, on guard duty only yards away, had not appeared. "Where the hell is Dietrich?"

Jack ran to the lookout post, returned a moment later to report that the Swiss was also missing. "What's going on?" he asked in a baffled growl. "I can understand Ramos trying to tip off the Jap—he never did like what we were doing—but why would Harry go with him?"

"Just one way to find out."

Jack nodded curt agreement, went for his rifle. . . .

At first they made rapid progress toward the hill, since Tegasay quickly found a fresh, machete-chopped corridor through the brush. However, about twenty-minutes after they set out, the wind that had struck in widely spaced bursts all evening started accelerating, flailed the trees and undergrowth, making it difficult to keep to the trail. "We're going to catch it!" Jack shouted as rain began falling.

By the time they scrambled up the slope below the rock outcropping, Tegasay's dog leading the way, the downpour limited vision to two or three yards, even with the aid of Jack's heavy-duty flashlight. They lurched over the rim of the outcropping, saw nothing but Shimura's tent, its nylon sides billowing. Then the dog loped to a patch of banyan past the tent, began pawing at an object on the ground. They rushed over, realized it was a human body. The flashlight beam revealed the slack, mud-smeared face of Virgilio Ramos. His chest had been blown out by high-powered rifle slugs. The Marlin .444 he had borrowed at the plantation house lay inches from the stiff, bent fingers of his right hand.

"Start looking for Harry and the Jap!" Michael bellowed over the wind.

The second body was discovered minutes later, sprawled at the bottom of a nearby ravine. Since the form was partially hidden by tangled brush, they couldn't identify the man from the hilltop. Together, Jack and Michael slid down the loose, muddy slope, expecting to find Harry Dietrich. But the victim's bloodied face belonged to Takei Shimura—and the Japanese was still alive. . . .

They hauled the unconscious man up the hill, placed him in the rippling tent. Besides the deep, still-bleeding gash on his forehead, Shimura had taken a bullet in the left leg, just below the knee. "Why didn't we think to bring the first-aid kit?" Michael muttered. "We'll have to lug him back to camp. Too exposed up here. The tent could blow away any second."

"What about Harry?" Jack protested. "He might be wounded too!"

"No, he isn't."

"How the hell can you be sure of that?"

"Because except for Ramos, only one man out here tonight had a gun. And Ramos is dead."

"You think *Harry* shot them? Why, for Christ's sake?"

"That's what we have to ask Shimura."

CARRYING Takei Shimura on a stretcher improvised from the tent's support poles and covering, they took nearly two hours to struggle through the brief stretch of jungle between the outcropping and the hunters' camp. By now the storm had reached full force, temporarily blinding them with wind-driven waves of rain, turning the ground underfoot into a shifting, sticky mass, as viscous as heavy machine oil. All three men were close to exhaustion when they reached the hollow, saw that their two tents, shielded by heavy foliage, were still intact. Nevertheless, Michael ordered a halt at the edge of the trees.

"Wait," he told the others, unslinging his Browning. "Better make sure Harry isn't waiting to pick us off. He had plenty of time to get back here first."

He soon had proof that his caution had been justified. Two of their mules had been shot through the head. The third was missing, along with the party's food. "Why?" Jack asked again, dazedly, when they had laid Shimura on Michael's sleeping bag and opened the first-aid kit. "Did he go crazy?"

"I doubt it," Michael said, using Tegasay's bolo to cut away the mud-soaked trouser on Shimura's injured leg. The Japanese was now conscious, his eyes glazed with pain, face as gray-white as a rotting bedsheet. The slug had torn out a chunk of the man's calf but had apparently missed the bone and knee tendons.

"Major Ramos?" Shimura gasped weakly.

"Dead."

"The other man," Shimura said, after gagging on the brandy Michael poured between his lips. "The one who shot us . . . It was dark. . . . I could not see his face. . . ."

"Harry Dietrich," Michael said, starting to clean out Shimura's scalp wound with cotton and alcohol. The apparent clarity of thought of the Japanese indicated that he had escaped with, at worst, a minor concussion.

"A large man . . . Swiss?"

"Yes."

"The frightened fool . . . I would not have told . . . I did not even remember his name after so many years. . . ."

"Told what?" Jack Tully asked.

"Don't push him," Michael insisted. "He might pass out again."

Anger flared in Jack's eyes. "Mike, a guy I've considered a friend all my life just murdered a man and stranded us in this hellhole without any food! *I want to know why!*"

So do I, Michael silently agreed. Otherwise, I'd have left this son-of-a-bitch at the bottom of the ravine.

"I still am not sure precisely what happened," Shimura gasped, gritting his teeth against the pain as Michael cleaned out, bandaged and taped the gaping wound in his left calf. "I was lying in my tent half asleep. . . . I heard a noise . . . someone stumbling, perhaps . . . I left the tent, saw the outline of a man . . . a big man. . . . I thought it must be Kurusu . . . until I heard Major Ramos' voice yell a warning . . . from the banyans. . . . The man turned and fired, and I heard the major cry out and fall. . . . I ran. . . . The man fired again. . . . I felt a blow in my leg, went over the side of the ravine . . . struck my head . . ."

"Fits together," Michael said, fastening the last layer of tape around the wound, enjoying the agony contorting Shimura's face. "Ramos saw Harry leave camp and followed him, caught up just as he was about to attack Shimura. Harry panicked and opened fire, then bolted, figuring the rest of us might be behind the Major."

"But *why*?" Jack cried, garing at Shimura. "Tell us, goddamn you!"

"You were a *kempeitai* officer, weren't you?" Michael guessed. "And Harry was one of your informers?"

"I do not have the right to answer that question," Shimura murmured.

"Ramos died saving your life," Michael said. "You owe *him* the truth, Mr. Shimura, even if he can't hear it."

Jack Tully did not need to hear the truth. It had already struck him with sickening brutality. During the war, on a single occasion, he had violated Aurelio Villamor's most rigid security rule: Never ask help twice from the same civilian. But twice within a few weeks he had scrounged supplies from Harry Dietrich, foolishly confident that another white settler—and a family friend—would never betray him to the Japanese. And days after the second food pickup, the enemy had descended mercilessly on the Ticlac encampment. Suddenly Dietrich's generosity to him after the war, his unstinting help in rebuilding the Tully plantation made a new, revolting kind of sense. It had been a guilt-sodden bribe!

"I'm going after him," Jack said, picking up his rifle.

Michael jerked his head toward the tent roof, shaking under the impact of the driving rain. "You can't get around in a storm like this. You don't even *have* to. Right now he's holed up, waiting it out the same way we are. We'll find him in the morning."

Heedless of Michael's words, the enraged Jack Tully hurried from the tent, plunged into the wind-lashed darkness. For a few seconds Michael considered following him, saw it would be pointless; only violent restraint could halt a man possessed by such fury. The storm would do a far better job. When he realized that tracking was impossible in this weather, Jack would come back to camp. Besides, Michael was after the *amok*, not a pitiful, aging wartime collaborator driven out of his mind by fear.

"Why are you all here?" Shimura asked.

"For the same reason you are."

"To hunt Kurusu?"

"Of course. You feel up to answering a few questions? What made you decide the *amok* would come to this part of the mountains? Something you found in the cogon?"

"I no longer believe that he *is* here," Shimura said. "If he were, he would already have contacted me. I too have a question, Mr. Braden. Why do you hate me? Even as you tended my wounds, the hatred was there. In your eyes and your hands."

Reason and self-interest—he still needed the information stored in Takei Shimura's brain—told Michael to lie. But almost against his will, the story of the roundup of the Cagayan's American civilians spilled from his lips in clipped, icy, accusing bursts of words.

Afterward, Shimura remained silent for minutes, recalling the day Hisao Tanape had sent him to the countryside with a detail of armed troops and six trucks. It had been the most uncomfortable task he had ever undertaken: stiffly reading the prisoners' names off a clipboard, explaining to each family where they were going, trying to hide his pity as the soldiers herded frightened men and women and children into the trucks, aware that the slightest show of concern for his charges' plight would be reported to Tanape. The convoy's destination had been Aparri, where the civilians were to board a coastal steamer. A propaganda team, headed by a fat, officious major, had been waiting at the dock. Reluctantly, Shimura had obeyed the major's orders to pass out bags of candy to the children, while a cameraman snapped countless photos. . . .

"I am sorry," he said at last. "I was given the assignment because I was the only officer in Tuguegarao who spoke English. And the ship and crew were not under the authority of my regiment. My responsibility ended at the dock."

"Always the same shit!" Michael bitterly shook his head. "Always somebody else to blame!"

"I had an uncle who immigrated to California in the twenties," Shimura replied. "He owned a florist shop in San Diego. On a morning in nineteen forty-two, American soldiers came and, at gunpoint, ordered him and his family and all their neighbors of Japanese ancestry aboard a bus. They spent the remainder of the war in tar-paper shacks, behind barbed wire, in the Utah desert. I imagine that the soldiers who put them on the bus were under an officer's command."

Michael involuntarily flinched. "That was different."

"How?" Shimura asked gently.

"They were fed and clothed and given medical treatment—not allowed to rot in the open like animals!"

"Two of my uncle's daughters died of diphtheria in the camp, Mr. Braden. One was nine years old; the other, just four. No doctors were summoned until the third day of the epidemic." Shimura closed his eyes. "I believe I will try to sleep now."

Tegasay—who obviously hadn't understood anything that had happened—crouched patiently beside the cot. In Ilocano, Michael told him to return to his lean-to but remain on guard. When the tracker nodded and left, he switched off the battery lantern, chain-smoked as he listened to the relentless pounding of rain on the tent roof, waiting for Jack Tully to abandon his futile search.

A treetop-shaking clap of thunder rumbled over the jungle. He wondered if earlier thunder had awakened Eve in the plantation house's nursery, compelled her to run fearfully to her mother's room, seek refuge in Cara's warm bed. It was the normal thing for a kid to do. . . .

Shortly after sunrise, the wind died and the rain tapered off to a morose drizzle—and Jack still had not returned. Ordering Tegasay to look after Shimura, Michael set out to find him.

19

TAKEI SHIMURA was startled awake by the loud, angry barking of Tegasay's dog. He sat up quickly, felt a stabbing pain in his wounded leg, sank back on the cot. The barking ceased and, for seconds, the only sound he heard was the buzz of a green fly, aimlessly maneuvering around the top of the tent. Shimura decided it must be at least midmorning, since the night chill of the Cordillera had passed. Clear light streamed through one of the tent's narrow plastic windows, indicating that the storm had ended.

Despite his injuries and the brutal events of the previous night, he was strangely at peace—the same calm that had come over him in 1945 when, after his capture by American soldiers, he had realized that the enemy would spare his life. If Michael Braden's rage at old grievances had been strong enough to permit murder, Shimura would already be dead. But once again he had escaped annihilation. Perhaps, he thought, the world was not completely mad after all.

Then the tent flaps parted and Kurusu entered. The blade of his sword, held in the vertical attack position, dripped blood. To his amazement, Shimura felt no fear at the sight of the towering figure. Perhaps, in his heart, he had known that the encounter he had so desperately sought—and, only seconds earlier, believed he could finally avoid with honor—had been inevitable.

"Do you remember me?" he asked, staring up into the cold black disks of the giant's eyes. Scarlet specks fell from the upraised blade onto the bedroll.

The sword remained poised to strike.

"The other men in the camp?" Shimura said. "Have you killed them?"

Again he received no reply. Was it possible that after decades of isolation, Kurusu no longer understood his own language? "What do you intend to do with me?"

Sheathing the sword, Kurusu stepped forward, picked up Shimura as easily as if he were a starving child, carried him out of the tent. Within seconds, the jungle had enveloped them.

Shimura never had a clear perception of how long the grueling journey lasted. Several times, when his wounded leg was jostled, he lost consciousness, later struggled back to awareness that they were still moving beneath the dark, rain-dripping branches of great trees. Gradually the undergrowth thinned and Shimura sensed that they were climbing into the mountains high above the forest. By now the pain had become so constant that his vision was a searing blur. For a brief, terrifying period, the blur gave way to total darkness and he thought that he was dying, finally realized that they had entered some kind of cavern.

Kurusu lowered him to a reed pallet. A moment later a pitch-impregnated torch flared to life.

When the pain subsided, Shimura glanced around the obviously man-made chamber, shored with heavy logs. He was surprised at the cavern's neatness. The tattered flag of their Imperial Army regiment hung on a wall, above a log table holding an officer's short sword and a photograph of the Emperor that he dimly recalled seeing in Hisao Tanape's quarters at the New Reno Hotel. The effect was almost that of a religious shrine—and, of course, to Kurusu, it must be. Ten feet away, another handmade table was covered with stacked cans of food and water kegs, beside a fire pit lined with rocks. The pit was bathed in pale natural light streaming in from a narrow overhead opening that must run to the surface, serving as a chimney for cooking smoke.

"Why have you brought me here?" Shimura asked—and abruptly, chillingly realized that he was alone in the cavern. . . .

THAT morning Michael Braden had headed northeast—a course chosen on the possibility that Harry Dietrich would not risk returning to the valley of the Cagayan. The Swiss must have known that the loss of the food and mules would merely divert his pursuers until they reached Ticlac and obtained new provisions. In Dietrich's place, Michael had figured, he would have continued through the mountains to the jungle-edge trading town of Bayag, where he could easily obtain transportation to the port of Aparri—and boat passage out of the country.

The storm of the night before had altered the forest landscape through which Michael moved. Ravines and gullies, almost dry the preceding afternoon, were filled with often waist-deep water, still running down from the mountains in torrents. The newly created streams forced him to make wide detours.

It was nearly noon before he discovered proof that his hunch about Dietrich's plan had been right. In a steep-walled gully less than a mile below the mountain ridge, he found clearly defined mule tracks. He unslung the Browning, quickened his pace. Moments later, at a turn in the gully, he came upon the objects of his search. The face of the dead man at Jack Tully's feet was so battered that Dietrich was recognizable only by his clothing.

"You know what he kept saying after I caught him?" Jack asked in a dazed mumble. "*I was afraid.* . . . At least ten times he must have said it. . . ."

Michael returned the Browning to his shoulder, looked at Jack with pitying eyes. The hunt was over. Two men were dead, another wounded. And they had not even glimpsed their quarry. Now there was nothing left to do but bury Ramos and Dietrich, mark their graves, tell the Philippine Constabulary what had happened. He had again failed to conquer the *amok*—and he would never get a third chance. Even if he escaped imprisonment, the government would probably deport him for organizing this doomed expedition. The hunt was really over. . . .

"Was easy," Jack muttered numbly. "I spotted him from high ground. . . . Came up on him from behind, ordered him to throw away his rifle. . . . Villamor wouldn't have liked that part. . . . Never talk to them, he used to tell us. . . . I expected Harry to say what good friends we were, how he'd helped me out after the war . . . as if it would have mattered. . . . But he sat in the mud and cried and said over and over again: *I was afraid*. . . . I put down my rifle and hit him with my fists. . . . Probably never even felt anything after the first couple of punches . . . I *wanted* him to feel it . . . until I was done and I realized I'd turned into an animal again. . . . So fucking easy out here, turning into an animal again. . . . We were already in Ticlac before I was sure I could kill a man. . . . Wasn't supposed to be Harry, though. . . . Funny . . . Wasn't true, was it? Everything I was thinking?"

"I don't understand."

Jack uttered a ragged laugh. "I know you don't. Makes no difference. Wasn't another murder left in me anyway. . . ."

"Where's Harry's mule? We'll need the supplies."

"Kept going after he dropped the reins."

"I'll take a look. It couldn't have wandered too far."

Michael found the laden mule grazing on scrubby grass less than a hundred yards farther north. He had already gathered up the trailing lead reins when he realized that a long, unobstructed stretch of the gully lay ahead and that its floor assumed a sharp uphill slant. Intent on the search, he had briefly wondered earlier why the deep gouge in the earth wasn't flooded, like every other north-and-south-running crevice he had encountered, had decided that it must cut east or west at a farther point. Now he saw that, like the rest, it twisted high into the mountains, so there could be no natural reason why it held less storm runoff than flat jungle surfaces.

He heard a faint rumble, as if someone miles away had started the engine of a heavy earth-moving rig, suddenly remembered Jack Tully's warning at the New Reno Hotel poker game: *He must have worked out defenses and ways of hiding so tricky we can't begin to imagine them.*

He ran back down the gully. "Get out!" he shouted. "For God's sake, get out!" He saw Jack, sitting beside Dietrich's body, far ahead. The planter must have detected the bellowed message but couldn't comprehend its sense. He stood up, arms hesitantly half-raised. The rumble was louder now.

Realizing he had only seconds to save his own life, Michael veered right, frantically began climbing the gully wall, his fingers clawing at the wet earth. He was about twenty feet above the gully floor when a roaring wall of muddy water passed below. He saw Dietrich's mule turning over and over in the churning flood, legs kicking, like a tiny gray spider being washed down a bathtub drain.

The rim of the gully was now only six feet above him. *What if he's waiting for me,* Michael thought, imagining the *amok*'s sword slicing off his hands the instant they found solid ground. *No . . . he couldn't have had time. . . .*

His left foot came to rest on a jutting rock. He pressed down hard, hoping to gain momentum for the final, desperate lunge that would get him to the top. Then the rock spilled out of its niche, throwing him off balance. His fingers lost their tenuous grip on the earth overhead and he slid back into the rushing water. . . .

AT first, when Kurusu vanished from the cavern, Takei Shimura had thought he would soon return. But now hours had passed. During this period of terrifying solitude Shimura's gaze had been locked on the torch, which had almost burned out, its guttering flames sending longer and longer shadows across the chamber's rock walls. Soon, except for the dim light from the chimney, he would be trapped in endless darkness.

Then, as silently as it had left, Kurusu's massive form materialized at the other end of the cavern. He squatted on his haunches, virtually invisible except for the whites of his probing, suspicious eyes.

Unsure that his words would be comprehended, Shimura said: "I have come to take you home. The war has ended."

The statement produced no reaction, not even a blink of Kurusu's staring eyes.

Takei Shimura went on to tell of the atomic destruction of Hiroshima and Nagasaki, of the painful years of Japan's postwar recovery, of the alliance between their countrymen and the former American enemy, of the great office buildings and industrial complexes that had risen from the ashes of Tokyo. When he had finished his plea for surrender, tired from the effort, he lay back on the pallet, waited for Kurusu's reply.

For minutes the cavern remained silent. Then he heard a voice—deep and echoing and growling, like the sound produced by wind rushing through a subterranean tunnel:

"Have you ever been to the island of Shikotan?"

The words came hesitantly, dredged one by one from the depths of the speaker's immense body. How could it be otherwise? This must be the first time in more than three decades that he had talked to another human being.

"No," Shimura said.

"Even in the spring, on Shikotan, the winds are cold. Once my youngest sister and I were walking in a light, warm rain. The wind roared off the sea and the rain turned to ice that covered our bodies. I remember how the ice crystals tinkled against each other on the folds of my sister's clothing, like little silver bells.

"I would have been a fisherman, like my father, if the soldiers had not come. I wanted to be a fisherman, working alone on the sea, where I could not hear the laughter of the others. Even as a child, I was taller than the largest grown man on the island of Shikotan. The soldiers came from the mainland at night and roused everyone from their sleep, took the young men away for the army. My mother and my sisters cried and told them I was not yet a man but the soldiers would not listen. . . ."

On and on flowed the strange, disjointed stream of reminiscence, with increasing clarity and assurance. Shimura slowly grasped the truth: that Kurusu was describing past events in order to bridge the years of silence, gain a foothold on the present. He told of being sent to a conscripts' training camp, of being put into a labor battalion because no army uniform was large enough to fit him, of the voyage in the hold of a cattle boat to the battlefields of northern China. He told how he and other men declared unfit for regular military duties had been harnessed to artillery pieces when mules or horses were unavailable. Finally, he told of the day a young *kempeitai* officer had watched him single-handedly lift the front wheels of a truck out of a boghole, had gone to the commander of the work force, asked to have Kurusu transferred to his unit. "I was a beast," he said, "and Colonel Tanape made me a man."

The reverse is true, Shimura thought, imagining Hisao Tanape studying Kurusu with his fanatic's eyes. Undoubtedly he had simply been seeking another oversized peasant for the *kempeitai*'s strong-arm squads. But what quality had Kurusu possessed that had set him off from other men recruited into the military police, caused Tanape to make him his chief aide, elevate a despised, illiterate, freakishly large out-islander to the rank of warrant officer?

Suddenly he knew.

"Kurusu," he asked, "how old were you when Colonel Tanape found you?"

"I am not sure. Does it matter?"

"Yes."

"I was nine when the soldiers took me from Shikotan. I believe I was with the labor battalion no more than two years, so I must have been eleven. Or nearly eleven."

To create a human "pure weapon," Tanape would have needed a child, Shimura reflected: someone ignorant, malleable, fully responsive to both kindness and threats—the same way a master swordmaker fashioned a fine blade from the purest steel he could obtain.

"Kurusu, it is time to go home," he said in a voice laden with pity.

"There is nothing for me in the world you spoke of. Colonel Tanape's order was to fight on until death. I will obey that order."

"The order was *mine*. And I have withdrawn it."

"You were merely his messenger."

"I lied to you," Shimura said, knowing that the admission might cost him his life. "Tanape died before I told him you had murdered those soldiers in the brothel. The order came from me!"

Kurusu rose, stepped out of the shadows, approached the pallet. Shimura involuntarily cringed beneath the gaze of the giant's impenetrable black eyes. "That is not important," Kurusu said calmly. "It is the order Colonel Tanape would have given—to you as well as to me. It was our duty to resist until all hope was gone—and then to die."

"All hope was gone thirty-two years ago!" Shimura cried, waiting for Kurusu to draw his sword from its sheath, strike the blow that would end his life.

"That will make what I have to do easier." Kurusu went to the table beneath the regimental flag, picked up the short sword. "I shall leave you most of the food. I will need little for the journey."

"Journey?"

"To a white house with red tiles on the roof. The man I killed twice lived there."

"No man dies twice."

"This man did." Kurusu dropped the short sword on the floor, within Shimura's reach. "The first time, he told me that the war had ended and I could go home. The second time he did not speak at all. I believed I had lost my senses. But perhaps it was a divine sign that my mission should be completed—and where."

I have failed, Takei Shimura told himself in despair. He *is* mad.

"I found this short sword in Colonel Tanape's room after you released me from prison. If you wish, you may use it to wipe out the dishonor you brought upon yourself and your comrades when you surrendered to the Americans. Or you may take the food and seek to find your way back to the valley of the Cagayan. It is of no concern to me."

"The men who followed me here?" Shimura asked. "What has happened to them?"

"All dead, the last only a few hours ago. For many days I watched them, waiting for an opportunity to slay the betrayer, but I was never able to catch him away from the others. And then one of his own friends killed him. Do you know why?"

"For the same reason," Shimura said, "that you have remained in these wretched mountains for thirty-two years."

Kurusu filled a burlap sack with supplies, slung it over his shoulder. "Goodbye, Captain Shimura. I shall not return."

"Goodbye, Kurusu."

Kurusu disappeared into the darkness, and Takei Shimura was alone. Staring at the guttering torch, he estimated his chances of survival. There must be other torches in the recesses of the cavern, and the food and water Kurusu had left him would last for weeks. But what would be his fate afterward? Long before he could walk again, Sacda would bring Dr. Mapitang, and they would discover at least a few of the hunting party's bodies, reduced to naked bones by insects and vultures. With no evidence that Shimura was still alive, the physician would start back to Tuguegarao, inadvertently leave him to perish of hunger and thirst. . . .

With a hoarse, self-mocking laugh, Takei Shimura picked up the short sword, tested the keenness of the blade against his thumb. He might, after all, be compelled to die like a proper Imperial Army officer. . . .

THE sun was going down when Michael Braden reached the rock outcropping where Shimura had made his camp. Gagging at the stench of Major Ramos' body, already so covered with insects and grubs that its shape seemed barely human, he searched for the Marlin .444, left behind in his and Jack Tully's haste to get the wounded Japanese back to their own tents. As he feared, the weapon had vanished; so had Shimura's machete.

Every step, Michael thought in enraged anguish. *He followed us every step of the way, knew everything we did. . . .*

The flood's battering crest had already passed when he fell back into the gully. Nevertheless, he had been swept almost a mile by the relentless force of the water, was barely conscious when the current slammed him into a tangled cluster of broken tree branches and brush. Somehow he had secured a grip on the mass of debris, had clung to it until the man-made deluge dissipated itself and he was able to crawl to higher ground. For minutes he had lain motionless, so tired that even raising his face out of the mud far enough to breathe required wrenching effort. *Have to get a weapon,* he had told himself. *Any kind of weapon. He'll find me soon. He's bound to. . . .* The .375 Browning had slipped off his shoulder when he tumbled back into the water, was now buried under feet of muck, along with Jack and Dietrich and their rifles. His hunting knife still rested in its sheath but what good would it be against the sword of the *amok*? At last he had struggled erect, stumbled through the jungle toward camp, reached it by midafternoon, discovered the corpses of Tegasay and his dog a few feet apart. The tracker's bolo knife and machete were missing, and Takei Shimura had disappeared from the tent. On the slight chance that the murderer had overlooked the weapons left behind at Shimura's campsite, he had pushed on to the outcropping—and had his last hope dashed. . . .

All he could do now was try to reach Ticlac before the *amok* caught up with him. If he made it, the villagers would give him enough food to continue on to the valley of the Cagayan. Perhaps—if he lied to the Philippine Constabulary, told them the other members of the party had died in a flash flood caused by the storm—he might even avoid deportation. Who could prove him wrong, without the bodies of the missing men? The chance of a new life with Cara and Evie and his grandfather—the life he had dreamed of since he had first realized he was in love with his sister-in-law—was still possible. . . .

And the *amok* would still be in the Cordillera.

He sat on the rocky ground, rubbed his sweating, mud-caked face with his blunt fingertips, his mind seething with the knowledge of his own grinding humiliation. The first time he had tested himself against the monster and failed, he had been able to argue that he was too young for the task. Now he was about to flee again—without a convenient, self-serving excuse.

In his pride and stubbornness, he had been more to blame for the deaths of Jack and Ramos and Tegasay than the *amok*. At the plantation house, Ramos had warned him that the circumstances of Luz Dietrich's murder were suspicious, implied that her husband could not be trusted. Consumed by his headlong need to track the *amok*, he had ignored the ex-policeman's warning. Last night he could have followed Jack into the storm, persuaded him to turn back—but he had not, simply because the revelation of Dietrich's wartime treachery seemingly had no bearing on his quest for the killer.

Now, because of his willful rashness, other innocent men and women would die horribly in the months and years ahead. He thought with grim inner laughter of the .375 Browning he had carried on the hunt, only to lose it in the flooded gully. It had been as much a talisman to him as that old samurai sword must be to the *amok*—and he had fired it only once! At a load of groceries!

No, he brooded. *I have to finish it somehow.*

Once the choice had been made, a peculiar calmness replaced the tremors of rage and fear that had racked his body for hours. He was able, at last, to rationally examine the task ahead, decided that the situation might not be hopeless. Almost certainly, the *amok* assumed that he had perished in the flood. If he were hunting Michael, he could have murdered him two dozen times by now.

Until weariness forced him to snatch a few hours of sleep, Michael headed back toward the gully, his hunting knife clutched in his hand. The fact that the *amok* had dammed the northern end of the crevice indicated that it must run close to the murderer's monsoon stronghold. It might even be the most obvious approach, the one that an attacking force would use; otherwise, setting up so elaborate a trap didn't make sense. But the big problem remained: If he found the *amok*'s hiding place, what could he do afterward? Lie in ambush somewhere, wait for a chance to sneak up on the bastard? That would be playing a game at which his opponent was far superior.

The sun had risen behind the ever-present mantle of gray clouds when he reached the gully. Rather than chance betraying his presence by entering it again, he crept through the heavy trees and brush on the eastern rim, gradually making his way higher into the mountains. Neary half a mile past the spot where he had first heard the rumble of the approaching flood, he was able to look down at the remains of the *amok*'s dam, an apparently crude assemblage of logs and branches and boulders. He must have erected it in such a way that with the shifting of a few key pieces the entire center of the structure would collapse, pouring trapped monsoon waters on anyone below. Another week of steady rain would have raised the makeshift reservoir to a level where Michael could not possibly have survived after falling back into the current.

His gaze rose to the mountains beyond. About seventy yards away, the already-thinning foliage surrendered to a region of bare volcanic shale, affording slight cover. Somewhere above, the *amok* might already be on guard, watching for new intruders. *You're spooking yourself again,* he thought. *He has to sleep and eat like other men. And he thinks I'm dead, has no reason to believe that anyone else is after him.* Michael took the chance, darted out of the brush to a nest of tall, jagged boulders, rested briefly, then dashed into the shadow of an overhanging cliff. . . .

Nearly an hour later, hundreds of feet above the tree line, he saw a black trail of smoke rising from the top of a rounded bluff ahead, stared at it in puzzlement. He couldn't believe that the *amok,* even if he considered himself momentarily safe, would build so conspicuous a fire. Then he remembered the blaze Takei Shimura had kept going on the rock outcropping. Was it possible that the Japanese, certain to be the *amok*'s prisoner if he was still alive, could have managed to set up another signal fire, intended to attract the hunting party? If so, why had the *amok* kept so careless a vigil over him? Michael had no time for doubts. Without food or an effective weapon, he had to move fast or not at all. He headed toward the smoke. . . .

The entrance to the cave was a slanting fissure in the side of the bluff, so narrow that he circled the base of the rock formation half a dozen times before spotting it. His knife held in front of him, he slipped into the opening, moved stealthily along a winding passage. It ended in a wide, shored chamber, where he found Shimura sprawled on the ground, feeding the leg of a wooden table into the fire pit's glowing coals. He glanced around, saw no side passages in which the *amok* could be hiding, ran to the side of the Japanese.

"Where is he?" Michael barked.

"Gone . . . since yesterday," Shimura gasped as Michael carried him to the pallet. "He told me you were all dead but I thought *someone* might see the smoke. . . . No other chance . . ."

"He just pulled out?" Michael asked incredulously. "No explanation?"

"It was all garbled . . . something about a man he had killed twice. But there is one thing of which I am certain: he left here to die."

"Why?"

Shimura directed a weary headshake at the American. "You do not understand the torture this man has suffered. He is not a mindless, accidental monster—but a monster of his own and Hisao Tanape's creation. For thirty-two years, he has been performing an act of repentance, turned himself into a living symbol of the Empire's eventual victory over its enemies. As long as he survived—and was feared—the people of this country would be reminded that the war still went on. Yesterday I took that belief from him, destroyed the entire core of his life. He no longer has a reason to fight or to live—and the greatest privilege a soldier can attain is to choose the time and place of his own death. Those words were spoken to me by a *true* madman!"

Michael checked Shimura's leg. Although stained, the bandage was still in place, and the exposed flesh above and below so far looked free of infection. "He gave you no idea where he was headed?"

"The house of the man he killed twice—a white house with a red-tiled roof. But hundreds of buildings in the valley of the Cagayan must fit such a description."

Michael now understood what had drawn the *amok* to his family's home the night that the floodlights had caught him. "He took weapons from our camp," he said in a harsh, choking voice. "Do you know what he did with them?"

"No. What is the matter?"

Michael spotted the Japanese officer's short sword on the cave floor; Shimura had been using it to pry apart the table for firewood. If nothing else, the foot-long blade would be of use in hacking through thick brush. He swept it up, rushed toward the mouth of the cave. The last thing he heard before entering the narrow passage was Shimura fearfully calling after him: "You will send someone back? Please, Mr. Braden, answer me!"

He went on without replying, reached the open air, skidded down the rocky slopes below the *amok*'s hiding place, began the desperate race he knew he could not win.

20

EVER SINCE Michael's departure for the Cordillera, Cara had been forced to take an active, if still superficial, role in the day-to-day workings of the plantation: checking the accounts, authorizing expenditures proposed by Romolo, visiting the fields in the foreman's jeep. She was glad that with the coming of the rains, crop production would be at a standstill for months, concealing her embarrassing lack of knowledge. Nevertheless, she found herself intrigued by her new duties—the first adult responsibilities, she had realized, of her life. Even simple household tasks—cooking, cleaning, the more unpleasant aspects of raising a child—had been in the hands of others.

The day after the storm finally moved south from the Luzon Straits, she had gone with Romolo to inspect wind and rain damage to the tobacco, returned late in the morning to find Lenore Tully's Volvo parked in front of the house. Her face red and puffy from crying, Lenore was waiting on the veranda. "What's happened?" Cara asked.

"Not too loud," Lenore whispered. "Evie or the old man might hear us. I tried to telephone but the lines are still down from the storm."

"All right," Cara said, leading Lenore farther along the veranda, away from the open, screened double doors.

"Walt Lydecker is dead," Lenore said when they reached the corner of the house. "I went into Tuguegarao to shop and the word was all over town. A couple of government geologists found his body three days ago, but they didn't reach the valley until last night."

"Was it the *amok*?" Cara asked, steadying herself against the veranda railing.

"Yes."

"And the others?"

"Why would they have looked? No one outside the families even knew they went up there." Lenore hesitated. "Cara, can I stay with you awhile? You were right before, when you asked me to. I don't want to be alone when the police come to tell me about Jack. If they find them at all."

"Of course."

"I'll go home, pack some things."

"Yes," Cara said numbly, telling herself that Michael *had* to be alive. It just couldn't happen again. Not so soon. . . .

NOT until the man spoke did Mr. Mapitang recognize Michael Braden. Face and arms encrusted with grime and stale perspiration, exposed skin swollen by festering insect bites, the young American probably would have been incapable of standing without Sacda's support.

Less than an hour earlier, Mapitang had returned to Ticlac, where the village headman told him how the hunters had appeared, learned where Takei Shimura had gone, set out after him. His mind saturated with dread of what he would find, he had told Sacda to prepare for a forced march north as soon as the mules were rested. He had been in the medical hut, unpacking all but the gear necessary for the trek, when a child had rushed in, told him that a stranger had arrived in the barrio. A moment later, the tattered figure had been led into the hut.

"Do you have a radio transmitter?" Michael Braden asked, pulling away from Sacda's grip.

"Sit down," Mapitang ordered.

Reluctantly, Michael sank onto one of the sleeping pallets. "A radio," he said again. "We have to reach the constabulary, tell them he's on the way . . . to my house."

"The *amok*?"

Michael nodded jerkily. "Been trying to get here for two days. . . . At first I started for the valley, then I changed my mind. . . . He was hours ahead of me, knew all the trails, shortcuts I'd never find. . . . Only chance was to contact you . . ."

"I do not carry a transmitter. We could start a signal fire, try to attract a plane or a helicopter—but they seldom fly low over the jungles in this weather."

Michael stood up, swayed weakly. "Have to go on, then. Can you lend me a rifle?"

"I have no weapons," Mapitang said, placing both bony hands on Michael's shoulders, forcing him back on to the pallet. "And the Ilocans are not permitted to own guns. You must have food and sleep, Mike. You won't last another day without them."

Despite his frenzied urge to continue the journey, Michael realized that the physician was right. But every second he wasted, the *amok* would be nearer his goal. There had to be a way to cut down the murderer's lead.

Then, through the hut's open rear window, he glimpsed the narrow river, the dugout canoes lined up on its muddy bank. By now, he realized excitedly, all the tributaries of the Cagayan must be navigable. In a canoe, he could ride the swift, monsoon-fed current all the way to the big river. The *amok* woud not have dared go by water, since it would mean repeatedly exposing himself to the barrios along the banks of every stream. In a day and a half, with luck, Michael could reach civilization, head off his enemy before the destruction of the Braden family was completed.

He quickly told his plan to Mapitang. "Just give me food and a couple of men to help paddle," he said. "I can sleep after we start."

"First I must know what happened out there," Mapitang insisted. "Where are the others?"

"Dead."

"Even Shimura?"

Michael pictured the Japanese surrounded by the fetid darkness of the *amok*'s cave, gradually understanding that he would die amid it—the way Michael's sister had lingeringly perished in the black, stinking hold of the Aparri death ship. . . .

"Well?" Mapitang snapped.

The lie would not form on his lips. "He's injured," Michael said, "holed up in the *amok*'s hideout. I'll draw you a map before I leave. . . ."

Half an hour later, Mapitang watched Michael Braden and two powerfully built young Ilocans shove a dugout canoe into the nameless brown stream, scramble aboard, plunge their paddles into the water. The physician waved goodbye but Michael, staring intently ahead from the middle of the canoe, did not return the gesture. In the barrio's communal area, villagers were piling wood on a fire, despite the drizzling rain.

Mapitang waited until the canoe was out of sight, then

turned and nodded to Sacda, who was holding the lead reins of a pack mule. It was time to begin his own journey against death.

ON the fourth day after leaving Captain Shimura in the stronghold, he reached the valley on the Cagayan. Heavy rain had been falling for hours and the late-afternoon sky was almost night-dark, enabling him to cross open fields, scuttling between rows of tobacco like a great dusky beetle, confident no one would be working in such a downpour. Even if he were seen—and the witnesses escaped his sword—it did not greatly matter. . . .

When he was within view of the house of the man he had killed twice, he threw himself on knees and elbows, crawled with snakelike speed until the building came within range of the binoculars he had taken from the body of the American he had slain on the highland savanna. He focused the lenses, saw no armed guards posted around the verandas. He doubted that the occupants had kept up the precaution after the monsoon; nevertheless, he decided to stay in hiding until past sunset, when the house's interior lights would afford a clear view of what awaited him within.

Although he knew that probably only hours of life remained to him, he felt at peace—except for the nagging mystery of the man he had killed twice. When he solved it, he would be fully prepared for the utimate act of *gekokujo*. They would again send a horde of soldiers after him—but this time would not be like the battle in the cogon; this time he would meet them face to face, allow Colonel Tanape's blade to savor enemy blood until he died with the sword in his hand, when and where he chose, just as his mentor had wished.

It was not men who had defeated him but the curse of time, a curse he had escaped until Takei Shimura had brought it into the heart of his sanctuary. More shattering than the word that the war was lost had been the captain's gray hair and seamed face. He has grown old, he had thought as he studied Shimura from the darkness at the front of the cave. And if he has grown old, I must have grown old also.

Not since the very beginning of his mission had he considered the passage of years, allowing the seasons to merge into a single, unvarying continuum, like the icy waves that, winter or summer, beat against the barren cliffs of Shikotan. And now, unexpectedly, he had grown old. Soon the strength would start to drain from his body and the men of this peculiar, oppressively warm island would lose their fear, pursue him deeper and deeper into the forests. He would die not like a soldier but like a hunted beast, placing survival above duty and honor. Better to end it now, he had decided, wondering when he had begun to grow old. . . .

Now real night lay over the valley of the Cagayan. The rain had slackened, making it easier for him to see through the binoculars; lights shone brightly in the tall, broad windows of the plantation house's first floor.

He studied the figures that entered his magnified vision. The slim, graceful girl he had glimpsed twice before, once in a jeep that had halted near the *takotsubo* he had dug across from the cogon field; later, wearing a white silk slip, briefly framed in an upstairs window . . . A red-haired woman who bobbed into view at unexpected moments, as if she were moving erratically about the room . . . A gaunt, ancient man slumped in a black leather armchair . . . A tiny female child with pale yellow hair . . . But no men with guns.

He stood up, unsheathed his sword, strode toward the house of the man he had killed twice.

HE had made it, Michael thought with a dizzying surge of relief, pausing for breath at the edge of the family cemetery. Ahead lay the path between the eucalyptus trees, leading to the rear veranda of the plantation house. The exterior light was on, pouring a dingy yellow glow over the squat form of Inez, the cook, sitting cross-legged on a reed mat near the kitchen door, every few seconds raising the lit end of a cigar to her mouth, contentedly sucking the acrid smoke deep into her throat. . . .

Now that he was so close to home, the past two days of frantic travel along mountain streams were already taking on the aspect of a half-recalled nightmare. Within hours of leaving Ticlac, he had realized that his fate lay chiefly in the hands of the tribesmen whom Dr. Mapitang had instructed to take him to the valley of the Cagayan. Exhausted from his headlong flight to the barrio, he had spent the first part of the downstream journey slouched limply in the center of the dugout canoe, his head between his legs. During his infrequent periods of wakefulness, he had swallowed handfuls of cold rice and yam paste passed to him by the men expertly maneuvering the canoe, the forested banks of the stream little more than indeterminate dark green blurs at the edges of his vision. Worst of all had been the long, agonizing stretches when rainsqualls forced them to pull the canoe on shore, wait for the watery onslaughts to taper off, with Michael intensely aware that the *amok* would still be in motion. Then, at last, they had entered the broad waters of the Cagayan River. Even though the rain was again heavy, he had insisted that they keep paddling, remaining close to the east bank in case the canoe was swamped and they had to swim to land. When the red-tiled roof of the house had come into view above the trees, Michael had leaped into the hip-deep water, waded to the bank, run toward his home, slackened his pace only when he saw Inez calmly smoking her cigar on the rear veranda . . .

He continued on at a rapid walk.

It had been the most strained evening since Lenore had begun her visit, Cara thought, watching Sam Braden's lonely ascent of the stairway, slower than she had ever seen him move before. They had all gone through after-dinner rituals: Lenore constantly interrupting her pretended reading of a Jacqueline Susann paperback with pointless diversions—crossing the room to the coffee table where she had left her cigarettes, returning to her chair, remembering that her lighter was still on the table, rising again to fetch it. Cara and Eve, already in her pajamas, at a card table, working on a fifteen-piece jigsaw puzzzle of brown and white rabbits in overalls pushing wheelbarrows full of carrots, Cara pretending to be as baffled as she had been on two dozen previous assemblages. Sam slouched in the flaking leather armchair, lost in his impenetrable thoughts.

Until yesterday, she and Lenore had managed to preserve a ragged illusion of household normality. Then Lieutenant Díaz of the Philippine Constabulary had come to the house, asked the two women where Jack Tully and

Michael had gone. Even though they realized the discovery of Walt Lydecker's mangled body made subterfuge impossible, they had persisted in the story that the men were boar hunting with friends. "And Mr. Dietrich?" Díaz had inquired in a tone of exaggerated patience. "He too went off to shoot wild pigs? A few hours after his wife's murder?" "My brother-in-law didn't mention Harry Dietrich," Cara had said, wondering why she continued to tell foolish lies. Like Lenore, she had begun to reluctantly accept the possibility that Michael and the others would never be seen again. So, she sensed, had Sam Braden, although he never questioned her about the policeman's visit. . . .

"Mama, Grandfather's sick," Eve cried.

Halfway up the staircase, Sam Braden had abruptly sunk to the steps, his withered hand clutching a banister rail, his face gray, a line of spittle running from the corner of his mouth. Thinking Sam had suffered another stroke, Cara rose quickly, knocking over the card table. She heard a rattling whimper, realized the sound was being made by Lenore, staring with glazed eyes at the archway separating the parlor from the front entrance hall. Cara turned to follow her friend's catatonic gaze, saw the gigantic figure, grabbed Eve into her arms. . . .

She had heard the grotesque stories told over and over by the Ilocan servants, but no words could have prepared her for the physical reality of the *amok*. The form was too overwhelming to be accepted as an entity. As she backed across the parlor, pressing Eve's face against her shoulder, she perceived him in fragmented images: the black-bearded face, skin so dark and thick and gnarled that it might have been stitched together from pieces of blemished, ill-matched leather; the huge torso, covered with clothing so old and faded and stained that it seemed part of his body, like a layer of reptilian scales; the immense, hairy hands, clutching a long samurai sword, extending straight before him. She felt a hard surface against her back, realized she had reached a corner, sank to the floor. Evie squirmed partially free of her sheltering arms, turned her head toward the advancing *amok*. . . .

Again, time had betrayed him, he thought, peering at the little girl's fair hair and white-skinned, freckled face: a delicate, feminine replica of the face of the man he had killed twice. The motionless old man on the stairs possessed the same features, corroded to near-disintegration. It was so ridiculously simple: they had been father and son, welded into a single person by the telescoping years of his existence. The mystery had not been a mystery at all!

"Leave this house," he shouted in Japanese to the woman holding the little girl. Perhaps, like the man he had killed twice, they spoke his language. However, when the woman did not obey, he realized that she had not understood. Neither had the red-haired woman or the old man on the stairs. Paralyzed by fear, they did not know he wanted them to flee, bring back the soldiers, enabling him to die in battle. He released a frustrated growl, gestured toward the hall archway with his sword. . . .

RATHER than confront the chronically ill-tempered Inez, Michael would have preferred to circle the house and enter through the front door. However, realizing he could not get past her without being seen, he had mounted the steps to the rear veranda. She had taken a draw on her cigar, looked at him with no more interest than if he had just returned from a routine trip to Tuguegarao.

"Good evening, *Patrón*," she muttered.

"Good evening, Inez."

He was about to open the screen door to the kitchen when he heard the *amok*'s commands to his captives. At this distance, filtered through two heavy walls, the incomprehensible words could be perceived only as a threatening subhuman snarl. But Michael instantly knew that he had been wrong once again. The enemy had arrived before him! He pulled the Japanese short sword from his belt, eased the screen door open just far enough for him to slip through it, padded across the kitchen tiles, reached the ground-floor hall.

"What do you want from us?"

Cara's half-whispered plea came from the front parlor. The illuminated archway to the room lay only a few feet away, between Michael and the passage to the study, where the plantation's rifles were kept. He realized that it would probably be impossible to reach the study without being detected. Even if he did, the metallic clatter of unlocking the gun cabinet and removing its trigger-guard chain was certain to reach the *amok*'s ears. The short sword would have to be his sole weapon.

To obtain an unobstructed view of the parlor, he was forced to dart to the opposite wall. He saw the *amok* standing above Cara and Eve, Lenore rigid in a chair, his grandfather immobile on the stairs. Although the *amok*'s back was to him, Michael was temporarily helpless. More than twenty feet of open space lay between him and the madman's intended victims—and his sister-in-law and niece cowered only inches from the killer's blade. If Michael charged—and made even the slightest of noises—the *amok* would have enough time to slay the woman and child before wheeling to meet the assault. . . .

Why is he waiting? Cara thought, forcing Eve's face back against her shoulder. "Finish it!" Her cry began as a scream of helplessness, ended in quivering rage. "Why don't you finish it?" While the words were still erupting from her throat, she saw Michael in the hall. . . .

It will happen again, Sam Braden told himself in despair. The way it happened with the first Eve. They will die before my eyes and I will have to watch. Then he remembered the Ilocan crossbows and spears mounted on the wall of Michael's bedroom, at the south end of the second-floor hall. Aware that if he reached the primitive weapons, he was probably too frail to use them, he nonetheless released his grip on the rail, began crawling up the steps. . . .

Michael saw his grandfather start to move an instant before the *amok* heard the faint rasp of the old man's fingernails against the stairway wood. The murderer turned away from Cara and the child, took three steps toward the stairs. Michael lunged through the archway, the short sword at hip level, drove the weapon into the *amok*'s lower belly, ripped upward, sticky liquid warmth gushing to his elbow. The samurai sword flew from the *amok*'s hands, rang loudly as it skidded over the floor tiles.

The blade of the short sword had lodged in the *amok*'s rib cage, refused to pull free no matter how hard Michael tugged. Then enormous, callused hands closed on his shoulders with crushing strength, effortlessly lifted him high, flung him across the width of the room. He crashed into a paneled wall, was unconscious even before his limp body crumpled to the floor. . . .

There was no pain yet—merely a great heaviness, as if a chunk of granite had been implanted in the center of his body—but he knew that it would start soon. He gazed dazedly at the gold-ornamented handle of the blade, realized it was the short sword he had given to Captain Shimura. Reeling, he looked around for his own weapon, determined to finish off the man who had attacked him, blinked in astonishment when he saw that the slight, gentle-faced, brown-haired girl had darted over and picked it up.

"Run, Evie!" Cara cried, raising the sword in both trembling hands as she backed away from the *amok*.

The child went past her, started up the stairway, paused beside Sam Braden, who had reached the top step. She reached down to help him.

"Run! Run! Run!"

Shrieking, Eve fled along the landing to the nursery, slammed the door behind her. Cara continued toward the stairway, staring defiantly into the *amok*'s eyes as he shambled after her. "Go away!" she yelled, wondering if she possessed the strength to make a lethal swing of the heavy sword. "Leave us alone!"

He took another step—and then, inexplicably, halted. His mouth opened to release a rumble of grim laughter.

Suddenly he had known that this was the correct way for his mission to end. He would die the way Shimura told him Colonel Tanape had died, beneath the finely honed cutting edge of the weapon cherished by both of them. He sank to his knees before the girl, bowed until his forehead touched the floor. His long, tangled hair fell away to expose the back of his neck.

Cara raised the sword straight overhead, uttered a scream that mingled fury and release and sadness as the blade arced downward. . . .

The *amok* toppled on his side, blood spurting from his decapitated body with relentless, unending force, like pressurized water exploding from a broken main. The scarlet flood washed over Lenore Tully's feet, broke in miniature waves against Michael's inert form. Cara dropped the sword, ran up the stairs, as if she feared the torrent would inundate the entire house.

21

A LIGHT RAIN was falling on the Tuguegarao airstrip when Ken Tisak brought his Cessna in for a landing, then immediately taxied into takeoff position.

"He's in a hurry," Michael told Cara. "Must be even worse weather on the way."

They sat in the front seat of a plantation jeep, parked on the edge of the field, next to the Philippine Constabulary command car that had followed them from Dr. Mapitang's clinic. They must want to make sure I leave right on schedule, Michael thought, glancing over at Lieutenant Díaz' grim face, dimly visible through the water streaming down the official vehicle's windows.

"It isn't fair," Cara said, her eyes moist. "You didn't commit any crime."

"Their country and their laws," Michael replied wryly. "If I were a Filipino, they'd have thrown me in jail. And maybe they'd be right. Five men are dead who didn't have to be. . . ."

NEARLY two weeks had passed since the night the *amok* had invaded the Braden home. Until an hour ago, Michael had been confined—on government orders—to a room in the Tuguegarao clinic, although the precaution baffled him. In a cast from abdomen to neck to immobilize eleven fractured ribs, he would have been the slowest-moving escapee in Philippine history.

Even more racking than the constant physical pain—and the cancellation of his visa, effective as soon as his physician pronounced him well enough to manage air travel to the United States—had been the need to face the families of the men he had taken into the hills. One by one they had come to his narrow, antiseptic hospital room, seeking the truth about how his companions had perished: Anson Lydecker, struggling to hide his resentment that only Michael had been spared; Tegasay's tiny, wrinkled wife, her expressionless features failing to acknowledge his promise that the Braden family would support her for the rest of her life; Mrs. Ramos, tall and cool and remote; finally, Lenore Tully, who arrived with her sixteen-year-old son, Kevin, home on summer vacation from his Manila boarding school.

"Is it true what the newspaper said?" the boy asked. "Dad found out Mr. Dietrich set up the Ticlac massacre? And tracked him down right through the typhoon?"

"Yes," Michael replied, wishing he had the courage to describe the look of poisoned self-hatred on Jack Tully's face when he had found him with Harry Dietrich's battered body. However, he had made enough enemies in the valley of the Cagayan without disillusioning children about heroically dead fathers.

When Kevin had left the room, Lenore asked quietly, "Did Jack ever tell you why he went along?"

"No, Lennie, he didn't," Michael said, puzzled by the question.

"I'm glad," she murmured, squeezing his hand before joining her son in the hall. . . .

His most frequent visitor was Cara, who appeared every day, occasionally with his grandfather or Eve, more often alone. He had anticipated that she would still be in a state of sickened shock over the grisly act she had been forced to commit. From the first, however, her manner was surprisingly calm, almost cheerful, as if the *amok* had never existed.

"I've spoken with Luis Delgado on the phone," she told him on her second visit. "He's sure he can get the deportation order reversed within a year."

"He was sure the Philippine Supreme Court wouldn't uphold Laurel-Langley, too," Michael said with a rueful smile. "We'll deal with it when we have to. Now I have a really important question. If we were home, I wasn't in a body cast and Sam and Eve were off on a picnic, would you be in bed with me?"

Michael had made the remark only to divert her from further talk about his deportation, was surprised when he wasn't able to provoke even a faint smile. "I'm not sure," she replied, seriously.

"Academic, anyway," he said. . . .

On the last night before his forced departure from the Philippines, he received a visitor he hadn't anticipated, even though he had known for days that Takei Shimura occupied a room only three doors down the hall. A constabulary helicopter had flown Dr. Mapitang and the Japanese out of the jungle as soon as Michael was coherent enough to give Lieutenant Díaz the location of the *amok*'s stronghold. However, five days of lying unattended in the mountain cave had led to a serious infection of his leg wound, as well as pneumonia. For more than a week, Mapitang had told him, the staff had feared Shimura might die, implying that Michael's interference with the surrender plan of the Japanese was the primary cause of his distress.

Michael was nearly asleep in his semidarkened room when he heard the slow drag of crutches over the floor, opened his eyes to see Shimura's stocky, bathrobed form at the foot of his bed. "You leave tomorrow, Mr. Braden?" he asked.

"Yes."

"I will be here a little longer, I fear. Thank you for sending Dr. Mapitang to me in the jungle."

"But not for failing to tell you I was going to do it?"

"Were you certain that you would?"

"Not until I was in Ticlac," Michael admitted. "I'm sorry."

"It is of no importance." Shimura swiveled about on the crutches, started toward the door. "Good luck on your journey."

"May I ask a question?" Michael murmured.

Shimura paused. "Of course."

"Do you believe, if my friends and I hadn't messed it up, that you really could have persuaded him to surrender peacefully?"

"No," Shimura answered.

"You're not a very convincing liar."

"On the contrary," Shimura said. "I am an extremely

convincing liar, Mr. Braden. If I were not, Kurusu would have died in nineteen forty-five and many, many innocent people would be alive today. Guilt is not a Western monopoly, by the way. Good night. . . ."

The following morning, after making his farewells to Sam and Eve at the clinic, Michael was driven to the Tuguegarao airstrip by Cara—with the constabulary command car a discreet distance behind. . . .

"Looks like no other passengers," Michael said when Ken Tisak revved the Cessna's engines to signal all-aboard. He kissed Cara goodbye, lingeringly. "Take good care of Evie and my grandfather."

Cara shook her head, clutched his upper arm. "Do you really think I can do it, Michael? Run the plantation?"

"You can do anything," he said. "You killed the *amok*."

Grunting with the effort of moving his imprisoned torso, he lifted his flight bag from the rear seat, slid out of the jeep, started limping toward the waiting aircraft. He had taken only a few steps when Cara caught up, kissed him again. "Even *with* a body cast," she said, smiling. . . .

"I heard about the deportation order," Ken Tisak said as he helped Michael into the front seat of the plane. "Lousy break, Mike. I'm sorry."

"No need," Michael said, buckling his seat belt. "I went into exile a long, long time ago."

The pilot gunned the engines and the Cessna roared down the airstrip, lifted off, flew straight south between the green, mist-shrouded mountains on either side of the valley of the Cagayan. . . .

SHE watched until the plane was out of sight before pulling away from the field. He'll be back, she told herself. He *has* to come back. Suddenly she wished she had told him of that frenzied morning after the *amok*'s death when, refusing the servants' help, she had gone on her hands and knees, used carbolic soap to scrub the encrusted blood from the parlor floor, not stopping until she had obliterated the last brown fleck—and the last vestige of her own fear. . . .

Cara Braden headed toward Tuguegarao, where she would pick up Sam and Evie at the New Reno Hotel, drive on to the plantation that, finally, had become her home.